Yours Always

by

Wendy Lawrance

First Published in 2018
by GWL Publishing
an imprint of Great War Literature Publishing LLP

Produced in United Kingdom

ISBN 978-1-910603-39-0 Paperback Edition

GWL Publishing
Forum House
Sterling Road
Chichester PO19 7DN

www.gwlpublishing.co.uk

Wendy was born and grew up in Surrey, attending school in Esher, where she developed an early interest in English Literature, especially that of the First World War. After twenty years running her own business in the graphic design industry, Wendy decided to fulfil her life's ambition and become a writer, which she has now been doing professionally for over ten years, becoming a recognised academic authority on First World War Literature.

Wendy lives near the beautiful West Sussex coast and is married with two grown-up children.

Dedication

For The Few

Acknowledgements

A book such as this cannot be published without acknowledging the debt which is owed to the men and women who fought, served and sacrificed so much during the Second World War. Nothing that is written today can hope to do justice to their courage, forbearance and quiet acceptance. Our debt is too great.

On a personal note, I would like to thank Claire Edge for once again taking the time to read through the final proof of the book and give me an invaluable reader's perspective. I'm indebted to you, dear friend.

I would also like to thank Chloe Hilton at Novo Editing for her customary diligence in picking up my many flaws. The value of a good editor should never be underestimated.

My love and thanks goes to my children, C & C, who have – as always – born my obsession with their usual patience and tolerance.

Finally, I wish to thank my husband, Steve, not only for his encyclopaedic knowledge of all things related to the RAF and their flying machines, but also for his unstinting love and support.
I am – as ever – yours, always.

Chapter One

Summer 1939

The body lay on the bed, thin grey hair surrounding a greying face, eyes closed and wrinkles fading. "I can't believe she's gone." Rose's words resounded in Harry's ears as she clung onto him. "How can granny really be dead?"

"Granny was just old, sweetheart," Harry said quietly, stroking his daughter's auburn hair. "She'd been unwell since granddad died. Her heart gave out, in every sense."

"She meant everything to me," Rose whimpered. "She's always been there."

Her words tore through Harry, crushing him in that far too familiar way she always managed whenever she spoke of her childhood. "I know, Rosie. I know." He spoke the words, despite the lump in his throat threatening to mute him. Still holding his daughter's head to his chest, Harry glanced across the bed, across the lifeless body of his mother, to the figures standing on the other side of the room. Elise, Harry's wife, looked at him, her dark eyes filled with tears, while his younger daughter, Amy, a youthful mirror-image of Elise, stood transfixed by the sight of her grandmother's ashen face and whitening lips. Catching Elise's eye, Harry motioned with his head towards the door.

"Amy?" Elise said, taking her daughter's hand. "Come along. Let's go downstairs, shall we?" Amy nodded and allowed her mother to lead her from the room. Alone in the still silence, Harry rocked Rose gently as she sobbed into his chest.

"Did my mother look like that when she died?" she asked, eventually.

"A little, I suppose," Harry replied, releasing her. He thought of his first wife Bella, lying on the bed they'd briefly shared a lifetime ago, unaware of the beautiful life she'd just created in sacrificing her own. He remembered her auburn hair, fanned across the white pillow, her pale beautiful face, and he closed his eyes, just for a moment. "Mummy was much younger," he continued. "She looked just as peaceful though. I'm sorry she never knew you, or you her."

"So am I."

Harry took her hand in his and kissed it before releasing it and picking up his walking stick that had been resting against the bed. "We'll go downstairs now, shall we? Matthew will be arriving soon... his train's due any time."

Downstairs, the french windows were opened onto the sunny garden. The flower beds were filled with plump roses, their scent pungent and heavy; a little sickening, Harry thought. The grass was cut neatly and the shrubs all well trimmed. Harry knew that Polly and her husband, Dennis, had always taken excellent care of his parents and his mother's beloved garden. Elise and Amy sat quietly on one of the two sofas, neither speaking.

"Are you all right?" Harry asked of them both, as he and Rose entered the room.

"Yes," Elise answered.

"Amy?" Harry enquired.

"Yes, Daddy," she replied quietly, looking up and waiting a few seconds before continuing, "She went so suddenly."

Harry crossed the room to her and sat down, while Elise went to sit next to Rose on the opposite sofa.

"I know she did, sweetheart," he said. "But it was better that way – for her."

They sat in silence for a while, the still warmth of the late July afternoon punctuated only by the sound of the clock ticking on the mantlepiece above the unlit fireplace.

"I'm going out for a while," Rose said, her voice little more than a monotone whisper.

"Where to?" Harry asked.

"Just into the garden."

She walked to the french windows, stepping out onto the terrace and down the steps. Harry stood and, unthinking, left his stick behind, limping over with some difficulty and leaning against the doorframe to watch her. Crossing the lawn, she looked elegant and slim in a simple blue summer dress, her long auburn hair loose over her shoulders and Harry was immediately reminded of Bella again. Rose sat down on the old rope swing and remained completely still, her pale face raised to the sky and her green eyes staring into the branches above her. As Harry watched, the guilt rose in him, not for the first time, and he felt the lump returning to his throat. He was aware of Elise behind him, even before her arms entwined around his waist, her head resting on his broad back.

"Don't worry so much, Harry," she said, her French accent less obvious after nearly twenty years of living in England. "She will come through this." He turned and she looked up into his tired brown eyes and tanned face. His jaw-line was still as strong as the first time she'd seen him that warm spring evening in 1916, and his lop-sided grin still made her heart miss a beat, just as it had back then, but his hair was now more grey than brown and there were wrinkles where none had existed before the Great War took its toll; his nightmares had aged him prematurely.

"I know. But I can't help worrying." He put his left arm around her, the stump of his right one hanging in his sewn-up shirt sleeve. He looked down at her, noticing the concern in her dark brown eyes and the few strands of hair which had escaped the loose bun at the back of her neck. He loved her informality, the way she ignored the current fashion for neatly curled and coiffed styles, and allowed her hair to do as it pleased, its natural curls either left loose or tied back casually, framing her tanned face and slender neck. She looked at him, her full lips slightly apart, and he wished he could lean down and kiss her. Instead he pecked her lightly on the cheek, before limping across the room and sitting back down again, next to Amy on the sofa. "Are you sure you're all right?" he asked softly, taking her hand in his. "I'm still not entirely sure it was wise to let you see that."

"I think it was, Daddy," Amy replied firmly, nodding her dark head. "You can't keep everything from me, you know. I'm nearly sixteen."

"Hmmm, I know."

Elise was at the door almost before the taxi had pulled up outside the house.

"Hello, Matthew," she said, quietly.

"Elise," he replied. One look at her face told him everything he needed to know. "I'm too late, aren't I?"

"Yes, I'm afraid so. Margaret died about an hour ago." Matthew entered the hallway, placing his small suitcase against the wall, then turned and kissed Elise on both cheeks.

"I'm so sorry. How is Harry?"

"Harry seems fine. He'll deal with it later, in his own way. At the moment he's more worried about Rose. She's gone quiet on us."

"Where is she?"

"She's in the garden."

"I'll go to her."

Matthew went through to the sitting room. Harry got up slowly, using his stick for support.

"Hello," Matthew said, crossing the room to where Harry stood. He didn't try to shake hands, but put his arms around Harry, patting him on the back affectionately. "Are you all right?" he asked.

"I'm fine," Harry said, glancing through the open french windows. "Please go to Rose," he continued. "She's not taking it well. She needs you."

"Leave her to me," Matthew said, releasing Harry and moving across the room to where Amy sat on the sofa. She looked up at him as he crouched before her. "Chin up," he said, taking her hands in his and rubbing her knuckles gently with his thumbs. She smiled at him. As brothers-in-law went, Matthew was one of the best, Amy decided. He was a bit of a dish, very tall and thin, with prominent cheek bones and neatly cut mousy brown hair, and hazel eyes that twinkled when he smiled; and he was a doctor, so he knew just about everything, but he was also very kind and, right now, with tears threatening once more, she needed someone kind.

Matthew stood again and crossed to the french windows, exited and, with his hands in his trouser pockets, strolled down the garden towards his wife. He'd only got halfway when Rose looked up, saw him and bolted from the swing, throwing herself into his arms. Harry, watching from the door, nodded his head and turned back into the room.

He didn't, therefore, see Rose pull away from Matthew, see him reach out for her, or her turn again and the whispered argument that followed between them.

"I'm twenty-seven years old. I shouldn't be crying like this," Rose said, sniffing into her handkerchief as they sat drinking coffee after dinner.

"Rose," Harry said, calmly, "Granny meant more to you than to any of us."

"That's silly. She was your mother."

"She was yours too for a long while, when you needed her most."

Rose sobbed again and Matthew moved closer, tightening his hold around her shoulders. She tensed and Matthew pulled away again, sighing deeply.

"I know," she continued. "But why does it have to hurt so much? I mean, first granddad and now this." She sniffed. "On top of everything else," she whispered so no-one could hear.

"It always hurts losing someone you love," Harry murmured, his words barely audible. Elise left Amy's side and walked to the fireplace, where he was standing, placing her arm around his waist. They remained in silence until Amy announced she was going to bed.

Lying in the darkness of the guest bedroom, lit only by the moonlight seeping in through the open window, Elise rested her head on Harry's broad bare chest, her fingers toying with the sprinkling of greying hair.

"How are you, really?" she asked.

"I'm upset, obviously," Harry replied. "But I'm glad she didn't suffer. At least it was quick."

"Yes."

"Rose is taking it very hard."

"Well, I suppose it's like you said. Margaret looked after Rose from a very early age. She's probably Rose's first memory of a woman in her life."

"I shouldn't have stayed away so long," Harry said, softly.

Elise sat up abruptly, resting her hand on his chest. "Stop, right now, Harry," she said. "You went to fight in the war; you were wounded, badly wounded. It wasn't your fault you couldn't come back. None of what happened to Rose was your fault. She wasn't neglected. She had your parents, so I wish you'd stop blaming yourself."

Harry pulled her back down into a hug, remembering the dark days at the end of the war, when nothing had made sense and Rose had been the last thing on his mind. "I know, I know. I just feel responsible. I can't help it."

"Then try harder, because you're not responsible. It was a war, for heaven's sake."

"Hmmm. And I think we're bound for another one any day now." Harry gladly changed the subject, and then, feeling Elise's shoulders tighten, wished he hadn't.

"Don't talk about it. I can't bear to think of it all happening again."

"Have you heard from Henri lately?" It was another quick change, hopefully more successful this time.

"Not since last month, no. I'm worried about them all, especially Luc." She thought of her wayward nephew and the likelihood of him getting into some kind of trouble if the Germans invaded France.

"Do you think they can be persuaded to come over here?"

"Henri says he won't leave the farm, which is stupid. He may be my big brother, but that doesn't stop him from being incredibly stubborn."

"Oh, so that's where you get it from, is it?" Harry spoke softly, trying to distract her from her worries.

"Harry Belmont!"

"Yes, Elise Belmont?"

"I am not stubborn."

"Really?" Harry turned towards her. He liked the way her figure had rounded with the passing years. Unlike him, her hair hadn't greyed at all, and was still as close to black as it was possible to get, but he knew she worried about the small amount of weight she'd gained, although he didn't even think about that: he loved every inch of her feather-soft skin, and the way her eyes, so dark and captivating with their flecks of amber, could still arouse him with nothing more than a simple look, just as they always had. "At times, I've known brick walls move more easily," he said as he ran his fingers lightly down her back, making her shiver slightly. He smiled at her involuntary reaction, pulling her closer.

"And yet, you still love me," she whispered, toying with him.

"Hmmm, I don't know why, but I do," he said between deepening kisses. "Desperately."

****

"Well, that was a fine turnout," announced Reverend Morris, clutching a cup of tea in his slightly shaking left hand and holding out his right, before realising that a handshake was impossible for Harry, who raised an eyebrow, coughing gently.

"Yes, wasn't it?" Matthew replied. "I wonder, Reverend," he continued, "if you'd like to have a look around the garden. Margaret was always so proud of her roses."

"Oh, yes," the vicar replied, blushing and awkwardly placing his cup and saucer on a side table next to the sofa. "I'd love to. I'm a bit of hybrid tea fanatic myself. My mother used to grow…" His voice faded as Matthew ushered him out of the french window and onto the terrace.

"Thank God for that," Harry said. "I know he means well, but he's not like Reverend Slate."

"It must be hard for him," Rose cut in. "He's young and he's only been here for six months."

Harry smiled. "I know, but he's so ungainly. Don't they train them how to handle people at funerals?"

"I think it's probably something they have to learn with time," Elise replied.

"Let's hope he hurries up," Amy put in, managing a smile, before settling into one of the armchairs.

"I must say, Matthew's very brave," Harry said.

"I'm not sure if he's brave or foolhardy," Rose replied, lowering her head and her voice, and looking at her patent black leather shoes.

Harry noticed the distant expression on her face, recognised it of old and sighed, feeling a momentary sense of pity for Matthew.

"Is everything all right with Rose?" Elise asked, coming and standing beside Harry, as Rose went off to talk to William and Charlotte, her uncle and aunt on her late mother's side, who were sitting with their son George and daughter Anne. "I know she's been reminded of Bella, and she feels the loss of your mother very deeply, but she looks so sad."

"I'm not sure. I think there's something wrong between her and Matthew, but they'll sort it out, providing she can refrain from crying long enough to have a conversation." He took Elise's hand in his and kissed her palm gently. "I do wish you'd remember that Bella may have given birth to her, but they never knew each other, and you've spent the last seventeen years being her mother."

"I know I have, but Bella came first and Margaret was special to her."

"Well, you're more than special to me." Harry kissed her forehead. "I'm surprised Ed's not here yet," he said, coughing and looking at the clock on the mantlepiece.

"I don't think the RAF is overly concerned about family commitments," Elise murmured, keeping hold of his hand.

"Mother wasn't really his family, though," Harry said. "So it probably doesn't count to them. The death of your honorary guardian's mother doesn't really count, does it?"

"I think you're a bit more than an 'honorary guardian' to Ed, Harry. You know you mean..."

A figure appeared in the french window and Harry looked up to see a tall, young man in a sharp blue uniform, his cap tucked under his arm.

"Ed!" he called out, taking his stick and moving towards the door. "How are you?"

Ed didn't try to shake Harry's hand, but patted him gently on the shoulder. "I'm fine, thanks, Harry." He glanced around the room. "How are you? I'm sorry I couldn't get here sooner, the C.O. was very nice about it, but..."

"It's fine," Harry said. "I didn't expect them to give you leave for the funeral of someone you weren't actually related to."

"She was like a grandmother to me too," Ed said, noticing Amy sitting on one of the chairs by the fireplace, gazing into its cold, empty darkness. "Is Amy all right?" he asked.

"She's been very quiet all day," Harry replied. "Try and cheer her up, will you?"

"Gladly, especially if it means I don't have to talk to him." Ed nodded towards a medium-sized, balding man, standing in the corner of the room, next to his mother, Isabel.

"Shouldn't you at least say hello to your mother? No-one minds if you ignore Charles," Harry said.

"I'll talk to her later," Ed replied, crossing the room and sitting down on the floor in front of Amy.

He tugged at the hem of her neat black dress to get her attention and she smiled down at him.

"Oh, it's you," she said, pushing away the few tendrils of loose wavy dark hair which had escaped her pony tail.

"Yes, it's me." He grinned up at her. "And you might sound a little more pleased to see me, kiddo. It's been ages."

"I know it has, but I'm not really having a very good day – for obvious reasons."

"It'll be better when this bun-fight is over and everyone's gone home. You can get back to normal," Ed said.

"You're staying, though, aren't you?" Amy asked, trying to hide the desperation in her voice.

"I've got a weekend pass," he replied. "We can spend it together, if you like. Now, come and fetch me a cup of tea and tell me what you've got planned for the holidays." He got up and pulled her out of her seat.

They walked together to the sideboard, where refreshments had been laid out. "Well," she began, "we're normally here for the whole of August anyway, so I suppose we'll just carry on as usual. I imagine there will be some clearing out to do, and then I guess we'll go back to Cornwall and I'll go back to school."

"It's a shame I couldn't get down there to see you earlier in the summer. I've missed the beach." Amy poured hot tea into a bone china cup, added milk and a spoonful of sugar, giving it a quick stir and handing it to Ed.

"I miss it already," she said wistfully, "and we've only been here a few days. I can't wait to go home."

"I'm sorry. Am I not good enough company for you?"

"Of course you are." She laid her hand gently on his arm. "But it's all so sad here now. It's not like all the other summer holidays. It's not the same anymore."

He placed a finger under her chin, lifting her face towards his. "Don't be sad, little Amy," he said. "Granny Margaret wouldn't want that."

"I know." She gulped back her tears.

"Hey," he said, pulling her into a hug. "Come on. Let's go outside and enjoy the sunshine. We can sit on the grass and you can tell me all the village gossip." Taking a handkerchief from his trouser pocket, he wiped away her tears, then took her hand and led her out into the garden.

****

"Why did you want to join the RAF?" Amy asked. It was the following morning and she and Ed were walking along a dusty lane, to nowhere in particular. Amy was picking the occasional poppy from the hedgerow, Ed had his hands in his pockets. She looked up at him and held her breath for a moment. He was so handsome; his slightly curly blond hair was tousled, like he'd not bothered to comb it, his eyes were an intense shade of blue, which seemed to grow darker the more animated he became, and his smile… She caught her breath again and tried to concentrate on his reply.

"There's going to be a war, Amy, everyone knows that. And I want to do my bit right from the off, fully trained and everything, not wait to be told. I didn't want to join the army and be a slogging foot soldier, and you know perfectly well that I'd make a shocking sailor." He looked at her, his eyes daring her to laugh as he knew she'd be recalling the time when they'd gone sailing off the coast in Cornwall the previous summer, and he'd been violently sick, leaving her to do all the work. "So I thought I'd try my luck in the RAF. It's fun."

"What does your mother think?" Amy enquired.

"I've never really asked her."

"Why not?"

"You know why not."

"Because she married 'him', you mean?" Ed nodded. "Why do you think she did… marry him, I mean?"

Ed thought about her question for a moment or two. "When my father died, she was still very young. She had me to take care of…"

"Yes, but daddy helped with all that, didn't he?"

"Harry paid for everything and helped as much as he could, but it's not the same, is it? After ten years on her own, I imagine she was lonely. Why on earth she had to choose Charles Dobson, heaven only knows. The man could bore for England, Amy." She laughed and he stopped walking. Amy turned round and looked at him. "In a way, I suppose I should be glad they got married."

"Why?" Amy asked. "Didn't you miss your mother once Charles moved in and insisted you went to boarding school?"

"Yes, of course, but Harry arranged for me to be sent to Uppingham, then on to University. I got the best education going and I got to spend my holidays with you and Rose, and Harry and Elise. You've all been like a second family to me. If I'm being honest, I hardly think of Isabel as my mother anymore. Elise has been more of a mother to me."

"You're going to miss granny just as much as the rest of us, aren't you?"

"Yes, I am." Ed paused and glanced at his watch. "Come along, miss. It's time we got back. We can't be late for lunch. Matthew's got to get the train back to town this afternoon and I suppose I should visit my mother before I leave for the base." He looked wistful.

"Try and sound a little more enthusiastic, Ed. You're nearly twenty-one now. You can't still feel threatened by the man."

"Not threatened. Just bored." He yawned in an over-exaggerated fashion. "I'll race you back!" And with that he took off, leaving Amy to chase behind him, not that she really tried. She was marvelling that Ed had shared a real 'adult' conversation with her for the first time ever. *Maybe he doesn't see me as a little kid anymore. Oh, how exciting!*

"Have you decided what to do about the house yet?" Matthew asked, taking a sip from his coffee after lunch.

"I'm going to keep it for the time being," Harry replied, glancing at Ed. "Much as we might like to pretend otherwise, we all know there's going to be another war in the not too distant future, and I'd like Ed to have a base whenever he gets leave." He felt Elise grip his hand and brushed her knuckles with his thumb.

"Will we stay here then, Daddy? At granny's house?" Amy's voice was quiet.

"Do you want to?" Elise asked.

"I'm not sure. I miss Watersmeet." She thought of the whitewashed cottage on top of the cliff, the beautiful sandy cove beneath and the tiny harbour with its fishing boats bobbing on the water. Then she looked at Ed, recalled their earlier conversation and her heart flipped, just for a second. "But if there's going to be a war, I think we should probably be here, where we can be of more use."

"What are you planning on doing then, little sister?" Rose asked. "Are you going to join up?"

Amy looked her sister straight in the eye. "If the war goes on long enough, then yes, I am." Rose laughed. "I'm certainly not going to sit around doing nothing."

Elise and Harry exchanged glances. The two girls couldn't be more different. Rose, with her mother's pale colouring and red hair, was quiet and had become prone to mood swings in recent months; Amy, dark haired and dark eyed, with clear, fresh skin, which tanned easily, was generally much more happy-go-lucky. Matthew placed his coffee cup on the side table and got to his feet. "Well, at the risk of spoiling a lovely afternoon, I'm afraid I've got to be going. My taxi's due any minute now."

"I assume you're going with him?" Harry said to Rose. "You can easily get the driver to wait for you and I'll pay him when you get back here." His older daughter glared at him and Harry wondered, once again, what was wrong between her and her husband.

"It's fine. Rose doesn't have to come," Matthew replied on her behalf. "We can say our goodbyes here."

Harry just stared at Rose until she looked away, then she said quietly, "No, I'll come with you, Matthew. I'll go and find my shoes..." She stood up, reluctantly and left the room, closing the door a little too loudly behind her.

"What's her problem?" Amy said.

"None of our business," Ed replied. "And now, young Amy, I'm going to visit my mother, and you're coming with me, for moral support."

"If I must." Amy feigned unwillingness. "Luckily for you, I've already got my shoes on." She turned to Matthew. "See you soon," she chirped, leaning up and kissing him on the cheek. Matthew and Ed shook hands and Amy led Ed out of the french windows, and round the side of the house.

Elise looked up at her son-in-law. "Is everything all right between you and Rose?" she asked. "I'm not interfering, but she seems unhappy."

"She is unhappy," Matthew replied. "I'm just not sure there's anything much I can do about it."

Harry wondered if Matthew was about to say more when the door opened and Rose came back in

"Your taxi's here," she said abruptly. "Are you ready?"

"Yes, my case is packed. It's by the front door." He said goodbye to Harry and Elise, and that he would come back the following weekend to collect Rose and take her back to London with him. Harry noticed Rose didn't comment about the arrangement, or seem overly enthusiastic. He resolved that when she got back from the station, he was going to speak with her.

"What do you mean 'he's having an affair'? That's absolutely ridiculous, Rose. I've never met anyone less likely to have an affair than Matthew."

Harry and Rose were sitting together on the terrace overlooking the garden. Elise had decided to make herself scarce, and was in the kitchen helping to prepare a light tea, while Amy and Ed still hadn't returned from visiting his mother at Holly Cottage.

"He's never at home, Daddy." Rose sniffled into a handkerchief. "I know he's busy at the hospital, but it's ridiculous these days. It's been going on for ages and I know he's got another woman."

"How do you know?"

"I just do."

"Sorry, Rosie, but that's not enough. Have you spoken to Matthew about this?" Rose sat silently looking at her fingernails. "No? I thought not. For goodness sake. How do you expect to deal with a situation if neither of you speaks about it?" He breathed deeply. "Spend the week here if you want to; think things through and help with sorting out some of Grandma's things, but then when Matthew comes back next Saturday, you're going to sit down and talk, even if I have to tie both of you to chairs and lock you in a room together. Is that understood?"

"Yes," Rose whispered. "Do you really think he's not having an affair."

"I'd stake my life on it. In fact, I'd stake your life on it. He loves you, Rose, and he's a good man."

"I know he is, Daddy, for crying out loud! How can I forget? Everyone's always telling me."

The sound of voices brought their conversation to a stop and Harry turned to see Amy and Ed appear around the side of the house, laughing.

"I don't know why he's so pompous," Amy was saying, between giggles.

"I think it's genetic," Ed joined in.

"No need to ask who you're discussing," Harry said. "How was Charles today, then? On his usual form, I'm guessing?"

"Absolutely," Ed replied. "He told me that I'm wasting my time in the RAF; evidently it's highly unlikely that there's going to be a war, and I'd be better off using my degree to get a 'proper' job – ideally somewhere as far away from him as possible, I think was the general idea."

"Sounds like Charles." Harry rolled his eyes. "How was your mother?"

"I thought she was a bit quieter than usual," Amy said, glancing at Ed. "What did you think?"

"She seemed all right to me." Ed shrugged. Harry was disappointed that Ed seemed to care so little for his mother these days, but didn't blame the boy; being rejected in favour of Charles Dobson had been difficult to swallow. He knew that Ed's father, Edward – his dearest friend – would have been devastated by the turn of events, but then Edward hadn't known he had a son when he'd died in the Great War. Remembering Edward was still difficult for Harry, even after all these years. Everyone sensed the change of mood. "What time's tea?" Ed asked brightly. "I know it's not that long since lunch, but I'm starving."

"You're always starving," Amy replied, laughing and nudging Ed's arm.

"Your mother's in the kitchen," Harry said. "Why don't you go and ask her."

Amy led Ed into the house. "Promise me you'll try," Harry whispered to Rose once the others were out of earshot.

Rose hesitated for a moment. "I promise, Daddy."

The sun was setting, casting long shadows in the garden. Harry knew it was nearly time for Ed to leave. The two of them were standing alone in the living room, looking out on the garden. "After the conversation at lunch, I've decided we're not just going to keep the house; we're going to stay on here," he said.

"You don't have to, you know. I know how much you all love Watersmeet."

"Yes, we do," Harry replied. "But you and I both know something of what's coming. You're going to need somewhere to stay, but you'll need more than just a base, an empty house to come home to. You'll need some support, and I can't give you that if I'm in Cornwall."

"Are you sure Elise and Amy are happy with the arrangement?"

"Yes." Harry looked at his feet. "In any case, it doesn't really matter where we live, as long as we're together. You've already got your room here anyway, and Elise and I will move into my parents' old room – she'll like having an adjoining bathroom. She'll want to redecorate, I suppose." Harry turned and glanced about the room at the floral decor. "I'm not sure my mother's tastes and Elise's really coincide. And Amy doesn't mind where we live."

"I'm not sure she'd agree with that, Harry."

"Why? Has she said something?"

"Just earlier, when we were out, she said that she misses home."

"She always misses home," Harry said. "But I know Amy. She'll want to be where the action is. You heard her at lunch. She won't want to be stuck down in Cornwall, and she won't like the idea of not seeing you for a long time. She's very attached to you. We all are."

"She's a good kid," Ed replied. "I'm fond of her too. Where will she go to school? I'm sure she won't want to be sent back down to Truro to board."

"No. Being a weekly boarder is one thing, but she won't want to stay down there without us. There's a very good girls' school in the town. She'll go there until she's eighteen. I'm sure she'll hate it just as much as she hated school at home." Both men smiled.

"I'd best be off," Ed said, patting Harry on the arm. "Thank you, Harry. It means a lot to know you'll be here." He turned and crossed the room.

"I'll always be here..." Harry whispered to the empty space.

Chapter Two

Late Summer 1939

"When will Ed be back?" Elise asked, opening the door into the kitchen.

"Tomorrow around lunchtime, according to his telegram." Harry replied, following her into Polly's haven.

"And you're sure he hasn't guessed about the party?"

"Not unless he's a mind-reader. No-one's spoken to him for over a week."

They looked at the array of delicacies laid out on the kitchen table, but especially the enormous sponge cake which Polly had baked and which was now standing on a cooling rack, waiting to be filled and iced.

"I'm so glad he was able to get leave again so soon after Margaret's funeral," Elise said, dipping her finger in a bowl of strawberry jam, and placing it in her mouth. She closed her eyes, savouring the delicate sweetness. Harry looked across at her and wished Polly would disappear. He coughed and tried not to appear too distracted.

"How's the cake going, Polly?" he asked, tearing his eyes away from his wife.

"Nearly done now, Mr Belmont," she replied. "I've done a strawberry sponge, just like you asked. Master Ed's favourite. I've just got to decorate it. "

"That's if I stop eating the jam," Elise said, grinning.

Leaning his stick against the table, Harry took her hand and dragged her away. "Come on, then," he said. "Let the poor woman do her job." He shooed Elise out of the kitchen door before turning back and taking his stick again. "Thank you for this, Polly. Ed will be so pleased with it."

Polly blushed. "It's my pleasure, Mr Belmont," she replied.

In the hallway, Elise looked up at the decorations which she and Amy had spent the previous weekend preparing, ready for Ed's twenty-first birthday party. "It looks all right, doesn't it?" she said. "Do you think he'll like it?"

"He'll love it… but not as much as I love you." He walked towards her, not taking his eyes from hers. "Were you trying to look seductive and tempting in there, or was that my imagination?"

"Entirely your imagination," she replied. "I was merely intent on eating the jam."

"Really? You think I've got that much imagination?"

She moved a little closer and whispered, "I know you have…"

Harry chuckled and glanced at the grandfather clock in the corner of the room. He knew Amy had gone for a walk, and would probably visit William and Charlotte in the hope of some refreshments on the way back. "We've got at least an hour to ourselves…" he said, leaning down to kiss her.

"Plenty of time, then…" she grinned, moving towards the stairs. He followed, but she turned just before putting her foot on the bottom step, and placed her hand on his chest. "I need to wrap Ed's present and sort out my dress for tomorrow night, and you need to go and see Isabel. She didn't reply to her invitation and I think you should go and see her personally. Then later, we've got more decorations to put up in the sitting room…"

"You utter tease," Harry said, smiling, dropping his stick and grabbing her around the waist. She squealed and giggled at the same time. "Don't think I can't pick you up and carry you to the bedroom. I've done it before, at home…"

"Ah, but that's a bungalow – there are no stairs," she said.

He hesitated, thought about the logistics of the idea and said, "Okay, it might be a challenge, but I'm willing to try."

"Can we do it later?" she asked, looking up at him, her eyes flashing.

"Is that a promise, or another tease?"

She reached up, took hold of his shirt and pulled him down to her, kissing him deeply. "What do you think?" she asked, finally breaking the kiss, and turning to walk up the stairs.

"I'm finding it hard to tell," he replied, admiring the view.

"It's a promise," she called over her shoulder. "Give my love to Isabel."

Harry smiled, already looking forward to the evening.

Harry took a slow walk to Isabel's, partly to calm himself down and stop himself from thinking about what he'd rather be doing with Elise, and partly because he was wondering why Isabel hadn't replied to the invitation to Ed's party. On reflection, he had to admit it was strange that he and Elise had issued an invitation to Ed's mother to attend her own son's birthday party; but that was the path she'd chosen shortly after her marriage to Charles Dobson. Without any explanation, a few weeks after her marriage, Isabel had approached Harry and asked if he could arrange for Ed to be sent to boarding school immediately. Until that point, Isabel had always clung to the boy and refused to send him to any school, other than the one in the village, where she taught music, despite Harry's protests that he really should go somewhere which would offer him more potential. The change of plan had come as a huge surprise to Harry and, when pressed, the only reason she was prepared to offer was that Ed and Dobson didn't get on very well and she felt this course would be better for all concerned. Harry had marvelled then, as he still did now, at how distant she seemed to have become towards her only child; and remained grateful that Edward was blissfully unaware of the fate of his son. He'd made all the arrangements for Ed's education and, during each holiday, the boy had visited Harry and Elise, either at Watersmeet in Cornwall, or at Harry's parents' home in the village, where he would stay with the family and spend as little time as possible in the company of his own mother and step-father.

Harry opened the gate of Holly Cottage and walked up the path, grateful that it was a Friday afternoon and that Dobson would be at work. Dobson was an accountant, with his own small offices in the town, working for a few local firms. He wasn't particularly successful and Harry knew that, despite Dobson's objections that his wife shouldn't work, they relied on her income, as well as the allowance which Harry still paid her, and about which Dobson also frequently objected. Harry knocked on the door, which was promptly answered by Mary, who had been Isabel's maid for twenty years, ever since Harry had brought her and baby Ed back to the village after the war.

"Good afternoon, Mr Belmont," she said.

"Hello, Mary," Harry replied, allowing her to close the door. "How's Susan? I haven't heard from her in a while?"

"I had a letter a week or so back," Mary said. "Frank's been unwell again, so she's been looking after him."

"Is he better now?" Harry asked, concerned about his former maid's husband, who had occasional bouts of asthma, as a result of having been gassed in the trenches of Northern France.

"Oh yes, sir."

"Mary," Harry said, smiling. "It took me ages to train your sister, when she worked for me, not to call me 'sir'. Don't tell me you're still falling into her old habits."

"No, Mr Belmont," she replied, her face taking on a serious expression. "The master does like to be called 'sir', though, so I have to watch myself around him."

"Hmm," Harry said. "Well, he's not here now, and I still pay your wages, so I'll always be Mr Belmont to you. Have you written back to Susan yet?"

"No, Mr Belmont. I was planning on doing so at the weekend."

"Well, can you let her know that I'll write once this party is over and done with? In the meantime, ask her to let me know if she needs anything."

"I will do, Mr Belmont. Mrs Dobson is in the sitting room, sir. I'll show you in." She led the way and Harry followed, although he hated the formality of being 'announced', which he knew would have been at Dobson's insistence.

Isabel stood upon his entrance into the sitting room, placed the book she had been reading on the table beside her chair and waited for Harry to approach her. He noticed that her usually straight back and shoulders seemed to have drooped slightly. Standing in front of her, he balanced his stick against his leg, and took her hand in his, kissing it gently.

"How are you, Isabel?" he asked. "I rarely get the chance to see you alone these days." Once close to her, he saw that, although her now greying hair was neat and tidy, cut fairly short and curled around her face, her eyes were red-rimmed as though she had been crying. Her skin was pale and she looked tired and worried. "Is something wrong?" he asked.

"No, Harry," she replied a little too quickly and instinctively he knew she was lying. "How can I help you?"

Harry knew it was pointless pushing Isabel when she wasn't in the mood to talk. "We haven't heard from you about Ed's party, so I came to see whether you and Charles would be attending tomorrow."

"No, I don't think we will." Her voice was cold and Harry felt the ice of her words press into his own heart. "I've thought about it since receiving the invitation earlier in the week, and I think it would be best for everyone if we weren't there."

"You're his mother, Isabel. He'll want you there."

"That's as maybe, Harry, but I think it's better this way."

"If this is about Charles, why don't you come on your own?"

She almost looked as though she was going to laugh at his suggestion. "I can't… Not yet," she whispered.

"What are you talking about?" Harry asked.

"Oh, it's nothing," she replied, visibly seeming to pull herself together. "We really can't come tomorrow, but I do need to see Ed and yourself about something very important…" She paused. "Would it be possible for you to bring him over here the morning after the party?"

"Of course, but I wish you'd come. It would mean a lot to him."

"No, Harry. I can't. Please don't push me." He saw tears welling in her eyes and took a step towards her. "Please, Harry. I don't wish to be rude, but would you mind leaving now, and coming back with Ed on Sunday morning?"

"If that's what you want, yes." Harry couldn't conceal his disappointment or his confusion, but walked to the door and opened it. He turned just before leaving and saw that Isabel had slumped back into her chair, her head in her hands. He wanted to comfort her, but knew she wouldn't thank him, so he left, his head full of confusing thoughts.

"So, do you feel you've proved your point yet?" Elise was still breathing hard, lying face-down, naked across the bed, her skin glistening with sweat, her legs apart and her arms above her head, while Harry, collapsed beside her, raised himself up on his elbow, and looked down at her.

He'd managed, by lifting her onto his shoulder, to carry Elise up the stairs, leaving his stick at the bottom and limping with every painful step until, stifling her giggles, they'd reached the bedroom. At that point, he'd lowered her to the floor, feeling her body slide down his. Then, in a frenzy of triumph at his achievement, coupled with pent-up frustration at where their thoughts had been lingering since their encounter on the stairs that afternoon, they'd torn each other's clothes off and, without saying a word, he'd made love to her, hard and fast, and very satisfyingly. "Oh God," he said, suddenly concerned. "Was I too rough? Did I hurt you?"

She turned immediately, sat up and faced him. "No, darling. Not in the least." A grin spread across her face as she gently pushed him onto his back.

"You're incorrigible," he said, smiling up at her and pulling her down into a deep kiss.

"I think you mean insatiable," she replied eventually.

"Do I? I'm the one who speaks perfect English, remember?"

"Well, I think I mean insatiable." She bit her bottom lip, doing her best to look confused and seductive at the same time, and he chuckled. "I'm sure it's insatiable… You see, I was just thinking I'd quite like to do all that again…"

"Insatiable it is then. But, I'm fifty-five years old, for heaven's sake."

"And…?" She planted gentle kisses on his chest and slowly moved downwards, while he caressed the back of her head.

"And nothing," he replied, closing his eyes.

Later, she lay beside him, her hand across his stomach. "You've exhausted me," he said. "Actually, I think you might have killed me."

"I doubt it." She licked the salty sweat from his chest and felt him shiver. "I imagine that, by tomorrow morning, you'll be just as keen as ever. I'm not the only one who's insatiable."

"I'll always be keen and insatiable where you're concerned. Just don't be too disappointed if I'm not... well... capable. "

"I'm never disappointed," she said, leaning up and kissing his cheek. He turned and kissed her, feeling the softness of her tongue on his.

"Hmmm. I find that hard to believe. But thank you for saying it." They lay together in silence for a while until he felt her breathing deepen and knew she was asleep. His thoughts turned to Isabel. Amy and Elise had been just as confused as him, when he'd discussed his earlier conversation with Isabel, with them over dinner. They all agreed that Isabel's decision not to attend Ed's party must be something to do with Charles, but his presence had never prevented them from attending other functions, so it didn't really make sense that she should miss Ed's twenty-first birthday. Feeling his eyelids drooping, Harry decided there was no point in worrying about it. Tomorrow was about Ed and they'd find out what Isabel was hiding when they visited her the following morning. He drifted off to sleep, feeling Elise's soft skin against his and smiling gently as he remembered the touch of her tongue and her lips, and her gentle caresses.

****

"I can't thank you enough for the party," Ed said, over breakfast on Sunday morning. "I wasn't expecting anything like that. I think you invited half the county... It's just a shame my own mother couldn't be bothered to turn up." Harry heard the disappointment in his voice.

"We'll find out why soon enough," he replied. "We're due there in an hour or so." He glanced at the clock on the mantlepiece.

The door opened and Elise walked in. "Good morning," she said. "I'm sorry I'm late. Last night was exhausting, wasn't it?"

"Fun though," Harry answered.

"Is Amy not down yet?" asked Elise.

"No. It's the first time she's stayed up quite that late. It was nearly two o'clock before she went to bed, so I think we'll be lucky to see her before lunchtime."

"Hmm. I'm quite jealous," Elise replied, yawning and pouring a cup of coffee from the tall bone china pot in the centre of the table. "Thank you for letting me sleep in," she said to Harry.

"It was my pleasure. You looked so peaceful, I didn't have the heart to wake you. Do you want me to get Polly to make some fresh toast?" Harry asked.

"No, thank you," Elise replied. "I'll make do with what's here. She worked so hard yesterday, she deserves to have an easier day today." She picked up a slice of toast from the rack and spread a thin layer of butter onto it, before eating it slowly. "Besides," she continued, "I drank so much last night, I don't think I could eat more than half a slice anyway."

"I thought I might have to carry you upstairs again," Harry said, winking at her.

"I wasn't incapable." She held his gaze. "Just merry. We French can hold our wine, you know..."

"I'm not going to ask what you mean about carrying Elise up the stairs," Ed said, smiling and glancing between the two of them, noticing that neither of them blushed while he spoke. He never felt embarrassed by the intimacy displayed between Harry and Elise, and neither did they. Charlotte and William were equally happy and, given the strange and strained relationship between his mother and Charles Dobson, seeing couples who could share such obvious love and happiness always gave Ed hope for his own future – not that he had any notion of settling down – but at least he knew there was hope for when – or if – he did.

"I'll go and find my shoes and get ready to visit my mother," Ed said, then excused himself from the table and left the room.

"Did you notice how Anne was all over Ed last night?" Elise said, pouring herself another cup of coffee.

"It would have been difficult to miss," Harry replied.

"Charlotte and I were talking about it when she came for coffee last Thursday," Elise said, tucking into another piece of toast, her appetite clearly returning. "Evidently Anne's got a teaching job starting next month, but the boyfriend she had for the last two months at university has moved to America, so that's died a death. I don't think Charlotte or William were very disappointed."

"Is that why there's the sudden interest in Ed?" Harry asked.

"Oh no, according to Charlotte, the boyfriend was just a very casual thing. Nothing serious at all. Evidently, Anne's always had a soft spot for Ed, ever since they were children."

"I think you'll find that's news to Ed."

"I think you'll find Charlotte and William have always rather liked the idea of their daughter marrying him." Harry choked on his coffee. "What? Don't you think they're suited?"

"Ed and Anne? No, not particularly. She's a lovely girl, don't get me wrong. But she's far too serious for Ed; too steady. Plus she worships him far too much, and that's not what he needs. He needs someone who shares his sense of humour, who'll keep him grounded and in his place; and that's not Anne, I'm afraid."

"Well, as you saw last night, Anne has other ideas."

"Let's just hope she doesn't end up too disappointed then, because I don't think Ed's got the same perspectives at all." Harry got up from the table and walked around to kiss Elise. "I have to go over to Isabel's with Ed now," he said. "I don't know how long we'll be, but we should be back in time for lunch."

"That's fine," Elise replied. "I've got lots to do this morning."

"I love you," he said over his shoulder as he walked to the door.

Having been shown into the sitting room at Holly Cottage, Harry and Ed sat side by side on the sofa, while Isabel sat in the chair by the unlit fire. An awkward silence ensued while they waited for Mary to return with the coffee that had been ordered on their arrival. The moment she'd gone again, Isabel took charge of pouring the hot, dark liquid into small cups and handing them around.

"Where's Charles?" Ed asked, taking the cup from his mother.

"He's gone to church," she replied. "I made an excuse not to go, because... because I wanted to talk to you both alone."

Harry was even more intrigued, but tried not to let it show as he took a sip of coffee. Isabel sat in her chair, staring out of the window for a few moments. "This is very difficult for me, Ed," she began. "I owe you a huge apology."

"It's all right, mother. I suppose I didn't really expect you to come to the party. I can't say I wasn't..."

"I'm sorry, Ed, but this has nothing to do with the party."

"Then what are you apologising for?"

"Everything else... All of it." A tear fell onto her cheek and she reached into her handbag which was by her feet, found a handkerchief and wiped her eyes.

"Mother..." Ed began.

"No, please. I have to get through this. Then it will all make sense." The two men sat in silence for a few moments while she composed herself. She took a deep breath. "I've made a terrible mistake," she said. "Marrying Charles Dobson was the biggest mistake of my life." Silence shrouded the room. Neither Harry nor Ed knew what to say: they could hardly disagree, but they were astounded by her statement. "Ed, I've never really talked much about the time when Harry first brought us back here..."

"And you don't need to now," Harry interrupted.

"Yes I do, Harry. I can't explain what's happened now, if Ed doesn't know about back then."

"But I thought you didn't want to tell him all of that?"

"I've changed my mind."

"What on earth are you two talking about?" Ed's curiosity got the better of him.

Isabel took another deep breath and looked at Harry, who shrugged and nodded his head, looking at the floor. He was clearly not happy. "Harry found me," she said, dabbing at her eyes again. "No, I have to go back a bit further than that... As you know, Ed, I discovered I was expecting you just weeks after I received the news that your father had been killed in the war. What I've never told you is that, when I told my parents the news, my father threw me out onto the streets." She ignored Ed's gasp. Harry could see her reliving the memories. "It was a horrible time, when it should have been such a happy one. I'd lost Eddie, but I still had a part of him, because I had you. Eventually, I found somewhere to live, but it was a hovel; just a single room, very damp and dark, and freezing in the winter. I did laundry to make ends meet."

"Why didn't you tell me this?" Ed asked.

"I'm not proud of what happened and I suppose I've always preferred to forget. And Harry made that easy." Ed glanced at Harry, looking confused. "Harry found me – found us – living in that state," Isabel continued. "By that stage, I'd had you and we were just about getting by, but he offered me the chance to come and live here in this house, which he'd once shared with Bella, Rose's mother; he paid me an allowance, found me a job teaching music, and... well, he just made everything all right again." There was a pause. "He also made certain arrangements..." She paused, wringing her handkerchief between her fingers. "You see, I wasn't married to your father... That's why my father behaved as he did." She looked at Ed, expecting him to display some kind of shock, but he just continued to gaze at her. "Harry bought me a ring, and told everyone that Edward and I had married on his last leave, just before he was killed; that you were a honeymoon baby. I became Mrs Wilson, war widow, not Miss Murdoch, unmarried mother. He saved us and my reputation. Twenty years ago, especially in small villages like this, people would have shunned me for such a thing."

"Did no-one know?" Ed looked at Harry.

"I had to take my parents into my confidence, because I needed my father to draw up certain papers, which had to be in your mother's legal name; and I told Elise, because I don't keep secrets from her, but other than that, no-one else knows, to this day."

"Not even Amy... or Rose?"

"No, Ed. No-one."

"Well," Isabel said, gulping back a sob, "that's not strictly true. Charles knows."

"What? We agreed no-one would know, to protect Ed." Harry was incredulous. "How did *he* find out?"

"I told him shortly before the wedding." Isabel shook her head, anticipating Harry's anger and wanting to dispel it. "I had to admit I was a spinster and not a widow..."

Harry's head dropped. "Of course. Why didn't I think...?" he muttered.

"It didn't occur to me until I had to fill in the forms... I had no evidence of a marriage between myself and Edward. So, I had no option. I had to tell Charles the truth." Another tear fell down her cheek, but this time she let it tumble onto her blouse, where it leached into the pale green material, darkening it. "He took it well, or he seemed to. He said he loved me and it didn't matter." She looked up at him and smiled, although it didn't touch her eyes. "I was so relieved, Harry..."

"But?" Harry could sense she was holding something back.

"But... the night of our wedding, when we came back here, it... it was like he was a completely different man. He turned on me, calling me such foul names... and when I argued that I'd told him before the wedding, that he could've called it off if he'd wanted... he hit me."

"He what?" Ed's voice was a shocked whisper. Harry got to his feet and limped across the room. He stood next to Isabel and put his hand on her shoulder.

"Why the hell didn't you tell me?" he asked, gazing down at her.

"I'd married him by then. I—I thought it was a one-off. By the time I realised it wasn't and that he actually seemed to like hitting me, I... well, I thought that if I told you, you'd probably kill him."

"And you'd have been right." Harry's voice had taken on a tone that neither Ed nor Isabel recognised.

"I realised that my past, my not being married when I had Ed just gave him an excuse for his behaviour."

"Is that why you sent me away to school?" Ed asked, in a gentle tone.

"Partially. I was worried that he might turn on you one day, but the real reason was that he told me I had to." Again there was silence as both men tried to take in the information.

"What do you mean?" Harry was finding it difficult to speak.

"We'd had a particular bad argument one evening. He'd hit me very hard and I'd fallen and hurt my head. He'd stormed off and didn't come home until the next morning. I have no idea where he went, or who he was with... and I don't care. But when he came back, he told me Ed had to go away to school. I didn't want to do it and I argued with him but he said he wouldn't have my bastard child in the house. As soon as he started saying things like that, I knew it was safer to get Ed away, so I came to you, Harry, for help."

"Yes, but only for help with Ed. Isabel, I could have helped you as well."

"I know. I wasn't thinking straight."

Harry thought for a moment. "What's changed?" he asked suddenly.

"What do you mean?" Isabel asked in return.

"All of this happened years ago. You married that... that animal when Ed was nearly eleven years old and he's known about Ed since before then. Why are you telling us this now? What's happened?" He sat down in the chair opposite her, leaning forward and looking into her face. "Tell me, Isabel..."

"I will," she replied. "That's why I invited you both." She swallowed hard. "But if I'm going to tell you, then I have to tell Ed all of it..." She stared into Harry's face.

"Then tell him," Harry said. "I know we agreed to keep it a secret, but that was really your idea, not mine. If he needs to know for me to sort this out, then tell him."

"I do wish you two would stop speaking in riddles."

"We're not... well, not really." Isabel dried her eyes again. "I'll go back to the story." She took another deep breath. "When Harry brought us back here, he did some very generous things."

"They weren't generous, Isabel."

"It's my story, Harry. And yes, they were."

"Harry, stop interrupting and let mother tell the story." Ed smiled over at Harry, who was looking embarrassed.

"Harry had said I could live in this house and I'd offered to pay him rent once I was earning enough money, but instead, he gave me the house. He signed it over to me completely, so it's mine and no-one else's. As you know, Harry still pays me a monthly allowance and, if I'm honest," she lowered her voice conspiratorially, "I don't think Charles likes that very much, or the fact that I own the house we live in. Anyway, on the night we first arrived here, Harry also gave me an envelope, containing a legal document." She took a small key from her handbag, got up and went across to the walnut bureau by the window. Using the key, she opened the top drawer and withdrew a large, faded and slightly dog-eared envelope, which she handed to Ed. "This is really for you," she said. "Harry wanted to ensure you were always safe, so he put some money in trust for you." Ed looked at Harry, his confusion obvious. Harry nodded his head and Ed opened the envelope, looking down at the document in front of him.

"I studied Classics," he said. "I don't understand this at all."

Harry stood and crossed the room to sit back down next to Ed. Leaning across, he took the paper from Ed's hands. "Basically, what it says is that, when you reach the age of 25, or you get married – whichever comes first – you will inherit forty thousand pounds, plus the interest which has been accruing on that sum over the last twenty years." Harry glanced up at Ed and saw the look of shock in his eyes. "What's the matter?" he said.

"Forty thousand?" Ed whispered. "That's... that's... that's a bloody fortune, Harry."

"Well, it was about a quarter of my fortune in 1919," Harry said. "I'm worth a good deal more than that now, but I had to think of Rose at the time, and then Amy, so I couldn't be any more generous than that, I'm afraid."

"*More* generous? What the hell are you talking about? I can't take forty thousand pounds from you, Harry."

"Oh, here we go again. Just like your mother." Harry sat back, smiling lightly. "It's not negotiable, Ed. You're not 'taking' it from me. I'm giving it to you. Now, stop distracting me." He turned back to Isabel. "I still don't understand why you're telling us this now. What's changed?" Ed continued to stare at Harry for a moment, then turned back to his mother.

"After what happened when we got married, I'd decided not to tell Charles about Ed's trust fund. To be honest, Harry, as you know, I've never really understood how it worked. You did explain that I was the trustee until Ed came of age, but I've never really fathomed what that meant and I've never really had to do anything. Your accountants seem to take care of everything and send me annual statements, which are kept separately in there." She glanced across at the bureau. "Anyway, last Tuesday evening, I was sitting at the desk, contemplating your invitation to Ed's party and wondering how to reply, because I did so want to come, even though Charles had said we couldn't, when I heard a scream coming from the kitchen. I dashed out of the room, and left the drawer unlocked – which I never normally do. I found Mary had burned her arm on the stove. We bathed it in cold water and I dressed it and made her some tea and, after a short while, she was fine, so I came back in here to find Charles sitting at my desk, reading through the statements, with that envelope lying open on the desk." Harry sat forward again. Isabel looked across at him. "You probably won't be aware, but Charles' business hasn't been doing very well of late. He clearly saw this as a golden opportunity and told me in no uncertain terms that, either I gave him access to Ed's money, or he would tell the whole village all about Ed's parentage. To be honest, Harry, I wouldn't know how to give him access to Ed's money, even if I wanted to. But I've got no intention of letting that man get away with this." Her voice suddenly grew steely in tone. "He's bullied and beaten me for ten years, but I've had enough. I won't let him take Ed's future away from him."

Harry put the trust document on the coffee table in front of him, got up and walked across the room to Isabel. "What do you want me to do?" he asked, the gentleness of his tone taking Ed by surprise.

"I want you to protect Ed's money," she replied.

"But that's completely safe, Isabel. He can't get to that. He never could have done. My question is, what can I do for *you?*" He turned and glanced at the clock on the sideboard. "He'll be back soon. Do you want him to find us here? Do you want us to go? What do you want, Isabel? Just tell me and I'll make sure it's done."

"Oh, Harry," she stood and put her hand on his arm. "You've always looked after me. I just wish I'd listened to you all those years ago." For a moment, they seemed to forget Ed was in the room.

"You were lonely, Isabel. I understood that you wanted company and someone to share your life with."

"Why him, though? Why did I choose so badly? You warned me about him and I refused to listen." Harry didn't reply because he didn't know what to say. "He... He'd have been ashamed of me, wouldn't he?" Isabel continued, tears forming in her eyes again.

"God, no," Harry replied. "Isabel, Eddie loved you more than life itself. He would never have been ashamed of you... especially now. But please, before Charles comes back, tell me what you want me to do."

"I want him out of my life, Harry, for good. I can't bear to be in the same room as him. He makes my flesh crawl." She shivered as she spoke.

"Consider it done."

"Just like that?" Ed spoke and they turned, remembering he was there.

"Just like that," Harry replied. Ed stared at Harry for a moment and saw a man he barely recognised nod his head, just once.

****

"It was so unlike you," Ed said. They were having tea on the terrace later that afternoon and Ed had finished telling an abridged version of the story to both Elise and Amy, who'd finally got out of bed just before lunch. Elise and Harry were sitting close together on chairs at the tea table, and Amy was next to Ed, perched on the low wall surrounding the rose bed.

"What was?" Harry asked.

"The way you dealt with Dobson. Your whole demeanour changed when he came into the room. Remind me never to get on the wrong side of you!"

"I'm not sure you could." Harry smiled. "Look, all I really did was pay the man off. Bullies like him are always very easy to deal with. You just have to scare them."

"But you were so intimidating... I've never seen you like that."

"I have. I've seen him put a bully in his place before," Elise said, leaning in to Harry.

"And that story can definitely wait for another day." Harry glanced across at her.

"Do you think he'll leave her alone now?" Elise asked.

"If he knows what's good for him," Ed replied. "Harry left him in no doubt as to what would happen to him if he didn't. He was..."

"Oh, do be quiet, boy," Harry said.

"Did you really warn her against him?" Ed asked, recalling part of the earlier conversation.

Harry nodded. "Yes, but as she said, she wouldn't listen. We argued quite badly at the time and it caused a bit of rift. You were too young to know what was going on and I wouldn't let the argument come between you and I, even though your mother was being particularly difficult."

"Why did she marry him do you think?"

"I think Dobson has one of those personalities that captivate certain women, and at the time, your mother was vulnerable. He took advantage. I have no doubt he'll do it again to some other unsuspecting female... But at least it won't be Isabel." Harry turned to Elise. "She'll be fine once she gets over the shock of it. I've given her Griffin's name. He's still quite new to the area, but he'll be able to handle her divorce without any problem at all. The sooner she's free of that man, the better." Harry was referring to Robert Griffin, who had taken over Harry's father's law practice in the town, about six months previously.

"Changing the subject slightly, Harry... I'm still not sure about accepting this money, you know," Ed said, and then glanced at Amy, wondering whether he should have spoken in front of her.

"Don't worry. Amy knows," Harry reassured him. "Both Amy and Rose have always known about it, and they've known about their own trust funds and that Isabel wanted yours kept a secret from you."

"Not that I ever understood why," Amy said. "I'm glad you know now, though. I've always hated keeping it a secret from you." She nudged Ed with her shoulder.

"It's not our place to question Isabel's motives," Harry said. "I understood completely that she wanted Ed to grow up independently and make his own way."

"Yes, but knowing about my inheritance doesn't affect me wanting to earn my own money and make my own way," Amy argued.

"And everyone is different," Elise put in. "You have to remember that Isabel's father was a vicar; she was brought up in a more austere household."

"Austere? Her bloody father threw her out!" Ed raised his voice and then saw Harry look heavenwards.

"What are you talking about?" Amy asked, looking from Ed to her father and back again.

"Oh God, I forgot that no-one else knew about that bit," Ed said, looking apologetic.

Harry took a deep breath. "Amy, what Ed is talking about – which he shouldn't be – is that Isabel and Edward weren't married when Ed was conceived. Her father threw her out when he found out about it."

"And he had the nerve to call himself a man of the church?" Amy replied, getting up and helping herself to a second slice of sponge cake. "There was a war on. Surely there were lots of unexpected pregnancies happening all over the place at a time like that. Why would he be so surprised?" Elise nearly choked on her tea; Ed laughed out loud, and Harry just looked knowingly at his daughter as she sat down again.

"Well, it may not mean very much to you now," he said, "but twenty years ago, war or no war, it did. People, especially in small villages like this, looked down on unmarried mothers and, more importantly, they often treated their children differently to others."

"Really? That's dreadful."

"Yes, it is."

"But you say her father, this supposed man of the church, threw her out?"

"Yes."

"So, what happened?"

Harry took a deep breath and looked to Ed, who just shrugged his shoulders. "It's your story, Harry. I was only a baby."

"Thanks. Well, after I'd visited the vicarage and had the door slammed in my face, I found Isabel and Ed in a dreadful room, with no proper heating and not much food, so I brought them back here to Holly Cottage."

"Yes, where he promptly gave my mother the house and settled a cool forty thousand pounds on me." Ed paused for a moment, then continued, "Why did you do that, Harry? I mean, don't get me wrong, I know you're incredibly generous and everything, but it does seem like an awfully big thing to do for the wife – well, not even the wife, really – and child of a fellow officer. I mean, I've always known that my father and you were friends in the army, but I think giving me this large a sum of money goes above and beyond, don't you?"

Elise put down her cup and reached for Harry's hand, feeling the sweat forming in his palm. "Not necessarily," she replied. "Harry and Edward served together for a long time... There was a war on... Things were different then."

"Even so, Elise, forty thousand is a huge amount of money; giving someone a house is a big step. Most people don't do things like that, not even for someone they've known for a long time. Do I have to take the money?"

"Yes, you do." Harry found his voice at last. He stared down the garden, unable to look at anyone. "I had my reasons for giving you the money and for giving your mother the house."

"Then would you mind explaining them?" Ed seemed almost angry and Harry could see his friend Eddie in the young man in front of him. He was so reluctant to speak, to reveal any of his war, but he desperately needed Ed to understand and accept. He sighed and realised that he had no choice.

"As Elise said, Eddie and I served together from the beginning... We trained together, went to France together and stayed in the same Company all the way through." He gripped Elise's hand and she knew how difficult he would be finding this. He took a very deep breath and she felt him shudder. She glanced across at Ed, knowing he had no idea what this was costing Harry. "Two days before he died, we argued for the one and only time in our whole friendship. The argument was about me looking after Isabel. Eddie wanted me to promise I'd do it and I refused. I didn't see the need to make a promise like that, because I was convinced Eddie would make it back alive. I used to joke with him that I was such a big target, they'd be bound to hit me and not him." Harry tried to smile, but failed. He swallowed hard. "Eventually, he made me promise, but then I think he felt guilty. He'd shouted at me and said some things I think he regretted. I remember he said that he hadn't asked me to take care of Isabel because I was rich, and that I didn't need to buy her a house, or provide for her for the rest of her life."

"And yet, you have done," Amy whispered, looking confused.

"Yes." He looked at her for the first time and she noticed the tears in his eyes. "I told him I would do anything for Isabel. 'Whatever it takes' were my precise words." His voice cracked slightly. "When he was... when he... was... killed, she became my responsibility and she will remain just that until the day I die." He turned and looked at Ed. " And that applies to you too." His words were barely audible and, as he finished speaking, he let go of Elise's hand and got to his feet, muttering, "Excuse me," as he stumbled into the house through the french window.

"Oh God," Ed said. "Is he going to be all right?"

"I'll give him a minute and then go to him," Elise replied.

"That's the most he's ever told us about the war," Amy said, wiping a tear from her cheek with the back of her hand. Ed put his arm around her and pulled her close to him. "He finds it very hard still, doesn't he?"

"He always will, sweetheart."

"I wish I hadn't pushed him now," Ed said, offering Amy his handkerchief, which she accepted.

"He obviously thought you needed to know, or he would have found a way not to tell you, like he usually does. Trust me, he won't blame you."

"I hope you're right."

"I'd better go up to him now. Will you two be okay?" Elise asked, standing.

"Yes, we're fine," Ed replied. "Tell him I'm grateful for the money. I didn't mean to sound so ungracious. Please tell him I'm sorry."

"There's no need. You have nothing to be sorry for. And he understands – about the money, I mean."

Upstairs, Elise found Harry sitting on the edge of their bed, his shoulders slumped and shaking as tears ran down his cheeks. She sat next to him and simply held him in her arms while he cried and cried.

"Oh God, Elise. Like father, like son… They're so, so alike," he sobbed.

"I know. And you feel responsible for both of them."

Chapter Three

Early Autumn 1939

"This morning the British Ambassador in Berlin handed the German Government a final Note stating that, unless we heard from them by eleven o'clock that they were prepared at once to withdraw their troops from Poland, a state of war would exist between us.

I have to tell you now that no such undertaking has been received, and that consequently this country is at war with Germany…"

The voice on the radio continued, but neither of them really listened to anything further. Harry looked at Elise, who was sitting on the sofa, surrounded by swatches of material for the new curtains and chair covers. He noted the tears in her eyes and her wringing hands, clasped in her lap.

"Don't," he said, getting up from his seat and limping across the room, sweeping all the materials to the floor to sit next to her. "It will be all right."

"How do you know?" she whispered. "It wasn't last time, was it? Even now, you still have nightmares. You still have problems."

"We'll be together this time. Whatever else happens, we'll be together." He pulled her into him and held her tight. "I won't leave you. Nothing will happen to me, or you. It won't be like before, I promise."

"Will you be all right, though?" She remembered his breakdown just weeks before, following Ed's party.

"As long as we're together, I'll be absolutely fine. You'll mend me if I break, just like you always do, you know that."

"And what about Ed?"

Harry felt a frisson of fear grip his heart. "He'll be in the thick of things, I imagine," he said, surprised by the strength of his own voice.

"And you're happy about that?" Elise stared at him.

"No, darling, of course I'm not happy about it. I'm absolutely terrified, and if I could do this for him, I would, but I can't."

"Can't you stop him?"

"No. And even if I could, I wouldn't. Ed has to do what he thinks is right. The same as all the other young men and women… just like I did. I can't deny him that."

"But what if…?" Elise couldn't bring herself to say the words out loud.

"Then our hearts will break…" He kissed her and felt her relax, just as Amy came running in through the door.

"What's wrong?" she asked.

"Come and sit down," Elise said, wiping her eyes on the back of her hand. "They've just announced that we're at war with Germany."

"Does that mean I don't have to start school tomorrow?" Amy asked. Elise and Harry looked at each other and laughed. "What?" Amy said. "If there's a war on, then surely things like school don't matter any more."

"Nice try," Harry said. "You'll be at school tomorrow just as planned."

Amy feigned a sulk, then turned to her mother. "What about Uncle Henri?" she asked. "Is it too late for them to leave France and come here now?"

Harry understood Amy's interest and that she was really only asking because she cared about her uncle, aunt and cousin, but he wished she'd been a bit more subtle. Still, subtlety wasn't really Amy's strongpoint. He wondered if it was any fifteen year-old's strongpoint.

"I don't know," Elise replied, her fear and worry obvious.

"I doubt if anything will happen very quickly," Harry intervened. "I'm sure we'll hear from them soon enough. You must try not to worry about them. Henri will do whatever is sensible. Even he isn't so stubborn that he'll risk their lives."

Elise swallowed hard and Amy leant over and hugged her mother. "Dad's right, you know. Aunty Sophie won't let him do anything silly."

"Aunty Sophie will do anything that suits Aunty Sophie, or that foolish son of hers," Elise said, without thinking, then glanced at Amy.

"Somehow, I don't think you were supposed to say that in front of me," Amy said, smiling and Elise smiled back. "That's better, Mummy," she said, getting up. "I'm going to ask Polly to make some tea. I assume you'd like some?"

"Yes please, darling," Elise said. "And thank you."

"Anytime," Amy shouted as the door closed behind her.

"Do you think she realised I wasn't thanking her for getting the tea?" Elise asked, snuggling into Harry's chest and relishing the comfort of his arm around her.

"Yes. She's a wise girl, that one. Sometimes too wise for her own good."

"I am worried about Henri, though. Sophie's such a stupid, selfish woman. I thought she was quite nice when they got married, but once Luc was born, I realised she's… she's…"

"What?"

"I don't know the word in English."

"Well, say it in French, then."

"I want to say, *elle est espiègle.*"

"Oh. That's quite polite, really. I was expecting something a bit ruder than that!"

"That's as may be, but what does it mean in English?"

"It means she's mischievous, skittish. Are you sure that's what you mean? I'd say she was probably the most annoying woman I've ever met, completely absorbed in herself and her lawless son, and without any sense of propriety."

"And I thought it was just me she infuriated."

"No, I think she infuriates every sane person she meets. Don't get me wrong. I can see why Henri married her." He smiled. "She's an attractive woman…"

"Oh, is she now?" Elise sat up, pulling away from him, a grin beginning to form on her generous lips.

"Yes, she's attractive, in an obvious sort of way, but she's nothing compared to you, my love. You're beautiful." He lifted her hand to his lips and kissed her fingers, one by one. "Sensual, erotic…" He ran his fingers up her bare arm, towards the capped sleeve of her yellow floral dress. "Come upstairs with me…" he whispered.

"Now?"

"Yes, now. I want you."

"But what about…" her words were suffocated by his lips.

"I don't care," he murmured between kisses. "God, you feel so good." He kissed her more deeply and ran his hand up her thigh towards the silky white knickers he'd watched her put on that morning. "I don't care about anything except getting you back into bed."

She giggled and stood, just as the door opened and Polly entered, carrying a tray of tea things, followed by Amy.

"Miss Amy ordered tea, Mrs Belmont." Polly said, not noticing the speed with which Harry straightened his clothes and changed position on the sofa, while Elise giggled again, this time at his obvious discomfort and walked calmly to the mantlepiece where she adjusted her hair, and succeeded, in a way that nearly drove him mad, to look nonchalant. "I told her you normally have coffee at this time of the morning, but she insisted that tea was required." She placed the tray on the sideboard and looked over at them for the first time, taking in Elise's still-flushed cheeks. "Is everything all right?"

"Yes, thank you, Polly," Elise said. "Mr Belmont and I were just discussing what might happen to my brother, now that war's been declared…"

"Oh don't you start on about this flaming war," Polly began and then turned bright red. "I do apologise, Mrs Belmont," she said. "I don't know what came over me. It's just that my Dennis has talked of nothing else for this last half hour and I've had enough already. He seems to forget far too quickly that I lost my fiancé last time round. But he just talks about Hitler this and Hitler that, as if he's going to be able to do anything about it. I swear, if it goes on this time for as long as the last one, I'll have strangled him before we get half way through, and that's a promise. Would you like me to pour?" she added.

Amy hid her giggle, while Elise turned, managed to keep a straight face and declined Polly's offer. "We'll manage, thank you."

"Lunch at one..." Polly said as she left the room, more as a statement than a question.

"Good lord," Harry said, heaving a sigh of relief. "Poor Dennis."

"Poor Hitler, if he ever gets over here," Amy added. "I think he'll head straight back to Germany if Polly ever gets hold of him."

"Well, let's just hope it doesn't come to that," Elise said, pouring tea and handing out the cups.

"Are Rose and Matthew still coming down next weekend?" Amy asked as she mopped up the last of her gravy with a roast potato.

"Yes, as far as I know," Harry replied. "I think Ed's expecting some leave too, so it will be a fairly full house."

Amy perked up. "I didn't know Ed was coming too. That's good."

"Yes, you can tell him all about your first week at school."

"Don't remind me." Her face turned glum, but the expression didn't last for long. Polly came into the room, bearing a bowl of fruit salad and a jug of cream. "Oh thank goodness it's not a heavy pudding," Amy said. "I've eaten far too many potatoes, as usual."

"While you're here, Polly," Elise said, "You know we've got the family down next weekend?"

"Yes, Mrs Belmont. Everyone's arriving on Saturday morning."

"That's right. Well, on Saturday evening, we've also invited Mr and Mrs King over, together with George and Anne. So we'll be ten for dinner."

"Very good, Mrs Belmont."

"If you need any extra help, you can always get one of the village girls in."

"They're more trouble than they're worth," Polly said over her shoulder as she left the room. "But thank you for the offer."

"I didn't realise Uncle William and Aunt Charlotte would be coming too," Amy said, spearing a piece of apple with her fork.

"Well, George is talking about joining up. He doesn't have to, of course; farming is a reserved occupation, but he wants to go and

William does have enough help on the farm... William asked if he could have a chat with me about it and this seemed the best way of diffusing the situation," Harry explained.

"Don't tell me Uncle William's going to try and stop him," Amy said.

"I don't think he could, even if he wanted to. George is adamant he's going. But it's not for us to interfere, Amy, so don't you start anything. Understood?"

"Yes, Daddy. I'll be on my best behaviour."

"That's exactly what I'm dreading," Harry grinned at his daughter as she nearly choked on her apple.

Later that afternoon, upstairs in her room, Amy lay on her bed, resting her head on the pillow and looking out of the window at the branches of the trees. Just six more days and Ed would be home. She'd get Polly to wash and press her navy blue dress, the one with the white collar and belt. It had boxed pleats that showed off her hips and made her waist look smaller. On their last trip into town, Elise had finally given in and bought her some stockings, after months of pleading, so she wouldn't have to wear socks; she'd look more like a woman and less like a schoolgirl, at last. Maybe Ed might actually notice. Maybe he'd see her as more than the little sister that she wasn't. Maybe...

****

"Nice dress, kiddo," Ed called as Amy entered the sitting room. She blushed and wanted to cry. 'Kiddo?' Her plan hadn't worked then. She glanced around the room, deliberately trying to ignore Ed, who was moving across the floor towards her. Amy's eyes settled on Anne, sitting in the chair nearest to the window and she walked over quickly, sitting down on the floor by her feet.

"Hello, how are you?" Anne asked, leaning down slightly. "How's school?"

"It's okay," Amy said, desperately trying not to look in Ed's direction. "You went there too, didn't you?"

"Yes, for my sins."

"What did you think?"

"It was okay, except for the games mistress. What was her name...?"

"Not Miss Minter?"

"Yes, that was her. She's never still teaching?"

"Yes, she is."

"My goodness, she must be sixty if she's a day."

"At least. It's quite funny though. The girls run rings round her and she can't keep up without losing her breath."

"I'd love to see that. She made my life a misery. I hated games, especially cross-country running."

"Everyone seems to just walk... well, except the ones who actually like running."

Anne laughed, then looked up as Ed approached. "Here's the hero, then," she beamed, grinning at Ed. Amy noticed the glint in Anne's eye.

"I'm not a hero yet, and I might never be," Ed said, sitting down next to Amy. "Are you avoiding me?" he asked.

"No. I'm circulating. It's expected."

"You two are like brother and sister, aren't you?" Anne said.

"Evidently," Amy whispered under her breath, then cleared her throat. "Yes, we are, but I suppose that comes of growing up together..."

"Ed," Anne interrupted, seeming a little nervous, "George and I were thinking of heading up to London tomorrow, maybe going to a club or two. Would you like to join us?"

"Sounds like fun. Count me in," Ed replied.

"Great!" Anne positively beamed. "We can catch the train. We could stay over up in town... if you'd like?" Amy felt herself blush. Could Anne be any more transparent, she wondered.

"I can't," Ed replied. "I'm due back at base first thing on Monday morning."

Anne's shoulders fell. "Oh, that is a shame." She put her hand on Ed's arm. "I shall just have to make the most of you while I've got you, then."

Ed seemed confused, but replied, "Yes, I suppose you will." He looked around the room. "And now, if you'll excuse me, ladies, I'm going to follow Amy's lead and circulate." He got up and went over to where Harry was talking to George in the furthest corner of the room.

"Oh God," Anne said, once he was out of earshot.

"What's the matter?" Amy replied.

"I hope George doesn't give me away."

"Whatever do you mean?"

"Well, I rather made that up, about George and I having plans. We don't."

"You mean you lied? Why on earth would you do that?"

"Isn't it obvious? About Ed, I mean… I'm head over heels about him…"

"My father is expecting you to talk me out of this," George said.

"Well, I won't," Harry replied. "You must do whatever you feel is right for you. Your father's feelings don't really come into it."

"Didn't you consult your father before you joined up?"

"No." Harry recalled his own enlistment. "I took myself off into town one morning, walked straight to the barracks, signed all the papers, and came home, telling my parents it was a fait accompli. I had Rose to consider too… I had to do my duty by her and that meant protecting her the only way I could."

"That's my point, really. How can I sit on the sidelines, working on the farm, when I've got a perfectly good degree in engineering and can do something useful for the war? There are plenty of people who can plough fields."

"If this is what you want, George, you know I'll support you. I think I know why your father is trying to dissuade you and I'll back you one hundred percent."

"Why is he trying to talk me out of it?"

Harry paused for a moment, looking down at himself. "Because he's afraid that you'll end up like me."

"Dear God," Ed's voice interrupted their conversation. "I'm sorry," he said. "I didn't mean to intrude or eavesdrop, but that's ridiculous."

"No it isn't," Harry said. "It's not ridiculous at all. It's perfectly reasonable. Neither of you know what I was like when I came back. William does. He was here. No-one would want that for their son."

"Tell us about it," George urged.

"No," Harry said. "You know perfectly well I never talk about it." He looked at Ed and their eyes met for a moment. Harry turned back to George. "Your father might tell you some of it, if you ask him. He might tell what happened between us when I got back from Germany."

"Germany? Didn't you serve in France?" Ed asked

"Yes, but I was a POW for a short while, and before you ask any more, that's as much as you're getting out of me."

"If it was so bad you won't even talk about it, then why were you happy for Ed to go into the RAF? He's the closest thing to a son you could have," George asked.

"Because we should never allow our own feelings or fears to stand in the way of our children or those we love," Harry replied. "No matter how real those fears are. Everyone has the right to live their own life…" Ed noticed Harry's hand shaking slightly.

"You'll talk to my father?" George urged.

"Yes, I'll talk to him," Harry replied.

"Then when you do, will you tell him one thing from me?"

"Of course, but you could tell him yourself, you know."

"I think it will carry more weight coming from you, Harry."

"What is it you want me to tell him?"

"I'd like you to say to him that if his fear really is that I'll come back like you, he needn't worry." George blinked a few times and cleared his throat. "You see, I'd be honoured to be even half the man that you are, Harry." And with that, he turned and walked across the room, to join Anne and Amy, who were now deep in conversation with Rose and Matthew.

"Well, that wasn't at all embarrassing," Harry said after a few moments. "And if he thinks I'm repeating that to William, he can think again."

"Why?" Ed replied. "I'm sure William knows it already. I think most people who get to know you feel like that."

"Oh, be quiet will you, and get me a whisky."

"How can I be sure he'll be all right?" William asked, the nervousness in his voice apparent. He and Harry were standing alone on the terrace in the moonlight. They'd all enjoyed a marvellous meal and everyone else was drinking coffee in the sitting room.

"You can't, Bill," Harry replied. "But if you don't let him do this, if you force him to stay on the farm, he'll come to resent you and you'll drive a wedge between the two of you that you'll regret for the rest of your lives."

"And if he gets killed? Or… or injured?"

"Then you'll cope with it somehow, and I'll help you. But you can't stop him. And you shouldn't want to. You should feel proud that he wants to do this. I know what you're afraid of, Bill. Not everyone dies and not everyone gets badly wounded."

"Even if he comes back physically in one piece, he might not be all right. Not all your wounds were on the outside, Harry. We both know that. I remember you going off into the woods, and trying to kill yourself. I remember all those things you told me, about the sights you saw, the men you killed, the dead bodies. I remember every word of it. It haunts me still and I wasn't even there, for Christ's sake."

"I know and I'm grateful that you've never told anyone. It wasn't my finest hour."

"But I don't want that for him."

"Neither do I. And I don't want it for Ed either, but I won't stop him from doing what he thinks is right. It's their turn." He saw William's shoulders drop and knew he'd got his message through. "We have to let them take it," Harry said quietly.

"And if they don't…?"

"Then we'll deal with the consequences."

****

Early the next morning, Harry lay in bed, watching Elise sleep. He loved to do this and had done, ever since the first time he'd spent the night with her. Then, twenty or more years ago, he'd marvelled at her youth, her beauty, and why she'd chosen a man nearly fifteen years older than her as her first lover. Now, her spell over him was unbroken and was, if possible, even stronger. Her skin was so soft, he longed to reach out and touch her, but he didn't want to spoil the moment, so he just lay on his side, studying her, drinking her in. She turned slightly, pushing the sheet down. It was a warm morning and she seemed to be hot. Her hair looked slightly damp against her cheeks and forehead, and he noticed small beads of sweat on her neck, longing to lick them away, to taste her. Her movement had exposed her breasts and her nipples hardened as the breeze from the open windows blew across them. Harry smiled. He loved the way her body reacted to the slightest thing. Just his breath on her thighs was enough to make her moan and shudder with pleasure. She turned her head towards him and opened her eyes.

"Good morning," she whispered, her voice thick with sleep.

"Good morning." He leant over and kissed her gently. "You look so beautiful."

"I'm sure I look a mess. I'm very warm."

"Let me help you with that." Harry smiled and pushed the sheet further down the bed, exposing her naked body.

"Hmm, that's better." She stretched lazily.

"It certainly is. You look even more beautiful now." He moved carefully down the bed, running his tongue across her stomach and hips, before leaning in closer and blowing gently over the tops of her thighs. She moaned and parted her legs, her head rolling back into the pillow...

Much later, she lay across him, her breaths coming in short bursts, her hair dishevelled, her eyes closed and her cheeks pink and flushed. Harry ran his fingers along her still parted thighs, up across her stomach and higher. Elise caught his hand in hers, drew it to her lips and kissed his fingers gently.

"You have to stop," she said. "If we don't get up soon, everyone will wonder where we are."

"Do I look like I care?" Harry replied.

"You might not, but I need the bathroom." She clambered off the bed and wrapped herself in a pale pink silk dressing gown. They'd moved into the master suite a couple of weeks earlier, after Elise had arranged for it to be completely redecorated and refurbished, and it was beautiful. Harry loved what she'd done. The old, dated furniture had gone and had been replaced with new, modern pieces in a paler wood. There was a four-poster bed, with pale cream drapes which matched the curtains and there were a few chairs scattered around the room, which Harry needed to sit or lean on as he dressed and undressed, since he often didn't use his stick in the bedroom.

"Spoilsport." Harry smiled across at her as she walked to their adjoining bathroom. "I could always join you in there," he called.

"Not if we want to have breakfast before lunchtime," she replied from behind the closed door.

"You're no fun anymore," Harry said.

"Perhaps you should take a mistress," Elise teased. "I'm told a lot of French men do."

Harry got out of bed and limped across to the bathroom. "Well I'm not French. Besides, I'd never have the energy. And anyway," he opened the door to find his wife running a bath, "who else would put up with me?"

"Indeed. You can be very demanding at times." She flicked water at him as he started to brush his teeth.

"Do you really want to start playing games with me?" he said, slowly putting his toothbrush down by the side of the sink.

"You've left your stick in the bedroom, don't forget. So, I have the advantage. I can run faster than you."

"Only if you can get past me." He reached for her, grabbing her arm and pulling her towards him. "You're supposed to make some effort to get away," he said, kissing her.

"Except I don't want to." She deepened the kiss, running her hands down his bare chest and across his stomach. "We need to stop this," she said. "You're too distracting. I must have my bath. Now, out with you!" She tried to sound severe, but failed dismally.

"Why don't we save time and water and I'll get in the bath with you?"

"Because then we'll never get any breakfast."

"Personally, I think breakfast is overrated," Harry said, kissing her again and allowing himself to be shooed gently from the room. His leg was aching and he sat down on the chair by the open bathroom door.

"Is it bad today?" Elise asked, as she tied her hair into a loose bun behind her head.

"How did you know?" He turned in time to see her drop her gown to the floor and climb into the bath.

"I saw you wince. Besides, I just know. I'll give you a massage later, when our guests have left."

"Thank you. That might help. I think I stood up for too long last night."

"I'll be as quick as I can in here and then you can have a soak in the hot water. That'll be good for you."

"You make me sound like an old man."

She turned and grinned at him. "Well, you'll be sixty soon…"

"Um, not for five years yet, thank you very much."

"That's still pretty old."

"Are you putting me out for pasture then?"

"I'll think about it."

"Oh, will you now…" Harry got to his feet, ignoring the pain in his knee and went back into the bathroom, closing the door behind him.

Matthew sat with Harry and Elise, watching Amy and Rose play badminton on the lawn. Ed was on his way up to London with Anne and George, who had been persuaded by his sister to join in the trip, despite his initial reluctance.

"Is everything all right between you two?" Harry asked Matthew. "I'm not trying to interfere, but Rose still seems very low. I thought things might have improved by now."

"I think she's just taking a while to get over her grandmother's death, which is understandable. That and she's finding the talk of war worrying. I'm having to spend even more time at the hospital, which she hates. There's not an awful lot I can do about that, though. I suggested she might move down here to be with you and away from London, but she just laughed."

Harry decided to take the bull by the horns. "She told me in the summer that she thinks you're having an affair; that working extra hours at the hospital is just an excuse for you to see your mistress."

"What? That's ridiculous."

"That's exactly what I said, Matthew. I did tell her to speak to you about it, and she was going to when you came down to pick her up after mother's funeral, but then she made some excuse about wanting to have the conversation in private at home. If I know my daughter though, I'll bet she never did."

Matthew looked down the garden for a few minutes. "No, Harry, she didn't. But it's no wonder she laughed when I suggested she move out. She must have thought I was going to install my 'other woman' in our house." He leant forward, resting his head in his hands, then sighed deeply.

"You need to talk," Harry said gently and Matthew looked up again. "Explain how things are. She's not unreasonable, just insecure. That's my fault for leaving her so much when she was a child. I think she just expects everyone to abandon her. You know, don't you, that it took Elise and me, and my parents, nearly two years to convince her that she could trust me enough to live with us permanently after the war? Once Elise and I were married, we all lived here together until 1922 and only then could Rose be convinced to move to Cornwall with us. She trusted my parents, but not me, and was certain I'd leave her and go away again."

"But I'd never leave her. She must know that by now."

"Tell her, not me," Harry said, getting up awkwardly. "But do it soon." He went inside the house, shaking his head. Elise smiled at Matthew, but sensed a growing anger under the surface.

As soon as the badminton match finished, Matthew walked down onto the lawn and, much to everyone's surprise, almost dragged Rose back into the house, and through the sitting room. Their bedroom window overlooked the back garden and, as Amy and Elise looked blankly at each other, raised voices could be heard. They remained where they were for a few moments before Elise broke the awkward silence:

"Let's go indoors, shall we?"

Amy seemed reluctant. She wanted to try and hear what was going on between Matthew and Rose. "Come along," chivvied Elise. "It's Polly's afternoon off. You can help me in the kitchen."

"Really, Mother?" Amy moaned.

"Yes, really, Amy."

****

Ed was now stationed locally, at Tangmere, just a few miles away from the village, which was just to the north of Chichester, and had hoped this would mean he could see more of Harry and the family. He'd completed his training and was surprised to receive orders so quickly to be sent out to France. He'd been given a 24-hour pass and was due to set off across the Channel at some time in the next few days. He marvelled at how disorganised everything seemed, but at the same time, could barely contain his excitement.

He joined the family in time for dinner and found them discussing Henri, over drinks in the sitting room.

"You should write to him," Harry was saying to Elise. "They can come here. We can find them somewhere to live and I'm sure there would be work for Henri to do. William would help, I'm certain of it."

"How would they get here?"

"They can get out through Dunkirk or Calais," Ed said.

"Hello," Harry said, getting up. "I didn't see you come in." Ed helped himself to a whisky and soda, then went to Elise and kissed her on the cheek.

"How's everything?" he asked, looking across at Harry, pointedly.

"Fine," she smiled, giving Ed a slight nod of her head. Then she turned back to Harry. "What about money? Won't they need money for the journey?"

"If he needs cash, I'll send it."

"Won't that be more difficult now?

"Yes, is it even possible to send money to France now the war's started?" Amy asked.

"I've done it before," Harry said, and immediately wished he hadn't.

"When?" Amy enquired.

"In the last war," Elise replied, glancing at Harry.

"Why did you have to send money to France in the last war... you were there, weren't you?" Ed asked.

Harry looked at his feet. "It's a long story," he replied.

"Well, we're not in any rush," Ed said, sitting down on the arm of Amy's chair.

Harry stared at him. "I don't think they're going to let you escape until you tell them," Elise said, crossing the room and taking his arm. "Would you like me to start?" Harry shrugged and turned towards the fireplace. Elise looked at him for a moment and then turned back towards Amy and Ed. She sat down on the sofa.

"As you know," she began, "Harry visited me a few times on the farm." Amy and Ed both nodded: they knew that much. "Well, on his last visit, he found me in a mess. I'd received the news that Henri was missing, the harvest had failed because of the rain and we faced ruin. I was distraught. Harry... Harry dealt with everything. He convinced me that Henri would be fine – which, of course, he was – and then the next day, before I'd even woken up, he walked into Bethune, went to the post office and sent his father a telegram, telling him to send me a small fortune..."

"It was not a small fortune," Harry interrupted, turning to look at her.

"It was to me. It was enough to tide us over for six months... that's a small fortune," Elise continued. "Then he went to the bank and told them to give me access to the money when it arrived. He did all of this and then walked back to the farm, where he just announced his plan. Just like that." She clicked her fingers.

"How did you react?" Amy asked.

"I was stunned."

"Er… If you're going to tell the story, you should at least be accurate. You weren't stunned. You were angry." Harry limped across the room, sat down next to Elise and took her hand.

"I was only angry that you hadn't told me how rich you were," Elise said, smiling at him. "But you were rather keen on keeping things to yourself back then, too."

"Not the important things, if I remember rightly," Harry said, raising Elise's hand to his lips and kissing it gently.

"No, not the important things," she replied.

"And I'm not even going to ask what that means," Ed said, winking at Amy.

****

Early the next morning, Ed found Harry sitting in his study, staring into space.

"Sorry to intrude," he said.

"You aren't," Harry said. "I was just remembering."

"Happier times?" Ed asked.

"No, not happier… different. Another war." He sat up straight. "What can I do for you?"

"I wanted to talk to you. I've received my orders."

Harry felt his chest constricting. "Oh?" He swallowed hard. "I'm sure you're not supposed to tell me where you're going, but I think I can guess. I imagine there will be a stretch of water between us very soon?"

Ed laughed. "Well, at least I didn't actually *tell* you. Nobody says you're not allowed to guess."

"When do you leave?"

"Any day now."

Harry could feel his hand begin to shake and hid it from view beneath the desk. "How do you feel?" he asked.

"Oh, you know. Part of me is terrified; part of me can't wait."

"So, perfectly normal, then."

"Is it? Is that normal?"

"Definitely. I think you'll find that's how just about all your friends feel. A lot of them won't admit to the terrified part though."

"Anyway, I wanted to let you know. I haven't told the others, and I wondered if you could do it for me tonight, after I've gone. I'm rubbish at goodbyes, so I just thought I'd slip away this evening as usual, and pretend I'm going back to base like I normally would."

"No, Ed."

"But, Harry…"

"No. I'm sorry, it doesn't work like that."

"Oh."

"I know it's tough, but you have to say goodbye. If you don't, you'll regret it and it will be harder on everyone."

"Yes, but saying goodbye and walking away from you all is going to be impossible."

"Not impossible, just one of the hardest things you'll ever have to do. I should know, I did it often enough, so did your father. You get through it though." He nodded towards the door. "You have to, for them… just in case…" He heard the crack in his own voice and coughed to clear his throat. "I'll be with you and, once you're back with your friends, it honestly doesn't seem so bad."

"All right, Harry. I'll do it. Just don't leave me on my own with Elise and Amy, okay?"

"I won't, I promise."

Chapter Four

Autumn 1939

Polly's jaw dropped almost as soon as she opened the door and Marjorie Evans smiled, looking expectant. Behind Polly, Elise came down the stairs and stopped.

"What's wrong?" she asked, looking towards the open door and wondering why Polly was just standing there.

"Good morning, Mrs Belmont," called Marjorie Evans, over Polly's shoulder. "I've brought your evacuees."

"Oh, God! Is that today?" Elise was flustered. "I thought it was tomorrow they were arriving. Let them in, Polly, for heaven's sake."

Polly stood to one side and Marjorie ushered in a woman, carrying a bundled up infant, and holding the hand of a young toddler. "Well, it should have been tomorrow," explained the bustling Marjorie, depositing the large suitcase she was carrying to one side of the hall, "but in the manner of all things government these days, it's all gone to pot, and everyone's arrived a day early. I do hope it's not a problem."

Elise was acutely aware that they were talking about the evacuees as though they weren't there, and moved forward, her hand outstretched, "I'm Elise Belmont," she said, as the woman released the child's hand and she tentatively shook Elise's. "I'm so terribly sorry for the confusion. You're very welcome to our home. Please, do come in." She moved towards the sitting room. "Polly," she called over her shoulder, "can you fetch coffee and biscuits and some milk in a glass, please?" Polly scuttled off to the kitchen, but before she reached the door, Elise said, "Can you ask Dennis to come and see me? And let Mr Belmont know that our guests have arrived?"

"Yes, Mrs Belmont," Polly said, disappearing through the kitchen door.

Elise showed everyone into the sitting room and invited them to sit. "I'm so sorry," she repeated. "We've just had the new curtains delivered." She motioned to the empty windows, adorned only with black-out material, drawn to one side and then to the parcels scattered on the floor. "I've still got to hang them yet."

"This black-out ruins everything, doesn't it?" Marjorie Evans cut in. "My sitting room looks so funereal now. The black-out's longer than my curtains, so it's a constant reminder, even during the day." She turned in her seat and quickly made introductions, checking on her clipboard first. "Now," she said in her usual slightly nasal tones, "this is Mrs Sylvia Thornton, and her daughters, Linda and baby Jane." Sylvia nodded her head as her name was spoken. "They live in Poplar, which I believe is in the east of London?" Marjorie looked to Sylvia for confirmation, and she nodded again, still not saying a word. "And her husband is a London fireman." And with that, she tapped her clipboard, clearly demonstrating that she had reached the limits of her information.

At that moment, Harry appeared at the french windows, opened them and walked through, just managing to avoid tripping over the parcels still left on the floor. Immediately, Linda shied away, diving down behind her mother. Harry was used to this reaction in children and ignored it, approaching Sylvia and introducing himself. "I'm Harry," he said. "I'm so sorry for the confusion." He looked across at Elise. "Is Polly organising something to drink?"

Elise nodded. "I'll get her to arrange the bedrooms later on."

"We must seem so disorganised to you," Harry said, sitting in the chair furthest away from Linda. "Well, we are quite disorganised actually, but this is exceptionally bad, even for us." He smiled, and tried to make light of the awkward situation.

"It's really not your fault, Mr Belmont," Marjorie cut in. "The government has fouled up, as usual."

"Well, at least they're consistent," Harry replied.

Elise introduced everyone to Harry, although Linda still wouldn't come out from behind her mother, her face buried almost into the back of the sofa. Harry smiled and tried to look reassuring. At that moment, Polly entered, carrying a large tray, filled with cups, saucers and a coffee pot, with milk, sugar and a plate of biscuits, together with a glass of milk for Linda.

The arrival of the refreshments broke the ice a little, although it presented Sylvia with the problem of how to control Linda, take a cup and saucer and hold baby Jane at the same time. Elise offered to hold the baby while Sylvia drank her coffee and she reluctantly handed over the tiny bundle. Elise cradled her gently.

"Oh, it's lovely to hold a little one again," she said, caressing the baby's cheek.

There was a knock on the door and Dennis appeared, holding his cap in his hands. "You wanted to see me?" he asked, taking in the scene.

"Yes, Dennis," Elise replied. "Can you please take up the suitcase that's in the hall, and put it in the yellow bedroom? The second door on the right, at the top of the stairs… and then, can you bring down the old cot down from the nursery and put it in there too, over by the window?"

"Yes, Mrs Belmont. I'll do it right away." Dennis backed out of the room as he spoke.

"Thank you, Dennis," Elise called to the closing door.

"I'm sure your Rose will be having children of her own one day soon," Marjorie suggested, as though there had been no interruption.

"When she and Matthew are ready," Harry put in, getting up and coming over to look at the baby. "She's beautiful," he said.

"You 'ave kids of your own, then?" Sylvia said, speaking for the first time.

"Yes," Harry replied. "But they're much older. Our daughter Rose is married and lives in London with her husband. He's a doctor, so they can't really leave, unfortunately. Our younger daughter Amy is at school. She'll be home later and you'll meet her then."

Sylvia nodded. "How old is she? Your Amy?" she asked.

"She's nearly sixteen," Elise replied.

Marjorie finished her coffee, then delved into a large shopping bag, fishing out two leaflets. "These explain the protocol," she said, handing the pieces of paper to Harry. "There are details of what to do in the event of a problem, how much you get paid… It's all in the leaflets. Any problems, you can contact me; but not for the next day or two, if that's all right; I'm going to be up to my eyeballs finding homes for everyone." She closed her bag, got to her feet and straightened her jacket. "I'd better be off," she announced. "Plenty to do." Harry showed her out.

Sylvia put her coffee cup back on the tray and tried to encourage Linda to sit up and drink her milk. "Don't be so rude," she admonished. Harry came back into the room, and the little girl hid away again, much to Sylvia's embarrassment. "Linda!" she scolded.

"Don't worry," Harry said softly. "I'm sure it's all very strange for her."

"Why don't we go upstairs and you can see your rooms?" Elise offered. "The beds will still need making up, but you can have a look around, and I'll show you where the bathroom is."

Sylvia nodded and took the baby back from Elise before taking hold of Linda's hand and dragging her from the room, following Elise up the stairs. Harry remained in the sitting room, deciding that his presence was only serving to upset the little girl. At the top of the stairs, Elise guided Sylvia to the right and along the passageway, stopping at the first door on the right. "This will be Linda's room," she said, opening the door onto a pretty room, decorated in pale green, with a single bed, a dressing table and wardrobe.

"It's lovely," Sylvia replied, her mouth slightly open.

"Then if you come along here." Elise guided them back out into the corridor and opened the next door along. "I thought you and the baby could go in here." This room was larger, the walls painted in a bright yellow, with an ornate double bed, a fireplace, chest of drawers and a dressing table. In the corner, was a dark blue wing-backed chair and by the window, was the small cot which Dennis had just brought down from the nursery. "I'm so sorry the rooms aren't ready."

"No need to apologise, madam," Sylvia said.

“Please don’t call me ‘madam’,” Elise said. “My name is Elise, and my husband is Harry.” Sylvia nodded her head. “Now, I’m going to get some linen and then Polly and I will make up the beds.”

“I can do that, mad… Elise,” Sylvia said, correcting herself.

“Why don’t we do it together?” Elise offered. Sylvia smiled and nodded again. “Just give me a minute,” Elise said, leaving the room and returning a few moments later with a bundle of clean linen in her arms. “We don’t have cot bedding any more,” she said. “But we’ll make do.” She folded a single sheet, then used it to cover the cot mattress. Taking a second sheet, she placed it in the cot and covered it with a blanket, folded in half. “That should do,” she said. “Linda,” Elise suggested, “why don’t you sit down in the chair, while mummy and I make up the bed? Then we can go next door and see to your room.” The little girl obeyed quietly and Sylvia placed the sleeping baby Jane into the newly made-up cot. The two women worked together, making up the double bed and chatting about the family’s journey from London.

After a week, Sylvia, Linda and Jane had settled in. Linda had grown used to Harry and no longer shied away from him and Amy took every opportunity to play with the little girl. The curtains had finally been hung in the sitting and dining room, so Elise was beginning to feel as though she’d started the refurbishment. Instead of Margaret’s floral pattern, Elise had chosen simple stripes, in deep red and cream for the dining room and pale blue and yellow for the sitting room. New plain sofas and chairs, also in pale blue, had been ordered and would be delivered within the month.

At breakfast on Saturday morning, Sylvia was surprised to find Harry and Elise talking animatedly.

“I thought Marjorie Evans and Pru Langton were in charge of the Red Cross Committee?” Harry said. “Why is it all now falling on your shoulders?”

“I think they saw me coming,” Elise replied, spreading butter thinly onto her toast. “But it’s fine. I want to do something towards the war effort. Most other people are. Good morning, Sylvia,” she added.

“Good morning, Elise… Harry.”

"Good morning. Where are the children?"

"Amy has taken them out for a walk. I fed the baby earlier, and Amy gave Linda her breakfast. They've gone up to the tree? I'm not sure where that is?"

"Oh, it's just an old oak tree that Amy loves. It's in one of the fields on the farm. It's very peaceful up there," Elise explained.

"Amy said she was going to take some books and read Linda some stories," Sylvia said, helping herself to the toast Elise offered her.

"Now, back to this flaming committee," Harry said, pouring a cup of coffee for Sylvia. "If you're going to be taking charge, what exactly is involved?"

"At the moment, I've got no idea," Elise admitted. "And I don't know that I will be taking charge. All I know is that Marjorie phoned early this morning and explained that she can't manage it at the moment, with her work as the billeting officer, and that Pru's husband is ill, and would I take over for the time being."

"That damned woman. She takes on all these commitments, and then passes them off whenever it suits her," Harry said.

"It's fine," Elise put in.

"Can I do anything?" Sylvia offered. "I'd like to help out if I can. Do my bit while we're 'ere, you know."

"That would be splendid," Elise said, grinning at Harry and poking her tongue out. "I'm going to see Charlotte after breakfast, to try and get her to join in too. Why don't you come along with me? You can meet her."

"Who's Charlotte?" Sylvia asked.

"A very old friend," Harry replied, looking at Elise and sighing, knowing when he was beaten. Why couldn't she see? Why couldn't she understand?

"Charlotte is married to William," Elise explained. "And William was the brother of Harry's first wife."

"You were married before?" Sylvia asked.

"Yes, I was. But it was a long time ago," Harry replied, getting up from the table. "I'm going to find Stubbs to discuss the garden. I'll leave you ladies to it." He nodded and left the room.

"Did I say something wrong?" Sylvia asked.

"No, not at all," Elise replied. "He can be a bit touchy talking about Bella sometimes, that's all."

"Bella?"

"His first wife. She died."

"Oh, I didn't realise. I wish I hadn't asked now."

"Don't worry about it. You weren't to know. Bella is Rose's mother; she died in childbirth and Harry brought Rose up by himself, until the beginning of the last war, when he went to fight. He and I met in France and came back here after the war finished."

Sylvia finished her coffee. "I'm not surprised he doesn't like talking about it. I can't imagine what I'd do if anything happened to my Jack."

Elise looked up and saw the sadness in Sylvia's eyes. "Come along," she said. "We need to keep busy, don't we?" Sylvia nodded. "If we start out now, we can get to Charlotte's and back before Amy returns with the children."

"We've decided to hold a cake sale," Elise said over dinner that evening. "Well, cakes, biscuits, jams… you know the kind of thing. It's only a small event, but we think it's a good place to start and will get the whole village involved."

"When will this be?" Harry asked, trying to sound interested.

"Probably the first Saturday in November," Elise replied.

"Can I help?" Amy asked. "I can make up some posters, if you like."

"That would lovely, Amy. We're going to hold it in the village hall. I'll give you the details tomorrow, if you like."

"Okay." Amy helped herself to a second Yorkshire pudding. "We can plan what you want to say on the posters."

"I'll be doing some more work with Stubbs in the garden tomorrow," Harry said. "But then, it doesn't seem as though you need my input."

"What's going on in the garden?" Elise asked. "You've been very mysterious."

"We're digging up the lawn and the flower beds to plant vegetables," Harry replied. "It's part of this 'Dig for Victory' campaign the government is running. Leaflets were sent through earlier in the week, and Stubbs and I have been talking it through. If you want any fruit to make jam for this sale of yours, now is the time. We'll be taking out the gooseberries and strawberries. Stubbs says they take up too much space for too little yield."

"We will still have fruit, won't we?" Amy asked.

"We're keeping the apple and pear trees, so yes," Harry said. "I'm leaving the decisions to Stubbs as to what we plant and when: he's the expert."

"Perhaps I can make some jams with Polly?" suggested Sylvia. "My mum used to do it all the time."

"What a good idea," Elise enthused. "This is all coming together marvellously." Harry smiled. Despite his own misgivings, he loved her enthusiasm and the light it brought to her eyes.

A few days later, while the hot jam bubbled gently on the stove, Sylvia sat sipping tea with Polly while Linda played on the kitchen floor. The baby was asleep in a moses basket which Charlotte had lent them, balanced on two chairs.

"Can I ask you something?" Sylvia said.

"Yes." Polly sounded nervous.

"I'm just a little confused," Sylvia continued, but stopped speaking as Elise came into the kitchen, followed by Dennis, who was carrying a box.

"These are all the jam jars I could muster," Elise said. "I raided Charlotte's kitchen too for the spare ones she didn't need."

"I'm sure that'll be plenty, Mrs Belmont," Polly replied, taking the box from her husband and starting to remove the jars before placing them into the sink for washing.

"You were saying something about being confused?" Elise said to Sylvia.

"Oh, it doesn't matter," Sylvia replied, embarrassed.

"No, what is it?" Elise pushed.

"Well, I just don't understand why you and Polly call Dennis by his first name, but Harry mostly calls him 'Stubbs'. At first I thought they were two different people, until I saw Dennis and Polly together, and Harry called him over, and then I realised that her Dennis and Harry's 'Stubbs' were one and the same man."

"Oh, that's easily explained," Polly said, looking at Dennis. "Mr Belmont and my Dennis knew each other in the last war. Dennis served under Mr Belmont, in his company."

"Did you work here before the last war then?" Sylvia asked him.

"No," he replied, taking over the story. "After the war, Mr Belmont was travelling up to London one day and we met, purely by chance, on the train. I was out of work and, to be honest, I was struggling. Mr Belmont offered me a job here as a gardener. He paid my fare down here and gave me a bit extra to tide me over. I was that nervous when I arrived, but Mr Belmont was living here at the time and he helped me get settled in." He glanced at Elise. "I know Mrs Belmont won't mind me saying so, but Mr Belmont has always been a most generous man. Even back then, back in the war, he always knew the best things to do to make people feel at ease, to make it seem slightly less awful." He took a deep breath. "He looked out for us, did Mr Belmont. I... I lost a very good friend of mine, name of Alfred Hawks. He took a direct hit from a shell..." Dennis went quiet for a moment, then coughed. "It was Mr Belmont who took charge. Took care of everything, even cleaning down the trench... and then afterwards, he came and found me. I was in a hell of a state after seeing that, but he sat down with me and we talked, and I felt a bit better afterwards. And from then on, he made a point of checking up on me every so often, just to make sure I was all right." He smiled a little absently. "I remember, even when we was being bombed to blazes, with shells dropping down on us like rain, he'd stand there in the trench, bold as brass, his tin hat in his hand, laughing and joking, refusing to put his hat on, just to show us men he wasn't afraid and that we didn't need to be – even though we was all terrified. Always used to come round and see us, he did. Used to stop and have a chat, and a joke, share a cup of tea, if there was one on the go. Knew every one of us by name, too. All them that had families at home, he knew the names of all the kids, and the wives and sweethearts. You never had to remind him – he just knew. He remembered it all. It mattered, that kind of thing; it meant we mattered to him, see? We all used to say, he was the best officer we had, the bravest man we ever knew…" His voice faded as he looked up and saw the three women staring at him. Elise's mouth was slightly open. "I'd best be getting back to the garden," he mumbled, embarrassed, and put his cap on his head as he went out through the back door.

"Did you manage to get the jam made?" Harry asked. They were getting ready for bed and it was the first opportunity they'd had to speak all day, Elise had been so busy.

"Yes. We've got over twenty pounds of it. Charlotte's making cakes and biscuits, and a lot of the other villagers are contributing too, of course. I think the sale's going to be huge success." Harry sat down on the edge of the bed. "What's wrong?" she asked.

"Nothing," he replied. "I'm just struggling with my buttons." It was a lie, but he was surprised and a little disappointed that she couldn't work out the real reason for his recent mood.

She came across and knelt in front of him. "Let me help you," she offered.

"I'll be all right. I just needed to sit down and concentrate." He ignored her and focused on what he was doing, unfastening the buttons one by one, before shrugging off his shirt.

"You were very quiet over dinner tonight," Elise said, staring up into his face.

"I know, and I've apologised twice already. You don't have to worry, Elise. I'm perfectly well aware of all my shortcomings. I don't need to be reminded of them by you, or anyone else." He got up abruptly and limped into the bathroom, leaving her kneeling by the bed, staring after him.

He took a deliberately long time in the bathroom, but when he returned, she was still kneeling where he'd left her, leaving him with a quandary: to get to the bed, he had to pass her, but he didn't really want another confrontation. He just wanted to get into bed, go to sleep and pretend the last half an hour hadn't happened. Well, actually, he wanted to cross the room, kiss her deeply, lower her to the bed and make love to her very slowly. He wanted to tell her how much he loved her, feel her warm body beneath his and hear her whispered moans of ecstasy. Given his words to her, though, that wasn't likely to happen. She turned towards him and he saw the hurt confusion in her eyes.

"Sorry," he said immediately. "That was all completely uncalled for."

"No, it wasn't," she replied, getting to her feet. "I understand. I was a bit slow, but I do understand now."

"Do you?"

"I think so. You're feeling… left out?"

"No, Elise, I'm not." He switched to speaking in French, so he could be certain she'd understand what he was saying: "I'm feeling inadequate, useless, incapable… impotent, if you want me to be honest. Ed's flying in France; George is training; Matthew's working all hours… And now you're taking on this fundraising work; even Amy's helping out, and I don't feel as though there's anything I can do to really help. And I do want to help. I'm no different to anyone else. I want to 'do my bit' as well. Having one arm and a useless leg are a little limiting at the best of times, but… well, I know it's selfish and stupid, but I've never felt so superfluous in my entire life."

She crossed the room and stood in front of him. "My darling, you're not superfluous. You're doing all the work in the garden. That's helping."

"No, I'm giving Stubbs instructions, listening to his views, and I'm paying for seeds and plants. There's a difference…"

"Would you rather I stopped working on the committee?"

"No, of course not. I don't want to stop you doing what you do, any more than I want to stop Ed, or George or Matthew. I just wish I wasn't so bloody useless myself." He took her hand. "Just ignore me," he muttered. "I'm feeling sorry for myself, which is pathetic in the circumstances. It'll pass." He looked down at her. "I am sorry," he said. "I'm a curmudgeonly old devil, and I just need to give myself a good talking to."

"You're not old."

"Meaning I am a curmudgeonly devil?"

"Well, you can be devilish at times," she smiled up at him.

"And curmudgeonly?" He led her back to the bed and they sat down together.

"We all have our bad days. You're as entitled as the next man."

"That's no excuse."

"Stop being so hard on yourself, Harry." Elise leant up and kissed him gently on the cheek. He grabbed her by the waist and pulled her down onto the bed, rolling on top of her. She didn't bother to stifle her giggle.

"God, I love that sound," he said. "I may not be good for much else, but at least I can still make you giggle."

"Harry," she replied, kissing him deeply. "You're good for all kinds of things…"

The sale was a resounding success and Elise was praised by everyone in the village, although she was quick to point out how much everyone – including Harry, Amy, Polly and especially Sylvia – had helped out. The general view was that there should be another event as soon as possible, but Elise decided to wait until after Christmas before making any decisions as to what that should be. Sylvia thought that a bring-and-buy or a fête might be a good idea in the Spring, and she and Elise had a few private discussions as to dates and venues.

Sylvia's husband, Jack, had written regularly over the previous weeks, telling her that there had been none of the expected bombing in London. His letters, while not romantic or effusive, made it clear that he missed her and the children, especially as Sylvia's letters to him were full of her activities and the small changes in baby Jane and how many new words Linda had learnt under Amy's guidance. As the weeks wore on, it became clear that Jack felt he was missing out on his daughters' development.

In the third week of December, Sylvia received a letter from Jack. She opened it at breakfast as usual, then let out a slight cry.

"What's wrong?" Elise asked, concerned.

"Jack wants us to go home," Sylvia explained.

"Is that a good idea?"

"He says it's perfectly safe in London. There's been no bombings, like they said there would be. He says he's missing us... Well, I won't go into that too much..." She blushed. "He says it's not the same without us there." She smiled up at them, with tears in her eyes. "He never normally says things like that," she explained.

"Do you want to go back?" Harry asked.

"Yes, I think I do," she replied. "Don't get me wrong. We've been very happy here, but I miss Jack too."

"When do you want to leave?" Harry asked.

"I don't know," Sylvia replied. "Do you think we could be home by Christmas?"

"Of course." Harry smiled. "If that's what you want. I'll arrange tickets for the train and you can write to Jack and tell him when to expect you." Sylvia stood up. "I do have one suggestion, though," Harry added. "If things do start to get bad up there, I want you to feel free to come back, at any time. Jack sounds like a very sensible man, and I want you to tell him from me that our door is always open to you."

"Thank you, Harry." Tears pricked Sylvia's eyes again.

"Well, let's start thinking about packing," Elise said.

A few days later, at the station, Harry, Elise and Amy helped Sylvia and the children onto the train. Harry had paid for first-class tickets so that Sylvia would find the journey easier and Jack was going to meet them in London. Once the door was closed, Harry passed an envelope through the open window.

"What's this?" Sylvia asked.

"It's an early Christmas present," Harry replied. "Open it when you get home."

"You've all been so kind. I can't possibly take anything more from you."

"It's a Christmas present. I'll be offended if you don't."

"Very well. Thank you." The train started to pull away.

"Please write," Elise called. "I'm going to miss you so much. We mustn't lose touch."

"I will." Sylvia waved. "And thanks again."

That evening, with both the girls settled in their beds, Sylvia sat cuddled up to Jack on the settee in front of the fire.

"Harry gave me this," she said, reaching into her handbag and pulling out the envelope he'd handed her.

"What is it?" he asked.

"He said it was an early Christmas present and that I should open it when I got home."

"Well then, open it." He leant across and kissed her cheek.

Sylvia slid her finger under the top of the envelope and removed the card inside. She opened it and several bank notes fell into her lap. Jack reached over and picked them up, counting them.

"Bloody hell, Sylvie," he exclaimed. "There's fifty quid here."

"How much?"

"Fifty… fifty pounds."

She opened the card and read:

'The government has been paying us to keep you, when it has really been our privilege to have you all here. I thought it only fair that you should have that money, plus a little extra. I hope you all enjoy a very special Christmas together. Please remember, our door is always open and, if you ever need anything, just write or call. With very best wishes to you all,

Your friends, Harry and Elise.'

Chapter Five

Late Spring 1940

The Easter fête had passed off very successfully and raised a lot of money. Elise was willing to admit that she'd missed Sylvia's help, but the letter that had arrived from Poplar in the New Year had made it clear that she and Jack felt she was just as safe in London as she had been in the countryside and, with her mother nearby to help with the children, she believed she was justified in her choice to remain in the capital. Harry worried that the decision might be premature but Elise was quick to point out that, in Sylvia's shoes and, given the choice of remaining with her husband, she'd have done the same thing. Elise and Sylvia exchanged letters regularly, and Linda sent pictures to Amy, which were stuck on her bedroom wall.

Ed also wrote, although his letters were less frequent than Sylvia's and much shorter in length, often limited to just a few lines to reassure them that he was alive and still flying 'somewhere in France'. Harry worried constantly, but tried to keep his fears to himself. George's training was nearly finished, and Harry knew that William lived in fear that he'd be sent overseas at any time.

In mid-May, Harry and Elise decided to go away for a weekend to celebrate their twentieth wedding anniversary. They chose a small hotel in Bath and, on the evening of their arrival, ordered dinner in their room, after which they retired to bed early. The next day, they walked through Bath's old streets, admiring the architecture and remembering their wedding day.

"I'm glad we married in France," Harry said.

"Even though it meant your family having to travel out there?" Elise asked. "And probably not understanding a word of the ceremony?"

"Yes. I couldn't have married you in the village. I'd already done that once, with Bella. I needed our wedding – our marriage – to be different. I didn't want my memories to spoil your day."

"Nothing could have spoiled that day," Elise said, leaning into him. "It was perfect. It's been perfect. All of it."

"I find that very hard to believe." Harry stopped, leant down and kissed her, regardless of the prying eyes of passers-by. "I know I'm difficult to live with sometimes."

"Only sometimes?" Elise said, smiling up at him.

"You're asking to be slung over my shoulder again," Harry teased.

"You wouldn't dare… not in public."

"Really?" Harry dropped his stick and Elise let go of his arm and ran, squealing and giggling down the pavement. "Cheat!" he called after her, grinning. "I'll catch you later." A passing businessman looked sideways at Harry, who rolled his eyes, and said, "I'm still training her," before bending awkwardly to retrieve his stick and following Elise down the street.

The following morning, as Harry was shaving in the bathroom, the telephone rang. He heard Elise speaking and then the door burst open. She stood on the threshold, wearing nothing but her underwear.

"What's wrong?" He dragged his eyes away from the lace and silk confections and took in the worried expression on her face.

"That was Amy," she began.

Harry dropped his razor and it clattered into the basin, sinking beneath the soapy water. "Is she all right? Is it Ed?" He could hardly begin to think about what might have happened, let alone say the words.

"She's fine and Ed's okay as far as I know. Evidently my brother has arrived." Elise stepped forward.

"Henri? Arrived where?" Harry wiped the remaining shaving foam from his face.

"At home."

"And Sophie?"

"Yes, Sophie too."

"And the delinquent?"

"Amy didn't mention Luc, but probably. Sophie rarely goes anywhere without him, does she?"

"No. I'm assuming Amy needs us at home?"

"She didn't say so, but I got that impression. I don't think she'd have telephoned otherwise."

"Well, as much as I'd love to say to hell with your brother and his wife, our daughter needs us, so we have to go."

"Shall I pack?" Elise asked.

"Yes. I'll quickly finish in here and get dressed, and arrange a taxi for the station." Elise turned to go. "Hey. Come back here a minute," he called after her. She took the two paces towards him. "It's been a perfect weekend. Thank you."

"No. Thank you." They kissed briefly.

"I wish we could have just an hour or two more. There are so many things I want to do with you... to you..." Harry said, slipping the bra strap from her shoulder.

"Don't tempt me." She ran her hands down his bare chest.

"I'm not. I'm just saying..."

"You're standing naked in front of me... Of course you're tempting me."

"A fifty-six year old broken man is standing naked in front of you. I'd hardly call that tempting."

"Harry. The man I love is standing in front of me... naked or otherwise, that's tempting. And don't call yourself broken. You're beautiful to me." She reached up and, placing her hands behind his neck, pulled him down and kissed him, her tongue softly delving into his mouth, searching for his and finding satisfaction in his heated response.

"Christ, Elise," he muttered into her mouth, breathing heavily. "Stop, or we'll never get home."

"Later, Harry," she replied. "We'll carry this on later."

By the time the taxi deposited them at their own front door that afternoon, Amy was already standing waiting for them, looking exhausted. She ran down the steps and into Elise's arms.

"What's wrong?" Elise said. Harry looked concerned.

"She won't shut up, Mum," Amy said. "She just won't shut up. She's so tiring. Nothing's good enough for her. She's constantly yelling at Polly in French, and of course Polly doesn't understand a word, so I'm having to translate everything. They arrived just after dawn this morning and we've been on the go ever since. Thank God you're home."

"Come here," Harry said, allowing Amy to throw her arms around him. He balanced his stick against the wall and hugged her. "You've done brilliantly," he whispered. "Now, I want you to go upstairs and lie down. Leave this to your mother and me."

"Thanks, Dad," she said, turning back towards the house. "Good luck," she called. "You're going to need it."

Elise looked at Harry and then back at the house. "Bon chance, cherie," he said, grinning at her.

"Oh, do be quiet!"

Over dinner, Amy watched her father closely. It seemed so odd to hear him speaking fluently in French. They could all speak the language, even Rose and Ed – Harry had insisted on them all learning to speak French – but she'd never actually seen or heard Harry speak it so fluently.

"So, where is Luc?" Elise asked. "I still don't understand why he isn't with you."

"We're not at liberty to say," Sophie said, trying to look secretive, but only succeeding in looking smug.

"We don't actually know where he is," Henri added. "He didn't want to leave France and decided to throw his lot in with the resistance."

"We promised not to tell," Sophie admonished.

"What does it matter?" Henri said. "I'm only telling 'Arry and Elise, not British Intelligence."

Harry smirked. "You must be so proud of him." His sarcasm was lost on Sophie.

"He is a true son of France," she gushed. "If only more men could be like him." She looked across at Henri, who ignored her remark.

"Was it a difficult journey?" Harry asked, desperate to avoid the topic of Luc if at all possible.

"Difficult? Difficult?" Sophie spluttered. "It was impossible! I've never been so uncomfortable in my life. And the way we were treated when we first arrived. We were made to feel like criminals."

"It was lucky we had your address to give them," Henri cut in. "Otherwise I dread to think where we'd have ended up."

"And this is such a lovely big house... so many bedrooms..." Sophie continued. "Why on earth do you live in that tiny place in Cornwall, when you could live here?"

"Well, we couldn't live here until recently, could we?" Harry said, looking at her. "This was my mother's house until she died, last summer. She lived here."

"Yes, but one old woman doesn't need so much space, does she?" Sophie looked around the large dining room. "Your house in Cornwall is so small," she said. "But this is, well, it's perfect."

Perfect for what, Harry wondered. Polly entered at that moment to clear away the plates.

"Girl," Sophie said, holding up her glass. "I need more water." Polly looked towards Harry, who shook his head.

"Sophie," Harry said calmly, "let's get a couple of things straight, shall we? Firstly, this is Polly and that is the name to which she answers, so please don't call her 'Girl', or anything else, for that matter. Secondly, Polly doesn't understand French and you don't speak English, so if you want something from her, then ask one of us and we will translate your request. Finally, if you want a drink of anything while sitting at the table, you can either pour it for yourself, like you do at home, or ask Henri or myself to pour it for you."

Amy put her serviette to her mouth to hide a giggle.

"Well, really!" Sophie was stunned, but unfortunately not into silence. "Do you speak this way to all of your guests?"

"No," replied Harry.

"I should think not."

"I've never needed to before," Harry continued. "You and Henri are very welcome to stay in our house, but only if you treat Polly and Dennis in a civilised manner. Do I make myself clear?"

"They're only servants," Sophie said, sulking. "I can't see what all the fuss is about."

"They're not 'only' anything," Harry replied. "And the fact that you don't understand says more about you than it does about them." He turned to Polly, who was standing to one side, looking quizzically at him. "Thank you, Polly," he said in English. "If you'd like to continue clearing away now. We'll have dessert whenever you're ready."

"Yes, Mr Belmont," Polly said.

"How are things in France?" Harry asked Henri, desperate to change the subject.

"Terrible," Henri replied. "Once the Nazis invaded, we just wanted to escape, like a lot of our countrymen. We could hear the bombing and the planes flying overhead. After the last time, I'm sure you understand, I couldn't bear to live under their rule again."

"No," Harry said.

"Many went south, but I'm not sure they'll be safe, even there."

"You think the Nazis will get that far?" Elise asked.

"It wouldn't surprise me," Henri replied.

"No, I'm sure they won't," Sophie interrupted. "I'm sure the resistance will drive them out of France."

Harry and Elise looked at each other. Amy got up from the table. "I'm going to bed," she said. "I'm too tired for pudding tonight."

"Oh, okay," Harry said, surprised. "Are you all right?"

"Yes, Daddy, I'm fine. I'm just exhausted." Amy glanced at Sophie, and Harry nodded slightly. "See you in the morning."

"Goodnight, sweetheart," Elise said.

Up in her room, Amy fell onto her bed. Sophie's attitude was next to intolerable, but what had really struck her was Henri's comment about the bombing and planes flying over France. One of those planes might be Ed's. She reached across to her bedside table and opened the top drawer. Inside was a bundle of letters, on top of which was a photograph of him in his RAF uniform, smiling at the camera, his eyes twinkling and his teeth showing between his full lips. She held the photograph in front of her face, staring at it and tracing his features with the tip of her forefinger. "Stay safe," she whispered. "Stay safe and come back to me." She didn't bother to wipe away the tears that dripped down her cheek onto the pillow.

"I'm not sure how much of this we can cope with," Elise said to Harry as she climbed into bed beside him, flopping down onto the pillow. "It's only been one evening and I'd already quite like to murder her."

"You'll need to join the queue," Harry replied, pulling Elise close to him and putting his arm around her. She rested her head on his chest and ran her fingers across his stomach. "I did wonder if she meant that her precious Luc was going to single-handedly defeat the Nazis at one point. Do you think she practices being that annoying?"

"Oh, no. I think it's a natural talent. Talk about ruining the moment. We were so happy this morning." Elise's fingers traced downwards and Harry inhaled deeply. He placed a finger under her chin and lifted her face to his. He kissed her, his tongue entering her mouth and tasting her soft sweetness. "I meant to tell you earlier, how utterly beautiful you looked when you burst into the bathroom."

"I've been thinking about that..."

"What?" He looked down at her, confused.

"My underwear..."

"What about it? It's very nice, but..."

"It's also French."

Harry thought for a moment. Elise always wore French lingerie. It was her one weakness. Every year, they'd take a trip to France, visit Henri and then travel on to Paris, where Elise would call at a very exclusive lingerie shop, while he would sit in a café, awaiting her return. Then they'd spend a couple of nights in a hotel, sampling some of her purchases, before catching the train back to Calais. "I see. Yes, it's going to be difficult to keep your lingerie supplies stocked up, isn't it?" He grinned down at her.

"I can't see what's so funny. The things I've got won't last indefinitely."

"Then you'll either have to make do with boring English underwear, or – better still – not wear any at all."

"Harry!"

"What? Only you and I would know." He winked. "Now, I seem to remember wanting to do all kinds of things to you at the hotel this morning..."

The following afternoon, William called round and asked to see Harry alone.

"I've heard that Elise's brother has arrived," he said, once they were safely in Harry's study.

"Then you've heard correctly," Harry replied.

"And, according to one of the farmhands, Norman, who was talking to Dennis, your sister-in-law is a bit... difficult?"

"Difficult would be putting it mildly. I'm worried Amy might leave home if Sophie carries on much longer. And as for Polly..." Harry smiled, but it wasn't sincere.

"I might have a solution, if you'll let me help you, for once."

"I'm listening," Harry said.

"There's a cottage, on the other side of the farm, on the way into town. It's nothing special, just two bedrooms, a kitchen, bathroom and a sitting room. It needs a bit of work, but I can get Norman onto that, and if Dennis helps out as well, it can be done even quicker. How about if you were to suggest that Henri and his wife move in there?"

"Really?" Harry jumped at the idea. "That would be marvellous."

"I could also give Henri some work," William continued. "I need all the farmhands I can get at the moment, and he's experienced, so he'd be doing me a favour. He does speak English, doesn't he?" William looked a little doubtful. "It's just that I don't speak a word of French, and neither do any of my other workers, as far as I know."

"Yes, Henri speaks some English – certainly enough to get by. But I'll pay you rent for the cottage and I'll pay Henri's wages, Bill."

"Oh, for heaven's sake, Harry, just let me do you a good turn for once, will you?"

"Well, I don't want you being out of pocket."

"I won't be. If I wasn't employing Henri, I'd have to take on someone else, and put them in the cottage, so this works out well for everyone. Plus they're far enough away that they won't be on your doorstep all the time, but close enough to keep an eye on."

"We can't thank you enough, Bill. Don't you want to put the idea to them?"

"I think it might be better coming from you."

"If you like. I'll call you later and let you know what they say."

"You want us to live where?" Sophie was incredulous. "A pokey little farm cottage? This is ridiculous. We didn't walk for miles and miles to live in some disgusting little hole."

"It's not a disgusting little hole, Sophie." Harry tried to keep his patience. "It's a very nice little cottage, not too dissimilar from your own place in France, if a little smaller. But as there's only the two of you, it will be absolutely fine."

"I'm sure it will be lovely," Henri said. "And this man is willing to give me work… and to pay me?" he continued.

"Yes. A lot of his workers have joined up, so he's short of help. Your experience will be invaluable to him."

"I hope he appreciates that Henri is not just a simple farmhand. He should show him some respect."

"Sophie," Henri said. "We should be grateful…"

"Grateful? You want me to be grateful as well now? And who is going to look after us?"

"What do you mean?" Elise asked, struggling to control her temper.

"You have a maid and a handyman. I want to know who is going to wait on us in this little farm cottage?"

"No-one, Sophie," Elise said. "You didn't have servants when you lived in France and you managed perfectly well. I'm sure you'll manage perfectly well now. The cottage is much nearer to the town than we are here, so you'll be able to walk there to go shopping, and meet people. I'm sure you'll be much happier there."

"But I don't speak English. How will they understand me?"

"I suggest you learn." Harry's coldness caught everyone by surprise.

It was a week before the cottage was ready. A week during which clothing had to be bought, being as Sophie and Henri had left France with very little; a week during which the cottage had to be equipped with furniture and bedding, crockery, cutlery, glasses and linens. A tiring week for all concerned, during which Sophie did little but moan, while others worked around her. At the end of that week, however, Elise, Harry and Amy settled down into their quiet sitting room, knowing that Henri and Sophie were safe and out of France, as well as out of sight, on the other side of the farm, on the edge of the town and that they had their own house to themselves again. The relief was palpable.

Chapter Six

Early Summer 1940

Amy walked down the dusty, dry lane towards the five-bar gate, stepping up onto its bottom rung and staring into the sky. It was the perfect pale blue of a late June afternoon and she took a deep breath, closing her eyes and savouring the silence, which that week spent in Sophie's company the previous month had made even more valuable. Clambering over the gate, she set off through the field, towards the brow of the hill and her favourite place beneath the old oak tree. She sat, resting her back against its gnarled bark and reached into her pocket for the envelope she'd placed there before leaving the house, containing Ed's latest letter, read and re-read over the last ten days since she'd received it. It couldn't hurt to read it through again.

Dear Amy,

How's everything going at home? I can't tell you how much I miss everyone. I keep thinking about how much I'd love to be there, playing badminton, going for our long walks, sitting in the garden in the summer sunshine, wandering up to the oak tree and reading away the hours. There's not much to do here when we're not flying. I can't tell you where we are at the moment, and we're moving around a lot anyway. I've been flying most of the time, so that helps to take my mind off being homesick and missing you all.

I'd better finish now, or I'll be too late for the post. Send my love to everyone.

Ed

She blinked back the tears, unsure why she was so upset. Was it because he was homesick and she wanted to make him feel better? Was it because she wished, oh how she wished, that he'd written of how much he missed her, and just her, rather than 'everyone'. It was an unrealistic hope, she knew that, but she couldn't help it. He'd been away for so long and, rather than forgetting him, she'd grown more and more fond of the memory of him. Now she knew, even better than she'd known before, that she was in love with him. She was in love with a man who saw her as a child. She desperately wanted him to come home safely and soon, but she wasn't sure she could stand seeing him and knowing that she'd always just be his little sister, and nothing more. She pulled her knees up to her chest, rested her head on them and cried, great sobs wracking her body. "Oh, it's so unfair," she wailed into her own lap.

"What is?" said a horribly familiar voice, and she looked up slowly to see Ed staring down at her. "Hey, Amy. Why the tears?" he asked, reaching into his pocket and handing her a handkerchief, as he sat beside her.

Filled with embarrassment, she took the offered hankie and wiped her face, while quickly hiding his letter in her pocket. "Oh, I don't know. The war, I suppose," she said, knowing it sounded a bit lame. "I want to do more, but I'm still too young. Mum and Dad both say I'm not allowed to leave school yet..."

"Your time will come," he said, nudging her with his elbow. "Don't be in such a rush to grow up. It's not all it's cracked up to be." She detected a sadness in his voice.

"When did you get back?" she asked, sniffing.

"Yesterday."

"And you didn't think to phone?"

"I thought I'd surprise you all. Your parents were thrilled to see me; Elise is talking about having a special dinner this evening. You, on the other hand, don't seem so pleased..."

"Of course I'm happy to see you. How did you know I was here?"

"If you're not in the house or the garden, then you're usually here," he said, standing and offering his hand to her. She took it and allowed him to pull her up. "Good heavens Amy, you've grown at least a couple of inches!" he exclaimed. "Bet I can still beat you back home though..." He took off down the hill and she sighed, following reluctantly. She knew he'd win. He always did.

William and Charlotte were invited for dinner that evening, as a special welcome home for Ed. They brought Anne, who Amy thought looked stunning in a beautiful, full-length pale green, low cut, floating dress that shimmered in the candlelight, with her blonde hair in a sleek chignon and bright red lipstick and long eyelashes, through which she gazed up at Ed. Amy felt even more dowdy in her dark burgundy belted dress with its pleated skirt, her hair loose around her shoulders and no make-up whatsoever. As everyone gathered in the sitting room before dinner, she watched Anne approach Ed, who was talking to William.

"Hello," she said and Amy noticed that her voice seemed slightly deeper than usual.

"Hello," Ed replied. "Would you like to sit here?" He stood up to let her sit next to her father and Amy saw the clear look of disappointment cross Anne's face. Ed moved to stand alongside William and continued his conversation, which seemed to be about William's difficulties getting untrained farmhands to understand what they were supposed to do and how useful Henri had been on the farm in the previous few weeks. The two men laughed and Anne tried to join in. Amy sat opposite, playing with the belt on her dress and watching, until she heard her name being called with some urgency.

"Amy!" Elise called. "That's the third time I've asked you."

"Sorry, Mother, I was day-dreaming," Amy said. "What did you want me to do?"

"Could you take Aunt Charlotte's glass and top it up for her?"

"Yes, of course." Amy got up and went over to Charlotte, who was sitting in the chair closest to the window, talking to Harry, who was standing beside her. "Dry sherry, isn't it?" Amy asked of Charlotte.

"Yes, thank you. That would be lovely, dear."

As she stood by the sideboard, she felt the heat of his body next to hers and didn't even have to turn to know that he stood beside her.

"Being as you're chief bartender this evening, you couldn't get me another whisky and soda, could you?" Ed said, grinning.

"You could get your own," she replied, smiling back. "But I suppose, just this once..."

"I say, Ed?" Anne's voice interrupted. "You wouldn't be a sweetie and make me a gin and tonic, would you?"

"Yes, of course," Ed replied over his shoulder. "And a gin and tonic, evidently," he whispered to Amy.

"On second thoughts," she said, replacing the stopper in the sherry decanter. "Why don't you get your own, and Anne's while you're about it." She turned and crossed the room, handing Charlotte her drink, before sitting back down on the sofa.

Ed shrugged and began pouring drinks, but had barely had time to open the gin bottle when Anne joined him at the sideboard and they started laughing and then clinking glasses. Anne threw her head back, exposing her long, pale neck and, looking at the expression on his face, Amy wondered whether Ed wanted to kiss her.

Anne sat next to Ed at dinner, while Amy sat at the furthest end of the table. She tried making conversation with Charlotte, but all the while she was watching Ed and Anne, observing how Anne kept touching Ed's hand and arm, how he leant towards her murmuring and laughing, how she giggled, holding her hand delicately over her mouth.

Not long after dinner, Amy announced that she had a slight headache and retired to her room.

Lying on her bed, staring at the ceiling, she realised, with a stark awareness that the five year age gap between her and Ed might as well be twenty-five years. She knew there was a much bigger gap between her parents' ages, but they'd met when her mother was nineteen and that made all the difference. At sixteen, Amy didn't stand a chance with Ed, and by the time she was old enough, he'd probably be married to Anne, with a couple of children in tow. A single tear rolled down her cheek and she brushed it away roughly, turning onto her side and huffing out a deep breath.

The following evening, not long after dinner, the doorbell rang. Polly answered it and came into the sitting room, announcing that 'Miss Anne' had called to see if 'Master Ed' was at home. Amy could feel her shoulders stiffen. Ed got up and went into the hallway. Amy heard voices and then both of them came back into the sitting room.

"Anne's just come round to borrow a book," he said.

"Oh yes?" said Harry, barely able to disguise the smile that was forming on his lips. "Any particular book, Anne?"

"It's for a lesson I'm planning," she said, seemingly embarrassed.

"Ed will take you through to the library," Harry said. "Help yourself."

Ed looked awkward, but showed Anne out of the room and Amy heard their voices fade as they went from the hall into the library.

"Do you think that girl could be any more obvious?" Elise said.

"No," Harry replied. "I find the whole..."

"Excuse me. I think I'll go up to bed," Amy interrupted, not wanting to hear her parents' views on how long it would take for Anne to persuade Ed up the aisle.

"Are you all right?" Elise asked. "It's still very early."

"I'm fine. I'm just tired." Once in her room, Amy flopped down onto her bed and sobbed into her pillow. Age gap or no age gap, against Anne she knew she didn't stand a chance, and she never would. Anne was so elegant and Amy was just... not. In her imagination, she pictured Ed and Anne in the library. In her mind, she saw him running his fingers through Anne's long blonde hair, kissing her neck and her ears, while she moaned, whispering his name, begging him to kiss her harder. He'd oblige, fearless of interruption, touching her, feeling her... "Oh God! I think if I didn't love him so much, I could probably really hate him," she whispered into the damp pillow.

Downstairs, Anne departed, with her book, not long after Amy had gone upstairs and Ed went back into the sitting room. "Where's Amy?" he asked.

"She's gone to bed," Elise said, looking up from her magazine.

"Oh. I was going to suggest we play cards."

"I think she was tired. Maybe she'll have a game with you tomorrow."

Ed sat down and picked up the newspaper. "How have things been here?" he asked, flicking through the pages.

"To be honest, you'd hardly know there was a war on most of the time," Harry replied.

"What about the Dunkirk evacuations? Surely, there was some activity at the marina?"

"I believe so, but it didn't really affect us, up here. The village is quite cut off, really. And we only found out about it in the newspapers, after the event."

"How are Henri and Sophie settling in?"

"Not too bad. I think Henri is proving useful at the farm. Sophie complains about something every time we see them, but that isn't too often, thank goodness," Elise replied. "I know he's my brother, but I'm glad they're not too close to us."

"It's been years since I've seen them. I'd forgotten how annoying Sophie could be until Amy reminded me," Ed said. "And as for Luc, well, I'm glad he's not here. He'd be sure to create trouble."

"Sophie is particularly upset now that France has surrendered," Harry said. "I'm sure she believed that Luc would drive the Nazis out all by himself, the stupid woman. I think she takes it as a personal affront that the plan didn't work."

"I have to admit, everyone was surprised by how quickly the French gave way," Ed said, staring into the empty fireplace. "It just seemed as though one minute they were declaring their strength and undying wish for freedom and the next, they'd handed the country over to Hitler on a silver platter."

"I think they believe the armistice is the honourable way out."

"Honourable, my ar..." Ed glanced across at Elise, who was looking at her clenched hands. "I'm sorry," he said. "I forget sometimes that you're French. It must be horrible for you to see your country occupied again."

"Don't be sorry," Elise said, taking a deep breath. "I'm as incredulous as everyone else. I just hope we don't live to regret their actions." Harry and Ed looked at each other for a moment, before Harry got up and moved across to sit down next to Elise and take her hands in his.

"Don't worry," he said. "You're safe here."

"Are we safe here though?" Harry and Ed could both hear the fear in her voice. "The Germans have taken so much of Europe now, what's to stop them from just crossing the Channel and invading England next?"

Harry didn't immediately know how to respond, how to reassure her, but he didn't need to worry. Ed took a breath and replied simply, "The RAF." His voice was quiet, but his gaze unwavering. "The Germans need to control the skies if they're going to invade... and we'll never let that happen. Never."

****

The next day, Amy got up early, bathed, dressed and left the house, with a piece of buttered toast in one hand and a book in the other. It was Ed's last full day before he returned to base early the following morning and, she decided, if she could avoid him as much as possible, it would be easier to say goodbye, knowing that he'd probably be writing love letters to Anne, and even less letters to her. The previous evening, having cried for nearly an hour, she'd decided that there were more important things in life than pining after what she couldn't have. And with that, being Amy, she had resolved to try and move on. It would be difficult and wouldn't happen straight away, but she'd manage it eventually. After all, what was the point, if Ed was never going to be interested? Today was a new day. The sun had risen an hour or so earlier and she approached the gate hesitantly. He'd find her here, if he came looking... but would he come looking? Probably not. He'd spend his last day with Anne, wouldn't he? And was she upset by that? Well, maybe, but only a little. She squared her shoulders and jumped over the gate, then climbed the hill, her stride assertive, and, having reached the old oak tree, she settled down to read. The book was Daphne du Maurier's *Rebecca*; she'd borrowed it from the library in town three days before and was thoroughly enjoying it. She particularly liked the character of 'the girl', thinking how clever it was to create a person in a book, but not actually give them a name. Of course, Mrs Danvers was absolutely terrifying, but she liked that too. It didn't do to feel too safe in a story. She liked a bit of mystery and suspense. She knew 'the girl' was much younger than the hero in the book, Maxim de Winter, and that thought reminded her of Ed. She sighed, and turned the page to a new chapter.

A few hours later, the rumbling of her stomach reminded her that she should have brought an apple with her. She was already ravenous and it couldn't be more than twelve o'clock. Ed would be with Anne, she guessed. She might be able to sneak back to the house, get Polly to make her some sandwiches, grab some fruit and return to her oak tree without her parents noticing and asking awkward questions. Could she take the chance, she wondered? She looked around the field, hoping for divine inspiration when her heart sank. Climbing over the gate below, was the instantly recognisable figure of Ed, carrying a basket and with a blanket tucked under his arm. He was wearing dark brown trousers, and a white shirt, open at the neck and he looked absolutely adorable, his blond hair catching in the breeze as he walked slowly up the hill. Perhaps her resolution to forget him and move on wouldn't be so easy after all.

She sighed deeply and buried her head in her book, trying to pretend she hadn't noticed him.

"How's the book?" he asked, throwing the blanket on the ground next to her. "You really should bring one of those with you, you know. You're ruining your skirts, sitting on the rough ground."

She got up and helped him spread the blanket. "My book's fine, thank you," she said, sitting back down again. "What brings you up here?"

"I thought you might get hungry. I saw you leave this morning, from my bedroom window, so I had Polly prepare a little picnic. There's sandwiches, some left-over chicken, and fruit, and ginger beer."

"How thoughtful." He sat beside her and retrieved his own book from the basket.

"Thank you for bringing the picnic, but you don't have to stay, if you don't want to," she said, not looking at him.

"Why wouldn't I want to stay? I brought the picnic for both of us."

"Well, it's your last day. I assumed you'd want to spend it with Anne." Had she actually said that? She could feel her cheeks burning red.

"Anne? Why on earth would I want to spend my last day's leave with Anne?"

"Because... well, because..."

He noticed her embarrassment. "You think I'm attracted to her, don't you?" Ed laughed out loud, throwing back his head. "Dear God. She's really not my type, Amy. Not my type at all." He opened his book, as though the subject was closed.

Amy stared at him. "I don't understand," she said.

"What don't you understand?" he asked, not looking up.

"If she's not your type, why do you lead her on?"

"I don't." He looked up. "What makes you think I lead her on?"

"The way you behave around her. You encourage her and *she* thinks there's something going on, even if you don't. She has done for years."

"But that's ridiculous. I don't encourage her. I'm just friendly with her. The same as I am with you."

Amy swallowed hard, blinking back her tears. "Except that I'm like a sister to you, and we've always messed around together, and she's a beautiful young woman, who happens to be in love with you."

"What?" He closed his book and put it on the ground beside him.

"She told me so herself, months ago. Everyone's known about it for ages. She's not exactly subtle, Ed."

"I'm sure that's rubbish."

"No it isn't. Even Mum and Dad have noticed it; they talk about it and I've seen the way they look at each other when Anne's around you."

"You're kidding."

"I'm not, Ed."

"Well, either way, it's not my fault if she's got the wrong end of the stick. I can't help how she feels, can I?"

"Oh, stop preening yourself!" Amy slapped his arm. "No, you can't help how she feels, but you can help how you behave around her. You shouldn't encourage her if you don't feel anything for her. It's not fair."

"I'd agree with you, if I'd realised; but I hadn't."

"Are you blind then?"

"I suppose I must be," he said quietly. He thought for a moment. "The question is, what am I supposed to do about it?"

"Tell her she doesn't stand a chance, if she doesn't."

"She doesn't. But how do I tell her? Oh heck, this is bloody awkward."

A silence descended and Amy took advantage of the moment, turned onto her stomach, and pretended to read. "Hang on, Amy," Ed said after a while. "I'm serious here."

"What?" she replied, not turning around.

"I need your help. You're a girl."

"Am I? I'm surprised you noticed."

"Very funny. No, seriously, I need your help. How do I tell her I'm not interested without hurting her feelings."

Amy turned onto her side and raised herself onto one elbow, looking up at Ed, who was sitting, with a pained expression on his face. She almost felt sorry for him and wanted to give him a hug, but she didn't. She thought for a moment. "I'm not sure you can tell her without hurting her feelings."

"Great. So I'm the villain of the piece, breaking the poor girl's heart, when I genuinely had no idea what was going on."

"You could write to her, I suppose. You could explain that you misunderstood and that might be easier in a letter than face-to-face."

"A letter? Isn't that the coward's way out?"

"Probably. I don't know; I'm not very experienced in these things. But what would you rather do? Stand in front of her and explain that you're an idiot?"

"Ouch. Thanks for that, Amy."

"Anytime."

Later that night, after she'd finished undressing, Amy stood naked in front of the full length mirror in her bedroom. So, Anne wasn't Ed's type? *Not his type at all…* She wondered what sort of woman might fit the bill – clearly more voluptuous than either her or Anne, she presumed, with more… obvious assets, maybe? Anne had a lovely figure, Amy mused. She stared at herself and ran her hands across her firm, small breasts and down her flat stomach, resting them on her neat, trim waist. *Certainly nothing to write home about, and not good enough for him.* She raised her head, sighed, then let her hands fall to her sides and turned towards the bed, pulling on her nightdress and climbing under the sheets.

****

Ed left very early the next morning, but Amy got up to see him off, trying her best not to cry and to remember that she was his sister, and would never be anything more, at least as far as he was concerned. Hopefully he wouldn't be granted any leave for a while and she'd be able to get used to the idea that she'd never be good enough for him to look at romantically. She just had time for breakfast before the long walk to school, but afterwards in the late afternoon, she took advantage of the warm weather and wandered down the lane towards the five-bar gate. She was surprised to see William standing there, looking up into the field. He turned on hearing her footsteps and smiled.

"Hello, Amy," he said.

"Hello, Uncle William. What brings you out here."

"I was just having a look at this old field," he replied. "I'm probably going to have to plough it up for planting."

"Not my field," Amy said, her face despondent.

"Probably. The County War Ags are surveying all the farms now, to find out how improvements can be made. All fallow land will have to be ploughed and planted."

"You won't have to cut down the oak, will you?"

"No. We'll work round it. That tree's been there for hundreds of years, it wouldn't be right to take it down. Besides, I know how much you love it. We don't need to take it down, so we won't."

Amy stared up at her beloved tree. "Can I help?" she said suddenly.

"Help with what?"

"Help on the farm."

"You're only sixteen, my girl. You're still at school. When would you have time to help? Besides, it's heavy work."

"You have other girls and boys of sixteen helping on the farm. I could find the time, at weekends and in the evenings. And I'm stronger than I look, Uncle Bill. Oh, please, let me help."

"Well," he hesitated, "only if your parents agree. And only if it doesn't interfere with your school work."

"I'll talk to them now!" Amy called over her shoulder as she ran down the lane towards the village. William smiled. He thought she had very little chance of persuading Harry and Elise, but he couldn't fault her enthusiasm.

Later that evening, William was surprised by a visit from Harry and Amy. Harry wanted to fully understand what Amy would be doing and he wanted Amy to hear it from William himself. They sat together in the large sitting room of Downwillow Farm, overlooking the terraced rose gardens. William explained that, being so young and inexperienced, there would be a limited amount for Amy to do, until it came to harvest time, when all the help they could get was needed. Amy was delighted. She was keen to do whatever she could and looked to Harry for approval.

"I'll agree to you helping out in the school holidays, with the harvest," he said. "But not during school time. Your mother would never agree and I think that's a fair compromise. You only have to wait another few weeks and then you can start coming up here each day. I'm sure William will find you something to do until the harvest starts in earnest. How does that sound?"

Amy leapt off her chair and flung herself at Harry. "Thank you, Daddy," she squealed. "I'll be helping with the war, at last!" She twirled around. "Oh, how exciting!"

"I wonder if you'll still be this excited when your back is aching and your fingers are raw, young lady," said William, grinning.

"Oh, I will, don't you worry," said Amy.

"Hmm. I have a strong suspicion that she might," Harry acknowledged.

When they got back, Elise was disappointed that Harry had given in, but she could see from the expression on Amy's face that her daughter was delighted and agreed it had been a fair compromise in the end. She didn't want to stand in the way of Amy 'doing her bit' as everyone was phrasing it these days. She pointed to a letter on the sideboard that had arrived by the evening post, addressed to Harry.

"It's from John Grainger," Harry said, resting it on his lap and opening the envelope.

Since they'd met in a German hospital after Harry had been injured, John Grainger had become one of Harry's greatest friends, probably closer to him even than William. And, as the man who had undoubtedly saved his life when he'd been at his lowest ebb, and had pointed him back to Elise, Harry felt indebted to Grainger and had a great deal of affection for him. He looked forward to their frequent correspondence and had bought a typewriter so that he could write to John himself without bothering Elise, even though he hated the formality of a typewritten letter.

"What does he have to say?" Elise asked. She too liked John and his wife Lillian, knowing that it was they who had persuaded Harry to seek her out again after the war, and had thus been the means of reuniting them.

"It's really just an update on Peter's activities," Harry said, scanning the lines of his friend's letter. "He's back home now, probably for a week or so."

"Does John say how badly he was injured?" Elise was referring to an injury which Peter had received during the evacuation of Dunkirk.

"Hang on," said Harry, "I'm getting to that bit..." He read on for a few moments more. "He was shot in the arm, but it wasn't a bad wound. He was evacuated early on and sent to a hospital in London, and now he's got some leave until he's fully recovered. Then he'll go back and be posted elsewhere, although goodness only knows where at the moment."

"Is John worried?"

"I think he's just glad to have him back in one piece," Harry said. "They're wondering if they can come and visit for the weekend. What do you think? Would it be all right?"

"Of course. You don't even need to ask, you know that. Write back to them and say we'd love to have them all."

"Can't they stay a bit longer, if Peter's got leave?" Amy said.

"I think John can only come for the weekend. He's headmaster now, don't forget, it doesn't do to go AWOL during term time."

"I keep forgetting he still works," Amy replied.

"Since most of the younger masters have enlisted, he's working harder than ever."

"Couldn't he employ some female teachers?" Amy asked. "Surely women can teach just as well as men. Anne does."

"She teaches in a girls' school, Amy," Harry pointed out. "John is headmaster of a very traditional, very old-fashioned and very expensive boys' school. It's a different world."

"Well, it shouldn't be. Not any more."

"I quite agree with you, and I'm sure John would too, but the parents at that school are quite a different matter, even if there is a war on."

"Well, more fool them."

Harry and Elise exchanged glances. There was no escaping the fact that Amy was growing up.

The following Friday evening saw the arrival of John, Lillian and Peter, whose arm was still in a sling, which he claimed was completely unnecessary, but Harry was more concerned by his red-rimmed eyes and his pale, sallow complexion. This, coupled with the greying hair at his temples and the far-away look in his brown eyes worried Harry deeply. After dinner, Harry suggested taking a walk around the garden and a look towards Elise made her suggest a game of cards for everyone else.

Once well away from the house, Harry spoke gently to Peter. "How are you, lad?" he asked.

"Oh, I'm fine, Harry," Peter said, and Harry knew immediately that something was very wrong. Peter's voice was just too hearty.

"How's the arm doing?" Harry offered, trying not to force the conversation.

"It's much better now," Peter said, looking away.

"Your parents are worried about you." Harry had known, just from the tone of John's letter that something was wrong and that his friend needed Harry's help. One look at Peter told him where his help was required.

"I know." His voice was barely audible, and Harry saw his Adam's apple rise and fall several times as he swallowed hard.

"Do you mind if we sit on the bench at the end of the garden?" Harry asked. "My leg plays up sometimes."

"Not at all," Peter said, allowing Harry to sit down first.

They sat in silence for several minutes, Peter shifting uncomfortably in his seat. "My mother is driving me insane," he said suddenly. "She fusses and… oh, well, you know…"

"Yes. I do. My mother fussed too at first. You mustn't blame her. It's difficult for her to understand. You could talk to your father."

"I don't think I could." He turned his head away and Harry sensed he was finding it difficult to speak.

"Why don't you try?" Harry suggested. "He's a good listener."

There was a pause while Peter collected himself. He coughed. "Yes, but then he'd only worry more, wouldn't he?"

"What is it you want to talk about?" Harry asked. "I might be able to help."

Peter looked back towards the house, then stared up at the darkening sky for a few moments, before speaking. "You have no idea what it was like out there, Harry," he said, the words coming out in a rush. "We were stuck on the beach for days on end, being dive-bombed by bloody Stukas. Two of my friends were shot to pieces right next to me… just shot apart." Harry heard the catch in his voice. "The boats kept coming in and taking some of the men off, but there was never enough space." Harry turned away as he noticed a tear track down Peter's cheek. "I was one of the lucky ones," he carried on. "Once I was injured, they got me off quite quickly. But there was a bloke I met. He was with a different regiment. Dave was his name. We spent two days and nights together on the sands, just talking and keeping each other going, and when I was injured, it was Dave who carried me to the aid post. He had to leave me there and go back to the beach. I don't know if he made it, or not. I haven't been able to track him down, because I didn't know his surname. I just knew him as Dave. He saved my life and I don't even know if he's alive or dead." Peter was crying openly now, his shoulders heaving up and down. "Then I got back here and everyone's calling it a bloody victory. A victory! If that's victory, I don't ever want to be anywhere near a defeat… not ever."

Harry placed his hand gently on Peter's leg. "It's all right, son," he said, his voice very soft. "I do understand." He allowed Peter to cry until his sobs subsided, then he delved into his pocket and retrieved a handkerchief, which he handed to the young lad. After Peter had dried his eyes and wiped his face, he looked at Harry.

"I don't want to go back," he said.

"I know you don't," Harry replied, remembering his own feelings and fears. "But you will."

"How will I?"

"Because you have to. For your two mates, and for Dave, and for all the others."

Peter swallowed hard again.

"How did you get through it last time?" he asked eventually. "I've only done one small battle… well, evacuation, really; you and dad did this for four bloody years. How, Harry?"

"Same answer. We got through it because we had to. We had friends who needed us, so we did it for them."

Peter hesitated again, then he spoke very quietly. "I know you don't like to talk about it, but what was it like?"

"It was the worst kind of hell you can imagine. I don't talk about it because if you weren't there, as you've already said, you can't begin to imagine it, and no words of mine can do it justice; and if you were there, then you don't need me to tell you. Your father and I rarely speak of it, because we don't need to rake it up."

"How did you and dad meet?"

"Don't you know?"

"He told me that you met in a German hospital, but I've always known there's more to it than that. Whenever I ask, he just smiles and says it's not his story to tell."

"That sounds like your father." Harry put his stick down beside him, leaning it against the bench, then took a deep breath. "I'll be brief," he said, "because I don't like to go into too much detail, but I think you need to know something about your father." He cleared his throat. "I'd been very badly injured and I met your father in a German hospital. He helped me write to my parents, he fed me and cleaned me up when I was sick, and when I soiled myself." Harry looked directly at Peter, unashamed. "Your father was like a guardian angel, really. He was released before me, but on the day they let him go, he gave me his address and said to look him up if I ever needed help. Once I was well enough, I was sent to a POW camp for a few months, until the end of the war. After that, I was very, very ill, not so much physically as mentally," he said, closing his eyes. "I reached such a low ebb and, just when I thought things couldn't get any worse, the piece of paper with your father's address on it sort of fell into my lap. It seemed like divine providence, if you believe in such things. I went to your father's house and, although I think your mother thought he was mad, he took me in. He put me back on my feet and persuaded me to go back to Elise in France. She thought I was dead, you see. Your father convinced me that I owed her the right to at least know I was alive, and that she should make the choice as to what she wanted to do. Fortunately, she wanted to try and make a life with me. I've been a very lucky and very privileged man, Peter, to have known your father. I owe him everything."

"I had no idea."

"Well, if he didn't think it was his story to tell, he wouldn't have told you. John is an honourable man."

"I know. He's a great man and that's why I hate the idea of worrying him."

"Parents always worry, Peter. It's part of the job description." Peter smiled up at him. "That's a bit more like it," Harry continued. "Now, I suggest we sit here for a while longer until you're feeling a bit better and then we can go back indoors."

"You won't tell my father what we've talked about, will you?"

"Not if you don't want me to. But I'd encourage you to. He will understand far better than you think, and he'll help you. I promise."

"I might try and tell him some of it, but I don't want him worrying. Can I... can I keep talking to you, though, Harry?"

"Of course you can, Peter. Anytime. Once you've gone back, you can write, or phone, if it helps. I'll always be here for you. Always."

Peter was staring at his feet, so didn't notice his father standing at the french windows, nor the nodding of his head and slight smile that he gave Harry, which Harry returned before John turned back into the sitting room to rejoin the others.

Chapter Seven

Late Summer 1940

At the sound of the aeroplanes overhead, all the farm workers in the field stopped what they were doing and watched the dogfight. Two Spitfires and two ME-109s were duelling in the pale blue sky, white puffy clouds forming the backdrop. The German planes flew out towards the coast, followed swiftly by the two Spitfires. As they disappeared behind the trees on the horizon, the farmhands returned to their labours. Amy, who was among their number, watched until the last speck of a plane had disappeared. She knew neither of the pilots could be Ed; he flew a Hurricane, not a Spitfire. Still, she couldn't help but worry. He might be somewhere else, in a dogfight over another piece of English countryside, or worse still, over the Channel. She shuddered at the thought. Try as she might, she was still struggling to think of Ed as the brother he wasn't, rather than the 'so much more' she wanted him to be.

"Lunchtime!" the foreman called, and the workers downed their tools and walked across the field to where Charlotte and Anne had arrived, bearing sandwiches and cold drinks in large baskets, lined with red and white checked material. Amy hadn't seen Anne for a few days, although Anne had been on school holidays for several weeks now. She'd been busy helping her mother and Elise with another fundraising event – a village cricket match this time, to be held the following weekend. Their paths had crossed during the summer, but not for long enough to hold a conversation. As Amy went across the field, she saw

Anne look up and the two girls smiled at each other. Anne picked up a couple of sandwiches and approached Amy.

"I hope cheese is all right," she said, as she came closer.

"That's fine. At the moment, I could eat a horse," Amy replied.

They sat together on the edge of the field, away from the others. "Do you mind if we talk?" Anne asked.

"No, not at all," Amy replied.

"It's just that there's no-one else I can speak to." She hesitated, looking around the field. "Have you heard anything from Ed lately?" Anne asked eventually.

"He calls whenever he's been on a sortie," Amy replied. "Just to let us know he's got back safely. And he writes from time to time, but I think he's been frantically busy. Dad says he always sounds exhausted."

"I didn't tell you I had a letter from him a little while ago, did I?"

"No." Amy bit into her sandwich, steeling herself for what was to come.

"It was a very awkward letter," Anne continued, pulling the crusts from her sandwich. "He wrote to tell me that he thought I might have got the wrong idea about his feelings for me. He said that, if I was under the impression he was attached to me in any way, I'd got it wrong and I shouldn't think of him like that. He said he was happy for us to be friends, but didn't want anything more." Amy heard the crack in Anne's voice and couldn't help but feel desperately sorry for her.

"Men are idiots," she said, and meant it.

"They are, aren't they?" Anne replied. "I didn't reply. I was too embarrassed and, if I'm honest, I thought he might change his mind. I wondered, do you think that's likely? You know him better than anyone else, except Harry, and I can't possibly ask him. Do you think he might change his mind, Amy?"

Amy looked across at Anne. "No, Anne. I'm sorry. If he didn't mean it, he wouldn't have written it. I'll give Ed one thing – he's honest. He's an idiot, but he's an honest idiot." Amy felt Anne's sigh as well as hearing it.

"Oh well," she said. "I had to ask. Just in case."

"I imagine he's like a lot of pilots," Amy said, trying to cheer Anne up. "They don't like to be too serious about anything, so he's probably got women scattered around all over the place." Even as she said the words, she hoped they weren't true.

Anne tried to laugh. "Probably," she said. "Thanks for listening, Amy. I'd better help mother to clear away."

"And I'd better get back to work," Amy replied. "I am truly sorry." And she was. Although she hadn't wanted to see Anne and Ed get together, she didn't want her friend to feel so sad.

"To be fair to Ed, he wasn't to know how I felt and I'm glad he told me now, before I made a complete fool of myself. At least I avoided that embarrassment."

"He got something right then," Amy smiled, getting to her feet.

"Did he call?" Amy shouted as she opened the door that evening.

"Yes," Harry replied. "Only about ten minutes ago. You just missed him."

Damn, thought Amy. "I assume he's okay?"

"Yes. He didn't say much, and he sounded exhausted as usual, but he's back safely."

"Good." Amy flopped down into an armchair. "What's for dinner?" she asked.

"Chicken pie," Elise replied.

"Thank goodness; I'm starving. Do I have time for quick bath?"

"You've got about half an hour."

"I won't be that long, unless I fall asleep," Amy shot out of the chair again and ran for the door. "If I'm not down in twenty-five minutes, bang on the bathroom door. If I don't answer, come in and shake me."

"I assume that invitation doesn't include me?" Harry asked.

"Of course not, silly," Amy called over her shoulder.

That night, lying in bed, Amy stared out of the window at the blue-black sky. Ed wouldn't be asleep, she knew that. He'd written to her once of how he often stared out at night, longing to fly up and touch the stars, and how he wanted to capture one and bring it back for her. It was the most romantic thing he'd ever said to her, not that he meant it that way. He meant it as an adventure. "Come back to me," she whispered. "I know you don't love me. I know you'll never love me, but please just come back to me."

Along the corridor, Elise lay in Harry's arms. "I'm so scared for him," he whispered. "Seeing the dogfights in the sky each day… It's terrifying knowing he could be up there. And I'm just sitting here doing nothing. I wish to God that I could do his job for him; take on the danger and keep him safe. Keep all of you safe."

"Harry, you've always done everything for him. Now it's his turn. You have to let him do this."

"I know, but this is so dangerous. There's so much at stake, and he's risking everything for us. They all are. And they're so young, Elise."

She snuggled into him. "Just trust him, Harry. Trust all of them."

She opened her eyes and knew instantly that something was wrong. The room was shrouded in darkness still, but she could sense the heat and fear coming from his body. Switching on the bedside lamp, she turned towards him and saw the beads of sweat on his face, the crumpled sheet sticking to his chest as his arm thrashed against an invisible foe. Silent words came from his mouth, his eyes were closed tight, and the furrows on his brow spoke of untold horrors. Kneeling up beside him, she gently placed her hand on his chest, feeling the dampness of his skin.

"Harry," she called quietly. "Harry, darling. Wake up."

He continued to thrash for a moment or two, then his eyes shot open and she momentarily saw the terror and panic reflected back at her. Grabbing her, he twisted her down onto the bed and rolled over to lie on top of her, kissing her neck, face and mouth furiously. The change in him was intense, unfathomable. She responded, kissing him back, running her fingers through his hair, down his neck and along his shoulders. His muscles were hard and tense, his lips and tongue urgent.

"I want you. Now," he whispered in her ear.

"Then take me," she murmured.

"Was it bad this time?" she whispered a while later, lying across his chest.

"No, you were amazing, as always." He twirled a few strands of her hair between his fingers.

"You know what I'm talking about, Harry." Her voice was serious.

He hesitated before replying, "Yes, it was bad."

"Do you want to talk about it?"

"Not really. I'd rather leave it in the darkness." She turned slightly, so she could see his face.

"Don't you think it might help? To talk about it, I mean?"

"Not right now, no." She sighed. "I'm sorry, Elise," he continued.

"Don't be sorry."

"I know you want me to talk about it, but it's not that easy."

"You've spoken more about it to various people over the last few months than over the previous twenty years. I know it hasn't been easy for you. It brings it all back."

"It's strange isn't it? It takes another war to make us talk about the last one..."

"Yes. The war even made Dennis quite chatty." She wanted to bite back the words as soon as they'd left her lips, and she felt Harry tense.

"Dennis? What did he have to say?"

"Oh, nothing. It was ages ago, when Sylvia was still here."

"And you haven't said anything? That was over six months ago now. It must have been bad if you've kept it to yourself all this time."

"Of course it wasn't bad."

"Then tell me what he said. And more to the point, why he said it."

"Don't be angry with him. Sylvia didn't understand why you called him Stubbs and everyone else called him Dennis. He was just explaining how you knew each other in the war." Harry wondered, just for a moment, whether to them it would always be 'the' war, and what that made the current conflict.

"Hmm. So, what did he say?"

She took a deep breath, blinking back the tears behind her eyes. "He told us about a friend of his who was killed... a man called Hawks. He said how much you helped him." She hesitated for a moment. "And then he said that you were the best officer he and the other men ever had; and the bravest man they'd ever known."

"What on earth made him say that?"

"I imagine he was simply telling the truth."

Harry paused. "Well, given tonight's performance, you know that's not the case."

Elise reached up and caressed his cheek. "You forget, I saw you with your men back then. I know how much you cared for them, so I don't know anything of the sort," she whispered. "It was nice to know they appreciated you though."

****

The almost constant drone of aircraft and worry about Ed sustained the nightmares over the coming weeks and, as the summer showed the first signs of waning into autumn, Harry and Elise were both exhausted from nights of interrupted sleep. Amy's work on the farm was finished, much to Elise's relief, as the early starts and late nights were playing havoc with the household in general. Much to her own disappointment, Amy had returned to school, and found she missed the camaraderie of working in the fields, as well as the fun she had chatting to Anne and Charlotte.

On her first Tuesday back, she walked slowly home along the lanes, watching the workers in the field and calling out to them. Henri came over to the fence and they talked for a while. The harvest was almost finished and William was delighted with how everyone had worked, Henri said. He seemed pleased and Amy was glad that he'd settled in, despite Sophie's continued disgruntled moaning. She dawdled along a little further, wondering what else she might be able to do to help with the war effort. She was going to be seventeen in a few months and had decided to leave school in the summer, whatever her parents thought. She'd been contemplating doing something with the Red Cross; perhaps helping at the hospital. She imagined Elise might object, but wondered whether the way round her objections might be to present her with several less favourable alternatives, thus making the Red Cross seem like an excellent idea. Her other option would be to get her father's agreement first, and then get him to work on her mother. As she approached the house, she contemplated which of these options might prove best and wondered what other war work she could present to Elise that she might find so much more objectionable than nursing.

"I'm home!" she called out, as she closed the front door, throwing her school bag into the corner of the hallway.

"We're in the sitting room." She heard her father's voice and headed towards it.

"Ed!" she cried almost as soon as she'd opened the door. He was standing by the fireplace, his hands in his pockets. Without thinking, she ran towards him, throwing herself at him. He caught her and swung her round.

"Hey, kiddo. You've grown again," he said, putting her back down on the floor.

"What are you doing here?" she asked. "Not that I'm not pleased to see you, but shouldn't you be off fighting the Germans?"

Ed looked at the carpet and kicked his heels for a moment, before glancing back at her. "My squadron has been a bit busy recently, and they decided we needed a rest. We've been sent to Wittering."

"Wittering? But that's great! You're just down the road."

"Yes. I'll be able to come and see you more often, just for a while. I don't imagine they'll let us stay here for long, but it'll be good to spend some time at home. I'm due back at base this evening, but I'll probably be able to get a pass this weekend."

At that moment, Polly opened the door and brought in a tray laden with tea things, including a sponge cake, something they hadn't had in ages. As everyone crowded around the table, Amy took advantage of the interruption to study Ed's face and noticed the black shadows under his eyes and the paleness of his cheeks. He looked very tired and she hoped the rest would do him good. Oddly, now he was home and safe, although he still looked magnificent, and gloriously handsome, especially in his uniform, she found the pull towards him slightly less potent. It was still there, but the intensity was less noticeable, less destructive. She shrugged her shoulders and helped herself to a slice of cake.

"Anne told me you wrote to her," Amy said. They were sitting under the oak tree the following Saturday afternoon. For the middle of September, it was surprisingly warm, the field had been harvested and looked barren, compared to its summer abundance. Amy was wearing a new skirt which Elise had bought for her, in a pretty pink floral pattern, accompanied by a white short-sleeved blouse. She'd tied her hair up loosely behind her head with a white ribbon, leaving a few stray tendrils caressing her cheeks.

"Yes, it seemed like the right thing to do at the time, although it feels like forever ago now. I was surprised I didn't get a reply, though. How did she take it?"

"Okay, I think. And she had a reason for not replying."

"Really? What was that?"

"She said she hoped you might change your mind. She felt that if she acknowledged your letter, you'd have no way back."

"That's a bit arrogant, don't you think? Not every man is going to fall at her feet."

"Well, I don't think she meant it like that."

"Oh? How did she mean it then?"

"I think she was probably just disappointed and hoped you'd... well hoped you'd see things differently after a while."

"I can't see why. If you're not attracted to someone, then you're not attracted to them. That's not going to change just because the other person wants it to."

"That was roughly what I told her."

"Really? She asked your opinion?"

"Why wouldn't she? She seemed to think I'd know you better than anyone else."

"And what did you say?"

"If memory serves, I told her that you would have meant what you said. I told her that you were honest."

"Well, that's a compliment, if nothing else."

"Yes, I told her you were an honest idiot."

"Trust you to spoil the moment."

"Well, I did also point out that you fighter pilots don't like to be too tied down. I told her you've probably got lots of women scattered around…"

He suddenly looked serious. "No, Amy. I don't have lots of women… I'm not like that. I'd have thought you'd know me well enough…"

"Yes… sorry." She felt herself blushing with embarrassment.

"Oh, don't worry about it. I don't have time for women right now anyway. It's been non-stop flying for weeks on end. I'm starting to forget what women look like."

Amy turned away. He'd obviously forgotten he was sitting next to one. When she turned back, he was staring up at the sky, with a far-off look in his eyes.

"Is something wrong?" she asked, touching his arm.

"No," he replied, turning back to her and smiling. "Nothing for you to worry about."

"It's been a tough few weeks, Mother." Ed was sitting in Isabel's living room, in a chair opposite hers, drinking coffee.

"We've seen our share of dogfights. It's worried me sick," she replied, and Ed knew he couldn't tell her what he was really feeling.

"I assume you haven't seen anything of Charles," he asked, changing the subject.

"No. Not at all. I don't know if he managed to sell his business, but Harry made sure he had enough money to start up again somewhere else."

"I hope the solicitor chap dealt with it all, and it wasn't too bothersome."

"Well, I can't say I warmed to Mr Griffin, but he was very good at his job. I much preferred dealing with Harry's father, but I suppose times have to change." She looked across at him.

"Why did you marry him?" Ed asked.

Isabel looked out of the window, then returned her gaze to him. "I don't expect you to understand at your age, Ed, but I needed someone in my life."

"I do understand that, Mother, better than you probably imagine. What I don't understand is, why Dobson?"

"We live in a small village, Ed. I wasn't exactly falling over men offering themselves."

"So you settled?"

"I wouldn't put it that way, but I suppose so, yes."

"Did he always hate me?"

"Hate's a bit strong. I think he was jealous of you. You and Harry. We were very close until he came along. He took advantage of the situation to get his own way and, to my shame, I allowed it."

"I don't blame you, Mother. I just wish you hadn't married him."

"So do I."

"I imagine he hated Harry paying your allowance and funding my education."

"Oh, yes." She smiled. "I won't repeat what he used to say about Harry. Suffice to say, it wasn't polite." They sat in silence for a few moments. "What's wrong?" she asked.

"What makes you think there's anything wrong?"

"You're still my son, Ed, even though we've been separated for a long time. I've always known when there's something wrong. You get a look in your eyes."

"I'll have to remember that."

"So what's wrong?" she repeated.

"Oh, it's nothing."

"It's not nothing. Tell me."

"I can't, Mother. It's to do with the war, and I wouldn't want to worry you."

"Now I am worried."

"You don't need to be, honestly. I suppose I just need to speak to someone who understands what this feels like. I thought I'd try speaking to Amy yesterday. You know we've always been close. But then I remembered she's just a child still really, and that wouldn't be fair."

"She's not a child anymore, Ed. She'll be seventeen soon. She's a young woman, with a very sensible head on her shoulders. I'm sure she'd be more than capable of listening, if you wanted to speak to her."

"No, I decided it wouldn't be right to burden her with my problems."

"What about Harry then?"

"Harry's having nightmares again. Elise told me. He looks quite ill. I can't possibly add to his worries."

"He'd be upset if you didn't, you know. And, if this is something to do with the war, he'll understand how you feel better than the rest of us. Your father always put a great deal of trust in Harry. You should do the same."

"I know. I always have in the past. I'm just worried about him at the moment." He paused. "They were very close, weren't they?"

"Oh yes. When your father and Harry first met, I used to be quite jealous of their friendship."

"Really?"

"Yes. Your father's letters were full of Harry. I felt as though I couldn't possibly compete. I didn't need to, of course..." She blushed. "It took me a while to realise that their friendship was different." She looked up and saw Ed nodding his head slightly and knew he understood, even better than she did. Getting up, she went to her bureau and opened the drawer, which had previously been kept locked. Reaching inside, she pulled out a bundle of letters and returned to her seat. "I want to read you something," she said, taking the top letter from the bundle. "This was your father's last letter to me. I'd let you read it yourself, but there are some personal details, which..." She left the sentence unfinished. "Well, I'll just read you a little bit..." She unfolded the letter and laid it on her lap.

"'Just back from the most awful raid,'" she read. "'Nothing went to plan and we had to retreat. Harry was marvellous, as usual. He took charge when the CO was killed, got us all back and saved my life – again. Harry turned up covered in blood, which put the fear of God into me that he'd been wounded, but it was the CO's blood: he'd died in Harry's arms, so he had a much better death than he deserved. Harry's gone back to HQ to report, now. He's exhausted, but he keeps going somehow, joking and smiling. I don't know how he does it, but he does. You know, Izzy, I trust him absolutely, even with my life, and there aren't many men you can say that about…'" She looked up and saw Ed's eyes were glistening. "Talk to him, Ed," she said. "He'll know what to do." He got up and kissed the top of her head.

"I will, Mother, just not at the moment. He's not infallible and I won't put any more problems on his shoulders. Not until I know he's feeling better."

"He'd want to help and he won't thank you for holding things back from him, Ed."

"He won't know."

"Hmm… I wouldn't be too sure of that."

It was a fortnight later before Ed could visit again. He found Harry sitting in his study, staring out of the window at what used to be the garden, which now resembled an allotment. The knock on the door brought him back to reality and, as it opened, Ed came in.

"Are you all right?" Harry asked, noting the even darker black shadows under Ed's eyes.

"Not really," Ed replied.

"I didn't think you were, but you've taken your time coming to find me. I've been expecting you to speak to me for weeks now." Harry sat up straight, smiling across at Ed and indicating the seat opposite him. "Why have you waited so long, when you know I'm only too happy to listen?"

"Because when I first got down here, Elise told me you're having nightmares. I didn't want to cause you any more problems."

"She didn't tell you that so you wouldn't talk to me, you bloody fool. She told you that so you wouldn't be disturbed if you heard me calling out in the night when you were staying."

"Sorry."

"Don't be sorry, just tell me what's wrong."

Ed looked around the room, taking in the shelves of books, the pictures on the wall, some of which were Harry's, dating back to the days when he could paint; scenes of the Cornish coast mingled with local Sussex landscapes. He glanced through the window as the sun shone through the branches of the silver birch trees at the end of the garden, casting dappled shadows across the rows of vegetables.

"I think there's something the matter with me," he said at last, not looking at Harry.

"If this is something to do with the women in your life, then I'm not necessarily the man for you," Harry said, grinning.

"No, it's nothing to do with women. I haven't got time for them at the moment."

"Okay, fire away then."

"Unfortunate turn of phrase, Harry, in the circumstances." Ed finally looked back at the older man and saw the concern in his eyes.

"I never said I was subtle."

Ed looked back down the garden and took a deep breath. "I don't understand myself sometimes. I can't work out how I feel. Do you know, I've watched at least four of my best friends die? They've been shot out of the sky, or they've bailed and their chutes have failed and they've fallen, crashed, either into the sea, or into fields, and I haven't felt a thing. I don't seem to react like the others."

"Why, what do the others do?"

"It varies. Mostly, they get drunk, some get maudlin', some sit and talk among themselves. I just lie on my bunk and read, or write letters. It's as though nothing's happened. That can't be right, can it, Harry? I lie awake at night wondering why I can't feel anything. I should feel something, shouldn't I?"

"Who says?"

"Well, no-one actually says, but it doesn't seem... well, normal to see that happen and just feel nothing."

Harry sat forward. "Ed, look at me." Ed turned his face and looked directly at Harry. "Pay attention to what I'm going to say because it's very important." Ed nodded his head slightly, so Harry knew he had his attention. "Absolutely nothing – and I mean *nothing* – about war is normal, Ed. No-one can say how you should react to anything." He swallowed hard. "I can remember..." He blinked, trying hard not to take his eyes from Ed's. "I can remember going out into No Man's Land and walking over bodies that had been lying there for weeks. I could recognise faces still, or tattoos sometimes, if there was no recognisable face, and I'd remember their names and that they had a wife, or a sweetheart and maybe children. But there was always a job to do; maybe some wires to mend or something, so we just had to carry on. Some men would vomit, there and then. Some would make the worst, rudest, most inappropriate jokes you can imagine. Others would break down and cry, recognising a friend. They all reacted differently."

"What about you, Harry? How did you react?"

"It was different for me, Ed."

"Why?"

"I was their officer. I couldn't let them see that I was affected, so I had to carry on as though nothing had happened."

"And how the hell did you do that?"

"The same way you do," Harry replied. "I just got on with it."

Harry heard the word "Shit," escape Ed's lips.

"I was lucky, Ed. I had friends. More importantly, I had your father and I'd never have survived without him. I can't imagine how you do the job you do. You're alone up there and that's the worst of it. Maybe what you're doing, is your way of protecting yourself."

"How do you mean?"

"I think you're deliberately trying not to get emotionally involved, so none of it touches you."

"But shouldn't it touch me? Shouldn't I be affected?"

"If it makes you a better flyer, a better pilot; if it helps you to survive, then you do whatever you bloody well have to do, Ed. Whatever it takes. Nothing is wrong, and most definitely nothing is ever right – not in a war. Just go with whatever feels natural to you, and don't ask too many questions. Get through each day, and do your damnedest to come out the other side."

The two men looked at each other for a moment. "Thanks, Harry," Ed said quietly.

"What for? I haven't really done anything."

"It just helps, knowing I can talk to you."

"You can always talk to me. Only next time, don't leave it so bloody long."

Chapter Eight

Early Summer 1941

"Nursing?" Elise wasn't incredulous, but she was getting there. "You want to do nursing?"

"Yes, Mum."

"But you've got no experience."

"Well, I'm not suggesting I'd be Florence Nightingale on my first day. That's the whole point. I'd be a volunteer with the Red Cross, learning the ropes."

"And where would you do this?"

"At the local hospital. I've already been to see the matron and spoken to her about it."

"Without speaking to us first?" Elise was disappointed, more than angry.

"Well, there didn't seem any point in speaking to you, if it wasn't going to be possible to do it."

"And is it possible?" Harry put in.

"Yes. They're always looking for volunteers, evidently. And working for the Red Cross, I'd be bit like you, Mum." Harry smiled inwardly; Amy had thought this through. "I'd only be doing very menial tasks to start with, but they offer training, so who knows?"

"That's what worries me," Elise said.

"There's nothing to worry about," Amy said. "I might not even like it. But I want to give it a try."

"But you're only seventeen."

"I'll be eighteen soon."

"In six months' time. And what about your education?"

Amy looked at both of them. "We all know I'm not really university material. I'm not sure what I'd study, even if I managed to get in. And I can go back and study anytime. I won't get this chance again... And I'll only be down the road if I do this. I'll still be living here, not abroad, not under fire, not in any danger," Amy added, trying to sound persuasive. Elise looked to Harry.

"I think your mother and I need to discuss this," he said. "You can't do it without our permission, so hold fire until we've talked it through, young lady."

"All right, Daddy," Amy replied.

"We can't let her do it," Elise said to Harry after Amy had gone to bed.

"I don't really see how we can stop her." Harry took the cup of coffee that Elise offered him.

"We can just forbid her from doing it."

"When we've encouraged all the others to do what they want?"

"The 'others', as you call them, aren't our children, Harry. Not even Ed is really your child. He's Isabel's and Edward's child. Amy is ours and I don't want her to be placed in danger."

"Nursing is hardly being placed in danger, sweetheart." Harry placed his cup on the table and moved along the sofa so he was nearer to Elise. "She wants to help out and she won't be satisfied until she does. If we don't let her do this, she'll just finish her time at school, resenting the hell out of us every single day, and then join the WRAF, or the WRENS or something, and then she really will be in danger."

"Do you think she'd do that?"

"Knowing Amy? Yes, I do. Just to spite us." He held her hand in his. "Look on the bright side, though, she's got no idea how difficult nursing is going to be. Once she's tried it, she might hate the whole idea."

"And then she'll wait and join the WRAF or the WRENS?"

"Well, maybe, or perhaps she'll go off the whole idea, but either way, we can't stop her."

Elise huffed a little and rested her head on his shoulder. "I just want to keep her safe."

"And you think I don't?" He pulled away from her slightly, looking down into her eyes. "I've only ever wanted to keep all of you safe."

"I know, Harry. Oh, why does she have to grow up so quickly?"

He kissed the top of her head. "Because that's what children do, my love."

Amy's first day was exhausting. She'd washed floors, cleaned bedpans, made beds and poured more cups of tea than she'd ever done in her entire life, but she returned home with red hands and a smile on her face.

"It was marvellous," she said, falling into the armchair nearest the fireplace. "I'm not sure I can stay awake long enough to eat supper, but I've had such a fantastic day."

"What have you done?" Harry asked from his seat on the sofa.

She repeated her day's experiences, telling them of the patient whose letter she'd read because he couldn't read very well, of the child she'd played with while his mother was examined by the doctor, of all the menial tasks she'd been given and carried out with gusto, and of Matron's congratulations on her first day's work.

"I'm going upstairs for a bath," she said, yawning.

"Dinner is in three quarters of an hour," Elise replied, glancing at the clock.

"All right," said Amy, getting to her feet. "I just have to wash the grime off."

"So much for her not liking the work," Elise said once the door had closed behind her.

"Hmmm. That backfired, didn't it? Who would have guessed she'd enjoy housework so much? If we'd known, we could have got her to do more here." Harry smiled at Elise and she tried to smile back. "Don't worry about her. She's clearly enjoying herself, and she's perfectly safe at the cottage hospital, so she's not likely to start looking elsewhere for something to do."

"I suppose you're right," Elise said.

"And we were never going to be able to keep her as our little girl forever."

It didn't take Amy long to settle into her new routine and, each night she would come home, full of stories. One Friday in late August, she walked through the door to find George, Anne, William and Charlotte clinking glasses with Harry and Elise. She looked around.

"Did I forget something?" she asked.

"No," Elise said calmly. "George has got the weekend home on leave and, when Charlotte called earlier, I invited them to come here for dinner. It's all very last minute, and they've only just arrived."

"I'll just nip upstairs to change. I'll be as quick as I can," said Amy, leaving the room.

"So," Harry said, turning to George. "How are things?"

"You don't all need to look so worried," he replied. "This isn't embarkation leave, or anything." Harry could almost hear William's sigh of relief. "I'm not going anywhere dangerous. I've just been given a few days off. I'm one of the lucky ones, I suppose."

"In what way?" Elise asked, motioning that everyone should sit down.

"Well, I can't say too much," George continued once they were all settled, "but I'm working on a few projects for a special department."

"This all sounds very hush-hush," Anne nudged him, playfully. Amy came back into the room and noticed the interplay between them. It reminded her of how she and Ed would mess around. She'd hardly thought of him in ages... well, not often, anyway. She'd been too busy.

"It is." George seemed slightly affronted that she wasn't taking him seriously. He fell silent.

"What *can* you tell us?" Charlotte asked.

"Just that I'm working in a house in a small village in Buckinghamshire. There's quite a big group of us, and we're all working on different things. It's fun, actually." His eyes lit up.

"I'm not being funny," Amy said, sitting on the floor next to her father's feet, "but you're young and fit and healthy... Why are you stuck in a house in the countryside, rather than fighting somewhere?"

"It's my engineering background," George replied. "And that's as much as I can say."

Amy was quietly impressed. She wondered what George could possibly be working on, that was so secretive and wished she could do something like that, something more… she didn't know what, just *more.*

That night in bed, Elise cuddled in to Harry and he put his arm around her.

"What's wrong?" he asked. Although they always fell asleep in each other's arms, he'd sensed there was something troubling her all evening.

"Amy," Elise replied.

"What's wrong with Amy?" Harry asked.

"Nothing that I know of, but did you see the look in her eyes when George was talking?"

"No, I was watching George. He seems very happy with the work he's doing."

"Yes, that's the point. It was rubbing off on Amy. She looked as though she'd happily jump in his suitcase and go back with him."

"What? You think Amy's interested in George?" Harry couldn't hide his amusement at the idea.

"No, I think Amy's interested in what George is *doing*, not in George himself. I'm worried, Harry. She'll be eighteen soon. She could easily decide to go and do something more dangerous."

"She's happy where she is."

"How long for? She terrifies me sometimes."

"You can't get so worried about something that hasn't happened yet. George will go back, she'll get busy and she'll forget all about it again." He ran his fingers down her back soothingly.

"Stop trying to distract me."

"It's working though, isn't it?"

"Yes," she sighed, "it is…"

Chapter Nine

Summer 1942

Ed walked slowly up the garden path. A whole five days. He sighed deeply. Five days to sleep, walk, rest, read a book, all of it without being interrupted. What utter bliss. He'd see his mother, of course, and chat to Harry, Elise and Amy, but he just craved some peace and quiet. Because he'd been flying night ops for months on end now, he had to catch up on as much sleep as possible during the day, so coming home had been difficult. On the three occasions when he'd been given a weekend pass and had managed to make it home, Amy had either been up in London visiting Rose or staying with her friend Pauline from the hospital, so he hadn't seen her since last Autumn, and he'd missed her eighteenth birthday in December. It was the longest time they'd ever gone without seeing each other and he missed their conversations. Letters kept him informed, but they weren't the same.

He still had to tell everyone he was being transferred to Northumberland and he knew they wouldn't take it any better than he was, but at least he wouldn't be flying at night anymore. Harry had been worried about that, although Ed had quite enjoyed it himself. It was just how he'd always imagined it would be. He enjoyed the mystery, the shrouding shadows and the complete isolation of night flying. Still, nothing seemed to last long these days… especially if you enjoyed it.

He opened the front door and let himself in, placing his suitcase by the wall.

"Hello!" he called. Elise was just coming down the stairs.

"Ed!" she cried, taking the final few steps a little more quickly. "I didn't realise you'd be here so early." She hugged him. "Oh, it's been so long," she said, releasing him. "We thought you'd be arriving just before dinner."

"Well, I thought I'd surprise you. Where's Harry?"

"He's in the garden. Dennis is having trouble with the beans, I believe." She raised her eyes heavenwards. "I sometimes feel as though the fate of the nation rests with the production of our carrots and runner beans."

"Dennis always was a bit prone to melodramatics."

She linked arms with Ed, pulling him towards the sitting room. "Well, to be honest," she said, conspiratorially, "I don't discourage him. It gives Harry something to do."

"And how's the fundraising going?" Ed asked, appreciating the meaning of Elise's remark.

"We had the summer fair two weeks ago. We raised even more than last year."

"I'm sorry I missed it. Last year's was such fun."

"I know. And now we're starting to plan for the autumn book sale. Those are our two staples. I think we might continue them after the war, you know? The whole village gets involved and everyone seems to enjoy it so much, it would be a shame to stop holding them just because the war ends."

"Well, I don't see why you shouldn't."

"Because I think Harry would probably kill me."

"I doubt that very much." They both looked down to the end of the garden, to where Harry and Dennis where standing. Dennis was pointing to something on the ground, then he knelt down and picked up some soil, then pointed at the sky. Harry was nodding his head.

"Harry!" Elise called. "Look who's here." Harry turned his head, smiled, spoke to Dennis and made his way up the garden, between rows of lettuces, beetroot, onions and radishes.

"How are you, Ed?" he said, as he reached the terrace.

"I'm fine. What's up with Dennis?"

"Oh, to be perfectly honest, I really don't understand," Harry whispered. "He's muttering on about the trees using all the nutrients in the soil, or something. I've got an awful feeling he's suggesting that we take the trees out."

"I hope you said no," Elise said.

"Of course I said no. Everything at this end of the garden grows absolutely fine. If we have to sacrifice the other end to the trees and grow a little less, then so be it."

"You could dig up the front?" Ed suggested.

"Do you know, I was going to put that to him," Harry said.

"Dig up the front garden?" Elise was astounded. "What would your mother have said?"

"Does it matter what mother would have said?" Harry asked. "I think she'd have agreed. She was always eminently practical when it came down to it. Better to keep the trees for the long-term and dig up the lawn at the front. It can always be replaced after the war. The trees can't. I'll talk to Stubbs later. Anyway, Ed, how long have you got?"

"A whole five days," he said, flopping into the chair nearest the fire. "And I can't wait."

"Five days? That'll be lovely." Elise sat down on the sofa. "Amy will be pleased. She hasn't seen you in ages. She's probably forgotten what you look like. Do you have any plans?"

"Sleeping mainly." Ed's eyes were already closed.

"Why don't you go up and have a bath and get some rest," she suggested.

"Please tell me you haven't planned a big dinner for tonight," he said.

"No, it's just us. I thought you might be tired."

"Good." He clambered to his feet. "I think I'll take you up on that offer. A bath sounds wonderful. When does Amy get back from the hospital?"

"She's usually home at around six o'clock. She phones if she's going to be later."

"She said in her last letter that she's learnt to drive an ambulance. I'd love to see that." His eyes sparkled as he smiled.

"I think she's been learning all kinds of things, apart from just driving an ambulance," Elise said, sounding wistful. Ed looked quizzical, but was too tired to ask anything further.

"Well, if she's lucky, I'll be out of the bath by the time she gets back," he said as he opened the door.

"You'll be a prune if you're not," Harry replied to his retreating back.

"Sorry I'm late!" Amy yelled. "I'm going for a quick bath. Down in twenty minutes." She kicked off her flat hospital shoes and ran up the stairs, straight into the bathroom, where she ran a bath, using only the regulation amount of water. God, how she longed to soak up to her neck in bubbles. Standing naked before the mirror, she pulled all the pins out of her hair and let it fall around her shoulders. Oh, the release of not having her hair restrained… it was joyous. She climbed into the bath and soaped up, washing away the smells of carbolic and iodine and other things she preferred not to think about. Her last job for the day had been to change the dressing on Mrs Hadley's ulcerated leg and, even now, the slightly nauseating smell seemed to fill her nostrils. Rinsing away the soap, she breathed deeply, feeling the relief of being at home. She wondered briefly as she dried herself, if Ed had arrived yet.

In her room, she put on some underwear, and went to her wardrobe. She was hot and didn't want to wear anything too formal. Rose had given her a beautiful summer dress when she'd visited London earlier in the year, so she pulled it out and put it on. It was bright red, fairly low cut with a lacy inlay, dainty capped sleeves, a thin white belt and a full skirt, which showed off her tiny waist. She'd worn it a couple of times before to parties, and knew it wasn't too warm. She checked her watch. She'd been nearly half an hour already. She brushed out her hair, then put on a pair of white peep-toe sandals and ran to the top of the stairs.

"Do you want me to go and find her?" Ed offered, putting his whisky glass down on the mantlepiece.

"Do you mind? Dinner will be late if she doesn't hurry up," Elise replied.

Ed left the room and had just started to climb the stairs when Amy appeared above him. She was rounding the corner of the landing, pulling her hair into a loose pony tail behind her head. She stopped at the top of the stairs and bent to fiddle with the buckle on the side of her right shoe. Then she stood up straight.

"Hello, you," she said, descending towards him.

"Um... Hello."

"Are you all right?" she asked, as she approached. "You look a bit pale."

He coughed. "No. No, I'm... I'm absolutely fine. You're..."

"I'm what? Late for dinner?" She smiled. "I know. You'd think mum and dad would be used to it by now. I'm late pretty much every night." She took his hand, and led him back towards the sitting room. "I've had such a day, but I'll tell you all about it over dinner." She let go of his hand and opened the door. "I'm sorry I'm so late," she said to her parents.

"Why didn't you phone?" Elise asked. "You usually do. We were worried."

"I'm sorry." Amy walked over and kissed her mother on the cheek. "There was a problem and I couldn't leave the patient to phone you."

"Is the patient all right?" Harry asked.

"She will be," Amy replied.

"We'll have to go straight in to dinner," Elise said, leading the way from the sitting room, through the hall and into the dining room. "What happened with your patient?" she asked, as they all sat down at the table.

"It was Mrs Hadley," Amy explained. "The lady with the ulcerated leg... Do you remember, I told you about her son?" She looked at Harry who nodded and turned to Ed.

"He was killed at Dunkirk and she just sort of gave up. Now she's in hospital."

"With an ulcerated leg, I gather?" Ed asked, watching Amy closely.

"Yes." She took the plate of shepherd's pie that Elise had just dished up, and placed it in front of her. "Anyway, I had to change her dressing just before coming home. It was the last job of the day." She took the lid off a dish and spooned out some peas onto her plate. "I took off the old bandage and noticed there was this horrible smell..."

"Do we need to hear the gory details over dinner?" Elise cut in.

"It's not gory," Amy explained. "Anyway. I knew something was wrong, and I should have gone to Sister Jenkins, but she was busy admitting a new patient on the other ward. Doctor Finch was just passing the end of the bed, so I grabbed hold of him – by the lapels of his coat, actually – and showed him Mrs Hadley's leg. He told me it was gangrene. He said I'd done really well to spot it as it was only in the very early stages, and I'd probably saved her leg. Could you pass the water please, Ed?" She looked up and saw them all staring at her. "What?" she asked.

"Amy, you've just calmly told us that you've saved a woman's leg and then you ask Ed to pass the water, as though nothing unusual happened," Harry said, as Ed picked up the jug of water and handed it to her.

"Well, I didn't actually do anything. I just grabbed the doctor and made him look at the patient. He did all the hard work. He's amazing, you know." She filled her glass with water before giving the jug back to Ed, who took it and replaced it on the table in front of his plate.

"Was this the new doctor you were telling us about last week?" Elise asked as they all started to eat.

"Yes. I don't think he'll be around for long, though, worst luck," Amy replied. "He's younger than all the others, newly qualified, fit and healthy. I'm sure they'll find somewhere much more exciting to send him. I don't think he likes being here much either, although he puts on a brave face whenever he's on the wards... he's absolutely brilliant with the patients." She took a mouthful of shepherd's pie. "Do you know?" she said, as she finished chewing, "he asked me out for a drink this evening? He said it was to congratulate me about Mrs Hadley." Elise went to speak. "Don't worry, Mummy, I told him I couldn't go because

Ed was coming home today... I'm not about to disappear straight after supper... This is wonderful," she added. "I had an early lunch today, so I'm starving."

Harry smiled and shook his head. "Will you be in trouble with Sister Jenkins?" Elise asked.

"Probably," Amy replied.

"Why?" asked Ed.

"Because I went to the doctor, not to her first."

"But she wasn't available and you helped the patient. Surely that's all that matters."

"Good Lord, no," Amy laughed. "There's a certain way of doing things in hospitals, and going above the head of the Sister isn't one of them."

"What do you think she'll do?" Elise asked.

"She'll probably rant a bit," Amy replied. "But Doctor Finch has said he'll back me up. She won't like it, but doctors carry far more weight than nurses, so she'll have to do what he says."

"She won't like him taking your side, Amy. You need to be careful," Harry warned.

"Oh, I don't know. Maybe I won't stay there much longer. Pauline got a transfer to the Swindon Ambulance convoy a couple of weeks ago. I'm wondering about doing the same."

Everyone stared at her and silence descended, until Elise spoke first: "Swindon?" she said.

"Well, probably not Swindon. I was thinking maybe Portsmouth."

"Portsmouth," Harry repeated quietly.

"Yes, it's not too far away."

"But, Portsmouth?" Elise whispered.

"Oh, don't worry, Mummy. I haven't decided on anything yet," Amy said, taking another mouthful of shepherd's pie. "Does anyone mind if I have a little more of this?"

After coffee, Ed got to his feet and stretched. "I think I'm going to take a short walk before bedtime," he said. "Fancy coming?" He turned to Amy.

"In these shoes?" She indicated the heels on her sandals.

"Then change your shoes." He grinned.

"Oh, all right. Give me five minutes." She got up and left the room, returning shortly afterwards wearing flat pumps.

"We'll probably go to bed before you get back. Elise has got a meeting tomorrow morning," Harry said. "So one of you should take a key."

"I'll put mine in my pocket," Ed replied as they left the room.

Outside, the sun had already set but its glow continued to light the sky in the west. They walked towards it, beneath the deepening blue directly above them, which faded into the darker purple haze in the east.

"It's beautiful, isn't it?" Amy said softly, staring up at the sky. Ed turned, looking at her. As she tipped her head back, he noticed her long neck, her delicate chin and cheekbones. She was smiling, a light gentle smile spreading across her full lips, and, as she spoke, she wrapped her arms around her waist, hugging herself.

"Yes," he replied, his voice almost a whisper. "I've never noticed before. I must have been completely blind."

"Do you know?" She turned to look at him. "Sometimes I think we're so busy, running around doing this and that, we don't have time to just stop and notice how wonderful the simple things are. Look at that tree." She took his arm and turned him around slightly, standing just behind him. She stood on tiptoes and he could feel her breath on his neck. "It's hundreds of years old. Just imagine all the things it's seen… And I know it can't see, before you correct me in your usual way. I know it hasn't got eyes, or anything. But I often wonder what trees would say if they could talk." She took a step back and laughed. He sighed, uncertain about what was going on in his own mind, but completely sure that he'd felt better when she was close to him. "And now you're going to tell me that trees can't talk either."

"No, I wasn't going to say that at all."

"You normally do, when I come out with daft things like that."

"It's not daft." He stared at her. She turned her head to one side, looking at him.

"Is there something wrong?" she asked. "Have I got food caught in my teeth? Or is my hair sticking up?" She rubbed her front teeth with her forefinger.

"No," he replied. "There's absolutely nothing wrong. Nothing at all…"

"Oh." She looked like she wanted to say more. "Shall we carry on?" She linked her arm through his.

"Sure."

They walked in silence for a while.

"You like your job, don't you?" he asked eventually.

"I suppose so. I'd rather do something a bit more… exciting, if I'm honest. Most of the time I'm cleaning floors and changing bedpans, but days like today make it all seem worthwhile. I actually felt like I made a difference today."

"Will you get into much trouble, do you think?"

"Not if Andrew backs me up."

"Andrew?"

"Doctor Finch."

"You're allowed to call him Andrew?"

She tapped his arm playfully. "Not on the ward, silly. Sister would throw a fit if I did that."

"But you call him Andrew off duty?" Ed looked down at her as they walked.

"Yes. He's much less stuffy than all the others. I'm sure he'll be gone by Christmas, though." She sighed and felt Ed's muscles tighten around her arm. She shivered.

"Are you cold?" he asked.

"Just a bit chilly. The wind seems to have picked up." He stopped, took off his tunic and placed it around her shoulders. "Better?" he asked.

"Thanks," she replied.

"So, this doctor leaving… is that why you want to transfer to Portsmouth?"

"No, not really. I mean, I can't be absolutely certain that he will leave, but I can't stay at the cottage hospital forever, can I?"

"I think your mother would quite like you to."

"We'll see." He sighed deeply. "Do you want to turn back?" she asked.

"I don't mind. Do you?"

"I'm on an early shift tomorrow, so I should probably get to bed."

"Why didn't you say?"

"Because it's your first night back. You seemed to want to walk, just like the old times."

"You really think this is just like the old times?" he whispered, so quietly she could barely hear his words.

"He was marvellous," Amy said the next afternoon, over tea. She'd finished work at three o'clock and they were all sitting on the terrace, enjoying the afternoon sunshine. "Sister Jenkins called me into her office before morning break," she continued. "I was nervous as hell, but Doctor Finch followed me in, bold as brass. She huffed and puffed and spluttered, but he wasn't having any of it and just told her, flat out, that I'd saved Mrs Hadley's leg and to hell with hospital protocol."

"So you got away with it?" Harry asked.

"Well, yes and no."

"What does that mean?" Ed said.

Amy smiled. "She's been laying into me all day, and made me scrub the floor in the kitchen twice because she said it wasn't good enough the first time. I didn't mind though, not really."

"Why not? It sounds dreadful," Ed replied.

"It could have been worse. If Andrew hadn't backed me up, I think she'd have kicked me out. It's not the first time I've defied her, you know."

"I hope you thanked Doctor Finch for saving your bacon," Harry said.

"Of course," she replied, her eyes shining. "We had lunch together, so I got to talk to him then. Could I have another cup of tea, do you think?" she added. "I'm absolutely parched."

On Saturday, Elise invited William and Charlotte for dinner. Anne came too and Amy was pleased to see that all the old awkwardness between her and Ed had disappeared. It made for a much more relaxing evening than Amy had feared. Not that she needed any help to relax. Amy was very tired. It had been a long and stressful week and she was disappointed that she hadn't been able to spend as much time with Ed as she would have liked, although they'd been together during most of her time at home. He'd taken her for walks and they'd sat reading together under the old oak tree. She'd had energy for little else, though. Now, she listened to the conversations around her, wishing she could find an excuse to go to bed early.

"You look tired," Ed said, sitting down next to her.

"I'm bushed," she replied. "I was just wondering whether it would be rude to sneak off to bed."

"I'm sure no-one would mind. Everyone knows how hard you work."

"I'll try and stay awake for another half an hour." She leant over and rested her head on his shoulder. "That's comfy," she whispered. "If I nod off, give me shove."

"No."

"Hmm?" she murmured, sleepily.

"You're fine just where you are." He placed his head lightly on hers.

On the other side of the room, William nudged Harry and pointed in the direction of the sofa.

"Something going on there?" he asked.

"I think there might be," Harry replied, focusing on Ed. "At least for one of them."

Not surprisingly Amy slept in late the next morning, only coming downstairs just before lunch. Afterwards, Ed took her out into the hallway.

"Please..." He hesitated. "Come up to the oak tree with me?"

"If you like," she replied. "Just let me grab..."

"No, come as you are." He took her hand and pulled her out through the front door. All the way to the tree, he didn't let go of her hand and she struggled to keep pace with him.

"What's wrong?" she asked when they finally reached the field, the tree ahead of them.

"In a minute," he replied. "I'll tell you in a minute." They climbed over the gate and he led her up towards the old oak tree. William had made a point of leaving a narrow track along the edge of the field, skirting the hedge and, at the brow of the hill, a thin pathway turned and led up to the tree, for Amy to use. She found it touching that he'd thought of her, and she actually preferred coming up to the tree now; in the height of summer, the high, ripe wheat offered her a degree of seclusion she'd never had before.

Once under the tree, Ed motioned for her to sit down, which she did, staring up at him.

"What's the great mystery?" she asked.

"You are," he blurted out, then looked as though he wanted to kick himself.

"Sorry? What do you mean *I am?* I'm not even vaguely mysterious. I'm an open book, Ed. Andrew's always saying that..."

"I don't want to hear about Andrew. And I especially don't want to know what he thinks about you," Ed snapped.

"Why not?"

"Because I'm not interested in his opinion of you."

"What's the matter with you? Why are you so angry with me? You're not making any sense at all, Ed."

"I know. Sorry. I'm not angry, really I'm not. But you're not helping."

She stood up, turning on him. "How can I help when I've got no idea what you're talking about, or why you've dragged me up here."

He looked up through the leaves of the tree and she heard him whisper, "Shit," beneath his breath. "Do you love him?" he asked suddenly, looking down at her.

"Who?"

"Doctor Andrew bloody Finch, of course."

"No, of course not."

"Does he love you?"

"No. Don't be ridiculous. I'm only eighteen years old. He's probably in his mid-twenties..."

"Which makes him about the same age as me, Amy."

"Precisely."

He stared at her. "Yes, precisely," he breathed.

He sighed, kicked his heels in the soft grass and looked down at her again. She seemed angry now and she never got angry with him – well, not often, anyway. "Don't look at me like that," he said.

"Like what?"

"Like a part of you wants to throttle me... while the other part—"

"Right now, I would rather like to throttle you," Amy interrupted. "You're being nonsensical."

"Sorry. I don't mean to. I'm just finding this really difficult."

"Shall we sit down?" she offered, her anger melting away. He let her sit first, then lowered himself down beside her. "We've always been able to talk," she said. "Tell me what's wrong, Ed. Something's obviously bothering you."

"It's different this time."

"Why? Is it to do with the war? Has something happened? Oh, don't tell me there's another problem with a woman. You can't have misled some other poor female into falling in love with you, can you?"

"Amy," he looked across at her. "Are you being deliberately dense?"

"Well thanks. I didn't let you drag me all the way up here to insult me."

"Sorry. But I thought I was making myself obvious."

"Not to me, you're not."

He pulled up a blade of grass and ran it between his fingers. "I... care... about you," he whispered, his voice faltering.

"I care about you too, you fool," she said, leaning into him. "Oh God." She sat bolt upright. "Has mum asked you to speak to me about transferring to Portsmouth? Is this your weird way of finding out how serious I am about it, whether I'm going to follow Andrew out to some God-forsaken battle-front or something when – if – he leaves? Because that's not going to happen, I can tell you that right now. I know she's worried but, look... I haven't really decided what I want to do yet. You can tell her..."

"Amy, will you please just shut up!" he raised his voice.

"All right. There's no need to shout."

"Well, honestly. Sometimes, talking to you is worse than pulling teeth."

"And we're back to the insults. You didn't have to talk to me, you know… It was you who insisted we come up here, if you remember?"

"It's not an insult; it's God's honest truth." He got up again. "Just sit there for a minute and don't say a word." He paced up and down and she watched him. The white shirt he was wearing, rolled up at the sleeves, and open at the neck, showed off how tanned he was. His hair was tousled as usual, as though he'd hardly slept and not bothered to even show it a comb, and now he kept running his fingers through it, making it look even more dishevelled. She wanted to stand up and straighten it just a little, but he'd told her to sit still. He stopped pacing all of a sudden and fell to his knees in front of her.

"I've never said anything like this before in my entire life," he began, "so I don't really have a clue what I'm doing, and I know I'm making a spectacular mess of things." He looked up at the tree again, as though hoping to find divine inspiration among its leaves and branches. "I'm leaving tomorrow," he said, glancing down again.

"Yes, I know."

"And I'm going to miss you." He looked into her eyes, searching.

"I'll miss you too, Ed." She reached out and touched his arm. "I always do, you know that."

"And still you don't get it," he said, sighing. "I mean I'll *really* miss you, Amy." He hesitated. "Do you remember, I wrote you a letter once?"

"You've written me dozens of letters, Ed. You'll have to be a bit more precise. Which letter are you talking about?"

"I told you I wanted to catch you a star."

"Oh." She blushed slightly, recalling her reaction to his words. "Yes, I remember."

"I've been flying night ops until recently and I wish I'd caught you a star while I had the chance. I wish I'd brought it back and could give it to you now. It might help me to say what I want." She swallowed. She was uncertain what he meant, so decided to say nothing. "I told you I was rubbish at this." She smiled but still remained silent. His shoulders slumped and it seemed as though he was admitting defeat. Then he leant forward and ran his finger gently down the side of her cheek. "Everything's so different," he said eventually. "Especially you. You're…"

"I'm still me," she whispered. "I'm still exactly the same as I always was."

"I don't think so. Or maybe I'm just seeing you differently. Either way, can you do something for me while I'm gone?"

"I'll try."

"Don't change any more. I'll be back again soon, hopefully, and I'd really like to find you exactly as you are now."

"Exactly?" She smiled up at him, trying to stifle a laugh. "You mean you want me to still be impossible to talk to, and annoying and obtuse and difficult?"

"Yes. All of that. I want to find you exactly as you are now."

Chapter Ten

Winter 1942

Dear Amy,

I can't believe it's been two days since I last wrote to you. They've kept us so busy, I've hardly had time to catch my breath, let alone pick up a pen. Please don't think it's because I've forgotten about you, or stopped caring about you, because I haven't.

The good news is, that I've got a three-day pass, starting on Friday. I missed your birthday last week and having leave now means I won't be home for Christmas, but at least I'll get to see you again. It's been so long and, as much as I enjoy writing to you and getting your letters, I can't wait to come home.

I've written separately to Harry, giving him my train times. I'll be home on Friday afternoon. Do you think you can get the weekend off? I have to come back here again on Sunday evening and I don't want to waste my leave sitting around waiting for you to come home from work. If you can't, then don't worry, but please try.

I'll see you on Friday.

Take care,

Ed x

She folded the letter and put it into her drawer, shaking her head. In all of his letters since the summer, he'd reiterated that he cared about her and that he thought about her all the time. She was very confused. After so many years of loving him and wanting more than brotherly affection, she'd given up on that and accepted his indifference. Now, she didn't really know how to take this change in his attitude, and she certainly didn't understand what he wanted from her. He was so muddled in his writing. One minute he seemed frustrated that he couldn't be at home, the next, he wrote of nothing but his excitement at flying. He always ended his letters now with a kiss, which was new and just as confusing as everything else, and he wrote much more frequently, sometimes every day. She got up and went to her dressing table, staring at her reflection in the mirror. Her skin was clear but pale and she pinched her cheeks to redden them slightly, then smiled. Brushing her hair back, she began to pin it up ready for work. She wasn't sure that Sister Jenkins would let her have the weekend off, but she would certainly ask.

"She's making me work Saturday morning," Amy said as they sat down to dinner that evening. "But I can have the rest of the weekend off. So, that wasn't a bad result, really."

"What shift are you doing on Friday?" Elise asked. "I was thinking of asking Henri and Sophie over."

"Really? Do you have to?" Amy asked. Harry tried to hide a smirk.

"We haven't seen them for ages. We can't behave as though they don't live here. It's awkward."

"I'm on a normal shift, so I'll finish at six," Amy said. "I suppose we can put up with them for one evening."

"Why don't you invite Griffin as well? That would take the focus away from Sophie a little," Harry suggested.

"Griffin?" Amy looked confused.

"Yes, you know. Robert Griffin. He took over your grandfather's practice."

"Yes, but that was years ago. We've never invited him to dinner before."

"That's because he's never lived in the village before."

"Oh, has he moved here then?"

"Yes, he's bought old Mrs Doughty's house."

"Doesn't that need a lot of work?"

"It did. He's been having it fixed up over the last couple of months, and he moved in last week."

"How do I miss out on all the gossip?"

"Because you're never here anymore," Elise laughed. "It's quite a good idea, but I think you should invite him, Harry. I've only met him once, very briefly. He knows you better, so the invitation would be more appropriate coming from you."

"All right. I'll phone him at the office tomorrow."

As usual, Amy was slightly late home and ran into the sitting room after her bath to find everyone enjoying drinks. Ed was standing by the fireplace, still in his uniform. He stood up straight as she entered, looking her up and down. She was just as he remembered, but if anything even more alive and beautiful, with her cheeks flushed and her lips pink and smiling, her eyes shining as she gazed around the room. She'd not bothered to tie up her hair and it was loose and wild, hanging around her shoulders. He almost reached out in his longing to run his fingers through it… He found his breath had caught in his throat and he coughed, trying to come back to his senses.

"Hello, everyone," Amy said. "I'm sorry I'm late. It's becoming a habit of mine." She turned to her aunt, who was sitting in the chair nearest the fireplace. "Hello, Aunt Sophie," she said, moving forward and kissing her aunt on each cheek. "Uncle Henri." He was standing by Ed and she turned to him and repeated the greeting. "Ed." She nodded to him and then moved towards the tall figure standing in the window between her mother and father. "And you must be Mr Griffin."

"This is our daughter, Amy," Harry said.

"Delighted," Griffin said, offering his hand. "You look just like your mother."

"I'll take that as a compliment," Amy said.

"Good," Griffin replied. "That's exactly how it was meant."

Ed cringed and moved forward. "Would you like a drink, Amy?" he offered, taking her arm and pulling her towards the sideboard.

"A gin and tonic would be marvellous."

"I'm sorry?" he said. "Since when did you start drinking gin?"

"Ages ago. You know mum's always let me drink a little wine on special occasions... well I graduated to gin. One of the doctors brought a bottle to a party someone had, and I found I rather liked it."

Ed handed her a drink and poured himself another whisky. "Well, here's to you, being all grown up," he said.

She took a large sip from her glass. "What do you think of him?" she whispered, nodding towards Griffin, who was talking to Harry.

"Smarmy," Ed replied. "What's more interesting is your aunt's reaction." Amy glanced at Sophie and saw she was watching Griffin's back, her eyes alight.

"Hmm. Interesting, as you say," Amy murmured into her glass as she took another sip.

"This is a very pretty dress you're wearing," said Henri, approaching them.

"Thank you, Uncle Henri." Ed wanted to kick himself. He'd meant to compliment her dress, but they'd been distracted by Griffin.

"Shall we go into dinner?" Elise called from the window.

Elise had positioned Griffin to her right and Henri to her left, and had sat Sophie next to Harry, for which she knew he wouldn't thank her. Ed was to Sophie's left, with Amy opposite, next to Griffin. It was a strange meal. Griffin spent the entirety monopolising Elise, discussing her work with the Red Cross Committee and praising her ideas. Sophie was torn between talking to Harry and Ed, neither of whom was particularly interested in speaking with her. Amy sat and observed, noticing occasionally the sad expressions which crossed Henri's face. She wondered if he was worried about Luc, or if there was something else playing on his mind. Every so often she looked at her father and saw him watching Griffin. She didn't like the way he was leaning in to speak to Elise; it was a little too intimate for her liking and she sensed that Harry was equally uncomfortable. With the exception of Griffin, she got the impression that everyone was relieved when the meal was over.

As they sat drinking coffee, Sophie managed to place herself next to Griffin on the sofa, while Henri sat in one of the chairs, observing them.

Ed and Amy perched on the window seat. Harry and Elise were on the other sofa.

"She's not exactly subtle, is she?" Amy said, as Sophie threw back her head, laughing at some comment Griffin had made.

"No, but then neither is he." He turned to face her. "I was thinking we could spend Sunday together," he said.

"If you like. I've got tomorrow afternoon off as well."

"I know, but I have to visit my mother at some stage, and I know Harry wants to spend some time with me."

"Naturally."

"Come with me to mother's?"

"If you want, but I'm sure she'd rather see you on your own."

"And I'd rather you came with me."

"All right. I finish at one. I'll be back by one-thirty."

"We can have lunch and then go over, if you like."

Sophie's shrill laughter filled the air again. Elise got up and topped up everyone's coffee cups. "How soon do you think they'll leave?" she asked as she filled Ed's cup.

"Whenever it is, it won't be soon enough," Ed whispered.

As they walked back from Isabel's late the following afternoon, Ed took Amy's hand. "I've borrowed William's car," he said, noting the confusion in her eyes as he squeezed her fingers.

"What for? I didn't even know you could drive."

"Of course I can drive. I can fly a plane; driving's no problem."

"Show-off. Do you know how long it took me to master changing gear?"

"I don't think I want to."

"So, why have you borrowed Uncle Bill's car?"

"Because I want to take you up to the Downs for a picnic tomorrow. I've arranged it all with Polly; she's going to prepare us a basket of food and we'll leave at eleven. How does that sound?"

"A picnic in December? It sounds insane. Are you mad?"

"Only sometimes. We can eat in the car, and then go for a walk."

"Okay." She sighed. "Your mother seems much happier now. She's a lot less tense."

"Yes, I think she is. I think she prefers being alone to living with that bastard… Sorry. For some reason which I really don't understand, I keep swearing when I'm around you."

"I don't mind. I like to think it means you feel more relaxed when you're with me. Besides, I'm not a child anymore."

"I had noticed." He smiled down at her. Did he feel more relaxed? He thought he did. He certainly liked holding her hand, it gave him a feeling like coming home; and he felt as though he could talk more easily to her than he had when he'd been here in the summer. Or maybe he'd just become more accustomed to his feelings for her.

"I was wondering…" Amy said, staring down the lane. "Could you do me a favour?"

"Yes, anything."

"You don't know what it is yet."

"I don't need to."

"Well, you might change your mind when you hear what I've got to say."

"Then tell me."

"I might need your help with something…" she began.

"What's that? You know I'll help if I can."

"I need to persuade my parents about something."

"Hmm?" Ed sounded doubtful for the first time.

"I've decided that I'm going to request a transfer to the Portsmouth Depot after Christmas. I know mum will kick up a fuss; I think dad might be alright with it, but will you be on my side?"

"Why do you want to do it?" Ed asked, stopping in his tracks and pulling her back.

"Because I know I can do more for the war effort than I'm doing now. They taught me to drive a flaming ambulance, but all I'm doing is washing floors and making tea and changing bedpans, which I've been doing for months."

"Why Portsmouth, Amy?"

"Because I thought they'd prefer it. Mum and Dad, I mean. It's not too far away."

"Yes, and Portsmouth has been bombed a lot. I think that's what would concern them."

"Do you think they'd be happier if I suggested somewhere else?"

"No."

"What *do* you think then?"

Ed stood looking down at her for a few moments, opened his mouth as though to speak, closed it again, sighed and then said, "I think you should do whatever you feel is right, Amy. I'll back you up."

"Thanks, Ed." She flung her arms around his neck. "I knew I could count on you." The feeling of her body touching his stunned him. Okay, so perhaps he wasn't as accustomed to his feelings for her as he'd thought he was. She released him and turned to walk away, leaving him standing, rooted to the spot, staring after her. "Come on, then," she called over her shoulder. "We'll be late for dinner, if we're not careful." He ran to catch up with her.

"When were you planning on telling them?" he asked.

"Not tonight, I don't think. Probably tomorrow. Although we're going out now… That makes it tricky."

"Wait until we get back from our picnic. I'll make sure there's enough time before I leave, so we can talk to them together."

"Okay, thanks." She linked her arm through his. "What would I do without you?" she said, resting her head on his shoulder.

At just after eleven o'clock the following morning, Amy climbed into William's Vauxhall 12, while Ed loaded the picnic basket onto the back seat. Getting in behind the wheel, he looked across at her. He'd spent most of the night lying awake, working out how to get everything right this time. He certainly didn't plan on a repeat of his performance under the oak tree, and he wasn't going back to base until he'd told her how he felt about her. He hoped that if he could stop trying too hard, and could be relaxed and they could be themselves, just like they'd always been, the rest might flow naturally.

"All set?" he asked.

"Yes. I've brought my warmest coat, my boots, gloves, hat, scarf and I've got my two thickest jumpers on."

"We're going up onto the Downs, Amy, not on a trip to the North Pole."

"I like to be prepared."

"Clearly." He started the car, put it into gear and they set off. The sun was shining, it was a clear day and, although there was still a frost on the hedges and the fields, it looked as though it might be reasonably warm. "I think you'll find you're overdressed," Ed said, looking out of the window.

"I'd rather be too warm than too cold," Amy said. "I can always take clothes off, but if I haven't brought them with me in the first place…" She left the sentence hanging.

"Very sensible."

"You're laughing at me."

"Only a little bit."

"When I'm all snug and you're freezing…"

"You can keep me warm." He smiled across at her.

"No. I'll laugh at you and let you freeze."

"Well, that's nice."

After half an hour's drive, they parked near South Harting and Ed turned to face her. "Walk first, or eat?" he asked.

"It's a bit too early to eat," she replied. "How about a little walk and then some food to warm us up?"

"You're determined to feel the cold, aren't you?"

"I'm just a realist."

He got out of the car, walked around to her side and opened the door. "Actually, it is quite chilly out here," he said.

"Who's laughing now?" she giggled.

"Well, actually, I am. I brought my great coat in the boot."

"Why you…" He dodged out of the way just before she managed to hit him on the arm.

The walk was bracing but they couldn't wait to get back to the car. Polly had packed them some cheese sandwiches, apples, some cake and a flask of homemade tomato soup, which they drank first to warm their hands.

"I can't believe you didn't think it would be cold up here," Amy said, blowing across the top of her soup to cool it.

"I've been wrong before," Ed said, looking at her. "I'll be wrong again, no doubt."

A few moments' silence followed while they both drank their soup, then Ed handed out the sandwiches. "Have you missed Andrew?" he asked tentatively.

"No. As I said in my letter, he needed to go. He was bored stiff at the hospital and it really wasn't the best use of his talents. I just wish I could do something that exciting."

"Going to North Africa is hardly exciting, Amy. It's bloody dangerous… and there I go swearing again."

"At least he's *doing* something."

"So are you."

"Yes, but not in the same way as you and Andrew, and Peter – and even George with his secrets."

"Amy, there is the slight difference that you're a girl."

"So?"

"So, the last time I checked, we don't actually expect girls to fight."

"I'm not suggesting I fight. I just want to do more than I'm doing."

"And that's the whole point of this transfer, isn't it?"

"Yes." Her eyes shone. "At least I'll feel like I'm serving a purpose. Well, hopefully I will, anyway."

"Doesn't the idea of being in danger worry you?"

"Does it worry you? You're in a lot more danger than I'd ever be."

"Of course it worries me, but not in the same way. It's different."

"Why? Because you're a man?"

"No… Well, maybe a bit." He thought for a moment and then made a decision. It was time to tell her. "No. It's because it's me and not you."

"I don't understand."

"I'm not worried about me being in danger; but I would worry about you."

"Well, I feel the same way."

"You worry about me?"

"You know I do."

"Why?" he asked abruptly, turning in his seat to look at her, but she stared straight ahead, out of the windscreen.

"Because I always have. You've been there all my life, Ed." He heard a slight crack in her voice. "I'd be lost without you."

"And I feel exactly the same, Amy. Surely you can see that, especially now."

"Why especially now?" She turned to look at him now, and he saw her eyes were glistening with tears.

"Because… I…" He faltered again. What was wrong with him? Why couldn't he just say the words? Perhaps if he couldn't tell her, he could show her. He reached across, placed a hand on her cheek and leant forward. "Tell me you know what I mean, Amy…" Moving closer, he kissed her lips, very gently.

She pulled back, looking into his eyes, then turned and opened the car door, bolting out and running.

"Damn!" he said under his breath. "Amy!" he cried, clambering from the car and chasing after her. "Stop! Come back." He ran behind her. "For God's sake, stop!" She'd almost reached the tree line before he caught up with her.

"What the hell?" he said, catching her by the arm and tugging her round to face him. Her cheeks were stained with tears. "Oh shit," he said, pulling her close and hugging her. "I'm sorry. I'm so sorry." She sobbed into his chest for a moment, then pulled away again, pushing against him. "Don't you dare bolt on me." He held her arms.

"Let me go."

"Only if you promise not to run." She nodded her head. He released her and she backed away from him. "Why did you run, Amy?" he asked.

"Why did you kiss me?"

"Because I wanted to. I've wanted to kiss you for months. I'm no good at explaining myself… I think I've proved that, but I thought if I kissed you, if I showed you, you'd understand how I feel…"

"But you've always acted like we're just brother and sister."

"Except we're not, are we?"

"I thought that was what you wanted."

"What *I* wanted?" It was Ed's turn to look confused. "Why? Did you want something different?"

Amy looked at her hands, twisting her fingers. "Years ago, yes, when I was younger. I used to idolise you. I wanted you to want me so much it hurt… But I knew I wasn't good enough for you, so I gave up on that idea and went back to thinking of you as my brother."

"I'm sorry, Amy. I had no idea that was how you felt." He smiled down at her. "I think we've already established that I'm an idiot when it comes to women… But is that what you want me to be now? Is that why you ran? Because you didn't want me to kiss you? Because you just want me to be your brother?"

"I don't know. God, I'm so confused."

He took a deep breath and moved towards her. "I know I made a hash of things in the summer. I wanted so much to be able to tell you… to explain, but I thought, with my letters, you'd understand… I guess not." He swallowed hard. He was in danger of messing it up again. Oh, to hell with feeling embarrassed by words. She needed to understand and that was more important than any amount of embarrassment. "Okay, so we've established that you don't really know what you want. Let me try and tell you what *I* want," he said. "It might help you make your mind up." She looked up at him. His eyes were staring into hers, the intensity of their blue even deeper than usual. "I want to kiss you here," he began, reaching out and running a finger down her cheek, then to her neck, and just below her ear, "and here." Then he brushed his thumb across her lips. "And here," he added, moving a little closer. He felt her shiver. "I want to hold you, when you're not crying, or needing a brotherly shoulder to lean on." He leant forward, not taking his eyes from hers, and undid the buttons on her coat, placing his hand on her waist and pulling her forward slightly. "I want to touch you, Amy… I want to feel you... all of you…" He ran his hand around her back, drawing her closer still. "It's quite simple really. I just want you," he whispered. "Desperately." He felt her exhale and knew she'd been holding her breath. "What do you want, Amy?"

She didn't reply, just stared up at him and he felt his heart sink to his shoes. "If you want me to be your brother still," he said, releasing her and moving back slightly. "I'll accept that. I'll probably avoid coming home for a while, just until I get used to the idea, but I will accept it." He saw the almost imperceptible shake of her head and felt hope blossom in his chest. "Did you just shake your head?" he asked. This time she nodded, and the movement was more obvious. He grasped her again, pulling her closer and leant down, just before feeling her hand clasp across his mouth.

"What the f…" he mumbled into her fingers. "What's going on?" he said, pulling her hand away.

"First, I have one question," she said, looking up at him.

"Okay." At least she'd said 'first'.

"Do you say all that to every girl you meet?" she asked. She had a slight smile dancing on her lips, so he felt safe.

"Yep, every time. It's never failed yet," he replied. Her smile faded as quickly as it had appeared, her shoulders dropped and her head fell. "Oh, Amy, you bloody idiot," he said, placing a finger under her chin and lifting her face to his. "I told you last time, when I tried and failed to get you to understand how I feel about you, I've never said anything like this before, not to anyone. I'm not saying there haven't been other girls. I'm a twenty-four year old fighter pilot. I don't think you'll find many of us who haven't been with a few girls. But that's different." He noticed her eyes glistening. "Please don't cry again," he said. "Oh, God. I'm making such a hash of this, as usual. Look… What I'm trying to say is that none of what's gone before has ever meant anything. And you, my gorgeous, beautiful, lovely, infuriating, Amy… you just mean… everything."

He leant forward and pressed his lips firmly against hers, drawing her closer. She raised her arms, placing them around his neck and, as she moaned gently and her mouth opened, he took advantage and delved inside, exploring for her tongue, which met his with a surprising desperation. Her soft body melded against his and he felt himself harden instantly. He deepened the kiss, changing the angle of his head slightly and groaned deeply. She responded, running her fingers through his hair, grinding her body even closer against his…

"Stop!" he said suddenly, pulling away and staring down at her.

"What?" she replied, breathing heavily.

"We can't... we can't do this."

She turned away. "I knew you'd see sense."

"Excuse me?" he panted.

"I knew it." She turned back, rounding on him. "I knew that once you kissed me, you'd realise you don't really want me. I told you, I'm not good enough for you, and now you know it for yourself. You'll only ever see me as your silly little sister. You're probably worried about what mum and dad will say, and how your fighter-pilot friends will react to you seeing someone who hasn't long left school, when you should be with someone..."

"Amy, stop!" he shouted. "Why do you do that?"

"What?"

"Jump to conclusions like that. You've got no idea what I was going to say, or what I was thinking."

"If I'm wrong, then why did you stop kissing me so suddenly?"

"Because there's such a thing as taking things too far too fast." She looked confused and he sighed, placing his hand gently on her cheek. "Let me put it this way. I'm only human, and you... you're incredibly sexy, even more so than I'd imagined... and I've got quite an imagination. I want you right now, about as much as I want to keep flying... hell, about as much as I want to keep breathing, for Christ's sake. And when I say I want you 'right now', I mean, *right now*, right here, in this slightly muddy, very frosty field, regardless of how bloody cold it is." She looked at the ground, blushing. "See?" he said. "You were about as far off the mark as you can get. I stopped kissing you, because if I hadn't stopped then, I couldn't have done... I'm just not strong enough." She smiled up at him, but his face was serious. "And that's twice you've said you're not good enough for me, Amy. I've got no idea what put that into your head, but please, don't ever say that again, because nothing could be further from the truth." He paused, staring into her eyes for a long moment. "Oh, please don't look at me that way," he whispered.

"What way? I'm not looking at you in any way."

"Yes you are." He took her hand and led her back towards the car.

"How am I looking at you then?" she asked..

He glanced down at her and saw the expression on her face. "You mean you really don't know?"

"No."

"Oh hell."

"What's wrong now?" she asked.

"That look."

"God, Ed. You've got me so confused. What's wrong with how I look?"

They'd reached the car and he sat her down in the passenger seat, leaning in, one hand resting on the dashboard, the other behind her head, his face just an inch or two from hers. "Nothing is wrong with how you look. You're perfect… completely and utterly perfect. But you just looked at me back there, and it's a look that makes me think you'd actually quite like me to touch you, and kiss you, and taste every single inch of you, and make love to you really, really slowly all night long. It's a look that makes me think you'd be happy to be completely mine… And if you don't even know you're doing it, Amy, then I don't stand a chance at keeping my hands off you." He kissed the tip of her nose, stood up and closed the door.

"You want to taste me?" she whispered, looking over to him as he climbed into driver's seat and started the engine.

"Oh God, yes." He grinned and turned the car around.

"I guess we need to speak to your parents," Ed said as he pulled the car up outside the house.

"You're going to tell them about us?"

"I wasn't planning to. Not tonight. But I thought you wanted to speak to them about transferring to Portsmouth."

"Oh, that."

"Yes, that." He looked across at her. "You do want to talk to them, don't you?"

She turned to face him. "I'm not sure."

"I thought this was what you wanted."

"But everything's changed."

"Has it?"

"Of course it has. You're going away tonight and heaven knows when you'll get leave again. But when you do, do you really want to have to choose whether to come here and see Harry and your mother, or to come to Portsmouth on the off-chance that I can get some time off to spend with you?"

"Hmm, I hadn't thought of it that way."

"I had. I've been thinking about it all the way home."

"But if this is what you want, Amy, you should do it."

"I'm not sure I want it that much," she said, placing her hand on his leg.

"Don't give up your dreams for me, Amy," he said, putting his hand over hers.

"I can't think of anyone else I'd give them up for," she replied and he stared at her.

"No, Amy. You must still do this, if it's what you want. We can work things out."

"I'd rather put it on hold for now and know that I can see you whenever you come home."

He took her hand, slowly raising it to his lips and, not taking his eyes from hers, he kissed her fingers one by one, taking the tips into his mouth. He felt her holding her breath. "Do you want me to talk to your parents?" he asked at last. She exhaled loudly.

"Ed, I thought we just agreed… were you not listening to a word I said?"

"About us, I mean." He grinned.

"Oh, sorry." Amy thought for a few moments. "No. Not yet. Can we keep it to ourselves for a while?"

He nodded his head, nibbling the end of her little finger. "As much as I hate keeping things from Harry, I think I'd like that."

"I'll drop the car back at William's and walk on to the station," Ed said to Harry as they all sat finishing tea.

"Why don't I drive you to the station, and then drop the car back at William's, then walk back here?" Amy offered.

"Because you're not walking back here in the dark on your own," Ed said, a little too sharply. Harry looked over the rim of his cup and smiled to himself. He was fascinated by how the two of them thought no-one had noticed their growing attachment. He and Elise had talked of little else all day, although their viewpoints differed. Elise didn't want Amy becoming too involved with Ed – but only because she was worried that if anything happened to him, their daughter would be devastated. Harry, on the other hand, thought they should take their chance at happiness. Since they'd come in from their picnic, he sensed something had changed between them, and watching the two of them trying their hardest to disguise their feelings, he knew they deserved to spend every moment together.

"Why don't I phone Bill and ask him to bring you back here once you've dropped the car off?" Harry suggested to Amy. He saw her eyes light up.

"Do you think he'd mind?" she asked.

"No. I'll go and phone him now."

At a little after six o'clock, Ed kissed Elise goodbye, gave Harry a hug and climbed into the car next to Amy.

"Are you sure you don't want me to drive?" he asked.

"Why? Are you scared?" She looked across at him and laughed, starting the engine and moving off.

"Bloody terrified, actually." She took her hand from the steering wheel and playfully smacked his leg.

"I'm a perfectly competent driver," she said, changing down a gear to take the slight hill out of the village.

"Hmm... You'll do, I suppose."

"I'll do? Have you ever tried driving down country lanes at night with no lights and no road signs?"

"Yes. It's fun, isn't it? Just drive carefully getting back to William's, will you?"

"You're about to go flying over occupied Europe and you're worried about me driving down a few country lanes in the dark..."

"Of course. I'll always worry about you." He turned in his seat to face her. "I..."

"Oh Christ, I missed the turning!" Amy interrupted, hitting the brakes sharply.

"Well, back up then." He laughed as she struggled to engage reverse. "Do you want a hand with that?" he asked, placing his fingers over hers on the gearstick.

"Will you please be quiet. You're not helping."

"I wasn't trying to."

When they finally arrived at the station, they had just a few minutes before the train was due to depart.

"Don't come onto the platform," he said. "I don't want one of those teary station goodbyes."

"Who said I'd be teary?" she goaded, swallowing hard and trying to put on a brave face. "For all you know, I might have several other boyfriends waiting in the wings."

"You'd better not." His tone was serious and he pulled her close, his voice deepening. "You're all mine."

"Entirely," she whispered into his coat. "Please take care of yourself."

"I will," he murmured into her hair.

"And come back soon?" She looked up into his face and he dropped his case, placing a hand on each of her cheeks, gazing into her eyes.

"Of course. I have to now..." he whispered, noting her quizzical expression. He kissed her hard and, as she opened her mouth to his, he murmured, "I love you."

Chapter Eleven

Late Summer 1943

My darling Ed,

Writing every day seems pointless sometimes when so little happens here, but at least I feel connected to you, knowing you'll be holding this piece of paper tomorrow, and reading my words. I'd hoped you'd get some proper leave by now. It's been over six months since I've seen you for more than a few hours at a time, and I miss you so very much.

Robert Griffin was here again today when I got home from work, which makes it the third time this week. I really don't know how dad puts up with him. He positively drools over mum, although she doesn't seem to notice. He's decided to help her with organising the book sale next month, which doesn't need much organising, as Charlotte has it all in hand. Frankly the man makes my skin crawl.

Another of my patients died yesterday. I didn't write about it last night as I was too upset. She was very old, but I'd got to know her quite well. I'm starting to feel as though I'm jinxed. Right now, I could really do with a hug and wish you were here to dry my tears.

I'd better go now.

All my love,

Amy xxx

Dearest Amy,

God, I wish I was there too; you sound so sad. I'm sorry to hear about your patient, but it's not your fault and you're not jinxed. It was just her time, and I'm sure she was comforted by your presence.

Griffin is an odious man, I agree. Maybe you should speak to Harry about it? If it's bothering you that much, I'm sure he'll set your mind at rest.

I've been kept busy here, (as usual, I can't say what with), but I am optimistic that I might be able to get a few days off in the next couple of weeks. I'll keep you posted. Don't raise your hopes though, as things have a habit of changing.

Please don't cry when I'm not there. I want it to be me who dries your tears. I want to kiss them away and make it all better. And I will do, very soon, I hope.

Please remember, I love you, Amy.

Yours always,

Ed xxx

She re-read the letter three times before finally folding it and putting it in her drawer. He always seemed to know the right things to say to make her feel just a little bit better. Glancing at her clock, she realised it was nearly time for tea. Sundays had become rather boring of late. Robert Griffin had developed a habit of arriving shortly after lunch and staying until late in the evening, so she'd taken to spending most of the afternoons in her bedroom, or walking in the lanes, thinking about Ed.

Downstairs, she opened the door and found Elise and Robert sitting on the sofa. He'd turned his long, slender body to face hers and they were laughing. Robert's hair was slicked back away from his tanned face and penetrating brown eyes, and he dressed well, in a fashionable suit, but the greying hair at his temples belied his age, which Amy estimated to be around forty-five. She looked around the room. Harry was nowhere to be seen.

"Where's dad?" Amy asked.

"He's gone over to William's," Elise replied. "He said he'd be back in time for tea, so he should be home any time now." She looked up at the clock on the mantlepiece.

Amy went over and sat on the window-seat, leaving Elise and Robert to continue their conversation.

"So, when the Will was read, it turned out that he had two wives. One in Manchester and one in London. Neither knew about the other and he somehow managed to run two entirely separate lives." Robert was trying hard not to laugh.

"But he'd sounded like such a nice gentleman. And isn't that bigamy?" Elise looked shocked.

Robert noticed her expression and quickly altered his own. "Naturally, but there was nothing anyone could do about that once he was dead."

"Those poor women."

"They weren't poor. Not once he'd left them both half of his fortune," Robert continued.

"He divided it between them?"

"Oh, yes. He married one before the last war and the other one during it. He couldn't decide between them, so he stayed with both, dividing his time by telling them that he was a travelling salesman, when really he'd inherited a decent amount of money from his father, and didn't actually work at all."

"Should you even be telling me this?" Elise asked.

"Oh, I was only a junior clerk back then. It wasn't my case." Amy wondered if that technicality really mattered. "Anyway," he continued, leaning in towards Elise, "it's not as though I've given you the names of those involved."

"No, I suppose not."

"Here's Dad," Amy announced, seeing Harry walking up the front path. She got up and went to the front door to let him in.

"I'll ring for tea," Elise said, as the door closed behind her.

"He's here," Amy whispered to Harry as she shut the front door behind him.

"Nothing new there, then," he replied, smiling down at her.

They both entered the sitting room and Harry noticed that Robert seemed to shift away from Elise in a rather obvious way. He smiled inwardly. Elise got up, came over to him and kissed his cheek. "Robert has been regaling me with tales of some of his old clients," she said.

"How interesting," Harry replied, sounding bored, and sitting down in one of the high-backed chairs.

"Not especially," Robert said. "We'd better move on to fundraising business soon, I suppose?" He turned to Elise, who was still standing by Harry.

She looked at the clock. "Well, I suppose so." She looked doubtful.

"I can always come over another evening, if that's more convenient," Robert offered.

"That might be better," Elise said, as Polly came in, carrying a tray. Elise set about pouring the tea.

"Shall we say tomorrow?" he suggested, taking a cup from Elise.

"Tomorrow might be difficult," Elise said. "I think it'll have to wait until Tuesday." Harry looked up at her, surprised. He sensed that something was wrong.

"Very well." Robert's disappointment was obvious.

"There can't be much left to do, from what Charlotte was saying this afternoon," Harry said, taking a sip from his cup of tea.

"No, I think we're pretty much there," Elise replied, resuming her seat next to Robert.

"And I'm sure Robert's help has been invaluable," Harry added. The younger man looked across at Harry, who was staring down the garden.

Robert seemed to take ages to leave, but as soon as he did, Harry turned to Elise.

"What's wrong?" he asked.

"Rose phoned while you were out," she replied.

"Is something the matter?"

"I don't know. She's coming down tomorrow. That's why I put Robert off, just in case Rose needs us for something."

"How did she sound?" Harry asked.

"I'm not sure. My initial reaction was that she seemed a bit down, but she cheered up while we were speaking."

"Perhaps she just wants a break from London?" Amy suggested.

"Maybe," Harry said.

"Well, I suppose we'll find out tomorrow."

"I'll go and speak to Polly and get her bed made up," Elise said, getting to her feet.

"You look tired." Harry took her hand as she walked past him.

"Oh, I'm fine. It's just this book sale. It's become gargantuan... Much more complicated than last year's." She crossed to the door.

"Or than it needed to be," Harry whispered under his breath.

"You don't like him either then?" Amy asked, once the door had closed behind Elise.

Harry looked up at her. "If by 'him' you mean Robert Griffin, then, to be honest, no I don't."

"He's not entirely subtle around mum, is he?" Harry lowered his eyes, but said nothing. "Well, don't you think it's out of order, Dad? I mean, she's a married woman. He should leave her alone."

"She's not doing anything wrong, Amy."

"I didn't say she was. He's the one doing the chasing; anyone can see that. Mum's just being her normal self."

"Yes, and I trust your mother, so nothing will happen."

"And you won't do anything about him?"

"What would you have me do? Challenge him to a duel? We're not living in the nineteenth century, Amy."

She smiled. "Perhaps it would be better if we were. I'd love to see you challenge him, Dad."

"Amy, I wouldn't stand a chance." She got up and crossed the room, kissing the top of his head.

"He'd be mincemeat, Dad." She left the room before she had a chance to see the expression on his face. It was a cross between frustration, anger and a deep, deep regret.

It was clear from the moment Rose arrived, just before lunch the following day, that something wasn't right. After lunch, Harry tried to talk to her, but she refused to say much, beyond how unhappy she was. So, he asked Elise if she would try to speak to her. The two women went out for a walk and were gone for most of the afternoon, arriving back just in time for dinner, which Rose decided she would eat in her room. Elise made it clear with a look, that she couldn't really speak in front of

Amy, so Harry was on tenterhooks until he and Elise went to bed that evening.

"What is it?" he asked as Elise closed the bedroom door.

"I don't really know where to start," she replied, sitting next to him on the bed.

"Well, start somewhere, for God's sake. I'm worried sick here."

She leant into him. "Oh, Harry. You don't need to worry too much. It's Rose, being Rose, really." She felt him heave a sigh of relief. "She started off complaining about Matthew's hours again. He's been promoted and is working even longer than before, evidently. I did try to explain that, as a doctor, that was only to be expected, but she won't really listen to reason. Then it all came out..."

"What did?"

"The real problem." She took his hand.

"Elise, tell me..."

"Rose wants to start a family. She has done for years, evidently, but nothing's happening. That's why she wouldn't talk to you. She found it embarrassing."

"Well, with Matthew at the hospital all the time, I'm not surprised nothing's happening. He does rather need to be in the same room." Harry smiled.

"And therein lies the problem."

"Don't tell me. They're not talking about it... Again."

"Precisely."

"My God, they need their heads banging together. I thought we'd ironed all this out."

"So did I."

"They're not going to solve their problems by her running down here, are they?"

"No. They need to sit down and work out what they both want."

"God, I hate being the referee in their marriage. It feels so intrusive."

"Why don't we take her home tomorrow?"

"What, just take her back to London and dump her there?"

"No, not dump her, but we could tell her that this isn't the answer. We could offer to take her back, say that you'll speak to Matthew..."

"Really? Must I?"

"No, but it's a way of getting her to go back home. Then we'll get Matthew in the same room and lock the door." She giggled.

"In the hope of what?"

"Well, either they'll talk to each other, or..."

"Stop it. She's my daughter."

Elise nudged into him. "I know, but it's worth a try. Her sitting down here sulking isn't going to achieve anything. London's quite safe at the moment and a day in town might be nice for us."

"What about your meeting with Robert tomorrow."

"I'll cancel it. I don't think there was really any need for it anyway." He leant across and kissed her.

"It sounds like a plan," he said, smiling. "Going up to town might be useful."

"Why?"

"I need to see the accountants," Harry explained. "Ed turns twenty-five very soon and I've got to see them about his inheritance and then talk to Ed about his plans when he's next on leave. I told Isabel I'd deal with it all."

"We could do it while we're up there, couldn't we?"

"Yes, I'm sure they'll fit us in sometime late in the afternoon, once we've dealt with Rose. I'll phone them and ask. Do you want to suggest it to Rose in the morning, or shall I?"

"I'll do it. We can leave after lunch, if she's agreeable."

"What about Amy?"

"She's working late shifts at the moment, so she'll probably sleep until mid-morning. She won't be home until after eight, so we'll probably get back before her." Elise paused for a moment or two. "Speaking of Amy... do you think I should talk to her about Ed?"

"To what effect?"

"To warn her of the dangers, I suppose."

"Do you really think that would put her off? They're so obviously in love, my darling, I don't think anything we say could have any effect on either of them."

"Yes, but..."

"But what?"

"I don't want her to get hurt."

"I know. You've already told me this, but he's not going to deliberately hurt her."

"I didn't say he was, did I?" She got up and started undressing, clearly annoyed.

"Come back here," Harry said.

"No."

"Don't be angry with me." He stood and limped towards her. "They couldn't help falling in love, or the fact that they fell in love during a war, any more than we could."

"Yes, but I don't want that for her, do I?" Elise shouted, then checked herself, stared up at him and rushed into the bathroom. Harry managed to catch up and push open the door just before she closed it.

"What do you mean?" he asked.

"Nothing. It doesn't matter."

"It clearly matters a lot." He waited as she stood in the middle of the bathroom, breathing hard. "Tell me," he said finally.

"I don't want her to have to go through what I went through, if anything happens..."

"I know, you've already said that. But there's more to it than that." Again he waited, blocking her exit. "Come back into the bedroom and tell me." He held out his hand and she looked up into his face, tears filling her eyes. She shook her head. "Then we'll stand in the bathroom all night," he said. Again, he watched her and, finally, her shoulders dropped and she moved towards him. He took her hand in his and led her back into their bedroom, sitting her down on the edge of the bed and taking a seat beside her. He waited patiently while she gathered her thoughts.

"It's not just about him not coming back and how that would hurt her," she said eventually.

"Okay. What is it then?"

"It's about how she's going to feel every single time he goes away. Every time she hears a plane overhead; every time the phone rings; every time the postman knocks." She took a deep breath. "I know those fears, Harry. I know how it feels to wake up in the morning and think that this will be the day you hear; the day the world ends; the day the darkness descends. Why should she have to go through that, when they could just wait?" He watched the tear trickle down her cheek and leant across to rub it away with his thumb.

"Wait for what?"

"The end of the war."

"But that could still be years away. They're in love now. They can't just forget how they feel for years on end."

"It might be better than living in fear and dread every day."

"I know how that feels too, you know."

"No, you don't."

"What? You think it was different for me?"

"You had a war to fight. Of course it was different."

"Okay, so I was occupied. I was busy. But I still woke up in the mornings and wondered if I'd ever see you again, or hold you, or kiss you. I wondered if I should ever have made friends with you, or made you love me, or made love to you, or whether it would have been fairer to you if I'd just tried to ignore how I felt about you. Do you think I didn't live my life in abject fear, just like you?" She turned and looked up at him.

"I suppose I thought it was easier for you, because you were away from me and had things to do."

"That's got nothing to do with how I feel about you, Elise. The thought of losing you, of never seeing you again was like torture, every single minute of every single day. Please don't think it was easy for me."

"Then why are you happy for them to go through the same thing?"

"Because I wouldn't change a single moment of it. I'd rather have had your love for ten seconds than never have had it at all. You make my life complete… Can't you see that? You always did. Do you really want to deny them the chance of a life like we've had, just because things might go wrong? Just because they'll have to spend some of their time worrying and living in fear? For crying out loud, Elise… They deserve their happiness. They're fighting hard enough for it."

"You make me feel ashamed." He grabbed her and pulled her onto the bed, staring down at her.

"I don't mean to. I just want you to see that they can't deny how they feel any more than we could have done. Dividing them now won't alter a thing. They're already in love. She'll still be afraid for him; he'll still miss her. If we try and split them up, all that will happen is they'll resent us, and they won't feel they can turn to us if they need someone to talk to. Let them enjoy their precious moments together. They need to grab them with both hands and cherish them, in case that's all they get... and if it is, then they deserve those happy memories. I think we owe them that."

Chapter Twelve

Late Summer 1943

As they sat on the train, looking out at the passing fields, Harry held Elise's hand. The sun was just starting to set, its golden hues dappling across the wide fields of corn.

"That went quite well, don't you think?" he said.

"As well as could be expected," she replied. "And everything was all right with the accountants?"

"Yes, it was fine."

Elise yawned. "I could do with a proper break, though. It would be nice to just go somewhere, find ourselves a hotel and pretend the world doesn't exist."

"Do you want to?" He put her hand to his lips.

"More than anything."

"Then let's do it."

"We can't. Amy's expecting to find us at home when she gets in from work this evening."

"Well, why don't we go at the weekend, then? We can go on Thursday evening, or Friday morning and come back on Monday. We'll book a hotel somewhere – you can choose where, and we'll indulge ourselves... just us."

She moved closer to him, leaning against his arm. "That sounds absolutely delicious. I can't wait. I do sometimes feel as though we're always having to help other people and it would be nice, just for a few days, to focus on ourselves." Harry felt his heart sing and, in his mind, he started to plan.

"When we get back," he said, "we'll sit down and you can decide where to go, then you can leave everything else to me."

"I like the sound of that," she whispered and tilted her head back so he could kiss her.

They hadn't even climbed out of the taxi outside the house, when the front door was opened and a familiar voice cried out, "Hello!"

"Ed!" Harry called back. "When did you get here?"

"About an hour ago," he replied, walking down the steps and picking up Harry and Elise's suitcase. "I was surprised there was no-one here. But Polly explained you'd gone to London. Is everything all right?"

"Yes, it's just fine," Elise replied.

"How long are you here for?" Harry asked, as they climbed up the steps and entered the house.

"Only until Friday night, I'm afraid. I left at the crack of dawn this morning and I have to be back by six am on Saturday." He put the suitcase in the hall while Elise closed the door.

"We'll wait for dinner until Amy gets in, shall we? Do you want to ask Polly to make some tea?" she asked. "I'm just going to our room for a moment." Harry saw the expression on her face, just before she turned and ran up the stairs.

"Is something wrong?" Ed asked.

"Maybe," Harry replied. "Get Polly to make the tea, will you? I'll be down in a minute." He climbed the stairs more slowly than Elise, leaving Ed standing at the bottom, looking up after him.

He found Elise in their bedroom, sitting on the edge of the bed. She looked up as he entered the room.

"I know exactly what you're thinking," he said.

"Do you?"

"Yes. You're thinking that now Ed's here, we won't be able to have our weekend away."

"I'm clearly very transparent. And I feel so selfish. I love seeing Ed, Harry, but just for once I wanted some time entirely to ourselves."

"And you'll get it, darling." Harry sat next to her. "We can still go away. Ed's leaving on Friday night anyway."

"Could we go on Saturday?"

"We can go on Saturday and come back on Tuesday, if you want."

She nodded her head. "I need this," she said, putting her arm around his waist.

"I know you do. And nothing's going to get in the way of it, I promise." He kissed her tenderly, then used his tongue to gently probe inside her mouth.

"You'd better stop that." She broke the kiss. "Ed will be waiting for us downstairs."

"Let him wait."

The tea was cold by the time they got downstairs, so Elise ordered some more and they sat and talked, telling Ed about their plans for the weekend. He sat in the armchair, with his back to the door, while Elise and Harry were side-by-side on the sofa, holding hands. Ed was pleased to see how close they looked, considering Amy's comments about Griffin in her letters.

"That sounds idyllic," he said. "Where do you think you'll go?"

"I don't know," Elise said, turning to Harry.

"I told you, it's your choice."

"Well, that's lovely, but I don't really know where to suggest. You took me to the Lake District on our honeymoon and, of course, I know Cornwall, but that's about it, and they're too far away. Besides, I'd like to go somewhere I've never been before."

"What about Somerset?" Ed suggested. "Or the Broads, or there's the Cotswolds… Or the New Forest?"

"I'm not sure you're helping," Harry laughed. "We'll look at a map later; it might be more useful than this one spouting names at you." He turned to Ed. "We went to see the accountants while we were in London," he said.

Ed didn't reply, but nodded his head.

"You'll be twenty-five soon," Harry continued. "You need to decide what you want to do with your inheritance."

"I haven't given it any thought at all," Ed said. "To be honest, I still haven't got used to the idea of inheriting in the first place."

"Well, we've got a couple of days before you go back. We can talk through your options."

"That sounds very business-like." Ed smiled. "And grown-up."

"An old man like you needs to think of such—"

The door opened unexpectedly and Harry broke off, looking to Amy, who was standing on the threshold of the room, still wearing her uniform, her eyes red and her cheeks stained. "Oh Dad, Mum," she cried. Harry jumped to his feet, almost as quickly as Ed. "Ed!" she whimpered and stood, looking at him, uncertain what to do. Harry hung back for a second, as Ed quickly moved forward. He stood before her.

"What's wrong?" he asked, his voice soft and calm. "What's happened?"

"Andrew's dead," she said, looking up at him, another tear trickling down her cheek. "He was killed."

"How?" he asked, taking her hand and leading her towards the chair he'd recently vacated. As she sat, he crouched at her feet, not letting go of her hand.

"I don't really know. Sister Jenkins found out. He was home on leave, of all things, and there was a car crash. Oh, Ed!" She leant forward and flung her arms around him. He held her tight and let her cry into his tunic, while Harry and Elise looked on. "Sister Jenkins was actually very nice about it," she whimpered eventually, sitting up a little and looking at her parents. "She said I could come home early."

"That was kind of her," Elise said, looking at the couple, who were still entwined. Amy noticed her mother's gaze and sat back in the chair, disentangling herself from Ed's arms.

"Would you like to go upstairs for a while?" Harry suggested. "You could probably do with a wash and a change of clothes. You'll feel better afterwards."

"Yes, I think I will," Amy said getting to her feet. She walked to the door. "I'll be back down soon."

"I'll just go and see that she's all right," Elise said, following her daughter from the room.

Ed sat back down in the chair and stared across the room at nothing in particular. Harry took the seat opposite him.

"Don't read anything into that, will you?" he said, quietly.

"Hmm?" Ed looked up. "Sorry? I was miles away."

"I know you were. I said, don't read anything into that. It's the first time she's actually come into contact with death, apart from her grandparents and the odd patient. But this was someone she knew and nearer her own age, which always makes it harder, doesn't it?"

"Hmm, I suppose so."

"Ed, stop it." Harry's voice hardened.

"What?"

"Stop imagining things that aren't there."

"What makes you say that?"

"Because I know how your mind works. You're thinking there must have been something between her and Andrew because of how she's reacted, but that's just Amy, I'm afraid. She shows her emotions – good and bad."

"I've noticed."

"I'm sure you have." Ed looked up, a quizzical expression on his face. "Ed, I've known about the two of you for months."

"How?"

"I'm not blind, Ed, and neither is Elise."

"Oh." Ed looked a little sheepish. "We were going to tell you."

"Well, there was no need to."

"And you're okay with it?"

"I am. Elise took a little more convincing."

Ed couldn't hide his disappointment.

"It's nothing to do with you personally," Harry continued. "She'd feel the same way about anyone in the forces. She knows what it's like to be in Amy's shoes, doesn't she? She knows what it's like to be left behind, to worry, to doubt, to live in fear, and she doesn't want that for Amy."

"And she thinks I do? She thinks I wouldn't rather be here with Amy every day, instead of flitting in and out of her life every few months? Doesn't she think I worry myself sick too?"

"Don't shoot the bloody messenger, Ed. And do you think I don't know how *you* feel?"

"Sorry. Is Elise going to stand in our way?"

"I told you, she took some convincing, but she's come round to the idea now. Besides, if she intended to do that, do you think you'd have been getting daily letters from Amy for the last eight months? She's worried, but she wants Amy to be happy, and you make her happy."

"Do I?" Ed whispered.

"Oh, stop it, Ed. Stop it, right now." Harry leant forward. "Let her get freshened up, then talk to her."

Ed closed the french windows behind him and joined Amy on the terrace. She looked up at him as he sat on the seat next to her.

"Where are mum and dad?" she asked, her voice little more than a whisper.

"Don't worry. They know about us."

"You told them? Without me?"

"No. They'd already guessed."

"Oh. So much for us thinking we were keeping it a secret."

"Elise wasn't too impressed, evidently."

"Why? What's she got against us?" He heard the indignation in her voice.

"Nothing. She just didn't want you getting hurt..."

"What, so I shouldn't be happy at all, on the off-chance that something might go wrong?"

"I don't think she meant it quite like that. You have to remember she's been there, Amy. She thought Harry was dead for months before he went and found her again. She knows what it feels like to live with that kind of fear."

"I suppose so." She sat forward.

"Besides, Harry says she's okay with it now."

"Good. At least we don't have to sneak around. I didn't like lying to them."

"Neither did I." He took her hand. "Speaking of lying..."

"What?"

"Andrew..." She pulled her hand away from his.

"What about Andrew?"

"Are you absolutely certain there was nothing between you?"

She stood and folded her arms across her chest and he knew immediately that he'd made a huge mistake. "For God's sake, Ed. He was my friend and he's just died. Are you so inured to death that you can't feel it?" She paced up and down a couple of times and then turned back to him, just as he went to get up. "Don't even think about it," she said, and he sat down again. "How dare you! How dare you accuse me of lying to you about Andrew." He heard a crack in her voice and longed to reach out to her, even though he knew she'd probably hit him, and deservedly so. "I've never had a boyfriend before, never been kissed even, until you. Meanwhile, you've evidently slept your way around several counties in England and parts of Northern France, using the excuse of being a handsome fighter-pilot to get into women's beds. I haven't once questioned that, but you... you accuse me of lying about a friend, who was just that – a friend. For God's sake..." She moved away, and stood at the top of the steps, staring down the garden, her shoulders heaving.

He waited until he felt it was safe to approach her, then he walked up behind her, placing his hands gently on her hips.

"I'm sorry," he whispered. She didn't reply. "Can you forgive me?" he asked. She made no sign, didn't move at all. "I was completely out of order," he continued, "and I apologise. It's the first time I've ever felt jealous in my life, and I didn't know what to do."

She turned on him and he took a step back. "What have you got to be jealous of? I don't have a past. I had a friend, that's all... nothing for you to be jealous of."

"I know that, and I'm sorry, Amy." He stepped towards her again. "It's just that you were crying... about Andrew, and you were perfectly entitled to, but all I could think was that I wanted your tears to be for me."

She looked at him. "Well, I don't. I don't want to ever have to cry like that about you." Again, he heard her voice crack. "It would be so much worse, Ed. I couldn't bear it."

He reached out and pulled her closer. "No," he said. "You misunderstand. What I mean is, I want all of you, Amy. I want every part of you to be about me… about us. I want your smiles, your tears…" He kissed her forehead softly. "… your laughter, all of it. I'm selfish and I want it all." He leant down and put his lips gently to hers. "Please forgive me for being a complete idiot."

"You have to trust me, Ed."

"I do. I promise. I'm just not used to feeling like this."

"And you think I am?"

"No." He pulled her down a couple of steps and they sat on the cold stone. "This would be so much easier if we had all the time in the world, but we don't."

"When do you go back?"

"Friday night, but that's not what I meant." He turned to face her. "We only get snatched moments together and then have to spend months apart."

"I know. It's so hard."

"I think it's probably harder for you than it is for me…"

"Why?" Amy pulled away and looked at him, suspicion filling her eyes. "What are you trying to tell me?"

"Nothing."

"You're not keeping secrets?"

"No, of course I'm not. I just meant that trying to stay alive tends to preoccupy the mind."

"And there's nothing else keeping you preoccupied?"

He looked at her and then smiled. "Oh, so I'm not the only one with a hint of green in their eyes." She went to pull away from him again. "Hey, don't," he said. He got up and moved to the step above her, sitting down again and pulling her back in between his legs, his warm arms tight around her shoulders. "You have nothing to fear, Amy," he whispered into her ear.

"Really..." She didn't bother to hide the sarcasm in her voice.

"Really. That trust thing you were talking about, it goes both ways."

"Yes, except that you've got a track record for playing the field."

"Oh, so that's what this is about." He leant back slightly and she twisted round to face him, looking up into his face.

"Well, if you must know, yes it is. You made a great point of telling me that, as a young, handsome, dashing fighter pilot, sleeping around is kind of expected. For all I know, that's precisely what you've been doing for the last eight months, while I've been sitting here, writing to you every day, dreaming about when we can be together. I've got no idea what you get up to when you're at your base, safely tucked away at a distance from me... You've probably got women stashed all over the place... one for every day of the week..."

"Amy, you're doing it again," he said patiently.

"Doing what?"

"Jumping to conclusions."

"And I'm probably right." She nodded her head and went to get up, but he pulled her back down.

"Listen," he said. "I didn't make a point of telling you that pilots often have flings with women, for any reason other than to let you know that I've never, ever been *romantically* involved with anyone in my entire life. I'm not saying I'm an innocent where women are concerned, but I wanted you to know that you, Amy Belmont, are the first woman I have ever actually loved. And just to be completely accurate, I have not slept my way around several English counties, or half of France. I haven't slept with anyone in the last year... not since that night I saw you on the stairs wearing that red dress, and you... you stole my heart. You've owned me ever since. I haven't even looked at another woman, and I don't want to ever again. And it's not just because I'm busy trying to stay alive, it's because I love you completely, and I don't want or need anyone else." He felt her lean back towards him slightly and kissed the top of her head. "You're an idiot too, you know." His voice softened. "I dream about our future all the time. I wonder what it will be like when the war's over and I can spend all my time with you, without worrying about what train I have to catch. I imagine taking long walks without checking the time every half an hour." He tightened his grip on her. "I want to hold you in my arms and kiss you all the time, not have to wait month and months between kisses." She nestled into him comfortably. He hesitated. "I want to watch you sleeping in my bed, Amy, and wake up next to you." He felt her tense slightly. "But I'll wait… until you're ready," he said softly.

"Will you?" He barely heard her muttered words.

"Of course."

"How long would you wait?"

"Oh, I think I'd wait forever for you."

She turned and knelt on the step, rising up to him. "Not forever… It won't be forever," she whispered. He grinned and kissed her, placing his hand behind her head as his tongue danced with hers. She ran her fingers through his hair, leaning into him and forcing him back onto the steps. She finally broke the kiss, breathless and knelt back, gazing down at him. "Wow," she whispered simply, her eyes alight, and they both laughed.

"I do wish you'd stop looking at me like that," he whispered.

"I'm not."

"Really?" She stared down at him. "You're doing it now."

"I'm not doing anything."

"Oh, dear God. Like I said before… I don't stand a chance." She went to get up, but he pulled her back down and kissed her hard before releasing her.

"By the way," he said, watching her and leaning back on his elbows. "I feel I should set the record straight."

"How?" She stood and straightened her skirt.

"At no stage did I say I was a handsome, dashing fighter pilot. I think I said I was a twenty-four year-old fighter pilot. You added the 'handsome' and 'dashing' parts in all by yourself."

"Did I? I can't think why…" She giggled and dodged as he grabbed for her, making it back to the french windows and into the sitting room before he could catch up.

At breakfast the next morning, Harry and Elise found it difficult to ignore the heat between Amy and Ed. Harry was secretly pleased that they'd made up so obviously the night before. Ed's dishevelled hair when he'd come in through the door had been the biggest give-away, although the light in Amy's eyes had helped to tell the story. No matter what Elise continued to fear for their daughter, he wanted them both to enjoy as much happiness as this war could afford them.

"We've decided on the New Forest," Elise said. "As we've only got a few days, we don't want to spend all of it travelling."

"I'm going to find us a hotel down there and book it today," Harry added.

"So, you're leaving on Saturday morning… and when will you be back?" Amy asked.

"Tuesday lunchtime probably." Elise took a second piece of toast, as Polly came in, carrying a telegram.

Everyone froze and looked at her. She passed the envelope to Harry, who ripped it open awkwardly and paled as his eyes scanned the flimsy page. Elise got up and went to his side, reading the few words on the piece of paper. "Oh no," she gasped, her hand covering her mouth.

"What is it?" Amy asked, as Ed also stood.

Harry said just the one word: "Peter."

"He's not?" Amy didn't need to finish the question. Harry nodded his head, placing the telegram on the tablecloth. Ed rounded the table in a few strides and lifted Amy to her feet, holding her tight while she sobbed into his shirt.

"Who's the message from?" Ed asked, over Amy's shoulder.

"Lillian," Harry replied, finding his voice at last, although it cracked. Elise placed her arm around his shoulder. "John needs me." He looked up at Elise. "I have to go. I'm sorry," he said, simply, taking her hand.

"What are you sorry for?"

"The weekend. I promised you… and I know how much…"

"Damn the weekend. John needs you, so we're going. I'll pack." She turned to Polly who was still standing by the door. "Can you phone for a taxi to take us to the station in half an hour," she said, "and send a reply to this telegram, to say we'll be there this afternoon."

"Yes, Mrs Belmont." Polly scuttled away, her head bowed. Harry kept hold of Elise's hand for just a moment longer, looking up into her eyes.

"Thank you," he mouthed, uncertain of his own voice.

"Don't," she said, wiping a lone tear from her cheek. "I need to focus on packing. I can't think about anything else for now."

Amy squared her shoulders. "Let me help," she said, sniffling. "It'll be quicker." She pulled away from Ed, but he dragged her back and kissed her lightly, ignoring Harry and Elise.

"Okay?" he asked, looking into her eyes. She nodded and tried to smile. He let her go and she and Elise left the room together.

"Harry?" Ed said. "What can I do?"

Harry shook his head, unable to speak for a moment. Ed moved his chair and brought it to sit next to Harry, although he said nothing. Harry took a deep breath, then looked up. To Ed, he seemed different. There was a look in his eyes that he didn't recognise, and he wondered how far away Harry really was. It took a few moments before Harry registered Ed's presence.

"I'm sorry," he said. "Did you say something?"

"I just asked what I can do to help."

"I'm not sure there's anything, really, thank you Ed," Harry replied. "I'm afraid you'll be gone by the time we get back. I don't know how long we'll be, but I can't imagine we'll be back by Friday."

"That doesn't matter."

Harry placed his hand on Ed's. "I need to just sort out a few things in my study. I want to contact Sister Jenkins and tell her what's happened. This coming on top of the news of Andrew's death yesterday will hit Amy hard. I'll try and arrange for her to have a couple of days off work," he said. "Look after her while we're gone, won't you?"

"Of course I will."

"Ed. I'm serious. Ideally I wouldn't leave her when she's this upset. She's known Peter all her life, but John and I... well, it's a long story.

I'll tell you all of it one day. Just don't let her down." It was the first time Ed had ever heard such a hard edge in Harry's voice, directed at him.

"Never." He looked up as Harry rose from his chair. "She means everything to me, Harry."

"Good, then you know a little of how I feel."

They only just managed to catch the train and Elise found them an empty compartment, into which she settled Harry. She noticed his hand shaking and took it in her own.

"It'll be all right," she said, stroking the back of his hand with her thumb.

"What the hell am I supposed to say to him?" Harry said.

"I don't know, but you'll work it out. You always do."

"I've never had to work out something like this before. Losing a child, Elise…"

"Just be yourself, Harry. That's all John needs. Someone he can trust and someone who understands." Harry nodded and she looked at him as he stared out of the window for a few minutes. "It's odd, isn't it?" she said quietly.

"What is?" He turned to face her.

"Whenever someone we know has a problem, they turn to you."

"That's just because I'm innately boring and sensible, and that gives people the impression that I can help them."

"And you do. Every time, Harry. You're still saving people, just like you always have."

"Rubbish, woman," he scoffed. "I'm terrified. I've got no idea what I'm doing and I've got every notion that I'm going to – excuse my language – bugger this up supremely. Tell me I've saved someone when I actually get it right."

"You will," she said, leaning her head on his shoulder.

The journey was all too short for Harry and, as the taxi dropped them outside the Graingers' cottage, he was reminded of the spring of 1919, when Grainger had most definitely saved him, brought him back from the brink of suicide and shown him how to trust others and live again. Now, he faced his hardest task and he didn't really know where to begin. Elise picked up their case and helped him forward, knocking on the door. Lillian opened it, her eyes red-rimmed and Elise stepped into the house, taking Lillian in her arms.

"Come here," she said, and leaving Harry, she led Lillian into the living room. Harry looked up and, ahead of him, sitting in the kitchen, he could see John, his head bowed over a cup. He walked into the house, closed the door behind him and approached his old friend. The first John knew of Harry's presence was the hand on his shoulder. He looked up, saw who it was and stood. Harry leant his stick against the table and held onto John as he wept in his arms.

"My boy," he sobbed.

Harry said nothing, but fought to hold back his own tears. It wouldn't help if both of them broke down.

"Do you know…?" John said, finally sitting down again, as Harry found a handkerchief in his pocket and handed it across the table, "I didn't even know for sure where he was until this happened."

"Where was he?" Harry asked.

"Burma." John looked at him. "So far away," he said.

Harry nodded. "Have they told you what happened?"

"No. Not yet. We just got a telegram yesterday." He looked up sharply. "How did you find out so quickly?"

"Lillian. She wired, asking us to come," Harry replied. "I'd have come anyway, as soon as I heard."

"I know you would… Burma…" he whispered.

An hour or so later, Elise emerged from the living room and made some tea for everyone. She raised her eyebrows to Harry, who shook his head. This was going to take some time.

****

The quietness in the house after Harry and Elise's departure was too depressing, so after lunch, Ed took Amy out for a walk. He explained that Sister Jenkins had been happy to give her the rest of the week off, in the circumstances.

"Maybe she is human, after all," Amy said, looking across the fields. "I hope he didn't feel too much pain," she continued. "He was always so gentle, so kind. I'd hate to think he had a painful end."

"Don't, Amy. Just don't think about it."

"How can I not think about it? I've known him all my life... Just like... Oh God, Ed," she wailed, the tears falling afresh.

"What?" He stopped and pulled her into his arms.

"First Andrew, now Peter..."

"What? You think I'm next? It doesn't work that way, Amy."

"But..."

"Please, Amy. You'll drive yourself mad thinking like that."

"I can't help it."

He lifted her face to his and kissed her. "Then try," he whispered. "I'm here now, and that's all that matters."

"But what about after... What about?"

"Stop it, Amy."

"Take me home," she said.

"We've only just started out."

"I know, but I want to go home."

"Okay." They turned around and headed back towards the house.

Once inside, they sat on the sofa, he kissed her gently for a while and then she curled up, her head on his chest. It didn't take long before he felt her breathing change and knew she was asleep. He rested his hand on her hip and closed his own eyes.

When she woke, she was lying alone on the sofa, a cushion beneath her head. She turned around, but Ed was nowhere to be seen. Outside, the sun was low in the sky. She squinted at the clock on the mantlepiece. It was nearly seven o'clock. She'd been asleep for hours. Just as she started to get up, the door opened and Ed came in.

"Ah, you're awake," he said. "I thought I'd let you sleep as long as possible. Polly's getting dinner ready for eight o'clock." He nodded toward the sideboard. "Gin and tonic?" he asked.

"Please," she replied. "I can't believe I slept for so long." She sat back and stretched her arms above her head.

"You obviously needed it." He poured the drinks and brought them over, handing hers to her. He sat and they clinked glasses and each took a sip. "How are you feeling?" he asked.

"Numb?" she replied. He put his drink down and took hers from her, putting it next to his own, before pulling her into him.

"That's okay," he said, then he twisted in his seat, lifting her onto his lap and holding both of her hands in his. "Now, I've got something to tell you, and I want you to let me finish what I'm going to say before you rip my head off."

"What's happened now?"

"Nothing's happened."

"What have you done, then?"

"I've been on the phone to William, while you were asleep. I told him about Peter… and Andrew, and that Harry and Elise have gone up to Oxford to see John and Lillian. He wanted to know if they could help."

"I don't suppose they can, really," Amy interrupted.

"You remember that bit where I asked you to let me finish?"

"Yes," she looked up at him sheepishly.

"Right. Well, I had an idea… I've asked William if you can go and stay with him and Charlotte…"

"What? Now? Why would I want to do that when you've only got until Friday night before you have to go back? Honestly, Ed…"

"Amy, let me finish, for Christ's sake." He took a deep breath. "Of course not now. Not until after I go back." He lifted her face to his. "I don't like the idea of you being on your own at the moment. I just want to know that you'll be safe when I'm gone, so I asked William if he'd take care of you once I've gone back to base, just until Harry and Elise get back." He noticed her eyes glistening.

"Thank you," she whispered.

"You're not angry?"

"Why would I be angry?"

"Because I know you hate it when people organise your life for you. I'm not interfering. I just love you too much to think of you being sad and lonely here."

"I know, and that's why I love you so much." She reached up and kissed him, it took him only a moment to deepen the kiss.

After dinner, they sat up, listening to music on the wireless until Amy couldn't keep her eyes open any longer.

"Why am I so tired?" she said as they climbed the stairs together. "I slept most of the afternoon."

"It's shock, probably," he replied. As they reached her bedroom door, he leant down to kiss her. "Goodnight, gorgeous," he whispered.

"Will you stay with me?" she asked. He looked down at her, turning his head to one side, an enquiring look in his eyes. "I don't mean like that," she clarified quickly. "Not yet, anyway, not after today. I just want you to hold me, until I go to sleep."

He nodded his head. "Okay. Just don't look at me like that."

"Like what?"

"Oh, God," he murmured, staring at the ceiling. He took her hand, opened the door and led her inside, then realised his mistake. Letting go of her again, he stopped. "I'll wait outside, until you're ready," he said. "Call me." He pulled the door closed softly, and in the darkness of the corridor, he paced for a few minutes. He knew he had to restrain himself; she wasn't in a fit state for anything other than sleep, but the idea of lying down in bed with her and not touching her was almost too much for him to contemplate. His one hope was that she'd be wearing hideous thick flannelette pyjamas that might enable him to temporarily forget his long-held dreams of the pleasures that lay beneath.

He paced, contemplating, giving himself a stern talking-to, and taking deep breaths, for about ten minutes before he heard Amy's soft call that he could go in. He entered the room and saw her sitting up in the bed, the covers over her legs. His hopes were in vain. She wasn't wearing a dream-shattering pair of flannelette pyjamas, but a dream-inspiring pale blue silk nightdress, with lace capped sleeves and a low-cut bodice, which appeared to him to be glued to her, showing off her figure and enhancing her pale, soft skin. She was in the middle of a single bed and he swallowed hard. Great. She looked like a goddess *and* it was a single bed.

As he walked towards her, she looked up with tear-stained cheeks and he realised she must have been crying again and he knew his feelings didn't matter in the slightest. He could and would do whatever it took to comfort her. She shifted down in the bed and moved across a little to make room for him. Without saying a word, he lay down next to her on top of the covers, then pulled her into him, wrapping his arms around her. "Okay?" he whispered. She nodded. "I'll only go when I know you're asleep." He felt her sigh. "Night night, beautiful."

The next morning, Amy was very late down to breakfast. Ed wondered if he should wake her, but decided to let her sleep. It was mid-morning before she finally surfaced.

"I'm so sorry," she said, sitting down at the table, where he was reading the newspaper and drinking coffee.

"Don't be."

"Did you sleep all right?" she asked.

"Yes. You only took a few minutes to nod off, and I went to my own room, as promised." He reached out and took her hand. "I enjoyed my brief sleep with you, though. You looked so beautiful." She smiled. "Do you want some breakfast?" he asked.

"No, just coffee." She poured herself a cup. "Do you really have to go back tomorrow night?" she asked.

"Yes. William said he'll come and pick us both up at seven, drop me at the station and then take you back with him. So, you'll need to pack in time." He looked up and saw tears in her eyes. "Don't cry," he said. "We've still got all of today and most of tomorrow."

She sniffed. "I know."

"After lunch, why don't we go up to the oak tree? We can take some books and read for a while and I'll get Polly to pack some food. We can stay up there for the evening and watch the sunset, if you like?"

"That sounds lovely."

The phone rang and Amy went to answer it. "Hello, Daddy," she said, tears filling her eyes again. "How's… How's… Oh, God." She waved the receiver at Ed who was at her side in moments, taking it from her and putting his arm around her shoulders.

"Harry?" he said.

"Is she alright?" Harry asked at the other end of the line, the worry in his voice obvious.

"Yes, she'll be fine. She's just a bit overwhelmed. How's it all going at your end?" Ed kissed the top of Amy's head, holding her close.

"Pretty bad, to be honest. John's a mess. Lillian's coping the better of the two."

"How are you and Elise?"

"We're fine. I'm worried about Amy, though. You're going back tomorrow..."

"Don't worry about her. I've spoken to William and, when I leave, Amy's going to stay with him and Charlotte until you and Elise get back here. I did think, last night while I was lying in bed, that I could have asked my mother to come and stay here, but then I realised that Amy probably knows William and Charlotte better, so I think I made the right choice."

"You made an excellent choice. Thank you, Ed."

"I made you a promise to look after her, and I will."

"I know."

"Now, you just concentrate on John and Lillian. And yourselves."

"Can you tell Amy that I don't think we'll be back until Monday or Tuesday at the earliest. Tell her I'll phone her at Bill's to keep her posted and make sure she takes John's phone number with her, so she can call us here if she needs to."

"Don't worry. I've already written the number down for her."

"I'm starting to feel redundant."

"That'll never happen."

"Ed. Thank you." Harry's voice was suddenly serious. "For everything."

"You don't have to thank me."

"Yes, I do."

As the afternoon wore on into evening, Amy looked up through the branches of the oak tree. The sky on the horizon was turning from blue to orange, with hues of pale pink. She'd already finished one book,

Agatha Christie's *The Moving Finger,* and had moved on to a second before the light faded too much to read anymore. She had her head in Ed's lap and he was leaning on the trunk of the tree, his eyes closed.

"Are you all right?" she asked.

"I'm absolutely fine." She put her arms around his neck and pulled herself up to him. "I'm even better now." He smiled and dragged her up onto his lap, and kissed her. He broke the kiss eventually, smiling down at her, looking deep into her eyes. "Do you know?" he said quietly, "I remember when you were born."

"Really?" She nestled into his arms. "Oh… yes, I was born here, wasn't I?"

"Yes, you were. Harry was scared Elise would go into labour down in Cornwall and, with the cottage being so remote, he wouldn't be able to get her to the hospital in time, and he didn't want you being born at home. He was worried after what had happened to Rose's mother, so he moved Elise and Rose up here in October, two months before you arrived."

"I suppose that was understandable."

"Completely." He kissed the top of her head. "In his shoes, I'd have done the same thing."

"I've always been told that he was terrified, right up until he knew I'd been born and mum was safe…"

"Again… completely understandable." He ran his fingers down her arm. "I remember, I was five, and my mother told me that Harry and Elise had a new baby, and that Elise had come home from the hospital and we were going to visit." He smirked. "I was much more interested in playing, than visiting a baby… especially when I found out you were a girl, of all things." Amy laughed. "But then Harry brought you downstairs and sat me in the corner of the sofa, and laid you in my arms… and I fell in love with you…"

Amy sat up. "What?"

"Not in the way that I love you now… but you were the most perfect little thing in the world, and even though you were a girl, and therefore unlikely to be much good at football, or much use with trains, I wanted to protect you, even then. You captured a piece of my heart." He pulled her back down to him, gazing at her. "And now you have all of it... it's all yours, Amy." He kissed her hard, exploring her mouth with his tongue, tasting and claiming her.

"Thank you for this afternoon," she said, smiling out of the kiss. "It's been perfect."

"Hmm, hasn't it? Do you want something to eat?"

"Not especially. I'm not hungry yet."

"I am." He twisted round, rolling her onto her back and raising himself above her.

"Well, Polly packed all kinds of things," she said, pulling herself up onto her elbows and glancing at the picnic basket. "What do you want?"

"You." He leant down and kissed her again. She hesitated for a second, then kissed him back, her back arching. He delved deeper into her mouth and she reached up and pulled him closer. Their breathing was ragged, bordering on desperate. He broke the kiss and knelt up, looking down at her, her hair fanned across the rug, her cheeks noticeably pink and flushed, even in the dimming light. "I want you more than I've ever wanted anything in my life," he said. "But if you tell me 'no'... if you want me to stop, I will." She looked up at him.

"I don't want you to stop," she whispered.

Without saying a word, he leant down and slowly undid the buttons of her blouse, and her skirt then removed them and placed them by the picnic basket. Then he undid her bra and removed that, not once taking his eyes from hers, and finally lowered her panties. She lay back on the rug, looking up at him. He quickly stood, pulled off his shirt, kicked off his shoes and socks, removed his trousers and underpants, then threw them to one side and lay back down, kissing her, and moving slowly down her body, exploring her. Time stopped, not even the brightening moon or the twinkling stars disturbed them as he slowly discovered her secrets, all of which were new to her too, touching, caressing, feeling, and especially tasting his way around her body, until she was moaning and writhing on the rug beneath him. He stopped, waiting for her to open her eyes.

"Are you sure about this?" he asked, finally poised. She nodded. "Please don't say yes just because you think it's what I want. You have to want it too."

"I do. I want this. I want you," she whispered.

"Not nearly as much as I want you."

Their breathing calmed eventually as they came back down to earth, and she looked up to find him staring down at her. Her eyes were glazed, mirroring his.

"Are you okay?" he asked, his voice filled with concern.

"Hmm." She managed to nod her head. "You?"

"Hell, yes."

She giggled. "Is it meant to feel like that?" she asked.

"Like what?" He leant down and kissed her, then moved back slightly, a worried expression on his face. "I didn't hurt you, did I?"

"No, not after the first bit, and even that only hurt a little. It… it just felt… like my whole body was coming apart and, sort of shattering into tiny pieces… but in a good way, if you know what I mean. Is that normal?"

"God, I hope so, because you looked so amazing when it happened. Are you feeling as though you're back together again yet?" he asked.

"Not completely."

"Well, do you think you can stand up?"

"I'm not sure… why?"

"Because I want to take you home, to bed."

"Oh." She couldn't hide her disappointment.

He placed his finger beneath her chin and tilted her face in his direction. "In my bed tonight, though." He got up, staring down at her naked, still spreadeagled body.

"Your bed?" she sounded breathless again.

"Yes, it's bigger than yours." Her mouth opened slightly and he noticed her eyes widen. "Let me help you." He offered her his hand and pulled her to her feet and into his body, enjoying the feel of her warm soft skin next to his, arousing him again. "I want to enjoy you properly," he said, kissing her. "God, I love every inch of your body." He gathered up her clothes and handed them to her, but just before she started to get dressed, he pulled her to him again. "You remember that feeling you had just now? The one where you felt like your body was coming apart and shattering into tiny pieces?" She nodded her head. "I take it you liked it?" She nodded her head again, very quickly, raising her eyes to meet his. He chuckled and leant forward, whispering in her ear, "Good, because once I get you into bed, I intend to make that happen… over, and over, and over again…"

The sunlight played across her body as she lay naked across the bed, face down, legs tangled in the sheets, her hair spread out across her shoulders, her arms above her head. He lay beside her, running his fingertips down her back and across her buttocks.

They'd slept very little, just in snatches and now, as she roused to his touch and slowly opened her eyes, he felt himself stirring again. "You're so beautiful," he whispered, pushing her hair to one side, exposing her neck and kissing it. She turned onto her side to face him.

"So are you."

He traced the outline of her mouth with the tip of his finger. "I've done something… I hope you don't mind."

"What have you done?" she sounded wary.

"I got dressed a little while ago, while you were sleeping, and went downstairs. I've given Polly and Dennis the day off. I want you entirely to myself today."

He saw the shadow cross her eyes. "Don't," he said, knowing what was passing through her mind. "Don't think about tonight yet. We've got the whole day together and I want it to be just us. They've gone into town for the day, so we've got the house to ourselves." She nestled into him. "I don't want to think about anything else, except us."

"Just us?" she whispered into him, her voice filled with a worrying uncertainty.

"Of course. Why? What do you mean?" He tried to make her straighten up and face him, but she stayed curled up, her head buried in his chest. "What is it, Amy?"

"You don't think about... about anyone else? When we're... you know?"

"Who else would I be thinking about when I'm making love to you?"

"The others..."

"What others? What are you talking about?" He took a deep breath and reached down, finally succeeding in getting her to raise her face towards him. In her eyes he saw such a depth of doubt, he was suddenly afraid that she'd changed her mind about being with him and what they'd done together. "Tell me," he urged.

"The other women you've slept with... You don't make comparisons?"

He laughed softly, mainly with relief, understanding her at last, but wanting to kick himself for being so slow. "Good God, no. Come here." He reached behind her and pulled her closer to him, feeling her along the length of his body. "Forget about them. I have."

"But... Am I...? I mean, wouldn't you rather have someone more sophisticated, who knows what they're doing?"

"No. Been there, done that. I like the fact that your knowledge is limited. I like teaching you. It means so much more." He kissed her very tenderly, reaching into her mouth with his tongue until she moaned into his. "I love your responsiveness." He rolled her onto her back and eased himself on top of her, parting her legs with his. "And I worship the fact that you're all mine."

"But am I enough?" she whispered, looking up at him.

He knelt up, looking down at her. "Enough? That's ironic." He leant forward and ran a delicate fingertip from her neck downwards. She closed her eyes, tilting her head back and exhaling loudly as his finger descended. "Earlier on," he continued, "before you woke up, I was wondering if you were too much. I wasn't sure if I could manage to keep going today, after everything we did last night, but then you woke up and I knew I had to have you again... and again... and again. I don't think I'll ever get enough of you, Amy. I want you now, and forever. No-one else. Just you."

"Promise?" She opened her eyes and he settled between her legs again, feeling her beneath him.

"I promise."

"And you're mine?"

"I'm yours… always."

****

Lillian sat at the kitchen table with Harry. Through the window, they could see Elise and John working in the garden, weeding around the vegetables. They didn't seem to be speaking much, other than to exchange the odd comment about the growth of certain crops.

"Elise is a marvel. It'll do John good to focus on something else, for a change," Lillian said, getting to her feet and filling the kettle with water.

"He won't forget about Peter while he's out there, but at least he's not sitting in here brooding about it."

"I wasn't just thinking about Peter. Well, not really." Lillian carried the kettle across to the stove and turned on the flame beneath it.

Harry looked up. "What do you mean?" he asked.

She came and sat down again with a sigh. "Oh, Harry," she said. "He's been fed up for ages… months and months. Peter's death is just the last straw really… I don't know how much more he – or we – can take…" Her voice trailed off.

"Why didn't he tell me?" Harry asked.

"It's the school. What could you possibly do about that?" Lillian continued eventually. "Things get on top of him, you see. He's been getting so low and then he snaps, losing his temper, usually with me. It's just not like him. It's been so difficult these past few months. He's been… well, nervous, I suppose you could say, since the last war. Not as bad as…" she stopped abruptly, looking down at her hands.

"Not as bad as me, were you going to say?" Harry smiled, putting her at her ease again.

She smiled back. "Something like that," she got up again and fetched the teapot from the dresser, placing it on the table. "But now, he's so much worse than I've ever known him. Being headmaster means he doesn't get to teach anymore, which is all he really wanted to do. Instead, he has to deal with irate parents, grumpy governors, an ambitious, over-zealous, downright nasty deputy head, and mountains of paperwork and only sees the boys when they've done something wrong and need chastising. It's not what he wanted. He's frustrated and fed up. He comes home each night and just sits in the chair staring into space, biting my head off whenever I speak to him. He used to love his job, but now we both hate it."

Harry stared at her. "He mentioned the deputy head being a problem, but he's said nothing about anything else... Couldn't he retire?"

"Not yet." She took a deep breath and spooned tealeaves into the warmed teapot. "He's due to receive a small pension when he gets to sixty-five, but that's a way off yet, unfortunately. We plan to sell up and move to a small cottage somewhere. We'll just about be able to make do with his pension and the proceeds from selling this house, providing we can find somewhere cheap enough to live." Having poured the hot water onto the tea, she placed the lid on the pot and covered it with a knitted cosy, then sat again for a minute. "I don't think he'd mind waiting if he was still teaching, but he hates his job, and now, what with Peter... I just don't see... Oh, I'm dreading September." Her voice cracked and she got to her feet and busied herself at the dresser, so Harry wouldn't see the tears in her eyes.

"Let me help," Harry said.

"He wouldn't take money from you, Harry, if that's what you're thinking. He'd see it as charity."

"I'm not offering money... I've got the beginnings an idea. Make him a mug of tea and let me take it out to him. If you don't over-fill it, I shouldn't spill too much."

"You'll have to walk without your stick."

"I can manage."

"I don't understand," John said, taking a sip of tea. "The place has been empty for over three years now. Why the sudden urgency to have someone fill it?"

"I told you. Mrs Bramwell wrote to me a few weeks ago and told me that her husband has been taken ill." Harry wasn't lying about this. "She said she can manage still, but I know she's just putting on a brave face. She's been looking after Watersmeet for me for years, whenever we go away, but it's getting too much for her now. You'd be doing us a favour. You need a break, John. You and Lillian. It would do you both good to get away from here."

"But I've got a job, responsibilities. I can't just up and leave and go to Cornwall to babysit your house until the end of the war – whenever that might be."

"Why the hell not? You told me that your deputy is after your job, so let him have it."

"And what would we live on?"

"Sell this place." Harry motioned back towards the house.

"I always intended to sell up when I retire," John said thoughtfully. "But I need the money I make from selling up to buy us somewhere else. I can't use that to live on."

"You'll be acting as my housekeeper and gardener. I'll pay you."

"Like hell you will."

Harry saw the set expression on John's face, but matched it with his own. "I'll pay you the going rate for those positions." A short silence followed. "Look, John," Harry continued, his voice softening, "I need someone to take care of the house. We've already had several birds' nests in the chimneys and there's been a problem with the roof over the studio, which worries me. And that's just the house. I imagine Elise's garden resembles a jungle by now. She'd be relieved to know it was being well tended and I'd like to know there was someone down there taking care of things. Mrs Bramwell is seventy-five if she's a day. She's a game old thing, but she's not as fit as she was. If you really don't want to take my money, what about finding some teaching work in the village? There's a local school… Amy went there before we sent her to the school in Truro, and I know from Mrs Bramwell that Miss Lewis is always struggling to cope. I believe her last recruit went off to join the ATS or something, so I'm sure she'd be only too glad of some assistance." He saw a flicker of interest in John's eyes. "It might not pay much, but if you invested the money from the sale of the house, you could earn some interest and I could just top it up, if necessary."

"What about my position here?"

"As I said, let your deputy have the run of things," Harry said. "It's what he's always wanted. He'll either sink or swim, but it won't be your problem."

"But I've been here all my working life."

"And that's a good reason to stay on, is it?" Harry asked, raising his voice a little.

"No." John looked around the garden at the neat rows of lettuces and tomato plants, tied up to canes, then back across the small tidy lawn and flower beds towards the house. "We've lived here since we got married," he said quietly, "but it's not... it's not the same, not now, not without..."

"I know."

John cleared his throat. "I'd have to discuss it with Lillian," he said. "It might not be something she'd want to do. Cornwall is a long way away."

"Naturally, Lillian has to agree," Harry replied. "I'll hobble back indoors and send her out, if you like?" John nodded, absentmindedly as Harry limped away, smiling gently to himself.

Inside the dining room, Elise and Lillian had been listening at the open window and, as Harry entered the room, Lillian rushed to him and threw her arms around his neck.

"Thank you," she said, barely holding back her tears. "Thank you so much. It's the perfect solution."

"Well, he seems to be coming round to it, so, if you're game, you'd better go out there and convince him. But for heaven's sake, act surprised when he puts it to you." She leant up and kissed his cheek.

"We'll always be indebted to you, Harry," she said.

"No. I owe John my life and my happiness." He glanced at Elise and smiled. "This is a very, very small recompense."

"This is everything," Lillian replied. "Just everything." She straightened her shoulders and smoothed her skirt, then left the room and went through the kitchen and into the back garden.

Harry and Elise stood at the window and watched as she approached John and he took her hand and walked her further down the garden.

"You did it again," Elise said, leaning on Harry's shoulder.

"What?"

"Fixed everything."

"Not everything. I can't fix the one thing they really want, can I?"

"Peter? No. No-one can fix that… except them. But you've just given them a way to make it easier. You've given them time and freedom… and each other."

"Well, he gave me you, my darling. I think that means I still owe him pretty much all I have to give." Harry turned and pulled her into a hug, looking over her head and down the garden to where John and Lillian stood, hand in hand, their heads touching.

Chapter Thirteen

Winter 1943

My Darling Amy,

I can't believe it's a week until Christmas and I won't get to see you – again. I'm hoping for a longer leave in the New Year, though, so keep everything crossed.

You're right, my letters are censored, but, as you may have noticed over the past few months, I don't care. I don't want you to forget how much I love you, so I put it in writing and I don't give a damn who reads it, or what they think.

Your last letter was incredible and keeps me awake at night, for all the right reasons. Write again, and tell me of your dreams, so I can add them to mine. I dreamt of our last day together last night… you feeding me lunch in bed, your soft white skin, your gentle kisses. I long to hold you in my arms and feel your body against mine. I want to taste your sweetness, and I ache for your touch and to hear my name on your lips. Thinking of you keeps me sane… amidst all this insanity.

I miss you so much, my darling, but hopefully I'll be home soon and we can snatch some time together.

In the meantime, dream of me, please.

Yours always,

Ed. xxx

Amy got up from her bed, feeling flushed. She knew she was blushing at his words and that he was prepared to put so much of himself into them. She was excited by what he'd said but also at the prospect of him coming home. They hadn't been together since the summer… those magical days. He'd had a few twenty-four hour passes in between, but that wasn't enough time to get home and back, so he spent his short leaves with a fellow officer, who had a wife and two children. Ed joked in his letters and phone calls that he spent most of his time babysitting the officer's children, so he could be with his wife – not that Ed resented it, but he clearly wished he could be with Amy instead. She put Ed's letter in her top drawer. She would write back later, when she'd had a chance to think about what to say. In the meantime, she knew dinner would be ready soon, so she went downstairs.

"Robert thinks we should bring the spring fête forward to Easter," Elise was saying, as Amy entered the room.

"Why?" Harry replied. "The weather's unlikely to be good enough."

"That was what I said."

Amy went and helped herself to a gin and tonic, then sat down opposite her mother.

"I thought you always had the spring fête in May," she said.

"We do, but Robert thinks we could fit something else into the year, if we moved it to Easter."

"And I think there's a limit to how much the village can be expected to do," Harry said. "There are only so many sales, fairs and bring-and-buy stalls people can donate to and spend money at."

"That was precisely what I said," Elise replied. "Unfortunately, the rest of the committee seemed to side with him, so, he's coming on Tuesday evening to discuss his ideas."

"Oh." Harry's reply was blank. He'd hoped they would have a rest from Robert for a while, now that the Christmas bring-and-buy was out of the way and nothing needed to be done for a few weeks at least. Amy noticed the expression on his face.

"If he's so keen, why can't he take over planning the event and leave you to do something else? After all, it's only a week until Christmas." Amy suggested.

"I don't think he has time to plan a whole event by himself, and I think he just wants to let me know his ideas before Christmas, so I've got some time to think about them."

"Well, what about palming him off on one of the other ladies and giving yourself a break? You're looking tired," Amy persevered. It was true. They'd never caught up on their weekend away. It seemed they'd no sooner returned from Oxford, than Elise had been thrown into arranging the next event, and then Rose and Matthew had come to stay, seemingly happier than they'd been in a long while. It felt to Harry as though they'd had almost no time to themselves for months.

"Oh, I don't mind. I do feel responsible," Elise looked at the clock. "Shall we go in to dinner?" she said.

The Tuesday before Christmas, Robert arrived within minutes of them finishing their evening meal, and Elise took him into the sitting room, where coffee was served.

"Is Amy not joining us?" Robert asked.

"No, she has letters to write," Harry replied. Amy had asked to be excused, knowing she would find it difficult to watch Robert fawning over her mother.

"To her young man, no doubt," Robert said, with a twinkle in his eye. He looked at Elise.

"Possibly," Harry replied.

"Young love… There's nothing quite like it." Robert took his coffee from Elise and sat on the sofa. As Harry went to sit down, the doorbell rang. They waited for a few moments, then Polly entered.

"It's Mr Martin," she said, standing to one side and allowing Henri to enter the room.

"Henri," Harry went across and Henri patted him on the arm.

"I'm sorry," Henri said. "I didn't realise you had a visitor." He looked up at Harry.

"Is something the matter?" Harry asked in French, his voice little more than a whisper. Henri nodded, almost imperceptibly, glancing beyond Harry to Elise and Robert.

"Henri has something he needs to discuss with me," Harry called over his shoulder. "I'll take him into the dining room and leave you two in peace." As he went out of the room, he turned and saw Robert moving his arm along the back of the sofa, behind Elise's head. He hesitated, but then glanced at Henri, whose face wore a pained, worried expression, and he closed the door softly.

Harry asked Polly to bring him and Henri some fresh coffee in the dining room and, while they waited, they discussed the farm, and the weather, and Amy and all manner of things except, obviously, Henri's real reason for calling. Only once Polly had gone, having deposited a coffee pot and two cups and saucers on the table, did Henri look up at Harry.

"What's wrong?" the older man asked, pouring coffee and handing a cup to Henri.

"It's Sophie," Henri replied.

"Has something happened to her?"

Henri tried to laugh, but failed. "Not really, nothing out of the ordinary, anyway." Harry couldn't hide his confusion. "She's having an affair."

Harry momentarily pictured Robert Griffin's arm lying along the back of the sofa, and Elise's head nestling into it. She hadn't actually done that, of course, but he wondered what might be going on in the room across the hall. He dragged himself back to Henri's problem, desperate to rid himself of the images swirling in his mind. "What on earth makes you think that?" he replied.

"She's done it before," said Henri, playing with the spoon in his saucer.

"What?" Harry nearly spat his coffee across the table.

"She's had at least three affairs to my knowledge during our marriage," Henri said. "Those are only the ones I found out about, so there are probably countless others."

"Why… I mean… why have you stayed together?"

"For Luc, I suppose." Harry knew he looked incredulous. Doing anything for the sake of Luc Martin seemed a fairly pointless exercise in his opinion. "Oh, I know, Harry. You're going to say he isn't worth it, and neither is she. But I made a promise, I took vows."

"So did she."

"That's not the point."

"It works both ways, Henri."

Henri shifted uncomfortably in his chair. "I didn't come here for you to judge me," he said.

"Sorry." Harry continued to look at Henri. "What do you want me to do?"

"I want you to speak to William."

"William? Why?"

"Because he's the one she's having the affair with, of course."

This time Harry did splutter on his coffee. He reached across the table for his serviette, left from dinner, and wiped his mouth. "You are joking?" One look at Henri's face told him otherwise. "Henri, I can't think of anyone less likely to have an affair than William. He and Charlotte are deeply attached to each other and I know he'd never do anything to hurt or betray her. Why, you might as well suggest that Elise or I would have an affair." The dark thought crossed his mind again and he shook his head, bringing himself back to the problem in hand. "I don't know how you got the idea that Sophie is seeing Bill, but you're so wide of the mark, I can't even begin to tell you."

Henri looked confused. "But…"

"What made you think it's William?" Harry asked.

"Because there's no-one else."

"Well, maybe she isn't having an affair at all."

"Oh, she is." Henri's voice held a conviction that Harry couldn't doubt. "I know the signs. I've seen them too often before."

"Then it must be someone else."

"Yes, but who?"

"How should I know? Why don't you just ask her? If she's that brazen about it, just have it out with her."

Henri looked at Harry. "Oh, I don't think that would be a very good idea. The last time I did that, she left me and ran off with the other man."

"And is that such a bad thing?"

"I still love her, Harry. Whatever she's done. If I confront her with my knowledge, she'll feel backed into a corner, like last time and, in all probability, she'll disappear again."

"She came back last time though, obviously."

"After about three months," Henri said. "The worst three months of my life. He threw her out." Harry wasn't in the least surprised.

"Well," he said, feeling exasperated. "If we know it isn't William, and you can't confront her about who it really is, I don't see what else you can do…"

"I got your letter, Amy, darling." Polly had called Amy downstairs but Ed's voice sounded distant on the telephone. "Are you okay?"

"Yes, I'm fine. I'm just so fed up with Griffin. He's here again now, would you believe, and Uncle Henri's turned up with some kind of problem. Poor dad doesn't get a moment's peace. Mum's exhausted and the hospital is just flat-out."

"You sounded so down in your last letter, I had to call." She heard the concern in his voice and loved him even more, if that were possible.

"How are things with you?" she asked.

"Oh, just the same old, same old. But I don't want to talk about me," he said and she heard his smile even though she couldn't see it. "I want to talk about you. All of you." His voice dropped to little more than a whisper. "I miss you so much."

"I miss you too."

"I want to kiss you." His whispered words sent shivers down her spine. "Everywhere."

She shivered. "Oh, yes please," she breathed.

She heard a slight chuckle. "Tell me you're not having this conversation in the hall, or the dining room."

"Of course not, silly," she laughed. "I'm in dad's study."

"Please God, don't let him be in there with you. If you're reacting how I imagine you are, he'll kill me."

"No. I'm on my own. Dad's ensconced with Uncle Henri in the dining room and mum and Griffin are in the sitting room."

"Good. I wish I could be there with you."

"So do I. Where are you, by the way?"

"I'm on the phone in the hallway just outside the Mess.

"Won't someone overhear you?"

"No. They're all in the Mess drinking, but I don't really care if someone does overhear. Now for some good news… I've been told today that, unless something drastic goes wrong I'll definitely be getting five days' leave after Christmas. No dates confirmed as yet, but keep your fingers crossed."

"It can't come soon enough."

"No. I really can't wait to see you… well, and to touch you. I want you naked in my arms… I want to taste you… feel the tip of my…"

"Oh, stop," she breathed, heavily, her eyes shuttering closed. "What if someone hears you?"

"Like I said, I don't care, and I don't want to stop. I'm not even with you and I know how you're reacting." There was a pause, then he lowered his voice so she had to strain to hear him. "I… I know you're wet, Amy. Really wet. I love that. I just wish I could be with you."

"It's you, Ed… You make me…"

"I know. I feel the same."

"I really need you to come home soon." The thought of his touch, his kisses, his nakedness made her hot and flushed… and, yes, wet. She stopped suddenly. "Oh, but… oh no…" She couldn't keep the disappointment out of her voice.

"I know exactly what you're thinking," he whispered.

"Do you?"

"Yes. You're thinking that, when I come home, your parents are hardly likely to let us share a bedroom, or go away by ourselves."

There was silence on the end of the line.

"Is that what you were thinking?" he asked, and she thought she detected his smile again.

"Am I that obvious?"

"No, not really, except to me. Amy, listen to me. I don't care about any of that, not really. It's fun to think about, and dream about… and I do, all the time… and I'd do all of it, if I could, but as long as I can see you and kiss you, and talk to you, and hold you in my arms, I'll be more than happy. Everything else can wait."

"Really? But all those things you've just been saying…"

"I like saying those things to you. I like knowing I can get you that aroused just with my words."

"You can..." she breathed, "you really can."

He laughed. "Good. But we've got our whole lives to make love and when the war's over, I fully intend to; right now, I just want to be with you. That's all that matters. If we can snatch a few hours alone, that would be wonderful, but I'll take whatever I can get."

"I do love you, Ed... so much."

"I love you too. And I'll be home soon, my darling. I promise... Very soon."

By the time Henri and Harry had thrashed the argument back and forth, it was nearly eleven o'clock. He said goodbye to Henri at the front door and found Elise alone in the sitting room, thumbing through a magazine.

"Is everything all right with my brother?" she asked, looking up as Harry entered the room.

He rolled his eyes. "Not really."

She put her magazine down. "What's wrong. You look... fed up."

"I am. I can't believe I've wasted an entire evening... I assume Robert's gone."

"Yes. About half an hour ago."

"Did you get everything done?"

"Yes, I think so. What's the matter with Henri?" Harry would have preferred to discuss her meeting with Robert, but he knew she wouldn't rest until he'd revealed his own conversation. It took him just a few minutes to explain.

"How... how could she do something like that?"

"Four times," Harry added.

"You seem to think it's funny."

"No, I don't. I feel sorry for Henri. But I can't believe he's put up with her all these years, regardless of her affairs. Add those into the equation and it makes even less sense."

"My brother's a good man, Harry. He doesn't deserve this."

"I agree." He could feel her fuming. Now would definitely not be a good time to discuss Robert Griffin and her feelings towards him. That would have to wait.

"Someone should give that woman a damned good talking to," she huffed. "Or a damned good thrashing – either would do."

"If you say so, dear." Harry couldn't help but smile, and he saw her mouth twitch with his. "But I think we'll leave that to Henri, if you don't mind."

Two days later, the day before Christmas Eve, the festive preparations were well in hand. A large tree had been erected in the sitting room and, after lunch, Elise planned on decorating it. She and Harry had discussed waiting until Amy came home from work and doing it together, but decided that she'd probably be tired and would want to write to Ed anyway, so they'd got Dennis to fetch the decorations from the attic.

"Did I see a letter from John arrive this morning?" Elise asked, opening up the first box of ornaments.

"Yes." Harry said, limping across to the sideboard and picking up the envelope that had arrived in the first post. "I'll read it to you, if you like."

Elise nodded, starting to hang the delicate baubles on the tree.

"It's dated the twenty-first," Harry said.

"'Dear Harry and Elise,'" he began, sitting down on the sofa. "'How can it already be Christmas? We've been down here for over three months now and it feels as though we've never lived anywhere else. Lillian and I take daily walks on the beach, whatever the weather, and have found it very restful and curative to be here. The locals have made us welcome and tomorrow evening, we're going carol singing – Lillian has warned them of my tone deafness and they're still willing to let me tag along, brave souls that they are.

"Miss Lewis and I are getting along famously and she's been able to split the classes, with me teaching the older children – thank goodness! I did have a couple of scary days when she was off sick and I had to teach the younger ones as well. They're very crafty and tried to convince me that they were allowed to play games all morning, but two of the older girls put me straight, so I let them help with taking the class and they seemed to appreciate the trust I'd placed in them. I can't wait to tell you some of the stories, but I'll save that for when I see you and Amy together... She'll appreciate them just as much as you – if not more.

"There isn't very much to report with regard to the house. The garden is now completely dug over and ready for planting in the spring, so Elise will have to let me know what she wants put in. She's more familiar with the climate and soil down here and I don't want to get it wrong. There have been no more mishaps with the roof and the repair carried out when we arrived is holding firm, despite the strong winds last month.

"I'd better close now, as it's time for supper, but I wish you all a very happy Christmas and that next year will see us at peace once more.

"Your faithful friends, John and Lillian.

"Wednesday 22nd December. Since writing the above yesterday evening, the strangest thing has happened. I had already sealed the envelope containing this letter and put it on the side to post, when a letter arrived early this morning, with the most remarkable piece of news, and I felt I had to tell you.

"It appears that an anonymous and very generous gift has been made to my old school by the parents of a former pupil who has evidently done well for himself, on the understanding that I, personally, am to receive a lump sum of £5,000. The letter came from the board of governors, containing this information and a cheque! I simply can't believe it, but now, when the war is over, we'll be able to settle comfortably wherever we like – although Lillian has taken a shine to this part of the world, and I'm very attached to it myself now, so you'll probably have some new neighbours when you get home.

"I felt I had to share our good fortune with you as I know you will understand, more than anyone, how much this means to us and, once again, wish you all a very merry Christmas.'"

Harry folded up the letter and replaced it in the envelope as Elise came and sat beside him.

"It was you, wasn't it?" she asked.

"What?"

"The anonymous parents. You're the anonymous parents."

"Whatever gave you that idea?"

"Because I know you. You knew he wouldn't take your money directly, so you found another way."

"Was it wrong of me to want to help them?"

"No."

"My money's never really felt as though it belongs to me anyway, Elise," Harry explained. "I inherited it; I didn't earn it. So, when someone needs help, I'm happy to use what I have to do what I can. You can never tell him."

"Of course not."

"Never tell anyone; that way he can't find out by mistake. Things have a habit of slipping out, so this must be our secret." She leant across and kissed him on the cheek. "What was that for?" he asked, looking down at her.

"Because you're so…"

"So what?"

"Oh, I don't know… but you are, anyway." She got to her feet again. "Now, rather than just sitting there, what about helping me with this tree? We haven't exactly got very far, have we?"

"You've only put up the newer decorations. Mother and father bought those not long before father died," Harry said, studying the tree. "What about the old ones?" He leant forward and rummaged through the boxes on the floor until he found what he was looking for. "There are some in here that are older than me."

"Really? They're *that* old?" He looked up at her, seeing the mischievous grin and the glint in her eye, and he suddenly realised how much he'd missed that look. Putting the box to one side and getting up, he limped across the room towards her and she backed nearer to the tree.

"Are you suggesting I'm ancient?" he said, smiling.

"Me? Would I do such a thing to my beloved, gorgeous, generous and kind husband?"

"We both know perfectly well that you would. And flattery will get you nowhere." He took another step and was now only inches from her, staring down into her eyes, which were shining and alight.

"Now, Harry," she said. "I've got the tree to finish."

"A feeble and pathetic excuse." He grabbed her waist, pulling her towards him. She squealed and he laughed. "God, I've missed you."

She looked confused. "How? I've been right here," she said.

"I know… But I've missed this." He pulled her in closer and kissed her deeply. When he released her, her face was flushed and her eyes were sparkling.

"But we haven't stopped…"

"I know we haven't stopped making love, but it's not the same. I've missed the fun. I've missed hearing you giggle and laugh, and make fun of me. I've missed that look in your eye… the one that says you're mine and you want me and you don't care who knows it." He saw her shoulders drop and raised her face to his. "I'll take you any way I can get you, Elise, but this…" He kissed her again. "This is us – it always has been. This is what we're all about."

"I'm sorry. I've been so busy, so pre-occ—"

"I don't want you to be sorry. I just want you." He looked around the room, at the scattered boxes and decorations. "Come on," he said, taking her hand. "We're going upstairs."

"Now?"

"Yes, now."

They stumbled towards the door with difficulty. Harry was without his stick but the main reason was their joint anticipation and desire. As Elise put her hand on the door knob, Harry turned her and pushed her back hard against its oak panels.

"We won't make it upstairs if you do that," she murmured into his mouth as he kissed her.

"I don't care. I told you… Anyway I can get you." He placed his hand behind her head, pressing his body against hers. She giggled and groaned, feeling his tongue delve deeply, tasting her. At that precise moment, they felt a nudging behind them, and the door knob twisted in Elise's hand. They broke apart, stepping away, breathless and flushed, and Polly poked her head around the door.

"Excuse me," she said. "This has just come."

"I didn't hear the…" Harry stopped dead, seeing the telegram in her hand. "Can you open it for me?" he said to Elise, his voice little more than a whisper. She took the envelope, which was addressed to Harry, opened it, and handed him the flimsy piece of paper inside. He unfolded it and read the words.

Although Elise moved forward quickly, it was Polly who really caught him as he stumbled backwards. In great confusion, between the two women, they helped him to the nearest chair. Elise could just about hear him muttering, "No… Please, no," under his breath.

"Sweet tea, quickly." She turned to Polly, who ran from the room, leaving the door open.

Elise knelt at his feet and took the piece of paper that was hanging from his hand. She read:

> *'REGRET TO INFORM YOU THAT FLIGHT LIEUTENANT EDWARD HARRY WILSON IS MISSING IN ACTION FOLLOWING OPERATIONS ON 22ND DECEMBER 1943. STOP. ANY FURTHER INFORMATION RECEIVED WILL BE COMMUNICATED TO YOU IMMEDIATELY. STOP. PENDING RECEIPT OF WRITTEN NOTIFICATION NO INFORMATION SHOULD BE GIVEN TO THE PRESS. STOP.'*

She looked up again. Harry was a blur before her. She felt his hand on the back of her neck as he pulled her into him and he held her close while she wept. Polly arrived with the tea, which she poured, adding more sugar than was strictly necessary. Then she waited, wiping away the tears that were trickling down her cheeks. Eventually, Harry and Elise separated and Harry looked up at Polly and, in his eyes, she saw something she recognised, something vaguely familiar, as he stood and took the two paces required to stand before her.

"It's Master Ed, isn't it?" she whispered. Harry nodded and Polly was transported back to the spring of 1915 as, for the second time in her life, she felt his arm close around her and she cried into his chest, lamenting a young man lost.

They sat together in silence. Polly felt awkward to begin with, sitting with them, but then realised she didn't want to be anywhere else. About half an hour passed before Elise suddenly sat upright. "Amy!" she said, her hand darting to her mouth.

"I know. I've been thinking about what to do."

"Should we phone the hospital?"

"No. This isn't something she should hear over the telephone." He glanced at the clock. "She'll be home soon. We'll tell her then." Harry stood. "In the meantime, I have to go and see Isabel."

"Oh, God. Of course. I'll come with you," Elise replied. Polly began to clear away the tea things.

"No." Harry's voice was firm. "Stay here, in case there's any further news… a phone call."

"But…"

"I know." He waited for Polly to leave the room. "I fully expect her to blame me."

"Harry."

"It's all right, Elise." He leant down and kissed her gently. "I'll be all right."

When he got to the door, he turned back and looked at her. "I won't be long," he said. "I promise I'll be back before Amy gets home."

It was only when Mary answered the door of Holly Cottage that Harry realised he'd been holding his breath. He asked to see Isabel and was shown into the living room, where she was sitting in front of the fire, listening to the wireless. She glanced up as he entered the room and, one look at his face told her everything she needed to know.

"No," she said simply. "Please, not Ed."

Harry crossed the room quickly, allowed his stick to fall to the floor, lifted her to her feet and held her in his arm while she sobbed. After several minutes, she calmed and pulled away from him.

He gave her all the details he had.

"Why you?" she asked eventually. He looked at her quizzically. "Why did they tell you and not me? I'm his mother." Her voice cracked on the last word.

"He gave me as his next of kin," Harry explained. "Remember, Isabel? When he joined the RAF, you and he weren't getting along too well. You were still married to Charles then."

"Don't remind me..."

"I suppose he just didn't get around to changing the records. It probably didn't seem that important to him."

She nodded her head and sat down again. Harry took the chair opposite.

"It does only say he's missing, Isabel. Keep that in mind. I won't believe he's dead until it's confirmed."

She looked up at him. "Really? You really think that?" Tears welled in her eyes again.

"I have to. It's all we've got."

Harry arrived home a few minutes before Amy was due to return. "How did it go?" Elise asked, taking his hand.

"Better than I expected."

"Did she blame you?"

"No."

"What would she have blamed you for anyway?"

"Encouraging him to enlist; not standing in his way."

"I'm sure she doesn't blame you for any of that."

"I expected her to. He's her son, Elise. I wouldn't have blamed her if she felt I'd taken him from her and encouraged him to go to his death."

"No-one could think that, Harry." They stopped speaking as they heard the front door open and close.

Before Amy had the chance to disappear upstairs to change, Harry walked quickly to the sitting room door, opened it and called, "Amy, can you come in here for a moment, please?"

Amy stepped into the room, looking at her parents.

"Sit down," Harry said quietly. She stared from him to Elise and back again, then began shaking her head.

"No," she whispered, repeating the word, over and over, her voice becoming louder, until she was shrieking. She fell forward onto the floor, kneeling. Then, clutching her stomach, a feral wailing noise came from her mouth. Elise stood rooted, her mouth open, her face pale. It was Harry who went to Amy, leaning his stick against one of the chairs as he passed. He couldn't crouch any more; his leg didn't bend enough, so using his one arm, he placed it around Amy's waist and lifted her to her feet, manoeuvring her to the sofa, where he sat beside her, cradling her as she howled.

He looked up and saw the expression on Elise's face. Reflected back at him was fear, longing, heartache and, something else, which took him a while to understand. She was remembering. This scene was familiar to her and it hurt.

After a while, Amy's cries became quieter, her sobs less wracking and she allowed him to soothe her gently, stroking her hair. They sat for hours. Elise and Polly brought food on trays, which no-one felt like eating. As bedtime neared, Amy finally sat up.

"I'm going upstairs," she said, her voice hoarse.

"Is there anything we can do? Anything you want?" Harry asked.

"Just Ed," she whispered. And with those two words, his heart broke.

Up in her room, Amy sat on the edge of her bed. She didn't think she had any tears left, and yet they still kept flowing. She went to open her drawer, but couldn't bring herself to look at his letters… not yet. After a while, she got up, opened her door and walked along the corridor to Ed's bedroom. Everything was as he'd left it on his last visit, when they'd spent the night and most of the next day in here. Should they have done that, she wondered. Would this pain be easier if he'd never kissed her, touched her, held her… tasted her? Of course it wouldn't. Because he'd loved her. She sat on the chair by the window, staring down the garden, into the darkness.

Perhaps if they'd had more time… Perhaps if they'd been married. If only she was pregnant with his child, she mused. She ran her hand across her flat stomach. Then she'd still have a part of him to cherish. She didn't care that the telegram had said 'missing'. She didn't care what her father said about waiting for news. She knew Ed wasn't coming back. The empty hole where her heart had once been told her that.

"I can't stay here," she muttered to herself, glancing around the room. "Everything reminds me of you." With a deep sigh and considerable resolve, she decided she had to get away. She'd apply for the transfer to Portsmouth. She'd do it the very next day.

The bed was made, and she crossed the room and lay down, curling up and sobbing into the pillow. 'We've got our whole lives to make love,' he'd said. But they hadn't, had they? They'd had one day. Just one day. It wasn't enough. She wished the sheets hadn't been laundered, wished she could smell his scent. But she couldn't. Because he'd gone.

"How are you?" Elise asked as she and Harry undressed for bed.

He looked at her. "I'll be all right," he said simply. His voice seemed a little distant and she turned to look at him.

"You've been so strong today. You don't have to be strong in front of me, you know."

They climbed into bed together and he pulled her across to him, holding her, while she rested her head on his chest. "I know. I'm just trying to hold on to some hope. I keep telling myself that, if I can do that, if I can believe he's still alive out there somewhere, then everything will come right in the end."

"Missing doesn't mean dead," she said, remembering his comforting words in 1917, when Henri had gone missing.

"Exactly. I have to hope. It's all I've got left of him. I won't mourn for him until I know for sure." he said, kissing the top of her head. She felt his chest heave beneath her and she knew he wasn't just thinking of Ed, but of Ed's father. They lay still for a while. "Something else happened this evening which confused me, and I need to ask you a question," he said eventually.

"Of course. You can ask me anything, you know that."

"I need to know, was it like that for you?"

"Was what like that?"

"When it was me? When you thought I was dead."

"Oh…" She hesitated, uncertain what to say. She decided on the truth. "No, it was different, I suppose."

"Different? How?" He recalled the look of anguish on Amy's face, the wild screams, the torment in her eyes and hoped against hope that Elise's 'different' was a good thing.

"I clung onto hope, Harry, for so long. I'd done it with Henri, when you'd said he wasn't dead, and he came back to me. I did the same when you didn't return. I waited for month after month, watching for a letter, looking out for you on the lane, hoping and praying you'd come back. You said you would... You promised, and I knew – or I believed – that if you could have got back to me, you would have done. So, I kept believing. Then the war ended and I realised you must be dead."

"What happened?" She didn't answer. "Tell me." She shook her head. "Tell me, Elise."

She took a deep breath. "I'd tried so hard to convince myself you couldn't be dead. So, when it hit me... I... Seeing Amy tonight, brought it all back. I was rather useless to her this evening, because all I could see was myself, lying on the ground in the snow outside the farmhouse, feeling that same pain, like a knife running through me, twisting inside, and hearing myself screaming your name into the darkness, over and over." She heard the hitch in Harry's throat as he breathed in. "I've never wanted to tell you any of this," she said, looking up at him. "You don't need to know."

"Yes I do."

"But it doesn't matter now."

"Yes it does. I need to understand." He pulled her closer. "Carry on... Tell me."

"Henri found me. I remember his arms around me, carrying me into the house and sitting me by the fire, wrapping me in blankets. It felt warm... he felt warm, but I was still so cold. The next thing I really remember clearly was when Luc was born, which was probably about four months later, I suppose... just a few weeks before you returned. Everything in between is just... lost."

She felt him shift beneath her, felt him turn towards her. Then she saw the look in his eyes. "How can you ever forgive me?" he asked.

"Because there's nothing to forgive. You came back to me. Nothing else matters."

"But I was alive... All those months. I should have written... I had so many chances... In Germany, at the nursing home in Shropshire, when I got back here... I thought about you all the time. Every waking second. I put you through that, and even then, it took John to make me realise how utterly selfish and stupid I was being."

"It's not important now."

"Seeing Amy like that, though, knowing you went through that pain because I was too... too wrapped up in my own problems. I'm a complete... a complete bastard, Elise and I don't know how or why you ever wanted to be with me again. Or why you'd want to now. What I did you you... it's inexcusable. Please, please say you forgive me."

She ran her finger down the side of his cheek. "I won't have you say those things about yourself, Harry. You were in a very, very dark place, and I think you were keeping everyone on the outside. I think you were protecting us from the darkness... protecting us from you. Your parents, Rose and me. You didn't speak to any of them and you didn't come to find me; not until you were ready. You went to John because you knew he was the only one who could understand that darkness and then, when you needed my help, you let me in again. I understood that then, and I understand it now."

He stared at her for a long moment, then covered her mouth with his. The urgency of his kiss took her breath away. His tongue delved deeply, pouring his longing, his fear, his regret into that one kiss. "Say you forgive me," he murmured.

"There's nothing to forgive."

"Please, say it. Please," he choked.

"I forgive you." She felt the relief flowing from him. "And now, Harry, I want you to forgive yourself."

Chapter Fourteen

Winter 1944

Amy stared out through the slightly misted window of the surgical ward. There was a light spattering of snow on the ground and the shadows were lengthening already as darkness fell. She turned and sighed. She couldn't believe she was still working on the ward, three weeks after the worst Christmas ever, three weeks after applying for her transfer. Matron had told her that she'd have to wait for a slot to become available, but she'd hoped the wait wouldn't be too long. Every day, waking up in her bed, eating breakfast, taking the familiar walk to the hospital… all of it reminded her of Ed, and she knew she had to get away.

She felt tears prick behind her eyes for the hundredth time that day and shook her head. Mrs Chantry needed more water. She'd fetch some and get herself a glass while she was about it. In the kitchen, she drank down the icy cold liquid, trying to feel something… anything, other than the numbness that surrounded her every thought and breath and movement.

Carrying the jug back into the ward, she deposited it beside Mrs Chantry's bed and tucked her sheets back in, then turned as she heard the door to the ward swing open. A man stood there, his pristine army uniform telling her that he was a Major. The Sister, who was at the other end of the ward approached him and he whispered to her. She looked up at him, he said something else, she shook her head, checked her watch, spoke a few more words and walked away. Then he leant back against the wall next to the door, his cap under his arm, and surveyed the ward. Amy shrugged. She assumed he'd come to visit a patient and had arrived early. Sister Jenkins was a stickler for punctuality and, although visiting was due to start in fifteen minutes, she felt sure the Sister had told him he'd have to wait. What surprised her was that the Sister hadn't made him wait outside. She resumed her duties, but she felt his eyes on her the whole time and it made her uncomfortable.

At four o'clock, she was due to go for her tea break and, having checked with Sister Jenkins, she left the ward, and headed towards the kitchen, passing the Major on her way. He nodded to her and she noticed the light scar down the right side of his jaw, and the green tint of his eyes as he watched her.

She got to the kitchen, retrieved a cup and saucer from the draining board and washed out the teapot. She put the kettle on to boil and turned, nearly jumping out of her skin when she saw the Major standing in the doorway. He was at least as tall as her father and just as well-built and his presence seemed to fill the room to the point where she felt a little intimidated. It wasn't a feeling she particularly liked.

"Hello," he said. "Sorry, I didn't mean to startle you."

"You didn't." He raised an eyebrow. "Alright, you did... You seem to be a bit lost. Visiting has just begun. If you're looking for a particular patient, one of the nursing staff can help you." She hoped her words were kind but dismissive.

"I'm not looking for a patient. I was looking for you, Amy."

Hope rose inside her. "Is this about Ed?" she said, holding her breath.

"No," he replied. She could have kicked herself for being so stupid. Why would they come to tell her anyway? They'd go to her father... and it would be someone from the RAF, if they sent anyone at all. But, they wouldn't send anyone... they'd write. She felt the tears rising again. "I'm sorry," he said and his sympathy sounded genuine, his voice soft and concerned.

She didn't reply, afraid her own voice would betray her feelings. "Do you think you could manage a second cup?" he asked, pointing to the teapot. She still didn't reply, but reached up into the cupboard and retrieved another cup and saucer, placing them next to her own. "Thank you." He pulled out a chair and sat down at the table. In the electric light, she noticed that his hair, which she'd thought was light brown, had tinges of red running through it and his eyes were actually a piercing bright green. She made the tea, not saying a word, then sat down opposite him.

"Don't you want to know why I was looking for you?" he asked eventually.

"I assumed you'd tell me eventually." He raised his eyebrow again. She guessed he was in his late twenties or early thirties, but he had lines around his eyes that made him look a little older.

"My name is David Harrison," he said. She wondered if she was supposed to know him. "Neither of us has very long," he continued, looking at the clock on the wall, "so I'm going to come straight to the point. I work for a special department of the government and we're looking to recruit people who have particular talents."

"What particular talents?" Amy tried to pretend she wasn't interested, but the distant light in her eyes gave her away.

David suppressed a smile. "People who can speak fluent French, have an understanding of living in France… that sort of thing."

"People like me, you mean?"

"Precisely."

"And what sort of work are you looking to recruit people like me for?" she asked, pushing her half-empty tea cup away.

"I'm not going to tell you that right now," he said. "I want you to come up to London the day after tomorrow. You'll meet my boss and he'll explain what's involved."

"And if I don't want to come to London to meet your mysterious boss?"

"But I think you do." His voice was quiet, purposeful, his eyes boring into hers. She didn't reply. He handed her a card, with an address printed on one side. "That's where you need to be," he said. "Two o'clock, Friday afternoon. I know that's your day off, so it shouldn't be a problem. And, by the way, you mustn't tell anyone about this." He got up, placing his cap back on his head. "I'll look forward to seeing you then, Amy." He turned and left and, as he did, the room suddenly felt larger again.

She noticed he hadn't drunk any of his tea and, as she got up and poured it down the sink, she suddenly wondered how he'd known her name.

The large hotel looked ominous to Amy, but she entered with her head held high, uncertain if she was being watched from a window above. She checked the room number on the card and replaced it in her pocket, climbing the stairs and walking along the corridor until she stood outside the door. Taking a deep breath, she knocked once in what she hoped was a confident manner and was startled when the door was opened immediately. Major Harrison stood to one side to allow her to enter, and she crossed the threshold into a sparse room, where the bed had been removed and a desk stood in the centre of the space that was left. Behind it sat a small, rather fat man, with a bald head and round, metal rimmed glasses. He was wearing a dark suit and a bow tie, which was a little crooked. He looked up as Amy entered and smiled genially.

"Good afternoon." His voice was high pitched. "I'm glad you decided to accept our invitation."

"Let's just say you piqued my curiosity," Amy said, trying to sound disinterested. "But I'm not sure I've accepted anything yet." She heard Harrison's muffled laugh as he pulled a chair from next to the wall, and placed it directly behind her.

"Very well," the bald man said. "Please take a seat."

Amy did so, and Harrison walked around to the other side of the table and sat down next to the bald man.

"My name is Wallis," the bald man said, and she wondered if he was telling her the truth. "Harrison here works for me." Amy didn't react at all, just stared at the two men. Wallis opened the file that was lying on the table in front of him. "Your mother is French," he continued. "And you speak the language fluently." Amy nodded, but noticed he wasn't looking at her. It hadn't been a question. "You've spent a great deal of your childhood in France and your uncle, before Dunkirk, lived there with his wife and son." Amy's mouth fell open, but she remained silent. "Your father is English. He served in the last war and was wounded…" He turned the page, raising his eyebrows. "Quite badly. He was a man of great courage."

"He *is*," Amy corrected. Harrison looked at her, noting the hard line of her mouth.

"Indeed." Wallis didn't take his eyes from the file. "You have a sister, living in London. She is married to Doctor Matthew Shaw." He turned another page and looked up at her. "Your boyfriend, Edward Wilson." He looked down again. "Shot down…"

"This is all very well," Amy interrupted, her voice cracking. "You've proved that you know everything about me. But why have you summoned me here?"

"We didn't summon you. We invited you. You accepted our invitation. The point is," said Wallis, putting the file down, but not closing it, "that we think you're eminently suited to the role we have in mind for you."

"And what would that be?" Amy asked.

"We're looking for couriers."

"Couriers?"

"Yes." Wallis stood up and Amy nearly laughed, despite the tears that had threatened just a few seconds before. He was so short, he looked almost the same height as he had when he was sitting. She reached into her handbag for a handkerchief to cover her smile. Harrison noticed and tried to look serious, although he too failed. "Couriers," Wallis continued, walking across the room to look out of the window. "We drop them into France. They deliver money, pass messages, that sort of thing…" He waved his arm in the air.

"When you say 'drop', do you mean what I think you mean?" Amy asked. Her face had paled slightly and she looked from one man to the other.

"Yes. We parachute them in." It was Harrison who replied. He was studying her closely.

"Parachute?" This time Amy did laugh, out loud, and didn't bother to use her handkerchief to hide it. "Parachute? Are you serious? You want to parachute me into occupied France? My mother would have kittens… My father, on the other hand, would probably kill you." She looked from Harrison to Wallis. "Both of you."

"Oh, you can't tell your father," Wallis said. "You can't tell anyone."

"What? So, I'm supposed to drop into Nazi-occupied France, deliver a few messages for you, somehow get back out again, and not tell anyone? Do you not think my parents might notice I've gone?"

Harrison stood, walked around to Amy's side of the desk and leant against it, stretching his long legs towards her and crossing them at the ankles. He sighed. "We'll provide a cover story for you." He saw her mind working things through.

"But, if I went away somewhere… If I transferred, or whatever the cover story was, I'd still write to them, wouldn't I? They'd notice if I didn't write and I presume I couldn't write from France without making it obvious where I was…"

"You presume correctly. Don't worry about the details, Amy. We've done all of this before."

"The point at the moment is," Wallis turned back into the room, "do you think you can do it?"

"What? You want an answer now?"

"Well, no, actually we don't," Harrison replied. "But we do need an answer fairly soon."

"So I've got some time to think about it?"

"Yes," Harrison replied. Wallis huffed and sighed deeply. "Amy…" Harrison leant forward, getting her attention. "What we're asking you to do is very dangerous. We'll train you. The training is very intensive and, afterwards, if we don't think you're up to going, we won't let you. You have the weekend to decide, but I'm afraid you can't discuss this with anyone… not even your father, and certainly not your mother. You have to make your decision on your own." She nodded her head, looking up at him. "I'll contact you on Monday. You can give me your answer then." He pushed himself away from the desk and held out a hand to her. She took it and stood. "I believe you can do this, but you have to be sure in your own mind, Amy," he said. "Think it through."

"She looked older than I thought," Wallis said once Amy had left, before crossing the room and sitting down in his chair again.

"Well, I suppose hearing that your boyfriend's been shot down and is missing in action can do that to a person." Wallis didn't miss the sarcasm in Harrison's voice.

He looked up, his eyes narrowing. "Is there something you're not telling me, David..." He left the sentence unfinished, but Harrison didn't answer. "I saw how you were looking at her and if you're letting your dick lead you around..."

"Don't be so vulgar," Harrison snapped.

"Since when did a little vulgarity worry you? Oh... So, it's not your dick; it's more serious than that." He closed the file. "In that case, we can't use her."

"We have to. You know that... Besides which, you don't get to decide, Rupert, you little shit." Harrison leant across the desk, his face inches from Wallis's. "I know we tell them all that I work for you, but I don't, do I? The interview's over. The role play is done."

"David, you'd be insane to take someone with you on this mission who you're involved with... whatever that involvement might be."

"Who I take with me is my choice and I'm not involved with her." He sat down in the chair vacated by Amy. "To be honest, I'm not that keen on taking her either," he said, his shoulders falling. "But what choice do we have?"

"We can work out another way."

"We don't have time, not when you take the training into consideration."

Wallis knew he was right. "Then you're going to have to control your libido."

"My libido is just fine. What I need now is for you to get on with the plans and get the paperwork under way."

"We don't know that she'll agree yet."

"Oh, she'll agree."

"How do you know that?"

"Her eyes." Wallis looked up at him.

"She told you with her eyes?" he asked.

"She has a very communicative face."

"And don't you think that might be a problem... given what we want her to do?"

"I'll be with her. I won't let it be a problem." Wallis knew David could conceal a lie. He was trained to do so. He just hoped that this time he was telling the truth, or the whole mission was going to go to hell, and Harrison was taking an innocent twenty year-old girl with him.

On Sunday afternoon, Amy wrapped herself up in her thickest winter coat, her boots, scarf and gloves, placed a woollen hat on her head and wandered up to the oak tree. She'd avoided it since hearing the news about Ed, just as she'd avoided looking at his letters and going into his room, after that first night. She thought of him as dead, despite everything her father said. She couldn't believe in his hopes. Couldn't keep hanging on... It was too painful. Better to make a clean break and deal with the pain of losing him once, than continue to hope and face losing him again in the future when his death was finally confirmed. If her father wanted to do it that way, that was up to him, but his determination to believe that Ed was still alive was starting to grate on her. Standing underneath the bare, gnarled branches, she looked up at the grey sky. Maybe Major Harrison was giving her the perfect opportunity? If there was as much danger as he seemed to be implying, he might be giving her a way out. A permanent one... Right now, under the tree where she and Ed had shared so much, the prospect of never having to feel again felt very enticing.

"Oh, tell me what to do, Ed," she whispered. There was no reply, but there couldn't be. The dead don't talk. She looked down at her boots, sinking into the wet grass where they'd lain together that night. "I can't do this any more," she said. "It's too hard."

On the Monday afternoon, Sister Jenkins informed her, with a frown, that she had a personal telephone call, which she could take in the Sister's office.

Amy went inside and closed the door, then picked up the receiver, which had been left lying on the desk.

"Hello?" she said, although she knew whose voice she'd hear at the other end.

"It's David Harrison," he said. "Have you reached a decision?"

"Yes," she replied, holding her breath.

"And?" She wondered why he seemed to sound nervous.

"My answer's yes." Had she imagined the sigh on the other end of the line? She must have done.

"I'm pleased," she heard him say.

"So, what happens next?"

"You'll receive instructions in a day or two. For now, you do nothing. And tell no-one. I mean no-one, Amy"

"I understand."

There was a pause and, for a moment, she wondered if he'd hung up. Then she heard him speak. "Amy," he said quietly. "You've done the right thing." And then the line went dead, so she didn't hear him whisper, "I hope so. Dear God, I really hope so."

"Cranleigh?" Elise was shocked. "I thought you'd applied to Portsmouth."

"Nothing was happening at Portsmouth, so when this came up at Cranleigh, I accepted." Amy hated lying to her parents.

"And what will you be doing at Cranleigh?" Harry got up and turned off the wireless.

"It's a complete change," Amy said, crossing the room and sitting on the window seat, so both her parents had to turn to look at her. "I'm joining the First Aid Nursing Yeomanry."

"Amy, this is all very sudden," Elise started.

"I know, Mummy." The crack in her voice was genuine. "But I can't stay here. There's too much of him…"

"But, can't you wait for something at Portsmouth?" Elise asked.

"I thought you'd be pleased. Cranleigh's much less dangerous. It's only a little further away than Portsmouth, but I don't think it's been bombed."

"I suppose…" Elise seemed doubtful.

"I have to do this," Amy said.

“I know.” Elise tried to sound more cheerful.

“The FANY?” Harry asked, joining in the conversation at last. He looked at Amy and she turned away from him, pretending to have an itch on her leg.

“Yes,” she replied.

“What made you choose them?” he continued.

“Oh, I just felt like a change.”

“When do you leave?” Elise asked.

“On Sunday.”

“But that’s only three days away.”

“Well, they offered me the chance, so I took it.”

Elise nodded, getting up. “I suppose we’d better think about packing,” she said, walking towards the door.

“I don’t think I have to take too much…” Amy crossed the room after her mother, and both women went out.

Harry sat back down again. He’d heard something about the FANY… He just couldn’t remember what it was. He shook his head. He was going to miss Amy. He understood her reasons for leaving. The reminders of Ed must be difficult to bear and he knew she didn’t share his optimism for Ed’s survival. He just wished, for lots of selfish reasons, that she wasn’t going right now. Robert Griffin had spent three of the previous five evenings at the house, ensconced with Elise over various committee matters, and Harry was beginning to find his presence intolerable. His only ally and solace had been Amy and, with her gone, he wondered how he would keep his temper.

Chapter Fifteen

Spring 1944

"It's lovely to see you again. It's been so long." Elise hugged Amy to her. "You feel different. Thinner… or more muscular."

Amy had known she'd have to behave as normally as possible when she got home, but she didn't expect the deception to begin the moment she walked through the door. "We have to lift stretchers and carry all manner things." Amy thought quickly. "I don't think I've ever been so fit." She flopped down into the sofa. "Or so tired. Where's dad?" She gladly changed the subject away from herself.

"He's down in his studio."

"Oh?" Amy looked up.

"Yes, he's gone back to sculpting."

"He hasn't done that for ages. Not since we left Cornwall." Elise sat in the chair by the fireplace and turned towards Amy. "And how are you?" the younger woman asked.

"Oh, you know. I'm ruing the day I ever agreed to take over this committee, and the day I put my foot down about keeping the Spring Fête in May. We moved it to early May, as a compromise and we've got three weeks to go, and I've never been so busy."

"Can't any of the others help?"

"Oh, they are, but there just seems to be so much to do. Would you like some tea?"

"Hmm. Yes please."

"Why don't you go and let your father know you're here and I'll get Polly to make the tea?" Elise got up again.

"Or you could sit down and put your feet up. I'll go and get Polly to make the tea and then I'll run down the garden and fetch dad."

"Would you mind? I really am exhausted."

"Stay there then. I'll be back in a minute."

The door to the studio was open and, as Amy approached, she heard her father cursing. She'd never really heard him swear before and it brought a slight smile to her lips. She took a few more steps forward, then she heard the sound of something crashing and she hastened towards the open door. Standing just outside, she saw a piece of moulded clay on the bench in front of him. It resembled a horse's head, but she could see where he'd gone wrong. The nose wasn't working. It was too long and out of proportion with the rest of the head. Harry was sitting on a stool, leaning on the bench, his head in his hand, breathing heavily and, beside him, on the ground, were his tools.

"Having a bad day?" she asked.

He jumped, then turned. "Amy!" he said and got up. He took his stick and walked towards her, smiling. "When did you get back?"

"About ten minutes ago." He hugged her. "What's the horse done to offend you?" she asked, pulling away and nodding towards the statue.

"Oh... that. Don't ask."

"Well, I am asking."

Harry looked down at her and sighed. "Well, to be honest, I seem to have lost my touch."

"Never!"

"I must be getting old, or something." He smiled, but it didn't touch his eyes.

"Or out of practice, maybe? It's been a while, Dad. You can't expect to get it right first time when you haven't touched a piece of clay for years."

"Oh, I've been coming out here for a while now, Amy. Since just after you went away. Needs must, and all that."

"Needs must?" She turned to lead the way back up the garden.

"Anything to get out of the house." Amy stopped abruptly and faced him.

"What's wrong?" she asked.

"Oh... Nothing like that," he replied. "Nothing between your mother and I. It's just that bloody man... It feels like he's here morning, noon and night."

"Then tell mum to tell him to bugger off."

"Amy! Language!"

"Sorry, but the man needs telling."

"I couldn't agree more and, to be honest, I think she's had enough now as well."

"She does look tired."

"I know. She's exhausted. I'm just waiting for this damned fête to be over and done with, and then I'm going to sit her down and have a talk with her. She needs to take a step back, and if Griffin doesn't let up, I'll have a word with him too. There's no point in even trying to speak to her beforehand, though. She's too wrapped up in it to even begin to listen."

"Poor old you," Amy said, leaning into his arm.

"Less of the 'old', if you don't mind."

"How long are you here for?" Elise asked as she poured everyone a second cup of tea.

"I've got until Thursday morning," Amy replied.

"Four days. How lovely."

"Hopefully you haven't got too many meetings booked. It would be nice to spend some time together." Amy looked at Harry as she spoke.

"I'm seeing Robert on Wednesday afternoon, but other than that, I think I'm fairly free. Most of our work this week is booked in for after Thursday... and as for the weekend, well..." Elise finished drinking her tea and stood up. "Would either of you mind if I went up and had a rest before dinner? I'm so tired."

"Not at all. Are you okay?" Harry's concern was obvious.

"Yes, darling. I'm just exhausted." Elise let herself out of the room.

"I see what you mean," Amy said, once the door had closed. "She can't keep this up."

"I don't mind her being on the committee, but she needs to delegate a bit more, and worry a bit less."

"And Griffin needs to take up less of her time," Amy agreed.

Harry smiled. He'd missed his ally.

"So, how's Cranleigh?" he asked.

"Oh… It's a bit boring, really," Amy replied. Harry looked at her. She'd turned her head away from him when she started to speak, and he knew she wasn't telling the truth. He wondered, just for a moment, if she'd met someone – another man – and didn't want to tell him.

"Nice crowd?" he asked, fishing a little.

"Okay, I suppose," she replied, as evasively as possible. He noticed her fidgeting with her fingers, and that she then sat on her hands. Perhaps he was wrong. She seemed nervous… agitated, even. Meeting someone new wouldn't cause that reaction, or he didn't think it would.

"What have they got you doing up there?" he asked outright.

"Oh, nothing much, really." She was being far too evasive. Now he knew she was lying. She'd turned her head again, but her voice had given her away.

"Amy, you're a bloody useless actress," he said.

Her head flipped back. "What?" she said. "What are you talking about?"

"You."

"What about me?"

"Who are you trying to kid, telling me you're doing 'nothing much'. You're up to something."

"No I'm not."

"Have it your own way, then." He looked at her and, eventually, she turned away.

On Wednesday afternoon, Amy decided to go and visit William and Charlotte. She didn't want to be around when Griffin was in the house. She suggested that Harry accompany her, but he declined. He preferred to be close by, he said, and took himself down to his studio.

Robert arrived at a little after two o'clock and he and Elise went into the sitting room together. He sat beside her on the sofa, and brought a file of paperwork out from his briefcase.

"Really, Robert?" she looked at him. "We can't possibly have that much to discuss."

"Oh, this is about something completely different." He smiled down at her.

"What?" she asked, sighing.

"Well, I thought I could put forward my plan for an outing…"

"An outing? Why? Robert… I…" Elise turned her head as Polly came into the room.

"I wondered if you'd like some tea, Mrs Belmont. And the afternoon post has just come." Polly handed Elise two letters.

"Yes, we'll have tea, thank you, Polly." She looked down at the envelopes in her hand. One was obviously a bill, addressed to Harry. The other was addressed to her, in a hand she didn't recognise, but it bore a London postmark. Desperate to put off her conversation with Robert a little longer, she got to her feet. "Would you just excuse me," she said. "I need to open this. It might be something important." She didn't for one minute think it would be, but the thought of arranging an outing to heaven knew where for an inordinate number of probably ungrateful people was beginning to overwhelm her, and she hadn't even heard his ideas yet. She tore across the top of the envelope and pulled out the single piece of paper inside, then unfolded it. There was no address at the top, so she looked at the name on the bottom of the sheet and read 'Jack Thornton'. She felt her blood run cold and forced her eyes to start at the beginning:

Dear Mrs Belmont,

I hope you don't mind me writing to you, but I thought you'd want to know, being as you and Sylvia became such good friends when she stayed with you and she's been writing to you since then. I've got some very bad news, I'm afraid and there's no easy way to tell you this, but Sylvia and our Linda were killed in an air raid two weeks ago. The shelter they were in took a direct hit and they didn't make it. By some miracle, Jane survived, completely unharmed.

I'm sorry I haven't written before now, but I've been staying with my mother and I had to go home to find Sylvia's address book so I could write to you.

I was very broken up to start with, but I'm finding it easier now and my mother is helping me with Jane. I don't know what I'd do without the two of them. I'm keeping busy at work too, which is probably a good thing.

I'm sorry to be the bearer of such bad news.

I hope you and Mr Belmont are keeping well.

Yours sincerely,

Jack Thornton.

"Oh my God, no," she cried, and clutched onto the mantlepiece for support.

"What is it?" Robert jumped to his feet and was in front of her in seconds. "What is it, Elise?"

"I can't believe it. They can't be dead." Tears were pouring down her cheeks.

"Who's dead?" he asked, putting his hands on her shoulders, turning her towards him and looking down into her face.

"Sylvia and Jane."

"Who are Sylvia and Jane?"

"Our evacuees. They stayed here." She looked around the room, as though searching for something. "Oh, God."

"Your evacuees? But why…?" He stopped, noticing the distress in her eyes. "Elise, my dear." He reached out for her and pulled her closer. "Let me help you."

"It's too much," she sobbed and she let him hold her, crying into his jacket.

Harry was sitting in his studio when he heard footsteps approaching. Polly poked her head around the door.

"I've brought you some tea," she said, placing the cup and saucer on the bench.

"Oh, thank you, Polly," he replied. She hesitated and he looked up. "What is it?"

"It's not really my place to say..."

"Say it anyway," Harry encouraged her.

"Well, I took the post in to Mrs Belmont a little while ago and, as I was passing the window to bring out your tea..." She paused for a moment. "I could have sworn I heard her crying. You don't think there's been any news about Master Ed, do you?"

Harry had already grabbed his stick and was out of the door before Polly realised he'd gone. He made quick time of getting back up the garden path, climbing the steps to the terrace as fast as he could and approaching the french windows before he stopped dead in his tracks. Through the opening, he could see Robert cradling Elise in his arms. In her left hand, which was by her side, closest to Harry, she held a piece of paper. Robert's arms were both around Elise's waist, pulling her close, her breasts hard against his chest, where Elise had rested her head. Harry felt a long-forgotten pain, tearing into his core, drawing the breath from him. He remained still. He heard Elise sigh deeply and saw her stand back a fraction. Robert whispered something, but her eyes remained closed. The pain increased, cutting into him a little deeper, a little harsher. Robert tilted her head upwards, and moved his down, their lips perhaps two inches apart. He brought his hands up, resting them on her cheeks, holding her tenderly, as his lips brushed against hers. Harry couldn't breathe, the pain was now too intense and he could feel himself beginning to fracture internally. Harry was torn; part of him longed to move away, to hide from the reality in front of him, but he was acutely aware of the blood rushing through his veins, urging him to fight for her... At that very moment, Elise pulled back, staring up at Robert. Harry couldn't read her expression, he wasn't sure he wanted to... but then she turned towards him and their eyes met.

"Harry!" she cried and ran to him. Dropping his stick, Harry caught her as she flung herself at him. "Thank God. Oh, Harry!"

"What? Tell me what's wrong?" His concerned voice belied the continuing pain which echoed around his chest.

"It's Sylvia... Sylvia and Jane. They're... Oh, God. How can this happen? She was just a little girl. And Sylvia too. That poor man..."

"You're not making any sense, Elise." Harry kept his voice calm and, letting her down to the ground, released her and took the letter from her. She nestled into him, and he wondered why the feeling of her body so close to his didn't make the aching in his chest lessen, even in the slightest. Looking down, he read the letter and his own pain diminished, just a fraction. "Come here," he said to her and pulled her close again.

"She was just a child," Elise sobbed into his chest.

"I know." He held the back of her head, stroking her hair. After a while, he turned her around and helped her back into the sitting room. "You need to sit down," he said. He was surprised to see Robert Griffin sitting in the chair by the fireplace, as bold as brass.

"You're still here?" Harry said, not bothering to disguise the disdain in his voice.

"Is Elise all right?" Robert ignored Harry's comment.

"She will be. I think it would be best if you left." Robert looked to Elise, who sat, impassive on the sofa, holding Harry's hand. She didn't look at Robert and, eventually, he gathered his papers together and, without saying another word, left the room.

"That poor man… his wife *and* his little girl…" Elise said.

Harry pulled her across to him and wrapped his arm around her.

Lying in bed, as dawn approached, Harry listened to Elise's breathing. She'd eventually gone to bed with a headache straight after dinner and, having sat up until Amy went to bed, herself quite upset by the news, Harry had come upstairs to be with Elise. He'd found her asleep and had climbed into bed next to her, lying awake all night, watching her sleep and mulling things over and over in his mind.

Throughout the evening, he hadn't dared to think about Robert and Elise, and how their lips had touched. He'd not dared to remember Robert's hands on her face, the look in his eyes, or the way he'd angled her head and leant down towards her, possessive and controlling. But lying in bed, with her soft body next to his, those were the images that filled his mind. He remembered, so long ago, the feeling of placing two hands on Elise, back when he had two hands. Now, for the first time in years, he recalled a snatched leave spent with her in the spring of 1917, when he'd lied to his parents and told them he was going to spend a couple of days in Paris because there wasn't enough time for him to return to England. In reality, he'd travelled back to Elise at the old French farmhouse, feeling a mixture of guilt and excited, almost breathless anticipation. Within just a few minutes of his arrival, they were upstairs in her bedroom, both naked, with her back against the closed door, and he was holding her up, supporting her, with his hands beneath her, her legs wrapped tight around his waist, kissing her ferociously, taking her so hard and fast, he'd thought his thighs would burn up and his heart would burst out of his chest. He recalled them both collapsing, breathless and satisfied to the floor afterwards, in a heap of arms and legs, laughing, kissing and then picking her up and carrying her in his arms, across to the bed, where they'd slept, just for a little while, until she'd woken him with her mouth… Oh, how easy she'd made it to forget the horrors of the trenches.

He looked across at her. She'd twisted and pulled the cover down slightly, exposing the top of her breasts. She'd always been so receptive, so open to pleasure and to any ideas or suggestions, so willing to try anything, and she'd never disappointed him. He wondered if she'd be able to say the same of him… He laughed, half-heartedly. Of course she wouldn't. Why wouldn't she want a man who was whole? A man who could please her completely, with no limitations? He turned, raised himself up on his one remaining elbow and looked down at her. He leaned across and kissed her very gently on her cheek and she mumbled something, then settled again.

He watched her until it was nearly daylight, then, as he contemplated getting up, he suddenly thought of Jack Thornton, having his wife and daughter snatched away from him, without warning, and he felt ashamed. He lay down on his back again, staring up at the ceiling.

He knew Griffin was pursuing Elise, he'd known it for ages, and he'd also known he should probably have put a stop to it months ago. He'd let it slide, though, because he trusted Elise, but he had no idea whether she'd been flattered by his attentions, had her head turned and had developed an interest in the man, or whether she'd opened that dreadful letter and was just upset and had turned to Griffin for solace. He hoped... God, how he hoped it was the latter. But, the thought of her eyes, looking up into Robert's haunted him, the image of their lips touching, tore at his mind. Now, though, as he turned his head and stared across at her, he realised that, even if he had to lose her to Griffin, even if he had to face the unthinkable pain of living without her, as long as she was alive and happy, somewhere in the world, and as long as Amy and Rose were safe, then he was a luckier man than Jack Thornton, and for that, he thanked God.

Harry was sitting at the breakfast table when Amy came downstairs.

"How's Mum?" she asked, sitting next to him.

"She's a little better," he managed to say, surprised by how normal his voice sounded. "She's having breakfast in bed, but she'll get up before you have to leave."

"Good." He heard a slight hitch in her voice. "I don't like the idea of going away, thinking of her being unwell." Harry looked up at Amy.

"What is it you're not telling me?" he asked. "I've been wondering since you got back here if there's something wrong with you and now I know there is."

"No, there's nothing wrong." She reached across and picked up the coffee pot, pouring herself a cup. "What makes you say that?"

"Because you've been on edge whenever we ask you anything. You're nervous and twitchy, Amy, and that's not like you at all. Despite what happened to Ed, you're not normally nervous."

"Well, I think you're imagining things," Amy took a sip of her coffee.

"I don't have that vivid an imagination." Harry took a bite from his slice of toast and continued to stare at her. "Okay," he said eventually, "so you're not going to tell me."

"Because there's nothing to tell."

He ignored her reply and continued, "But that doesn't mean I can't guess..." She looked up sharply and then shrugged. "I've still got a few military connections, and I knew I'd heard something about the FANY, so I did a big of digging and if I were to hazard a guess that your job has very little to do with nursing, and quite a lot to do with intelligence, would I be close to the mark?" Amy said nothing and took a piece of toast from the rack in the middle of the table. "And if I were to suggest that, fairly soon, you'll be going overseas?" She dropped her knife and it clattered loudly onto her plate. "So I'm right, then."

"No." He could hear the edgy tension in her voice. "Why on earth would I do something like that?"

"Because you're convinced that Ed is dead, that he's not coming back, and you want… what? Revenge?" She didn't reply. "Look, I know that if I'm right, you're not allowed to tell me anything," he said, "but if I ask questions, will you just nod, or shake your head." Amy looked at him and slowly nodded, just once. He took a deep breath. "Are you going overseas?" She nodded again. "Soon?" he asked. He saw the slight incline of her head and sighed. "I'm assuming you're going to France." This time she didn't respond. "Okay, you're not going to give that away."

"I can't."

"Amy, why are you doing this?"

"It's difficult to explain."

"Then try."

What could she tell him? It had to be something convincing and as far away from the truth as possible, or he'd just lock her in her room and forbid her to go anywhere. "It is to do with Ed," she said quietly, "but it's not about revenge."

"Then what is it about?" She didn't reply, so Harry continued, "You need to work it out, Amy, because if you're going where I think you're going, you at least need to know why, and have that straight in your head, because you're going to want to understand it when you get there."

She knew exactly why she was going, but she was intrigued by his words and their passion. "What do you mean?"

"You're likely to see things… Things you've never seen before; death and killing, destruction, maiming… maybe even torture." He looked at her, but she didn't flinch. "War's not pretty, Amy. You have to know why you're fighting it. You have to understand the reason, the purpose behind it."

"Why were you fighting?"

"That's complicated."

"King and Country?"

"Dear God, no."

"Then try and explain it to me." He saw the confusion in her eyes. "Please?"

He took a deep breath and reached across the table to take her outstretched hand. "I joined up," he began, "because of Rose, because I felt a duty to protect her and I did all my training with her in mind. But once I got out there, in the mud and the death, I realised I couldn't protect her at all, and anyway she was safe back here with granny and granddad. She didn't need me. But by then, I wasn't fighting for her anyway. I was fighting for the man standing next to me, and the one beyond him… for the captain, for my sergeant – a damned good man, by the way – for Stubbs, and Canter and Travis and Hamilton…" He reeled off names that meant nothing to her. "But most of all, I was fighting for Eddie. Keeping him alive became the most important thing in my world. You have to have a purpose, Amy."

"I do."

"Revenge for Ed? If he's even dead? It's not enough."

"I know. I said, it's not about revenge." She hesitated, trying to find the right words. Words that he might believe, words that might convince him to stop asking. "I'm doing it for myself."

"Sorry, but I don't believe you," he continued. "Oh, Amy. Whatever is going through your mind, please believe he's never doubted you. Not for a second… You've got nothing to prove to him."

"I'm not trying to prove anything to him. Whatever you think, I know he's gone. It's been four months now, and it's too late to hope anymore. I'm trying to prove to myself… I need to prove to myself that I'm strong enough. That I'm brave enough." She didn't add 'to carry on', although the thought was a constant in her mind. "Like he was…" she said aloud, then she lowered her head. "Like you were."

Harry stood up and towered over her. "Don't you dare go and risk your life to prove a damned thing to me, Amy."

"I'm not. Don't you see? I'm proving it to myself. You've always been so strong. Ed was the same. Now I need to prove to myself..."

"No, you don't," Harry interrupted.

"Yes I do. I feel so uncertain about everything. I need this one certainty... that I can do this and get it right. I'm doing it for me, Dad. Not Ed. Not you. Me." She hoped he was convinced.

He took a deep breath and came round to her side of the table. "I don't really claim to understand," he said. She looked up at him. "But I won't stop you going. I'll worry about you every second of every day and, if anything happens to you, I'll never forgive myself. But I won't treat you any differently to Ed. You say you need to do this for yourself, so do it." He put his hand on her shoulder and squeezed her tightly. "Just, for God's sake, come home again, Amy, or I'll never be able to live with myself."

She put her hand over his, and looked up at him. "You can't tell mum."

He thought of Elise and the image of her with Griffin crossed his mind again. "I've never kept a secret from her, Amy. I can't start now."

"I'm sorry, Dad. You can't tell her. It's important. They really stressed that on me. Maybe they guessed that you might work it out, but they were adamant that mum couldn't know. Think about it... Henri... Sophie... I suppose it's because Luc's still in France, working for the Resistance."

"You can trust your mother to keep a secret," Harry said. "Anyway, I don't think Sophie and Henri have heard from Luc since they got here."

"Please, Dad. It's safer for everyone if she doesn't know, especially me."

Harry thought for a few moments. "I'm not happy about this," he said eventually. "But, if you put it that way, I won't tell her. Not if it's that important."

"It is. They made it very clear."

He squeezed her shoulder again and removed his hand. In a way he felt grateful to her. As much as he hated keeping secrets from Elise, at least she wouldn't have to share his worries.

When they returned in the taxi from the station, Elise lay down on the sofa and Harry covered her legs with a light blanket.

"I really should get on and pull myself together," she said. "I do hope Amy doesn't leave it so long before she comes home again… and that she writes more often this time."

"Well, I imagine they keep her very busy, and there are probably a lot of other young people there to take her mind off things," Harry replied. So, the lies were beginning already. "I've just got a couple of calls to make. I'll let you rest." He needed to escape. He needed a few minutes to himself. He left the room quickly and went across the hall to his study, where he closed the door and leant back against its oak panels. He felt as though she was slipping away from him. That image was branded onto his eyes; their lips touching, that man's hands on her… He tried to breathe, tried to pull the air into his lungs, but the pain was becoming too much. Ed was missing, and they'd heard no word for four months. Everyone was losing hope for him, and even Harry was starting to have his doubts; Amy was about to go overseas to face dangers he didn't even want to think about, and Elise… He couldn't bear the thought of her leaving him, but, as the images seared into his mind, he realised he might just have to.

Chapter Sixteen

Late Spring 1944

They'd had to wait ten anxious days for the moon to be right but now, as she felt the wind rushing past her and stared out at the stars in the clear deep purple sky, she thought the darkness seemed almost absolute. She glanced up twice. The rigging was clear. Her parachute was open and she enjoyed the sensation of falling, drifting, feeling free. In the distance, she could just about make out the outline of a town, and a hill behind it. She couldn't see David, although she knew he was there somewhere, either above or below her. She twisted in her harness. Still nothing. Where was he? Uncertainty shrouded her mind and it was with a bump that she hit the ground, the impact taking her breath away. She waited for just a moment to gulp in some air and breathe properly again, then rolled onto her side and climbed to her feet. She began gathering in her parachute, working quickly. As she started folding the canopy, she heard a voice right next to her ear, which made her heart stop.

"How many times did I tell you to watch for the ground, not keep looking up at the bloody stars?" It was David. She hadn't even heard him approach.

"I wasn't looking at the stars," she said, offended. "I was looking for you."

"I'm touched." She fumbled with the canopy. "Here," he offered. "Let me help." He took over and made light work of finishing the job of folding her parachute, then handing it to her. "Follow me," he said and led the way across the field.

They'd almost reached the boundary, a small copse, when she heard a whistle, which David returned, and out of the trees, two men appeared.

"Patrice!" one of the men cried, slapping David on the arm and pulling him into a hug.

"Put me down, Thierry," David said, in perfect French and, when released, he turned to the other man and was greeted with equal enthusiasm. "We don't have time for this," David said eventually. "Which way?" The man named Thierry looked in Amy's direction, but David shook his head. "I'll introduce everyone later. We need to get out of here." Thierry nodded, and led them back into the copse.

They walked for about half an hour before reaching a farmhouse, where further greetings took place. Amy stood by the door, watching, as David was hugged by another man and a woman stepped forward and kissed him, firstly on both cheeks and then on the mouth, taking perhaps a little longer than was strictly necessary. David held her away from him and then let her go. "Hello, Katriane. It's good to see you again too." His voice was cool. He turned to Amy and pulled her forward. "This is Yvette," he announced. "Yvette Babineaux." Amy nodded her head, still unused to her codename. Thierry approached and handed them both a mug of steaming coffee. Amy clasped her fingers around the cup, surprised to find that her hands were shaking. David glanced at her. "It's been an eventful evening," he said calmly. "I think we'll get settled for the night and discuss everything tomorrow."

"Aren't you going to introduce me properly?" Amy asked.

"No. All that can wait until tomorrow." He turned and, taking her hand, pulled her towards a door beside the fireplace. "You'll sleep in here," he said.

"And where will you sleep?" she asked.

"Out, here." He knew he wouldn't sleep at all. There was too much to do. "I'll just be here, outside the door." He pointed to a chair near the window, knowing she needed the reassurance. It was all still new to her. "Now, finish your coffee and get some sleep."

She smiled and went inside the room, closing the door behind her. She looked around. A small lamp on a side table gave off a little light: enough to see that there were three mattresses on the floor, with blankets on each. The window was heavily curtained and next to the lamp was a basin, with a jug standing beside it. She chose the mattress nearest the door and sat on it while she drank down her coffee then, not even removing her coat or shoes, she lay down, pulling the blanket up over her. Her mind churned over the experiences of the day and she wondered what her first mission would be. She'd been told nothing, other than the fact that her name was Yvette Babineaux and that she was from Paris, but visiting a sick relative in Agen, a few miles from where they'd been dropped. She knew the paperwork in her pocket reflected this, but it seemed like scant information and, she'd not been given anything to deliver, which also seemed odd to her, given that she was supposed to be a courier.

A little later, she heard the door open and felt the presence of someone else in the room. A soft humming told her it was Katriane. Amy turned over.

"Oh. Sorry, I didn't mean to wake you," Katriane said, kicking off her shoes and sitting down on the mattress in the farthest corner.

"You didn't. I wasn't asleep," Amy replied.

"This is the first time Patrice has ever brought someone across with him. Whatever he's got planned for you, it must be something special."

"I've got no idea what he's got planned. He hasn't told me yet."

Katriane sighed. "Well, I'm sure you'll find out soon enough. He has a way of making things happen whenever and however he wants them to. But I'm sure you'll find that out for yourself." Amy could feel the other woman's eyes on her. Katriane sighed again. It was a wistful sigh and Amy wondered briefly about the history between her and David and what lay behind that kiss.

She lay down. "Goodnight," she murmured, and closed her eyes, hoping for sleep and that she'd find out what was wanted of her before her own curiosity drove her mad.

The following morning, as they ate a breakfast of eggs, bread and strong coffee, David introduced her to the other members of the group. In daylight, she could see that Katriane was a little shorter than Amy, with a figure that could best be described as voluptuous. She had shoulder length light blonde hair and sharp blue eyes, with a slightly turned up nose, and lips that most men would almost certainly want to kiss. Thierry was the polar opposite in terms of colouring, with very short black hair. His eyes were large and dark, beneath thick eyebrows and the slight growth of beard looked harsh as he rubbed his fingers back and forth along his chin. The oldest man present was Renaud, who was probably in his mid-forties. He was thin, tall and had iron-grey hair. He chain-smoked and paced the floor, stopping only to take gulps of coffee. Finally, there was Didier, who Amy estimated to be about her own age. His blond, tousled hair reminded her of Ed and she shook her head to erase the memory, until she looked up and discovered his deep blue eyes on her and felt her throat closing and the tears rising.

Finishing his coffee quickly, David glanced up at her. "We need to talk," he said and, taking her hand, he pulled her from the table. He opened the door and dragged her outside, leading her briskly away from the house until he was certain they couldn't be overheard.

"I need you to stop that," he said.

"What?" she tried to control the anger in her voice, panting hard.

"What you were doing in there. I can't help it if Didier looks a little bit like your boyfriend."

"How do you…?" He saw the tears forming in her eyes again and longed to pull her into his arms and hold her close. He blinked. He really needed to take better control of himself.

"I know more than you can possibly imagine." She folded her arms, glaring up at him. "I need you to be professional. I don't need you falling apart on me, Amy," he said.

"Firstly, I'm not falling apart. And secondly, I thought you weren't supposed to use my real name."

He moved a step closer so he was looking down on her. "Well, firstly, I'll be the judge of whether or not you're falling apart and secondly, I make the bloody rules while we're here, so don't start trying to tell me my job." He felt the anger pouring off of her, and calmed himself down. "Don't get in a mood with me, Amy. I'm only trying to help. Anger can be just as dangerous as sadness, or pleasure… or love. You have to control your emotions when you're out here. Emotions put you off your guard, and if you allow that to happen, you're as good as dead."

"Well, if you're offering professional tips, you might want to tell some of that to Katriane," she said, glaring at him. She was clearly still angry.

"What are you talking about?" he asked, remaining calm.

"I would have thought working with someone who has a crush on you is unprofessional."

"I haven't done much that work with Katriane. She's usually just a back-up, passing messages. I've only met her a couple of times and she won't be involved in this mission at all. But, be fair, Amy, if she's got a crush on me – and I'm not saying she has – then that's her problem, isn't it?" She took a deep breath and went to open her mouth again, but he forestalled her. "Look, you can call me all the names under the sun when we get home, but put a lid on it until then. Okay?"

She turned away and he saw, even in her shoulders, her struggle with her feelings. It took a few minutes before she turned back. "I think you owe me an explanation," she said at last. He looked quizzical.

"Of what?" he asked. "I've tried to explain…"

"Everything I'm doing wrong? Yes, you've done that perfectly, thanks. But what you haven't told me is what the hell I'm doing here."

He kept her waiting for another few hours. Despite her protestations, they went back into the farmhouse and, after a while, he gave the others tasks to do that would keep them away until later in the evening. He needed some time alone with Amy to explain what was going to happen next.

They sat at the table, Amy with her back to the fireplace and David to her right.

"You won't be aware," he began, "but the invasion into Europe is closer than you might think." Amy leant forward, her eyes widening. "I know the planned date and we need to have completed our mission before it begins. That's important." He drummed his fingers on the table for a few moments until Amy placed her hand gently over his. He looked up.

"Sorry," she said. "But that's very annoying. And it's making me nervous."

He smiled at her. "I apologise." She could see his mind working. "In a day or two, we'll leave for Paris."

"Paris? Why have we been dropped here, if we're going to Paris?"

"Because we don't normally drop agents slap bang in the middle of Paris… The Germans tend to notice."

She turned a sarcastic smile on him. "I realise that, but wasn't there somewhere a bit closer?"

"I had to deliver some money here, and pass on some messages to Thierry. It made sense to come here first, rather than drop someone else down here."

"But it'll take the best part of a day on the train, won't it?"

"Yes, but we've got time. And your cover story is that you've been visiting a sick relative here, so what difference does a train journey make?"

She thought for a moment. "None, I suppose." He waited while she turned things over in her mind. "Will we travel together, or separately?"

"Together." He coughed.

"As what?"

"Don't get too hung up on details right now, Amy. We'll talk about that later." She stared at him for a minute, then nodded. He took a deep breath, then continued, "We have a particular job to do when we get to Paris… There's a cell there, run by a man called Paul Mercier. He's French and has done some really good work for us over the years." He watched her closely. "His number one courier is Claudette Soucy, an agent I sent over about eight months ago. Which makes all this my responsibility." She looked at him inquisitively. "Within that cell we have a mole." He saw her eyebrows furrow and he stared at the crease between her eyes, yearning desperately to kiss the soft skin. "A leak," he clarified and heard her sharp intake of breath. "Too many lives have been lost already, so we have to find the leak and eliminate it before the Allies start to get anywhere close to Paris."

"Eliminate?"

"Yes. Now… here's where you come in. We've been monitoring this cell closely and we think the mole is Claudette."

"But she's English. Why would she do that?"

"You'd be amazed what people will do. I hand-picked her for this role and, when the evidence first came to light, I didn't believe it could be her either, so I sent one of my best agents in late last year to try and find out what was going on. I couldn't come myself– that wouldn't have worked, not with what I had in mind, I needed someone more… suitable. This other agent, well… he was one of my best: young, handsome and made for the part. Claudette, you see…" He swallowed and looked at the table, running his clean fingernails along its deep grains. "Claudette has always had very… healthy appetites, shall we say." Amy blushed and David tried to hide a smile. He paused for a moment.

"Can I ask a question?" Amy said.

"Yes."

"If you hand-picked her for the job, why couldn't you come and clean up your own mess?"

His eyes darkened. "Like I've already said, that wouldn't have worked."

"Why not?"

"Because…" He paused. "Because she already knew I wasn't interested in her." He got up, went to the stove and poured them both a cup of coffee. Sitting back down, he continued, "That's how I knew about her… her…"

"Appetites?"

"Yes." He smiled at Amy. "The training was different back then. Recruits used to spend several weeks doing various exercises and I used to turn up occasionally, to observe, sometimes join in. I found her in my room one night, in my bed – well on my bed, really. Stark naked and…" Now it was his turn to blush. "Well, let's just say she was enjoying herself. It was quite a show."

"What did you do?"

He looked at her sardonically. "What do you think? I threw her clothes at her and told her that, if she got out of my room within twenty seconds, I'd overlook her behaviour. I should really have kicked her off the course, but she was such a good student… Or so I thought." He stared across the room. "I was warned about her by another of the recruits… another woman. She claimed to have caught Claudette and two of the men together. Claudette was the top student in the group, better than any of the men, even. This other young woman didn't make the grade; she wasn't physically strong enough… I put it down to jealousy at the time, but perhaps I should have listened to her." He looked back at Amy. "In any case, if I'd turned up in Paris and claimed to be interested, tried to gain her confidence, she'd have known something was up." They both drank down their coffee. David continued, "This agent I sent across, he knew what he was up against, he knew what I was asking him to do, and I didn't think she'd be able to resist his very obvious charms. He was killed two weeks after he got to Paris." He paused for a moment. "She must have guessed… or else he wasn't as good as I thought and she wasn't falling for his attentions, or maybe she did and he gave himself away in the heat of the moment. I'll never know now." He shifted in his chair. "So, we're going to try a different tack this time. We're hoping that, if we use a woman – you to be precise – you might be able to befriend her, agent to agent, woman to woman. You won't have to get too close, but just close enough that she'll give something away. Anything. Just enough for me to be sure it's her."

"Then what?"

"Then you get out and I take over."

"Why don't you just recall her?"

"Because I'm not absolutely sure it is her and if it isn't, I might be able to use her to find out who it is."

"I see." Amy thought for a moment. "And how do I get close to her?"

"The story, as far as everyone in Paris is concerned, is that you're going to be based down here for a while, working with Thierry. You've come up with a message from Thierry, to Paul, which you'll deliver. I'm just tagging along because I want to have a chat with Paul about his activities prior to the invasion and then, the story is that you're coming back here and I'm moving on to another cell further north. We'll stay a few days in Paris, which is perfectly normal, to give you time to get acquainted with Claudette."

"What if she doesn't take to me?"

"She's the only woman in that cell, and, while she much prefers the company of men..." he hesitated, looking up at her, "she did used to enjoy certain aspects of the female friendships in training as well... mainly gossiping about men..." He coughed. "We can go over the details of that before you meet her."

"Okay. So, how do I go about this? Do I just approach her?"

"No. Not on your own. I'll introduce you. Once you've spent some time with her and got to know her a little, if she falls for the story we're going to give her, we'll be able to formulate more of a plan."

"Will that work? I mean, won't she be suspicious if you're there?"

"I don't think so. Not this time."

"Why not? If you thought she'd be doubtful about you last time, what makes you so sure she won't be this time."

"Because no-one will be *trying* to get her into bed. It'll be the exact opposite. Last time – using a male agent – that was our only chance of getting close to her. I plan on being very aloof with her."

"I see." She sounded doubtful, despite her words.

They sat in silence for a little while. "Do you have anything you want to ask?"

"Probably lots, but I'm still processing my thoughts at the moment. You've given me a lot to think about."

"Well, just remember, everyone here thinks you're going to be working in Paris. This is so hush-hush, even they don't know what's going on, so if you need to ask anything, make sure we're completely alone."

"Okay." He stared at her. "What's wrong?" she asked, feeling his eyes boring into her.

"You're a very remarkable young woman, Amy." She felt her face redden but said nothing, uncertain how to respond. "I've asked you to undertake one of the most dangerous missions I've ever instigated, and you're just taking it in your stride. You haven't even commented on the risk to you."

"I hadn't really thought about that."

"Well, you should." He stood up and walked around, standing behind her. He leant down and placed his mouth close to her ear. She could feel his breath on her neck. "We're going into Nazi occupied Paris. We'll be surrounded by Germans, and we have to find this traitor… If I'm right and it is Claudette, and she finds out what you're doing, she'll almost certainly try and kill you." He sighed and his breath whispered across her skin. "I'm taking you into the jaws of hell, Amy." He felt her shudder. "I want you to understand who and what you're going to be up against." He saw her swallow and slowly lick her lips. The sensation rippled down into his groin, settling there uncomfortably.

"Are you trying to scare me?" she whispered. "Because if you are, it's working."

"No. I don't want you scared. I want you alert. I promise, I'll be with you, Amy. All the time." *Even when you don't know it*, he added to himself.

Chapter Seventeen

Late Spring 1944

The ten days since Amy's departure had been difficult. Harry had found it hard to focus on anything and had slept very little. For once, it wasn't nightmares keeping him awake. When he wasn't thinking about Amy and wondering where she was and what she might be doing, imagining the worst possible dangers; he was worrying about Ed and pondering if he could still be alive after all this time, and why they hadn't been told anything. Every other waking moment was spent thinking of Elise and Griffin. Nothing made sense anymore and he wandered around the house, feeling as though he was in a permanent daze.

The fête had taken place the previous Saturday and had been an enormous success, raising more money than any previous event. Now, the following Tuesday lunchtime, Charlotte, Elise and Griffin were sitting on the terrace while Harry was in the living room, standing near the fireplace. The French doors were open, so he could witness them discussing the possibility of a summer dance. Griffin's earlier idea of an outing had been quickly abandoned once Harry had pointed out that petrol rationing made such things impractical. Now, it seemed, he'd come up with the alternative of a dance, and Harry felt his irritation rise, although at least Elise was sounding uncertain about it.

"We don't normally do another event so soon," she said. "And, as both Harry and I have pointed out before, there is a limit to how much the village can be expected to do."

"But we won't be expecting them to do anything this time, except we could maybe hold a raffle or something." Griffin said. "People will just have to turn up and enjoy themselves."

"I must say, it does sound like a good idea to me," Charlotte joined in.

"What about all the work, though?" Elise said. "We've only just had the fête and that was exhausting."

"I'll help you, my dear," Griffin said, leaning forward. "You know that." To Harry's ears, he seemed to be purring.

"Well, I suppose if you think we can manage it…" Elise seemed to be coming round to Griffin's way of thinking and Harry felt his mood dropping.

"I *knew* you'd agree!" Griffin sounded elated.

"I have my diary, shall we try and set a date?" Elise said.

"What about September?" Charlotte suggested.

"Don't you think that might seem as though we're celebrating another year of war?"

"August then," Griffin put in. "How about the Bank Holiday weekend? I think the Saturday is the fifth?"

Elise flipped forward to the correct page. "Yes, it is," she said. "Are we agreed?" Everyone murmured their agreement and she scribbled a note on the page.

"We can meet again tomorrow evening to start discussing the details," Griffin suggested.

"I can't make tomorrow," Charlotte said.

"Well, I'm sure Elise will be able to fill you in," Griffin replied.

"Or we could just meet another time? I'm available after the weekend." Charlotte offered.

"I think we should get started as soon as possible, don't you?" Griffin ignored Charlotte and addressed himself to Elise.

"I… I suppose we should, yes."

"I'll pop round tomorrow then, shall I?" Elise nodded, closing her diary. "I'd better get back to work," Griffin added, glancing at his watch. "I've been out for nearly an hour already."

Elise went to get up, but Griffin forestalled her, taking her hand and patting it gently. Harry watched the intimate gesture and sat down in the chair, facing away from the window. It was bad enough hearing the man fawn over Elise, he couldn't bear to watch it as well. "Don't worry, my dear," Griffin said. "I can find my own way out." Harry heard him saying goodbye to Charlotte, then his fading footsteps as he went around the side of the house and out through the garden gate.

"I'm so sorry," Elise said, once he'd gone. "I've got a dreadful headache coming on, Charlotte. Would you mind if I went upstairs?"

"Of course not. I'll show myself out."

Elise got up and went in through the French doors. She didn't notice Harry sitting in the high-backed chair and he didn't make his presence known to her.

Charlotte rose and followed Elise. As she went in through the door, Harry got up.

"Oh!" Charlotte said. "I didn't see you sitting there."

Charlotte sighed and noticed the look in Harry's eyes. They'd known each other for more years than she cared to remember and, while he was really William's friend, she felt he needed someone to talk to. She walked further into the room and sat down on the sofa, waiting for him to decide what to do. He turned and resumed his seat.

"Do you know?" Harry said suddenly. "I have his enormous temptation to..."

"Yes? What's that?"

"I've got this desire... this great wish... to go upstairs, delve to the back of my wardrobe, find my old service revolver, load it with bullets, go round to that bastard's office and blow his damned brains out." He looked up. "I apologise for my language," he said.

"I completely understand the sentiment," Charlotte said, ignoring his last remark. "But men like him really aren't worth it. He isn't really a threat—"

"You know he kissed her?"

"What?"

Harry couldn't believe he'd said the words out loud. Saying them a second time wasn't so difficult. "He kissed her."

"When...? I mean... What...? When?"

"It was a couple of weeks ago now. The day Elise got word of Sylvia and Linda's deaths. She was upset. I was down in the studio. I'd like to think she turned to him for comfort. I'd like to think it was because she was so upset, she just needed someone to lean on and I wasn't there. I'd like to think he took advantage of the situation. I'd like to think she didn't return the kiss, but from where I was standing, it was hard to tell... I don't know. I'll never know." Charlotte heard the hurt in his voice.

"Oh, Harry," she said. "I'm sure she didn't kiss him back... She loves you."

"Does she?" He looked up. "Then why can't she see him for what he is? I can. You can. But she keeps going along with everything he wants. It's like he holds her under some kind of spell." He could feel himself becoming angry. "I'm sorry." He took a deep breath. "This isn't your problem."

"Have you spoken to her?"

"No. We haven't spoken much at all recently. She's been tired and she keeps getting these headaches. I'm worried about her and, to be honest, I don't want to know the truth. I'm not sure I could cope with it. Not right now."

"Does she know that you saw what happened?"

"I don't know. I imagine she thinks I'd just arrived at that moment, not that I'd been standing there for ages, watching him with his hands and his lips all over my wife."

"Then talk to her, Harry. If you don't it will tear you apart, and I don't mean just you, I mean *both* of you."

Harry looked across at her, saw the sorrow in her eyes and knew she was right. He was falling to pieces himself. He knew the signs of his own darkness, but he also knew that, if he didn't find out the truth, whatever pieces were left of him would soon start drifting away from Elise, and then he'd never be able to find a way back.

Elise came downstairs before dinner. "Are you feeling any better?" Harry asked, looking up from the sofa, where he was reading the newspaper.

"Yes, much," she said, kissing the top of his head. "I think I had too much sun. I'm sorry I've been such a bore lately."

"You haven't."

She sat down next to him, taking his hand. "I hadn't anticipated organising anything else so soon, but I'm not going to let this get on top of me. I'm going to do everything I can to spend as much time with you as possible." She leant across and rested her head on his chest. He put his arm around her. He'd missed her but he'd found it impossible to make love to her since seeing her with Griffin and, because she'd been so tired, she'd not really seemed to notice. He longed to touch her and to feel her touch, but he needed to know the truth.

"Elise..." He couldn't disguise the emotion in his voice.

She raised her head, looking at him. "What is it?" she asked.

"We need..." The ringing of the telephone interrupted him. She clambered to her feet and went to the sideboard, where she picked up the receiver.

"Oh, hello, Rose," she said. Harry glanced over his shoulder, hoping nothing else had gone wrong. "Yes," Elise continued. "Wait a minute." She spoke to Harry. "Come here, Harry," she said. "Rose has something she wants to tell us both." Harry got to his feet and went to stand next to her, feeling the heat of her body close to his. "We're both here now," Elise spoke into the receiver again.

"Can you both hear me?" Rose's voice was audible to them both, but Harry's head was filled with Elise.

Unable to speak clearly, Harry nodded and Elise said, "Yes."

"I wanted to tell you both together... You're going to be grandparents."

"Oh, that's wonderful news!" Elise said.

"Congratulations, darling." Harry came back to his senses and raised his voice, so Rose would be able to hear him. "I'm so pleased for you... for you both."

"When is the baby due?" Elise asked.

"The middle of November, Matthew says. He's been wonderful."

Harry moved away slightly. He could still just about make out what Rose was saying but feeling Elise so close was becoming tortuous. The two women discussed morning sickness, and strange cravings for food and arranged that Rose and Matthew would visit as soon as possible.

"Isn't that wonderful," Elise said, when she finally put down the receiver. "They've waited so long. I'm delighted."

"So am I."

"Hmm. I'm not sure I'm ready to be called granny, though. You, on the other hand, you make perfect granddad material." She sat next to him and ran her finger down his cheek.

"Yes, I'm sure I do."

"What's wrong?" she asked.

"Nothing. Everything's fine." He kissed her forehead lightly. "It's time for dinner."

As they sat in the dining room, neither of them really eating much, the irony wasn't lost on Harry that, having nagged at Rose and Matthew that they needed to communicate better to make their marriage work, he was failing dismally himself to do just that.

That night, when they went to bed, Harry went through the bathroom first, then lay in bed and watched Elise undress, the day's events and Charlotte's words echoing around his head. The idea of becoming a grandfather had never bothered him before, but now it made him feel older than his years, reminding him of Elise's comparative youth. He knew he should talk to Elise about his worries, but the thought of rejection was almost more than he could take at the moment. Having taken off her dress, Elise sat on the edge of the bed.

"How can getting ready for bed be so exhausting?" she asked, her shoulders hunched over. "I feel like I've got no energy left at all."

"You're overdoing it," Harry said, getting out of bed. "Let me help." He limped around to her side of the bed and removed her underwear, then pulled back the covers and helped her into bed. She glanced up at him.

"I'm sorry," she muttered. "This probably isn't what you had in mind when you were helping me off with my clothes, but I'm so tired, I could sleep for a week."

"Don't worry about it." He turned out the bedside lamp and kissed her gently on the forehead.

"I wish my head didn't hurt so much, but I'm sure it will feel better in the morning."

Harry turned out his own lamp, then pulled back the curtains and the blackout and opened the window. "Some fresh air might help," he said quietly, then realised that her breathing had already changed and she was fast asleep.

The next evening, Elise went to bed before dinner, having her meal served on a tray, although she didn't eat very much. Harry went and sat with her, reading to her for a while, although she was tired and still suffering from a headache. "If you're no better after the weekend, I'm calling the doctor out," Harry said.

"I don't need to see a doctor. I'm just tired."

"And feeling sick, with a fairly permanent headache." Harry had wondered whether the headache was an excuse not to make love, until she'd complained of feeling sick as well. He couldn't even remember the last time Elise had been ill and was starting to worry about her, as if he didn't already have enough to think about.

She went off to sleep by nine o'clock, just before Polly knocked quietly on the door and informed him that Mr Griffin was downstairs in the sitting room. Harry had forgotten that the man was going to call.

On entering the room, he found Griffin seated in one of the armchairs, looking very at home, which merely got Harry's back up even more than it already was.

Griffin stood as Harry entered. "I was expecting Elise," he said.

"She's unwell," Harry replied, his voice a monotone.

"Perhaps I can rearrange the meeting for another evening, then."

Harry stared at Griffin, surprised by his lack of concern. "I don't think that will be possible," he said. "I suggest you liaise with Charlotte King for the time being. My wife is going to have to take a back seat for a while as far as the committee is concerned."

Griffin picked up his briefcase. "I'm sorry to hear that," he said, crossing the room. "Send her my regards." He passed Harry on his way out, not bothering to say goodbye. The exchange seemed most peculiar to Harry, who'd expected the man who'd been pursuing his wife for so many months to at least feign an interest in her well-being.

Now, he really wondered what was going on.

Chapter Eighteen

Late Spring 1944

"We're leaving tomorrow," David said quietly. Amy was standing outside the farmhouse, looking up at the stars and thinking of Ed.

She turned to face him, but didn't reply.

"Walk with me," he said, leading her away from the building. Once they were far enough away, he started to speak again. "There's one thing we haven't really covered," he said. "I need to tell you about our travelling arrangements, and our… erm… relationship on the journey." He patted his trouser pocket and wondered how she was going to react to his plan.

She looked up at him. The moon was bright and she could see a worried expression on his face. "Okay," she said, sounding dubious.

"As you know, my cover name is Patrice… Patrice Thibault. I am a doctor and I live in Paris, just a few streets away from you… and… we're engaged. We have been for three months." He reached into his pocket and brought out a ring, which he handed to her. She took it. Even in the moonlight, she could see it was beautiful. A small ruby set on a gold band, with tiny diamonds surrounding it, to form an oval. She stared up at him again. "Put it on," he said. She hesitated. "Put it on," he repeated slowly. It fitted perfectly. She looked up at him quizzically and he smiled. "Remember? I know everything about you."

She stared down at her finger for a few moments before returning her gaze to his. She couldn't fail to hear him suck in a breath. "I need an excuse to be travelling with you," he continued eventually. "So, we've been down in Agen, visiting your dying mother, and now we are returning to Paris because I have to get back to work."

He stared at her for ages, trying to read her thoughts. Eventually she spoke. "Couldn't we just be travelling as friends?" she asked. "This all seems very elaborate."

"It has to be elaborate. I weighed up all the options. We needed a reason for you being in Agen and travelling back to Paris. Visiting a sick relative is always a good one… we use it quite often. But I didn't want you to travel all the way to Paris alone, so this gives me an excuse to travel with you. Would a friend really come with you to visit your mother? It doesn't seem very plausible to me, but a fiancé might." She still looked concerned. "Trust me… I've done this before, Amy."

"What? Been engaged."

He laughed out loud. "No. What I mean is, I'm used to working out back stories and lying about who I am, when it's required."

"Oh." She wasn't sure how comfortable she felt with that, but he lifted her left hand and held it, looking down at the ring on her finger.

"I've never even thought about getting engaged before," he said. "There's a first time for everything, though. And who'd have thought it would be that easy?" He winked and smiled at her mischievously, and she couldn't help but smile back.

Having travelled up from the south, they'd left Poitiers station about half an hour earlier and, with the compartment now to themselves, David finally felt he could speak freely. He was surprised to find the train so empty on a Friday but was grateful for the solitude. They'd both taken off their jackets and he was wearing shirt-sleeves and dark green corduroy trousers. Amy had on a white short-sleeved blouse and a flared floral skirt, both of which were French. They fitted perfectly and she loved the feel of the fine cloth against her skin. They were sitting side by side, Amy in the window seat, staring out at the passing countryside.

"You haven't been able to think of a single question, then?" he asked.

"Not really. I decided if there was anything else to tell me, you would – other than the bombshell that I accepted your proposal, obviously. Where did you propose, by the way? Just in case someone asks…"

"It's unlikely that they will, but where would you have liked it to be? You can make that bit up, if you prefer."

Amy stared at her hands, twisting the ring and feeling self-conscious. "Oh, I don't know. I assumed you'd have thought of that."

"Well, let's say I took you out for a romantic dinner and got down on one knee. How does that sound?"

"A little dull, if you ask me."

"Thanks. I was doing my best. You didn't give me any time to prepare. Let's see if you can do any better..." He nudged into her and she looked up at him.

"I've always thought outdoors somewhere." She turned and looked out of the window at the passing green countryside. "There's a tree, near where I live..." she murmured.

"Sorry, I didn't catch that?"

"Nothing. It doesn't matter." She shook her head and turned back to him. "We'll go with the romantic dinner. That's probably for the best." He sensed her disappointment and took her hand.

"I'm sorry," he whispered. She didn't need to ask what for.

They sat quietly for a while, neither speaking, and he kept hold of her hand, resting it in his lap. After a while, she closed her eyes, although he knew she wasn't asleep. He looked across at her. She seemed very calm and he hoped it wasn't a façade. He hadn't been lying when he'd told her this was a dangerous mission, and he'd spent weeks trying to find an alternative to using her, without any success. He knew if he failed, they'd probably both be dead within the next few days. After a while, she opened her eyes and sat up suddenly, although she didn't pull her hand away from his and he found that surprisingly comforting.

"There is one thing I've just thought of..." She turned to face him. "I forgot to ask, when we get to Paris..."

The compartment door opened suddenly and David held his breath. Standing in the doorway was a tall man, wearing the black uniform of an SS-Standartenführer. He looked down at the two of them, and stepped over the threshold. The atmosphere turned to ice and David thought quickly, and turned towards Amy, his back to the

SS man, rubbing the backs of her fingers with his thumb and looking into her eyes.

"It's understandable that you wanted to stay, my love," he said quickly, and in perfect French. "But your mother is on the mend now, really she is. I spoke to the doctors before we left and they have every confidence she'll pull through. And I do have to get back to work." He stared deeply into her eyes, willing her to understand. She took but the blink of an eye to comprehend.

"I know," he caught the hitch in her voice and smiled inwardly. She was good... she was very good. "But I hated leaving her alone. Now my father's gone, there's no-one else to care for her." Were those actual tears in her eyes? He thought they might be. The Standartenführer sat down opposite Amy.

"Come here," he said, pulling her closer and hugging her to him. She nestled into his arms, resting her head on his chest. "We'll be home soon and you can rest. And you can phone the hospital in the morning to check on her." She placed her hand on his leg and fiddled with her engagement ring. That was a nice move, he thought. He kissed the top of her head and rubbed his hand down her spine, feeling her involuntary shudder. He couldn't afford to look, but he could feel the officer watching her, his eyes taking her in. He couldn't be certain whether the man was suspicious, or appreciative and he couldn't take the chance on finding out. He'd have to up the ante, just in case it was suspicion filling the officer's mind. "It's such a shame I have to go to work tomorrow," he said, his voice suggestive, as he moved her hair to one side and nibbled her earlobe.

"Do you really have to?" she asked, slightly breathy and entreating.

"I'm afraid so. I pushed my luck to get these few days off." He smiled into her hair. He knew she'd be good, but he'd really had no idea...

"What time will we get back to Paris, do you think?" she continued.

"About nine o'clock. Then I'll take you home... Unfortunately..." He kissed her neck, gently nipping the skin with his teeth.

She looked up at him. "You could..." she whispered, her voice almost silent, merely mouthing the words.

"Stay?" he mouthed back, grinning and raising an eyebrow. She lowered her head again, as though embarrassed, but he placed a finger under her chin, lifting her face to his. "Are you sure?" he asked, looking deeply into her eyes.

"I don't want to be alone," she murmured. "Not after the last few days." He leaned lower and saw her eyes flicker away from his. *Don't stop now*, he thought. *You're doing so well. He thinks we're young, desperate lovers… Just hang on a little longer. Please.* He kissed her gently.

"Then I'll stay," he whispered, and she smiled. He opened his mouth and claimed hers. He longed to delve into her and discover her with his tongue, but that wasn't necessary for the show they were putting on and he didn't know how she might react. He ground his lips onto hers and she responded, lifting her arms around his neck and running her fingers through his hair, fisting it hard as his breathing became more ragged. He grabbed her hips, reaching around beneath her and, before she knew what was happening, she was on his lap, astride him, his hands caressing her buttocks. He felt her tense as she realised his arousal, but her fingers kept working through his hair, while she moaned softly into his mouth.

They both heard the door slide open and click shut and they stilled. For a couple of seconds, his lips remained on hers, her fingers stayed tight in his hair. Once it became clear the officer wasn't coming back, she pulled away and he lifted her to her feet. She straightened her clothes, keeping her head low, not wanting to make eye contact with him.

"I just hope he hasn't gone to fetch his friends to come and watch the show," David said, smiling, desperate to lighten the mood. "They'll be disappointed that it's over so quickly, and my reputation will be shot to pieces forever." He tucked his shirt back into his trousers. Until that moment, he hadn't even realised that he'd pulled it out. Or maybe she had. He hoped it was her. "I was beginning to wonder if we were doing too good a job of that and he was going to stay until the end." He looked up at her. She was standing, twisting her fingers and staring out of the window. "Sit down," he said. She didn't move, so he leaned forward, grabbed her hands and pulled her down next to him, his arm wrapped around her. She continued to stare out of the window, her bottom lip trembling. "You were amazing," he whispered.

"Don't," she said.

"I'm not talking about that," he said. Although she had been absolutely amazing and had felt incredible beyond even his wildest imaginings, he didn't think that was what she wanted to hear. "I'm talking about the way you handled it. Those were real tears in your eyes, when you were talking about our visit to your mother. You played your part brilliantly." She kept her fingers entwined, gazing at the passing countryside. "Look at me," he said. She didn't move. He placed a finger under her chin and turned her face to his. The anguish he saw there caught in his throat. Her eyes were glistening and she looked so helpless. "I've been doing this for a long time, Amy," he said gently. "And that was one of the best performances I've ever seen."

"Behaving like a slut, you mean?" she said, her voice suddenly harsh.

"No," he said calmly. "Picking up the story from just a simple lead, running with it, making him believe in us, and then taking it to the next level with me, so he'd either have to stop us, stay and feel embarrassed, or leave. It was a gamble and it worked."

"Why gamble at all though? Couldn't we just have sat here? What did it matter if we had to share the compartment with a Nazi?"

"Because I knew I had to get rid of him. He was being a little too attentive to you and while I'm almost sure it was because he was attracted to you, I couldn't take the chance of being wrong." He paused for just a moment. "I've got several hundred bank notes tucked away in my case, Amy. If he'd decided he needed to search our belongings a little over zealously for some reason, I might have been arrested... And so might you. That's not a risk I'm prepared to take. We trained you for this... and I knew you'd be good at it. But you were better than good." She looked him in the eyes, the tears welling over and onto her cheeks. "And don't you ever call yourself a slut again, do you hear me?" he added, wiping them away with the back of his finger.

"What should I call myself then? I can't believe I did that. What would he have said?"

"I presume this is Ed we're talking about?" She nodded. "If it saves your life, Amy, I imagine he'd tell you to do whatever you have to do."

"How could I do that, though? I've never… I mean… There's only been Ed."

"And there still has, hasn't there? That wasn't much more than a kiss, not really. Okay, it was a pretty amazing, incredibly sexy kiss." He grinned at her, longing to see her smile. She didn't. "But it was, really, just a kiss."

"But you were…" She glanced down at his groin, reddening.

"Oh… I see." He raised her face to his again. "That."

"Yes… That."

"I couldn't help it," he said. "It was a natural reaction, way beyond my control. As I said… It was a very sexy kiss. And I'm only human."

"But…"

"No more buts, Amy. You haven't done anything wrong."

"And what if the German hadn't left? What if he'd decided to stay and… feel embarrassed?"

"Well, I wasn't about to have sex on a train with an audience," David said. "Even I have limits to what I'll do for the job… Now, stop this and just accept that we did a good job, and that you… you were just spectacular." He took her hand in his and kissed her knuckles, smiling up at her and she wished, she really wished, she could smile back.

She woke late the next morning, exhausted. Her dreams had been disturbing, filled with images of Ed, reaching out to her, and when she'd taken his hand, her heart full of love and hope, she'd found herself looking up at David. She'd woken several times, hot and dishevelled, breathless and tense, knowing that their kiss was bothering her. They'd been playing parts, she knew that. His arousal made it clear that she'd had an effect on him and, as much as she might like to deny it, she was flattered by that knowledge. Now, as dawn broke over the Parisian skyline, she was glad Ed wasn't alive to see what she'd become. However much David might like to pretend otherwise, she still felt cheapened by the whole thing… She still felt like a slut.

There was a quiet knock on the door and she sat up just as it opened. "You're awake then?" David asked. He was showered, dressed and clean shaven, his hair still slightly damp and dishevelled. He came into the room, but didn't close the door and stood to one side, leaning against the wall, his arms folded across his chest. "You don't need to hurry to get up yet," he said. "We're not seeing Claudette until this evening, but I've got someone else I need to meet up with first."

"Paul?"

"No. I'm saving him for this evening." She noticed a shadow cross his eyes, but thought nothing of it. She knew he was worried about the mission. "I'll be off soon. There's food in the kitchen. Just don't go out, okay? I'll be back sometime around four. I'll let myself in, so don't open the door to anyone." She nodded. He turned and left, closing the door softly behind him.

With the apartment to herself, she got out of bed, went to the kitchen and made some coffee, then sat in the small living room and looked around. The furniture was simple and basic, but comfortable. There was a fireplace with a small mirror above it, and a picture of a French country scene on the wall opposite her bedroom door. David had slept on the tiny sofa and she assumed he must have spent a very uncomfortable night, squeezing his large frame onto its small length. Still, he had offered.

After she'd showered and dressed, she ate a croissant and settled down to read one of the books which she found on the shelf. They were all in French, but she managed and was soon lost in the tale of a beautiful young aristocrat, her broken heart and the loss of her family's wealth to an old enemy.

"Wake up, sleepy head." The familiar voice brought her back to reality. She'd been wandering a field of cornflowers and poppies, with Ed holding her hand, under a clear blue sky. This time, in her dream, it had just been the two of them. She opened her eyes, reluctantly and found David looking down at her. "You must have been tired," he said. "You didn't even hear me come in."

"What time is it?"

"It's half past five. We've got to go out soon, so I had to wake you."

"What have you been doing?" she asked, stretching.

"For the last hour? Watching you sleep, and reading… but mainly watching you sleep."

"Should I change?"

"No. We're meeting them in a bar not far from here. You'll be fine as you are." She was wearing a cream coloured dress with short sleeves and buttons down the front, nipped in at the waist, with a narrow black belt. She looked down at her hand.

"Should I give you this back?" she asked.

"Yes," he said, taking the ring from her and putting it in his pocket. "I don't want Claudette to think there's another man in your life." Amy looked confused. "Well, she'd know I wouldn't bring my own fiancée out here, and I want her to think we're both free and single."

"Does that matter then?"

"Probably." He hesitated and saw the confused look deepen on her face. "In your tests, you showed really good adaptability… which you demonstrated to great effect on the train." He ignored the reddening of her cheeks. "I have no idea how Claudette will respond to seeing me: we haven't met since I sent her over here and, when I was briefing her to come and work with Paul, she made it very clear she was still interested in me." It was his turn to redden as he remembered the encounter. It was the only time, to his knowledge, that an agent had arrived to a briefing wearing a raincoat, high heels and absolutely nothing else. "As for meeting you… seeing another female agent with me… Well, anything might happen. I want to let her believe we're together. Not on a long-term basis, that wouldn't work, but she might believe in us as opportunistic lovers, snatching a couple of days together. I want to see what she does. She might want to scratch your eyes out, or she might want to get to know you better, to find out what your secret is… how you've succeeded where she failed. I'm hoping for the latter, obviously."

"And when were you going to tell me about this new relationship of ours?"

"I'm telling you now. It's no different to yesterday, really – nothing's changed, except we're not engaged any more." He smiled at her, trying to lighten the moment.

"Well, I don't think I like the idea of being a promiscuous lover. It makes me feel like even more of a sl—"

"Don't say it," he warned, an icy edge to his voice. "I told you not to use that word about yourself. None of this is real, Amy. Remember that."

Amy stared down at her now empty ring finger. "I don't want to get caught out. Is there anything else I should know about you and her before I meet her? Did you and she ever actually…?"

"No, we didn't. I've told you everything you need to know." He sat down beside her and took her hand. "If you want me to be honest, I wish we didn't have to go with this story. It doesn't make me feel too good about myself either. It makes me feel like something of a lothario, and that doesn't sit comfortably, especially around you. Still, look on the bright side, she might have come to her senses and realised she hates the very sight of me, in which case, we won't need to use that story, and you can just try and make friends with her, as one female agent to another. Talk about make-up, or hair styles, clothes, the theory of relativity, or something. I don't know… whatever it takes to get on friendly terms with her for a few days, just to see if we can find out what's going on in this bloody cell. It's important, Amy. Take your lead from her. Okay?"

"I hope I don't let you down."

"I know you won't."

They walked along the street hand-in-hand. "There's one other thing," he said. "There will be Germans in this bar."

"Well, I had assumed that," she replied.

"Just be on your guard," he said. "Be prepared for everything."

"That's very mysterious."

"It's meant to be. Remember, Amy… I'm taking you into hell… Here we are."

He pushed open the glass door and they entered the smokey room, filled with tables and people, either standing or sitting. The bar was busy, but then it was Saturday night, and Amy assumed that, war or no war, some things never changed. Amy noticed a couple of scantily dressed women, sitting on the knees of German officers, but she kept her eyes on the back of David's head as he led her through towards the back of the bar area, his eyes alert, scanning the room. Eventually, he saw who he was searching for and they made for a table in the rear corner. There was a woman sitting on her own and Amy wondered if something had gone wrong. They were supposed to be meeting Paul as well. She suddenly felt nervous, but David led her towards the woman, who Amy noticed was utterly stunning. She had ash-blonde hair, which was long and wavy, shining even in the low light of the bar. Her lips were full, painted red and, what could only be described as pouting and, as she looked up and saw David, they parted slightly, her deep blue eyes glowing, her hunger all too obvious. When she stood, and revealed the most perfect body Amy had ever seen, clad in a thin yellow sweater and a black skirt, both of which were moulded to her, she recalled David's story of this woman in his bed and was surprised he'd refused her invitation. She was surprised any man would do so.

"Claudette," David said. His voice was flat, far removed from the humorous tone she'd become accustomed to in their own conversations. "Where's Paul?"

"At the bar." She nodded towards a man who stood with his back to them. Amy turned and looked. He was tall and broad shouldered, with dark hair that grazed his collar. "He's getting some drinks." She looked at Amy.

"This is Yvette," David said.

"Hello." Amy held out her hand and Claudette took it. Her skin was as soft as silk and, as she shook Amy's hand, her eyes widened and locked with the younger girl's, and her lips parted slightly. Amy suddenly felt very uncomfortable and vulnerable, as though she was being visually consumed by this lioness.

"And who's this, then?" The deep male voice behind her made her drop Claudette's hand and turn and, as she did, she froze. She was filled with confusion. Her pulse was racing and she could hear the blood rushing through her ears. What was going on? This man wasn't called Paul. She knew this man; she knew him well. She was looking up into the face of her cousin, Luc.

The first half an hour was the hardest, although Amy was fairly certain she'd managed to keep her expression neutral, despite the pounding of her heart. She must have succeeded because Luc had ignored her after their initial introduction, evidently far more interested in speaking with David and, when they sat down, had twisted his chair around and turned his back towards her. David sat off to her left, facing her and, although she tried desperately to make eye contact with him, he seemed hell-bent on avoiding her gaze and talked exclusively to Luc. She couldn't hear what they were saying, their voices barely more than a whisper. Claudette, on the other hand, who was sitting opposite her, didn't seem to be in the mood for conversation. She was staring at David, her eyes alight. Amy was wondering what she was supposed to do, when she felt the other woman lean across to her.

"So, what's he like?" she asked. Her French was immaculate, so immaculate that Amy had to remind herself that this woman was actually English.

"Sorry?" Amy replied.

"I asked, what's he like?"

"Who?"

"David."

"You mean Patrice."

"Have it your own way." Claudette stared at her until Amy felt her mouth go dry. "So?"

"I'm not sure..."

"In bed."

"What makes you think I've been in his bed? You know the rules." Amy looked down at her hands, which she had clasped on the table so they didn't shake.

"Yes, I know them. He quoted them at me often enough. But maybe they don't apply to all of us." Claudette stared directly at Amy, who became aware of another pair of eyes on her. She looked over and saw David glance at her, noticing the reassuring nod of his head, as he looked away again and continued his conversation. Had she imagined that? It was so quick, she wasn't sure she'd even seen it. "Go on. You can tell me..." Claudette urged.

Amy dipped her head, just for a moment or two, then looked up at Claudette again, allowing a slight smile to form on her lips. "How can I?" she whispered, nodding towards David, who was still deep in conversation with Luc. She hoped this was what David had in mind. Claudette ran her tongue along her bottom lip, shifting forward in her chair.

"I knew it," she said. "Tell me… He won't be able to hear."

"No. I can't." She thought quickly. "Not here. Not now."

Claudette's impatient sigh was so loud, she knew David would have heard it. "Meet me tomorrow then," Claudette said.

Amy hesitated for what she felt was the right amount of time. "Where?" she asked.

"There's a café, on the Rue de Rocher. Meet me there at eight. Tell him we're having a girls' night out by ourselves." She raked her eyes slowly over Amy. "I'm sure he can spare you for one evening."

Just as Amy nodded her head, David stood and shook Luc by the hand. They said their goodbyes, but Luc was more interested in Claudette than in Amy and, merely said good evening to her, with a slight inclination of his head, before grabbing Claudette around the waist and dragging her towards the bar.

Outside in the street, David walked quickly, and Amy struggled to keep pace.

"We need to talk," she whispered.

"Not now," he said between gritted teeth and Amy wondered what she'd done wrong. She was sure he'd nodded to her; certain that he'd meant her to pretend they were lovers. What was wrong, then? "Take my hand," he whispered. She placed her hand in his and felt his thumb rubbing along her knuckles. Maybe things were okay after all… "I'm really sorry I have to do this," he said quietly. "Please, just go along with me." And with that, he glanced to his left, and then pulled her with him, into a darkened shop entrance, where he pushed her back against the panels of the shuttered door. She felt his lips on hers, hard and longing, and his hands on her body, seemingly everywhere. He reached down, and behind her, pulling her close. Then he moved, just slightly, his mouth next to her ear as he nuzzled into her. "I'm going to pull away," he whispered. "Pull me back, kiss me, and then I'm going to drag you back to the flat, as though I can't wait to get you into bed. Got it?" She nodded her head almost imperceptibly. He leant back, staring down at her. There was such an intensity in his eyes and she placed her hands behind his head, dragging him down and kissing him, entwining her fingers in his hair. She heard the groan deep in his throat, and wondered for a moment if that was really a necessary part of the act. Then, he stopped, stepped back and said a little louder, "Now. I want you, right now. I can't wait any longer." And he pulled her away from the wall, and back onto the street. They took just a few minutes to reach the flat and ran up the stairs, frantically, like desperate lovers. Surely they could stop now, she wondered. He opened the door to the apartment and, as he pushed her inside, she looked back and saw that he'd already pulled his shirt over his head and was undoing the buttons on his trousers. "I want you naked in the next twenty seconds..." he said loudly as he closed the door, breathing heavily.

"Are you alright?" he whispered, his voice returning to normal. She nodded. He did up his trousers and pulled his shirt back on, but didn't tuck it in.

"I assume she followed us?"

"Yes... She came out of the bar just a few moments after us, I saw her reflection in the shop windows. I figured if we're meant to be lovers, we'd hardly walk back chatting casually. But then, as we came inside the building here, I realised she was still with us. She was right behind us, on the stairwell, hence my little display outside the door. Sorry about that... about what I did and about what I said out there, but I wanted to give her something to think about, being as you've arranged to meet her tomorrow, to dish the dirt on what I'm like in bed."

"How did you know that?"

"It's a skill... I can have one conversation, while listening to another."

"Did I do the right thing, arranging to meet her again?"

"Of course. That was the whole point, wasn't it? For you to get friendly with her... and what better way than for you to discuss our torrid sex life?" They moved further into the flat, their breathing now calmed. "Coffee?" he offered, but she shook her head. "I hope I wasn't too rough with you back there," he said. "Stay away from the windows, by the way," he added, as she started to wander around the room. "Remember, we're supposed to be rolling around naked at this point. If she's out there watching, it wouldn't do for her to see you fully clothed and looking wistfully down onto the street." Amy moved back and sat on the sofa.

"I'm not being rude," she said, "but why is she so fascinated by you? I mean, the woman seems to be obsessed."

"Aren't my charms obvious?" he said, looking down at himself and grinning. Amy rolled her eyes. "No. I think – and this is only my theory – but I think, from what I've heard, that I'm the only man who's ever said 'no' to her, which makes me a challenge. And Claudette liked a challenge. Whatever task we set her, she had to come top; she was the most competitive person we ever had on the programme."

"And that's it?" He looked at her, raising an eyebrow.

"That's enough for some people. They become obsessed with the one thing they can't have." Amy nodded slowly and he stood in the kitchen doorway, watching her, waiting... She was mulling things over in her mind. "I'm sorry," he said quietly.

"What for?" She didn't look up at him.

"I know that must have made you feel uncomfortable."

"I suppose it was necessary."

"Well, not necessary, perhaps." Her head shot up. "Don't get angry," he warned. "It wasn't absolutely necessary, but I think it will prove useful. We need her to believe in us, Amy, and I don't think she had, otherwise she wouldn't have followed us."

Amy looked down at her fingers, twisting in her lap. "Well, judging by the way she was looking me up and down, I think she was having a hard time believing you'd choose me over her. Actually, I think most people would have a hard time with that one."

He moved across the room and sat down next to her. "Look at me," he said. She turned her face towards him. The aching sadness was still there in her eyes and he longed to help her see beyond her memories.

"Given the opportunity, if you'd let me, I would choose you over any woman... every time. Every. Single. Time. No hesitation." He saw the colour rise in her cheeks. "Now," he said, "you've had a tiring evening. I suggest you get some sleep." She got to her feet, feeling suddenly exhausted, and crossed to the bedroom. She'd just reached the door, when she remembered.

"Luc!" she cried, turning sharply and David's blood ran cold, his palms dampened and his tongue turned to dust. She came back towards him, sitting down again. "That man... Paul," she said. "His name isn't Paul. He's my cousin, Luc."

How could he tell her? What could he say? The truth was probably a good place to start...

"I know," he said, softly.

She shot to her feet.

"You know?" He got up, standing in front of her and looking down into her now confused eyes. He nodded.

"Just don't hate me," he said.

"You know?" she repeated. Then she shook her head. "I don't understand," her voice was a pitiful whisper. *Oh God,* he thought, *what have I done to you?*

"Sit down," he said.

"No." He moved a little closer to her.

"I know that Paul is Luc. I knew that before we came here. I knew that when I recruited you." Her mouth fell open and the look of confusion deepened. "That's why it had to be you," he said. "That's why I worked so hard with you, because you *had* to come here with me."

"But..." She didn't know how to form the multitude of questions.

"Sit down and let me explain," he said.

"I don't want to sit down." He found the hardness in her voice hurt far more than he'd expected.

He took a deep breath. "I'm going to tell you everything," he said. "Paul... or Luc, has been working with us for years. He's a remarkable man, ruthless, and deadly with both knife and gun. He's run this cell for nearly a year now, very successfully. Claudette arrived eight months ago and, although I hate to say it, in certain respects they've made an amazing team. When we discovered the mole, I contacted him and he thought he'd found the culprit quite quickly – a young man from Southern Paris. Paul… Luc, that is, executed him himself." He heard her intake of breath. "I told you he was ruthless. But, it seems he was wrong, because our information was still getting back to the Nazis. He continued to investigate but found nothing, so that's when we started looking at Claudette. The trouble only started a few weeks after she got here. I didn't tell Luc about that because I thought there was every chance they'd become lovers, knowing Claudette's track record, and I wasn't sure he'd be able to be impartial. I sent my agent out late last year. He only sent back one report before he was killed and he confirmed Luc and Claudette were lovers, so we formulated our plans with that in mind, and kept Luc in the dark from then on. It was only when we were going through the files on the members of the cell that we remembered Luc's family and found you…" He looked at her closely. Her face was expressionless. "I came to see you. We hadn't decided anything at that stage, but once I'd met you… once I'd spoken to you… well, I thought it might work." He turned and walked towards the kitchen, pacing the floor. "The plan was two-fold. Our first option was to use Claudette's attraction to me and make her jealous by having me come here with another female agent. Any reasonably attractive agent would have done for that part, but we couldn't be entirely certain how Claudette would react. She might not have cared about seeing me again, although I still thought that was our best shot; but she might have moved on, actually fallen in love with Luc… We had to have a secondary plan. And that was him and you."

"I don't understand."

"I was thinking that, if she was no longer attracted to me, and you couldn't use that to get close to her, then you'd have the family connection to Luc, and you'd be able to sow the seeds of doubt in his mind about Claudette, to make him question her actions and watch her more closely."

"But I'm not that intimate with Luc. I never was. Why would he believe me? He didn't even recognise me…"

"Yes, I noticed. I hadn't anticipated that."

"Then I suppose it's just as well that plan A worked, isn't it?" He couldn't miss the sarcasm in her voice.

"You're angry."

"Do you blame me? You used me and you lied to me."

"No. I just didn't tell you everything. I couldn't."

"Why?"

"Because that's how we operate."

"Then I don't think I like how you operate."

"I don't have the luxury of always being completely open."

She stared at him. "I'm going to bed," she said eventually. "I'm tired. We'll need to talk tomorrow." He looked across at her, his eyebrow raised. "Well, if I'm going to meet with this woman who's obsessed with the idea of being in your bed, and give her a description of your… abilities, then you'll have to tell me what to say. You can lie about that too, if you want… You lie about everything else it would seem—"

"I didn't lie," David said. "I left out bits of information, because I had to, but everything I've told you is the truth."

"That's just semantics… besides, it won't matter what you tell me about yourself; it's not like I'll ever be finding out the truth." She turned and stormed into the bedroom, slamming the door behind her.

He leant back against the wall, letting his head drop to his chest. He'd done some low things in his time, but he'd never hated himself quite as much as he did right at that moment.

Amy walked alone to the café. She was on time and didn't need to rush, but she still felt flushed, after spending the most embarrassing hour of her life, sitting at the kitchen table with David, while he described, in great detail, the sort of things he and she might do if they were in bed together. He told her that he was being creative, basing a lot of it on the performance he'd given the previous night outside the apartment door, and that making it up was easier than talking about reality. However, her comparative innocence with men made it harder for both of them. Claudette would expect her to be experienced, having embarked on a brief and casual affair with David, but in reality, she wasn't. Amy's lack of knowledge meant she couldn't just invent something herself and was relying on David to provide the right words, phrases and descriptions for her to use. It was deeply humiliating, but was made much worse as Amy was finding it hard to forget that he'd told her just the previous evening that, given the chance, he'd choose her over any other woman.

They went through several scenarios, and eventually they agreed that the best policy was for Amy to start off by being a little coy and then to build up the descriptions. The ultimate aim was to gain Claudette's trust, and hopefully arrange a second meeting at which Amy might be able to discuss something other than David.

When Amy arrived, she spotted Claudette immediately. She was wearing a very low-cut top, revealing full, rounded breasts and, as she stood, to greet Amy, she noticed that her skirt was so tight, she wondered how the other woman breathed, or walked, for that matter. Claudette ordered two coffees and leaned forward, eagerly. She clearly wasn't there to make polite conversation, but intended getting straight to the point.

"Where is he?" she asked, licking her lips.

"I've left him at the apartment."

"Good." Amy wasn't sure what that meant and remained silent. The waiter brought their coffees and Claudette took a sip before looking across to Amy.

"So… tell me more," she said.

"What do you want to know?" Amy asked.

"Everything. From what I saw and heard last night, he looks like he knows all the right buttons to press. Not that it surprises me."

"You followed us?" So David had been right about that at least.

Claudette nodded. "I wanted to make sure you were telling me the truth. He's tried fobbing me off before with fake lovers, but seeing you in that doorway… watching him with his hands all over you… I thought he was going to take you, there and then." She was breathing heavily. "I assume you got naked in twenty seconds for him? I mean, why wouldn't you? He was certainly keen; let's face it, he was pretty much undressed before he'd even closed the door…" She squirmed in her seat. "I always knew he was muscular, but that chest… My God…

What a chest." Claudette fanned her face and grinned. "I'd like to have a go at that with these." She held up her long, bright red fingernails and playfully ran them across the table. Amy planted a knowing smile on her lips. "Was it good?" Claudette asked, her eyes half closed.

"What? Oh… Good? No… it was… amazing." Amy dragged out the last word and allowed herself a loud sigh. "But then, it's always amazing."

Claudette's eyes closed slightly and Amy heard her exhale. She stayed that way for a moment, then seemed to shake herself awake again and looked at Amy, making her feel uncomfortable.

"Why you?" she asked at last.

"Sorry?" Amy said, taking a sip of her coffee.

"Well, I hate to point out the obvious, but I'm not sure you're exactly his type." Again, Claudette looked her up and down, taking in Amy's white blouse and blue skirt. Her skirt was tight, and she'd had to take small steps on her walk to the cafe, but it was nowhere near as clinging, or revealing as Claudette's outfit. Despite Claudette's unfavourable appraisal, Amy smiled inwardly, given David's responses to her and comments about his own preferences the previous evening. "You're very… quiet," Claudette continued.

"Didn't your mother tell you, you should always watch out for the quiet ones?" Amy felt pleased at her own response; one she hadn't practised with David.

Claudette finished her coffee, eyeing Amy over the brim. Then she replaced the cup in its saucer and looked out of the window. "At last…" she muttered and then Amy noticed her expression change very abruptly. "Would you excuse me, just for a minute. I'll be right back." She went to the front of the café and outside, where she crossed the street. Opposite and a little further down the road, Amy saw a man sheltering in a doorway. It was nearly dark now and she strained to see him until he stepped forward, and put his arms around Claudette, kissing her. It was Luc. They stepped away from each other, talking. Amy got up from the table and slowly walked to the door, opening it and passing outside into the shadows. She heard a slight laugh coming from Luc, a throaty sound which made her feel a little embarrassed. He leant down towards Claudette, whispering something and she giggled and pulled his lips to hers, kissing him ferociously, her hand moving down between them. Shocked, Amy stepped back inside the café and resumed her seat, waving to the waiter to bring her another coffee. She sat drinking it and watching the other customers, most of whom seemed to be French, much to her relief. She assumed that was why Claudette had chosen this venue. She didn't want to look outside again, in case she saw something she'd never be able to erase from her mind. She wondered why the scene outside had shocked her. After all, they hadn't been doing anything very different to what she and David had done the previous evening, except Luc and Claudette really were lovers, while she and David were just pretending. The waiter, an older man, probably in his mid-fifties, passed her table and smiled at her. She smiled back and ordered a third cup of coffee.

Eventually, Claudette reappeared, a little breathless, and resumed her seat.

"Do you want more coffee?" Amy asked, knowing she couldn't drink any more herself.

"No," Claudette said. "I was wondering… whether you'd like to come back to my apartment. We could open some wine, if you like, and talk some more? It's quieter there."

Amy felt the hairs on the back of her neck stand up. She had no idea why, but she felt suddenly wary, maybe even afraid.

"I haven't finished my coffee yet," she said, slowly taking another sip.

"Well drink up, and we can go and have some fun." The glazed expression on Claudette's face made Amy's mouth dry.

"What did you have in mind?" She was surprised how normal her voice sounded.

"Well, what do you think? I want details… I've always wondered how big he is… I'll bet he's huge, isn't he?" Amy smiled but said nothing. "Come on…" Claudette urged. Was this what David would want her to do? It must be, otherwise why had they had that embarrassing conversation in the kitchen earlier on… but at Claudette's apartment? He'd specifically told her to stay at the café…

She didn't know what to do, but her instincts were telling her this was a bad idea.

Amy took another sip, then checked her watch. "Gosh, I didn't realise it was so late," she said.

"I'm sure he can spare you for a little longer."

"No, he can't." The familiar voice behind her took her breath away and she was surprised by the sense of relief that flooded through her when she felt his firm, warm hand on her shoulder. Claudette looked up, clearly startled, but she recovered quickly.

"Patrice," she simpered. "We were just talking about you."

"I'm sure you were," he replied, his face blank. "And now, if you don't mind, Yvette and I have to go. We have plans." He looked down at Amy and smiled, a wicked, knowing grin, his eyes alight.

"But..." Claudette went to stand.

"No buts." He cut her off, pulling Amy to her feet and into a hug, his hand roaming down to gently squeeze her buttock. "Come on," he growled, his voice thick with desire. "I seem to remember you made certain promises before you left this evening and I've waited long enough to feel you underneath me again..." She looked up at him and smiled, rolling her eyes at Claudette, who scowled as David dragged Amy from the café.

"Walk very quickly," he whispered, "like you can't wait to get back to the apartment." The tone of his voice had altered completely. Gone was the playful lust, replaced by a strained urgency. Still, he grinned at her, as though nothing had changed, laughing and pulling her along, his eyes full of need, like his desire for her knew no bounds. He led her down the road to the junction and, as they rounded the corner, she heard the screeching of tyres behind them. He didn't hesitate, but with a firm grip on her hand, stepped out into the road. "Now... run!"

Chapter Nineteen

Late Spring 1944

On Friday evening, Charlotte and William came for dinner, bringing George with them. He was home for a couple of days' leave. Elise was feeling a little better and, after spending the afternoon resting in bed, managed to come downstairs just before their guests arrived. After dinner, while she and William were talking to George, Charlotte sat quietly with Harry on the window seat.

"Have you two managed to speak yet?" she asked.

"No," Harry replied.

"Oh." Harry could sense her disappointment, without her needing to express it.

"I have spoken to him, though."

"Really? What happened?"

"He came round on Wednesday evening, as expected, but Elise wasn't feeling very well. He was surprisingly unsympathetic. I told him that he'd have to leave and discuss committee matters with you for the time being. I hope you don't mind."

"Not in the least, but he hasn't been in touch. That seems a little odd, doesn't it?"

"Not really. Not if he was just using the committee as an excuse to see Elise. Take her out of the equation and he'd have no use for the committee anymore."

"I suppose so. But if he only came to the committee meetings to see Elise, why was he so uncaring about her being ill?" Charlotte paused for a moment. "You do need to speak to her, Harry... You need to tell her what you saw."

"Not at the moment, I don't. She's really not been at all well. I'm surprised she made it downstairs tonight."

"Is it still these headaches?"

"Yes, she has one most days, and she's feeling very sick a lot of the time."

"Has she seen the doctor?"

"She's refusing to at the moment, but I've said if she's still bad after the weekend, then I'm calling him out."

"Good. And then you need to talk."

"I've got something in mind for that... but I need George's help."

"Just ask him. He'll help if he can."

They were interrupted, much to Harry's relief, by the arrival of George. Charlotte moved away and sat down next to Elise.

"How are things going?" Harry asked.

"Alright, really," George replied, smiling. "I've got a feeling they'll be hotting up soon. All my hard work for the last year or so might actually be coming to something."

"Sounds interesting." Harry looked across at him. "Would you mind if I asked you a favour?"

"No. You know I'll do it if I can."

"I need to go into the town tomorrow afternoon and I could do with a lift. I don't want to be out for too long. Would you mind taking me?"

"No, of course not."

"I don't want to waste part of your precious leave, but there's something I need to do without having Elise with me."

"This all sounds very mysterious."

Harry and George had barely finished making their arrangements before Elise stood shakily and said, "Please, will you all excuse me. I'm feeling very tired. I think I'll go to bed."

"Do you want me to come up and help you?" Harry offered.

"No. You stay with our guests."

"We don't mind," Charlotte said, looking at Harry.

"No, I'm really fine by myself." Elise walked to the door and let herself out.

"She's terribly pale," Charlotte said once the door had closed.

"I know. She's so stubborn though."

"Maybe a restful weekend with no worrying will do her good."

"I hope so."

The following afternoon was warm for mid-May and, once Harry had finished his errand, he and George were walking past a row of empty shops, back towards where George had parked the car on the outskirts of the town.

"I'm sure she'll like it," George said.

"I hope so. We need to hurry back. I know Polly's at home, but I don't like leaving Elise when she's not well."

"Hey..." George cried out as a group of young boys ran past. "Slow down there!"

"Sorry, Mister," one of the boys called out.

"Surely you remember what it felt like to get out of school at the end of the day?" Harry said.

"I suppose so... What the...?" George stared up at the sky, which had suddenly darkened. For a moment, he and Harry just stood and watched, then he froze as he realised what he was seeing.

"Get down!" Harry cried, throwing his stick to the floor and grabbing George, just as the plane crashed behind the the building directly opposite them. The explosion was enormous – far bigger than anything George would have expected. Glass, wood and bricks flew about everywhere and flames shot into the sky. The sound was deafening and, for a few moments, it seemed as though all the noise was muffled. Then, slowly, sight and sound returned to normal. It took a moment for George to realise that Harry had covered him with his body, sheltering him from the blast. Harry stood, allowing George to get back to his feet. The two men turned and looked into the street which was covered with debris, the air filled with dust.

"Are you alright?" Harry said, quickly, looking George up and down. "You've got some blood on your arm."

George looked down, pulled back his sleeve and saw a deep gash just above his wrist. Harry reached into his pocket, took out his handkerchief and wrapped it tightly. "Stay here," he said.

"Like hell I will," George replied. Harry looked at him. "It's just a cut." Harry didn't argue with him.

"Those boys…" Harry said. "Where did they go?"

"I think they'd already gone around the corner."

"Go and check. Make sure they're alright. If you can't find any trace of them, come back here."

"Where are you going?"

"Over there." Harry pointed towards the burning building. "It's… It *was* a laundry. There will have been people working inside."

"Harry, the emergency services will be here soon." Harry was already limping away.

"There was no siren, George," he called over his shoulder. "They might not be aware yet."

George couldn't find any trace of the boys and, after hunting for them for nearly ten minutes, he made his way back towards the laundry. He found three women sitting on the pavement near where he and Harry had sheltered. They looked shocked, especially the youngest of them.

"Are you all right?" he asked. They looked up at him and one of them nodded. The other two just stared into the distance.

"George!" He heard a familiar voice behind him and turned to find Harry limping across the road, supporting a middle-aged man, who had his arm draped limply across Harry's shoulder. George ran forward and took the man from Harry, lowering him to sit beside the women.

"The boys?" Harry asked.

"No sign," George replied. "They must have got away. Anyone else in there?" he asked, making to return to the building

"Not alive," Harry said, grabbing George's arm. "Don't," he continued. "It's not pretty."

George swallowed hard. "Are there many dead?"

"Only two that I could find, but one of them was quite young... Little more than a girl, really."

"Not Millie?" The older of the women cried.

Harry crossed to stand in front of her. "I'm sorry," he said. "Was she your friend?" His voice was full of a kindness that George had never heard before, and it took his breath away.

"She was my niece. Oh God... How ever am I going to tell her mother." The woman sitting next to her placed an arm around her shoulder.

The youngest of the three women sitting on the ground started to cough.

"Where the hell are the ambulances?" George said.

"They'll get here, don't worry." Harry came across to him and looked into his face. "How's the wrist?"

"It's stinging a bit now, to be honest."

"Let me see..." Harry lifted George's arm, undid the handkerchief and inspected the wound. The cut had stopped bleeding. "It seems okay." In the distance, they could hear the sound of bells ringing.

"Oh, thank God," said the man sitting on the pavement. "They've taken their time."

Two ambulances pulled into the road and stopped. The crews jumped out and ran towards the huddled group. Harry approached them.

"Fire tender's on it's way," said one of the ambulance men.

"I don't think there's anyone else left in there," Harry said. "There are no obvious wounds on any of these people, except the young man over here." He pointed to George. "He's got a deep cut to his wrist."

"Very good, sir," said the ambulance man. "What was it?"

"A plane of some type," Harry replied. He suddenly felt a bit light-headed and clutched the sleeve of the man's uniform. "I'm sorry," he said, and everything went black.

When he woke, he could feel a comfortable mattress beneath his back and a pillow under his head. "Elise..." he murmured. He turned his head to one side. It didn't hurt at all. Beside him sat George, a look of fear and worry on his face.

"Hello," Harry said. "What are we doing here? What happened? Is Elise all right?"

"Blimey, Harry. That's a lot of questions. Firstly, Elise is fine. She's with my father. Secondly, you're here because you fainted."

"I fainted? I haven't done that in years. I wonder what made me do that?"

"Probably that bloody great piece of wood you had stuck in your leg."

"I thought it was hurting a bit."

"Hurting a bit? Hurting a bit?" George raised his voice and the nurse at her station looked up. "Shit, Harry, it was about six inches long, and three inches of it were stuck in your thigh." Harry reached around with his left hand to the outside of his right thigh – the leg that actually did work properly – and felt the bandage.

"How is everyone? The women…?" Harry asked, trying to sit up. The nurse came over and, between her and George, they managed to get Harry into a sitting position. The nurse propped up his pillows, took his pulse and left them alone again.

"They're all fine. The younger girl has got to stay in overnight, but everyone else has already gone home."

"And your wrist?" Harry asked.

"Bugger my wrist," George said, looking down at the bandage wrapped around his lower arm.

"The army's done nothing for your language." Harry smiled across at him. "Seriously, how is it?"

"It's all right." The door to the ward opened and Elise stood there, a small suitcase in her hand. She looked across at Harry and he stared at her, noting the tears in her eyes, and the black shadows beneath them. He nodded, and smiled and she walked quickly towards him. George got up and moved to one side, as William also entered the ward. Elise stood beside the bed and looked down at him.

"You're awake," she muttered.

"You're here," he said at the same time.

"Of course I'm here. Where else would I be? I just went home again to fetch you some things. You'll have to stay here for a while."

"I don't think so," Harry said. "I need to come home to look after you."

"Harry…" The warning tone in her voice had no effect.

"I'm not staying any longer than I absolutely have to," he said.

He placed his arm behind her and without a word, she fell onto him, laying her head on his chest. He felt the wetness of her tears and kissed the top of her head, running his hand across her back.

"It's okay," he whispered. "It's really okay." She shook her head. Then stood.

She stared down at him, still crying, but half smiling and running her fingers up and down his arm. "What on earth possessed you, Harry? You could have been killed."

"But I wasn't. You have to trust me, Elise. I wouldn't have done anything that would take me away from you."

"You walked into a burning building!" she cried.

"Well, yes, but…"

"Well, yes, but nothing!"

"There were people in there, Elise. What would you have had me do? Leave them to die? I knew what I was doing. The flames had largely died down by then. They were just trapped because of the fallen debris. All I did was get them out. I wouldn't have done it if I'd thought it would kill me. " He looked right into her eyes. "I love you too much to do that to you. But I couldn't just stand there and do nothing."

"Even though you had a six-inch piece of wood stuck in your only good leg, evidently."

"Well, I didn't actually know it was there. I just knew my leg hurt a bit. I'm sorry if I've frightened you." He reached up and wiped her tears away with his thumb.

She leant down again, her mouth next to his ear. "When William arrived and told me what had happened and that you were in the hosptial…" she whispered, "I thought… I thought I'd lost you… again."

He placed his hand behind her head, stroking her hair. "I'm sorry," he murmured. He yawned, feeling the drag of tiredness, and she stood again and turned to William and George, blushing. They looked on, unconcerned.

"Harry," William said, his voice full of emotion. "I can't thank you enough for what you did."

"What *I* did?" Harry looked genuinely confused. "I should be thanking you, for looking after Elise."

William moved to stand on the opposite side of the bed. "George told me what you did… that you put yourself between him and the blast." Harry heard the crack in William's voice. "I can't…"

"You don't have to," Harry said, his eyes drooping.

"I think the patient needs some rest," Elise said, smiling.

"Don't leave," Harry said, his voice thick with sleep.

"You'll see me tomorrow," she replied to his almost closed eyes, as she bent to kiss his smiling lips.

They let Harry go home the following evening, mainly because he insisted. The doctor was pleased with his progress; the wound, although deep, hadn't caused any internal damage, and his argument that the bed was needed for other patients didn't go unheeded.

Once home, Elise tried to fuss around him, despite her own tiredness, helping him into the house and initially insisting he go to bed.

"Absolutely not. I'm not having you running up and down the stairs after me."

"You're going to rest. If you won't go to bed, then at least lie on the sofa." He looked down at her.

"All right. I do need to sit down," he said.

"I knew it. You're overdoing it. Why wouldn't you use a wheelchair like they suggested?"

"I didn't use one when I first damaged my other leg, I'm certainly not using one for a little cut."

She guided him into the sitting room. "It's a bit more than a little cut, Harry."

"They stitched it up, didn't they? It just smarts a bit sometimes."

"Then sit down."

"All right." She lowered him onto the sofa. "Now, I want you to come and sit down too. You're exhausted."

"I was terrified... I thought..." She sat down and he put his arm around her, pulling her close.

"Shh... I'm home now. You feel good," he said.

"So do you." She put her arms around him and rested her head on his chest. He felt her shudder and sniffle.

"Don't cry," he said, knowing there would be tears falling without having to see them.

"I thought I'd lost you," she replied.

"I'm not that easy to lose."

"Don't you ever do anything like that to me again... do you hear?"

He raised her face to his, looking into her eyes. "I promised you I'd never leave you and I meant it. Whatever happens, I'll never leave... but, I can't promise not to do my best to help when my help is needed."

She blinked. "No, I don't suppose you can... and I don't suppose I'd want you to."

"Now, will you do something for me?"

She sat up. "Anything."

"Could you reach into my inside jacket pocket? I don't want to move my arm. It's kind of comfortable holding you." He grinned down at her and Elise obliged and pulled out a small box.

"What is it?" she asked.

"It's why I went into town in the first place. I wanted to buy this. Open it." She opened the box and gasped at the ring inside. It had a single round diamond in the centre, flanked on either side by two oval cut emeralds.

"It's... It's so beautiful. But why?" Releasing her, Harry took the ring from the box and placed it on her finger.

"I don't need a reason," he murmured. "But if I did, it would be because I want you to know that I truly, truly love you."

It wasn't everything he wanted to say and it wasn't the way in which he'd wanted to give her the ring, but it would have to do... for now.

Chapter Twenty

Late Spring 1944

Amy felt as though her lungs were going to explode. David had kept a hold of her hand the whole time as they pounded through the back roads, turning this way and that, down dank alleys, zigzagging their way through Montmartre's dark, shadowy streets.

"Stop!" She heaved the word out. "I can't…" She pulled him back.

He turned to her. "You have to." His eyes were darting everywhere, searching, desperate.

"But I can't..."

"We're nearly there. Please, Amy…" he begged.

"My skirt," she panted, "I can't run properly. It's…"

Without another word, David bent down and ripped the seam at the side of her skirt to half way up her thigh.

"Better?" She heaved a deep breath, nodding and, grabbing her hand, he set off again, running faster now down the cobbled street. She yelped as he darted into another passageway, barely wide enough to fit down, dragging her behind him. At the other end, they came out onto a narrow path, about a car's width, and he turned abruptly to the right, pulling her with him. Then, after a hundred yards or so, he turned again, this time into a doorway. The door itself was closed, but David pushed hard against it with his shoulder and it budged. He hauled her inside, closing it behind them. They were faced with a wide set of stone stairs and he took her hand again, leading her up to the first floor, where they were met with three doors. The second on the left, had a number

'2' in the centre and, as David fished in his pocket for a key, Amy stood bent over, with her hands on her knees, heaving air into her lungs. As soon as the door was opened, David dragged her inside, closing and locking it behind them. The room was in darkness and he went straight to the shuttered window and stood to one side, watching, listening. Below, there came the sound of running footsteps and Amy walked across and stood beside him, her breathing laboured and heavy. There was just enough light coming through the slats in the shutter to make out his features and he seemed to be holding his breath as the footsteps moved straight on past. She closed her eyes and leaned, with her back against the wall for support, trying not to collapse with relief.

"You're safe," he murmured gently and she felt the breath of his whisper on her cheek and his fingertips on her neck. She opened her eyes and found herself staring up into his, just for a moment, just for a blink. Then his lips were hard on hers, his tongue was probing into her mouth and he delved deeply, searching and taking what he'd needed for so long. He found her hands and held them above her head with one of his, while the other moved lower, discovering the tear in her skirt and, beyond that, the bare skin at the top of her stockings. He placed his feet either side of hers and pressed his hips into hers, knowing she would feel his arousal and, in that moment, not caring. Her breasts heaved against his chest and her tongue responded to his, twisting into his mouth. He groaned and nipped at her bottom lip gently with his teeth, devouring her, harder still, pouring himself into her. He heard her moan deep in his throat as he raised his hand up her thigh to cup her buttock and pull her closer. He wanted her, but not here… not like this. He let out a sigh and pulled away from her, releasing her hands and letting them fall back by her sides. He glanced down at her. She was breathing hard, but he couldn't read the look in her eyes. He took a small step back and she pushed herself away from the wall.

"I'm sorry," he whispered as she turned away. "I didn't mean for that to happen."

Silence descended for a few moments. Even in the dim light, she could make out a sofa in the middle of the room and she walked across and flopped down into it, letting her head rest on the cushion behind her. He watched her for a moment, then joined her. "What happened?" she asked. They still whispered, just in case anyone could hear them, although neither really knew who might be listening.

"I couldn't help myself, I'm sorry," he replied and she glanced across at him. "You're so… Amy, isn't it obvious? I'm in…"

"I don't mean that. I mean at the café, earlier."

"Oh." He turned towards her, placing his arm along the back of the sofa, behind her head.

"Where did you come from?" she asked.

"I didn't come from anywhere. I'd been there the whole time."

"What? I didn't see you."

"You weren't meant to. I was outside, watching."

"The whole time?"

"Yes, of course. I told you when we were at the farmhouse that I'd always be with you…"

"Then why did you let me think I was on my own?"

"Because I didn't want you to start looking for me. I needed you to act naturally."

"So, what happened?"

"It all went to hell."

"I gathered that, but why?"

"Because I got it wrong, like I've never got anything wrong before in my whole life." She heard his deep sigh.

She looked at him for a while, then said, "She met Luc, you know."

"Yes, I saw."

"They were… intimate. I didn't want to watch, so I went back inside."

"Luckily, I'm not as virtuous as you. I watched. And it wasn't what you expected." He took her hand and she tensed. "It's okay," he reassured her. "I'm only going to hold your hand, nothing more." She relaxed and his disappointment cut like a lance. "It seems we're not the only ones who can put on a show," he continued, after a moment's pause. "Luc must have been watching you over Claudette's shoulder. Almost as soon as you'd gone back inside the café, they stopped what they were pretending to do, and started talking. A few minutes later, I heard footsteps approach and then a Gestapo officer appeared. He walked straight up to them and they talked together for a short while. He seemed to be giving instructions to Claudette and, to start with, she didn't appear to be very keen, but Luc spoke to her and she nodded her head. Then she came back inside the café. Luc and the Gestapo officer spoke for a bit longer and then shook hands and they both left." He waited for her to realise what he'd said.

"Luc?" she whispered, eventually. "Are you telling me the mole was… is… Luc?"

He nodded. "Well, I think it could be both of them, working together. I'm not sure. But Luc is definitely involved and he's the one in charge. Claudette seemed unwilling to return to the café and it was Luc who did the persuading, not the man from the Gestapo."

"So she… she…"

"I followed her inside, but kept my distance. I could just about hear what you were saying. It seems that her instructions were to get you away from the café. I don't know if they'd have waited until you reached her apartment… I doubt it. They just wanted you away from the café to make it easier. Then they'd have arrested you."

"He gave me away to the Gestapo?"

"Yes."

"My own cousin?"

"Well, we can't be certain he'd recognised you. He didn't seem to. He just saw you as a threat." He could feel her confusion and pain. "I'm sorry, Amy. I got this so wrong. If I'd known…"

"You'd have brought me anyway. Don't kid yourself, David."

"Is that what you really think of me?" He dropped her hand and stood up, still not daring to raise his voice, but wishing he could. "You think I'd have brought you into this much danger if I'd known the mole was Luc?"

"Frankly, I think you'd do anything to get the job done."

"Then you really don't know me at all." She glared up at him, trying to disguise her sorrow with anger. "I'd never knowingly endanger an agent, especially not you… not when…" He stopped himself, calming and sitting down next to her again. "I'm sending you back to Agen first thing tomorrow. Thierry will get you back home."

"What are you talking about?"

"I can deal with everything now. I'm putting you on the first train in the morning."

"But… What about Luc?"

"What about him? I'll handle Luc."

"How?"

"Don't worry about that."

"But, you said… you said you were going to eliminate the mole." He didn't answer. "Are you?" He turned to look at her, staring into her eyes.

"Your job's done," he said eventually.

"If you think I'm going to leave and let you kill my cousin…"

"I can't let him live, Amy. He's too dangerous. If you knew what he'd done…"

"But…"

"This isn't up for discussion. I'm staying to deal with things here, and you're going. Tomorrow. First thing."

"Why?"

He sighed. "Because… I need you to." He rose again and started pacing the floor. "I can't let you stay."

"Why not?"

"Because you're too damned distracting, Amy." He stood above her and she heard the strength of feeling in his voice, even though it was little more than a whisper in the darkness. He ran his fingers through his hair. "I can't think straight when you're around and, right now, I need my wits about me. I've got to find a way to catch him without breaking up, or giving away the whole damned cell, then I have to question him, and then, yes, I'll kill him, and probably her as well. I can't do that with you here." He crouched down in front of her. "I'm putting you on that train, so I know you're safe and I can do my job without being reminded, every time I breathe in and out, that I'm not the man who fills your dreams like you fill mine and I'm not the man whose touch you long for, like I long for yours and I'm not the man you love… like I love you." He stood up, turned and walked back to the window, leaning against its wide frame. The room was filled with a silence so deep and overwhelming it threatened to stretch on to infinity.

"But… you can't love me," Amy whispered eventually. "That's not possible. I'm not worth…" She bit back the words. "I mean… you said we had to control our emotions out here; you said love was dangerous. Just as dangerous as anger, pleasure, sadness."

"You're easy to love, Amy," he whispered. "And I know I should show more control, but that's proving impossible around you."

She didn't reply. Instead, she got to her feet and went into the kitchen, where she poured a glass of water and drank it deeply. She stood there for some time, leaning against the sink. David was aware of her every move, even though his eyes never left the street. Eventually, she returned, came and stood next to him and took a deep breath.

"I'm sorry," she whispered, placing a hand on his arm. Her voice had changed; she'd calmed down, and now she just seemed sad. On reflection, David thought he preferred her anger to this dejected sorrow, because now all he wanted was to hold her and kiss again, and he was fairly certain she wouldn't like that. "I know you wouldn't endanger me. You saved my life, and risked your own to do it. So I had no right to say you would have brought me if you'd known the danger."

He gave a half laugh. "Well, I'm glad we got that straight, if nothing else."

"And I'm sorry, David… I'm truly sorry that I can't feel the things you do." She hesitated. "That kiss… it was…"

"I know," he said. "Your response, it was just a basic reaction… relief, mixed with fear. You didn't – you don't – feel the same things I do. I understand that."

"Part of me wishes I could, but it's only been six months since… I can't forget what I had with Ed, even if it was so brief…" He heard the catch in her voice.

"Hey," he turned towards her. "Don't be sorry for that. It's not your fault, just really, really bad timing. Chronically bad timing." He looked out through the slats again.

"In any case, how do you know what you feel is real? It could be just the danger, couldn't it? A heat of the moment thing, not real love at all…"

"I've been in danger before, Amy… lots of times, but I've never been in love. I've never felt anything like this before." He reached across and touched her cheek with his fingertips. She blinked up at him and he felt her blush, even though he couldn't see it. "Ed was a very lucky man."

"I don't know about that," she muttered.

"No, but I do." He smiled at her. "It's late. You should get some sleep. You take the sofa. I'll be okay on one of the chairs. We'll need to be up early to get you to the station."

"I'm not going."

"Amy. You're going."

"No. I'm. Not."

"Give me a bloody good reason why not."

"Because you might need me."

"That goes without saying. I've needed you since the day I first met you."

"That's not what I meant, and you know it. You might need me when it comes to Luc."

"I can handle Luc."

"And I can handle him better. Look, I don't want to talk to him directly, but I can help you talk to him better. I know him. I know his parents, his secrets, his past."

"And you think I don't? I know your secrets, Amy."

"Not all of them, you don't." She looked at him, her eyes widening slightly. "Trust me, David."

"I do, completely. But I also love you very, very much and that's not going to change any time soon. I want you safe, Amy. I know you don't love me, but I want there to be a chance, even if it's just a slim one, for us to have a future together at some stage, when this bloody war is over and your memories are where they belong." She looked up at the ceiling, blinking away the threatening tears. He reached out to touch her but she backed away slightly. "I do get it," he said. "I understand that you're not ready for me, or for anyone in your life right now. I know you're still grieving for Ed, and that's how it should be. You love him, you need to grieve. But one day, you'll want to move on, and when that happens, I want it to be me you move on with; so I'll wait..."

"That could take a long time."

"I don't care. I think I'd wait forever for you, Amy."

"Oh... Don't say that." Her tears were flowing freely now and she was thankful for the darkness.

"Why not? It's true."

"Because he said that to me once." She sniffled and he pulled her into a hug, letting her cry into his jacket. After a while, she quietened and he placed his finger under her chin, raising her face to his.

"I guess you're right." he whispered. "There are some things I don't know about you. But I'd really like the opportunity to discover them all... one day. Just remember, in the meantime, if you need me for anything at all, you can come to me, or send for me. I promise that I'll help you in any way I can. I won't pester you, but I won't ever stop loving you either. Give me your word that you'll come to me, if you need me." He waited until she nodded her head. "And I'm still sending you home," he added. She pulled away from him, wiping her tear-streaked face with the backs of her hands.

"But, you say you want me to be safe and, if that's the case, it seems the best thing for me to do is to stay right here, with you... not travel back to Agen on my own, anyway. Being with you has been the safest place there is since we left England."

He smiled. He liked the idea that she felt safe with him. It felt promising. It felt hopeful. "Amy, this is going to get really nasty. I'm not going to sit Luc down over a cup of tea and ask him polite questions, while we eat cucumber sandwiches."

"That's good, because he doesn't like tea."

He smirked. "Well, thanks for the tip."

"I remember, he used to make fun of my father for drinking so much of it."

"I can't imagine anyone making fun of your father."

"My mother does it all the time," she muttered, then her head jerked up. "You know my father?"

"No, not directly. I know of him. I've done some work with a man who knew your father quite well," he explained. "They served together in the last war. I was intrigued by what I'd heard, so I looked up his war record."

"What was his name, this man?"

"Newby."

"Oh. Dad's never mentioned him..." She sounded thoughtful. "But then, I suppose he doesn't mention any of it much. What does this Newby chap have to say about my dad, then?"

"I'll only tell you, if you agree to go home."

She narrowed her eyes and folded her arms across her chest. "Bastard," she whispered.

"I know your father wouldn't like you swearing," he said, smiling.

"Well, he isn't here."

"No, but it seems you are. So, what's it to be? I'll spill the beans on Harry, if you agree to go home."

"Nice try, but not a chance. I've lived for over twenty years knowing very little about his past. I can live a little longer."

"Blast. I thought that might work."

"Huh. And you think you know me?"

"Not as well as I'd like to." He took her hand, kissing it gently. "I'm not going to win, am I?"

"No, so you might just as well accept that and then we can get on with working out what to do next."

"Well, I think you should lie down on the sofa and get some sleep..."

"What are you going to do?" she asked.

"I'm going to take a cold shower." He grinned at her. "If you're staying, I'd better get used to them, and I might as well start now."

Chapter Twenty-one

Late Spring 1944

After a couple of days, Harry's leg felt a little better. He was still worried about Elise and wondered if he should try and take her away for a long weekend. Perhaps it would even give him time to talk to her about Griffin, away from the usual distractions of home. He'd spent the morning in his study, typing a few letters and had just popped into the kitchen to ask Polly to bring coffee into the sitting room. He knew Elise would be in there, hopefully resting. He would suggest a break in the New Forest, just as they'd planned. The journey shouldn't be too arduous. He smiled to himself for the first time in ages. Some time away was just what they both needed. He opened the door and was surprised to find that Elise wasn't in the room.

"Elise?" he called, going back into the hall, but there was no response. He went into the dining room, which was also empty, then returned to the kitchen.

"Polly?" he asked. "Have you seen Mrs Belmont?"

"No, not since breakfast." Dennis was also in the kitchen, having a cup of coffee and he shook his head when Harry looked at him.

"No, sir."

Harry went back into the hall and stood for a moment. He hadn't heard her go upstairs, but that didn't mean she hadn't; she was light on her feet. He'd just started to climb the stairs, when he noticed the door into the library was ajar. He descended, went across and opened the door, and let out a cry.

Elise was lying prone on the floor in front of the large bookcase, her head at an ungainly angle, and one arm awkwardly caught beneath her body. Without thinking, Harry dropped his stick, and half-limped, half-ran to her. He fell to the floor next to her, ignoring the pain in his knee and instinctively felt her neck for a pulse with his shaking fingers. Relief flooded him as a faint but steady beat coursed across his skin.

"Stubbs! Polly!" he yelled at the top of his voice.

The couple came through the door almost together, banging it against the bookcase and clattering into the room.

"Oh, Mrs Belmont," cried Polly.

"Please, help me... Please, lift her," said Harry desperately, looking up at Dennis.

"Yes, sir." Dennis leant down and, raising Elise's body into his arms, he carried her through to the sitting room. Polly, without being asked, helped Harry to his feet, and fetched his stick from the doorway where he'd dropped it.

"Call Doctor Blackwood," Harry said over his shoulder as he followed Dennis into the sitting room, where he was laying Elise gently on the sofa. Harry perched on the edge of the seat beside her and leant over, placing a hand on her forehead. She felt clammy and feverish.

"What on earth's wrong?" he muttered, frantically. "Wake up, my darling." He patted the back of her hand.

Dennis stood by, uncertain what to do.

"Doctor says he'll be round straight away and to keep her warm." Polly came into the room, wringing her hands.

"She's already burning up, though," Harry said.

"Keep her warm anyway," Polly said. "I'll fetch a blanket." She ran from the room again.

"Elise, darling... wake up... speak to me." Harry's voice was growing more frantic.

Polly returned within minutes with a blanket, which they placed over Elise and, then, very slowly, she opened her eyes, which were panicked.

"Whash... who's zat? 'Arr...'Arry?" Her words were slurred and she seemed confused.

"Elise? Don't worry. Everything will be fine." Harry said, as the doorbell rang. "Oh, thank God," he murmured. Polly left the room, returning moments later with the doctor.

"Move out of the way, Mr Belmont." The doctor didn't stand on ceremony, but knelt down next to Elise, pushing Harry to one side. He examined her briefly, taking her temperature. "Has she been unwell for long?" he asked eventually.

"She's had a headache for some while," Harry replied. "And she's recently complained of feeling sick and dizzy. She wouldn't come to see you. She just said she was overtired."

"Has she been tired as well?"

"Yes."

The doctor looked up at Polly. "I want you to telephone to the hospital. Tell them I'll be bringing a patient in my car." He looked up at Harry. "It'll be quicker than waiting for an ambulance."

Polly left the room quickly.

"Doctor," said Harry. "You're really frightening me. And I don't frighten very easily, or at least I didn't think I did, until today."

The doctor got to his feet and led Harry away from Elise. "I'm not going to lie to you," he said. "I think your wife is very sick. The most important thing right now is to get her to the hospital and I'll run some tests."

Harry allowed the doctor and Dennis to take Elise to the doctor's car and watched while she was lowered into the back seat. Then he climbed in himself and supported her head on his lap, while the doctor walked around and got into the driver's seat.

"Polly," Harry called out of the window, and she ran across and leant into the car. "Can you please telephone William King, tell him what's happened and ask him to come to the hospital." Harry had a feeling he was going to need his friend.

Several hours had passed and Harry felt as though he was going to wear a hole in the hospital floor if he paced up and down much longer. William and Charlotte were sitting in two very uncomfortable chairs, watching him, both looking as worried as he felt.

"What's taking so long?" Harry repeated for the umpteenth time. "Why can't I see her?"

"They said they've got tests to run," Charlotte tried to sound soothing.

A door opened at the end of the corridor and the doctor appeared, with a nurse by his side. At the sight of a sympathetic looking nurse, Harry felt his whole body start to crumble. His legs turned to water and he faced William and Charlotte, who both stood and came to his side, Charlotte placing her hand beneath his arm to offer subtle support.

"Mr Belmont," the doctor began, "I haven't got back all the tests results just yet, but I'm certain enough of my diagnosis to be able to say that your wife has something called Addison's Disease."

Harry nodded. He had no idea what the doctor was saying and kept looking at the nurse, half expecting her to tell him, in a sympathetic voice, that Elise was dying.

The doctor was still talking. "Ordinarily, Addison's Disease is something that a patient can live with perfectly happily, on medication, provided they don't overdo it. If they get overtired then they can have an adrenal crisis, which is what happened to Mrs Belmont."

"What does this mean?" Harry asked. "Is she…?"

The doctor placed a hand on Harry's shoulder.

"She'll be fine. We're giving her some fluids and have already given her the injections she needs. She should improve quite quickly now… But she'll need to take medication and be careful about getting overtired or if she becomes unwell. The nurse here will explain everything in more detail once you've seen your wife." He smiled at Harry, who could feel the tears welling in his eyes and didn't bother to wipe them away.

"Are you sure?" Harry asked, unable to believe what he was hearing.

"I'm certain she'll be all right, yes. She's already responding quite well, although she's still very tired. We'll keep her in for a couple of days and she'll need to rest at home until she feels better, but then, with the right medication, she should be able to lead a perfectly normal life."

"Thank God," Charlotte whispered next to Harry.

"Would you like to see her?" the doctor asked. He glanced at Charlotte and William. "I'm afraid it had better just be Mr Belmont for now."

"You go ahead, Harry," William said, patting Harry's shoulder. "We'll wait here."

He turned to his friends. "Thank you," he mouthed and then turned back and followed the doctor and nurse through the doors.

The nurse left Harry and Elise alone, after a brief explanation to both of them as to what would happen over the next few hours and days. Once she'd gone, Harry moved closer to the bed, placing his hand in Elise's.

"Don't you ever do anything like that to me again," he said, trying hard to control his voice.

"Are you angry with me?" she whispered.

"No, of course I'm not angry, but seeing you like that…" A tear fell down his cheek. "For Christ's sake, Elise, I can't lose you. What if I hadn't found you? What if I'd been out, or had decided to go down to the studio, instead of having coffee with you? What if… You could have… I couldn't carry on without you…"

"Stop it, Harry."

"These adrenal crises, or whatever they're called. They can be fatal. Do you realise that?"

"I do now, obviously. Stop sounding like you're so cross with me. If I'd known I was so ill, I'd have seen a doctor. I thought I was just a bit tired. Please, Harry…"

He took a deep breath. "I'm sorry. I'm just not sure I'm ever going to forget the sight of you lying there on the floor…" His voice cracked. "Oh, Elise." He leant forward and she cradled him in her arms.

After a while, he stood up again, reached into his pocket for a handkerchief and wiped his cheeks.

"From now on, you'll do as you're told," he said, sitting on the edge of the bed next to her and taking her hand in his.

"There speaks the most difficult patient in the world." She smiled up at him.

"That's got nothing to do with it. I'm not the patient now and when you come home, you're going to take it easy for a while."

"Don't wrap me in cotton wool, please. I couldn't stand it."

"After what happened today, I can't guarantee not to be a little over-protective." He squeezed her hand. Elise nodded, but didn't seem unduly upset by the prospect. They sat quietly for a few moments, until Elise suddenly tried to sit up.

"What's the matter?" Harry asked, concerned.

"Who's going to look after you while I'm cooped up in here?" Elise looked worried. "I mean, you've not long injured your leg, Amy's away, Polly can't manage everything by herself, and she has to have some time off. Oh God, and there's still the dance to organise… How on earth…?"

"Will you be quiet!" Harry raised his voice, just a little. Elise stared up at him. "To start off with, forget the bloody dance. Charlotte's already said she'll take care of the whole thing. Polly and Dennis will cope with the house… And, as for me… Well, while you're in here, I intend to spend as much of my time as possible sitting just where I am right now, so you can still watch over me, just as you always have done. So, will you please stop worrying."

"Sorry."

The door suddenly opened behind them and a voice said, "I don't mean to intrude, but the nurse said I could just stick my head in and see how everything is."

Harry turned and stood. "Rose!" he cried. "What on earth are you doing here?"

"Where on earth else would I be?" she asked, entering the room.

"But how did you even know?"

"Polly called." Harry nodded, giving her a hug. "So, I packed a bag, telephoned Matthew at work, told him what I was doing and jumped on the next train. I called Polly from the station, and she said everyone was still here, so I got the taxi to drop me off." She turned to Elise, leaning over and kissing her on both cheeks. "You're looking better than I expected."

"I'm feeling better than I did," Elise replied.

"But should you be here?" Harry asked, looking down at her slightly swollen stomach. "In your condition, I mean?"

"I'm pregnant, Dad. I'm not ill. I can take a train and organise a taxi ride."

Harry smiled. "It's lovely to see you," he said.

"Well, that's a good thing," Rose replied, "because I'm planning on staying for a while, at least until Elise is out of hospital and feeling better."

Elise smiled up at Harry. "I feel better already," she grinned.

When Elise arrived home a couple of days later, she was relieved to see that the house was exactly as she'd left it. Harry insisted that she go straight to bed and, for once, Elise didn't argue. Although she wasn't as exhausted as she'd expected, getting dressed at the hospital and the car journey had been tiring, and she didn't want to be difficult on her first day home.

"I'll go and help Polly make some tea and sandwiches," offered Rose. She looked at her father and he nodded gratefully.

"Can you manage the stairs?" he asked Elise once they were alone. "Or do you need me to carry you?"

"Don't be ridiculous," she replied.

"I've done it before."

"I'm not being slung over your shoulder."

"If you can't manage the stairs, then that's the only option."

"I can do it, if we take it slowly." He left his stick at the bottom of the stairs and offered her his arm. She looked up at him. "I said I can manage. And what about your leg and your knee? You need your stick. Please don't..."

"Don't what?" he asked, looking into her eyes.

"Don't wrap me up in cotton wool, remember?"

"I'm not. I just want to help you. You let me worry about my leg and my knee. They're both fine." He held his arm out again. "It's this or I carry you... You choose."

"You're going to be insufferable, aren't you?"

"Probably." She took his arm and allowed him to help her up the stairs, knowing that his knee must be hurting.

Once they reached their bedroom, he released her for a moment and she stood in front of him. "Come here," he said and pulled her to him. "God, I've missed you."

"I've missed you too." She put her arms around his waist and hugged him, resting her cheek against his chest and enjoying the feel of his arm cradling her.

"Do you want me to help you undress?" he offered, leaning back slightly and looking down at her.

"Now, there's an offer I can't refuse." She smiled up at him and raised her eyebrows.

"Not a chance," he said. "You're not well."

"I'm not that unwell." She pouted in a slightly exaggerated fashion. "I told you, I've missed you." She reached up and caressed his cheek, but he grabbed hold of her hand and kissed it, pulling it back down by her side.

"Come on, let's get you into bed before Polly and Rose come up." He turned and limped across to the bed, pulling back the covers. She began undressing, slowly and deliberately, not taking her eyes from him.

"I know exactly what you're doing," he said, re-arranging the things on her bedside table to make more space.

"What am I doing?"

He looked up at her. She'd let her skirt fall to the floor and had unbuttoned her blouse, and was standing at the foot of the bed with it undone, her silk and lace trimmed underwear on full display. He kept his eyes on her face. "I think that's obvious. Now, are you going to let me help?"

"No, thank you. I can manage just fine." From the tone of her voice, she was either hurt or angry and he wanted to bite off his tongue. Instead, he crossed to the windows and opened them a fraction to let in the gentle early evening breeze. When he turned, she'd disappeared into the bathroom, returning a few minutes later in a nightdress. *A nightdress?* She'd worn one in the hospital, but she'd never worn one at home before. She threw her clothes onto the chair near the wardrobe and climbed into bed, nestling down into the pillows and enjoying the comfort of her own bed.

"What do you want me to do with these?" Harry asked, crossing to the chair and picking up her skirt and blouse.

"Leave them. I'll get Polly to deal with them."

He limped to the bed and sat down next to her. "Don't be angry with me," he said, his voice little more than a whisper.

"You've never rejected me before. I can't believe you don't want me." Her voice cracked and she turned her face away to hide the tears that were brimming and which she knew would fall with her next blink.

He placed his finger under her chin and turned her back towards him just as she blinked and a single tear trickled down each cheek. "Please, don't cry," he said, brushing them away with his thumb, one by one.

"But I don't understand…" She stopped speaking as a knock sounded on the door and Rose entered, followed by Polly. They carried two trays, one with a teapot, cups and saucers, a milk jug and sugar bowl; the other with a plate of sandwiches and another of scones.

"It's lovely to see you looking so well, Mrs Belmont," said Polly, placing her tray on the chest by the window. "You did give us a fright."

Harry handed Elise his handkerchief. "What have we here?" he said, getting up and crossing the room, giving Elise time to wipe her eyes. "Those sandwiches look delicious, Polly."

"Thank you, Mr Belmont," she said. "Just some cucumbers out of the greenhouse. And I've made some carrot scones."

"Carrot scones?" Rose and Elise spoke together.

"It was a recipe in the newspaper. I thought I'd give it a try. The carrot bulks it out so you use less flour and sugar. I tried one downstairs and I don't think they taste too bad, even if I say so myself."

"Oh well… I suppose we can try anything… once," Harry put two triangles of sandwich on a plate, together with a sliced scone and carried them over to Elise, placing them on her bedside table. "Is that all right?" he asked.

"Fine, thank you." Her voice was stilted and distant and he cursed the interruption to their earlier conversation.

Polly left them to enjoy their tea and the three of them sat together, talking quietly for nearly an hour. Although Harry felt the tension in the room, Rose and Elise seemed happy to chat.

"Have you heard from Amy?" Rose asked, taking Harry by surprise. "I wrote to her on the day mum went into hospital, to let her know."

"You did?" Harry had no idea Rose had done that.

"Yes, but she hasn't replied." Rose seemed surprised.

"I know she's been busy." Harry wondered if his excuse sounded realistic.

"Too busy to even acknowledge her mother's illness?"

"I don't want so much fuss," Elise interrupted. "Maybe she didn't even receive the letter. You know how bad the post is."

"I suppose it's possible."

"I'll write again," Harry offered, hoping to throw Rose off the scent.

"Don't you have a phone number for her?"

"No. She's never given us one."

Elise yawned loudly and it became clear she was tiring. Harry stood and started to clear away the plates and cups. Rose took his lead and helped, loading the tea things back onto the tray.

"I'll take one down and come back up for the other," she said, in a low voice.

"No you won't," said Harry. "I can't believe you carried one up in the first place."

"Polly carried the heavy one."

"Hmmm. And Polly can carry them both back down later. You're pregnant, remember?"

"I'm hardly likely to forget." He glared at her and she backed down. "All right. We'll send Polly up later on, once Elise has rested. Now, I think you should come down with me and let the patient get some sleep."

"All right, I'll be down in a minute." Harry turned and was disappointed to see that Elise's eyes were already closed and she was breathing deeply and steadily. "I might as well come now," he whispered. "It seems as though the patient couldn't wait for us to leave." He nodded in Elise's direction.

"It's been a tiring day for her." Rose took her father's arm and led him from the room.

Downstairs in the sitting room, they sat with the curtains open, enjoying the sunset as it stained the sky with pigments of bright orange, mingling with pinks, pale blues and dusky purples. "That's quite spectacular," said Harry. "You should paint it." He looked across at Rose.

"I'd never do it justice, not like you could have."

"Oh, those days are long gone. But you have talent, Rosie."

"Not as much as you."

"Rubbish! I've seen your work, remember? You should make the most of these few months, before you're rushed off your feet. Take advantage of having some time to yourself, while you still can, and do some sketching."

"I might, while I'm down here. There's precious little to catch the eye in London, especially at the moment. I never found London particularly attractive, but what with taped up windows, sandbags and bombed out buildings, it's worse than ever."

"You'd be surprised. I sketched some things in the last war that I'd never have considered doing in peacetime. But they were there, so I drew them."

Rose looked at her father. He so rarely mentioned his war that she wondered if he was going to say more, but instead he continued to stare out of the window and she thought for a moment he might be too deeply lost in his memories.

They sat quietly for some time before Harry spoke again. "How's Matthew?" he asked.

"He's still busy, but it's not as bad as it was," Rose replied. "He said he'll try and come down at the weekend. I think he wants to check up on Elise."

"I'm sure he wants to see you too." Harry looked at her closely. She didn't look up, but nodded her head. "Things are better, aren't they?"

Now she looked up at him and smiled, and it was a smile that helped to heal his aching heart.

When Harry went back into the bedroom later that evening, having said goodnight to Rose, the moonlight filtering through the open window gave just enough light to see that Elise was still asleep. He crept around the room as quietly as he could, preparing for bed and then, as gently as possible, climbed in next to her. He turned onto his side and watched her sleeping, hating the fact that she'd put on a nightdress, presumably for decorum's sake, although she could have just put on a robe and taken it off when everyone had gone back downstairs. The fact that she'd chosen a nightdress worried him a little. It felt like a barrier between them. Griffin's kiss had already provided one… they didn't need any more.

He awoke early the next morning, surprised to find that Elise was staring at him from her side of the bed.

"Is something wrong?" he asked, confused by the expression on her face.

"I don't know. You tell me."

"What does that mean?" He sat up slightly in the bed, leaning up on his elbow and looking down at her, his head still sleepy.

"I'm not really sure what you're doing here."

"Um… Sleeping? Why?"

"Well, I assumed after yesterday, you'd choose to sleep in the guest room."

"What on earth are you talking about?"

"You didn't want me, Harry. For the first time ever... you didn't want me. I've been unwell for weeks… it's been ages since you've touched me." The hurt in her voice was so obvious, so cutting, he couldn't help but feel it. If only she knew *his* pain… *his* doubts. "I undressed in front of you. I—I thought, after what happened… I thought…"

"I know."

"Do you? You said you wouldn't wrap me in cotton wool, but you're different. You're treating me differently."

"Of course I'm treating you differently. You nearly died, Elise. I'm not going to just forget that."

"But..."

He pulled her across the bed, closer to him, placing his arm around her shoulder.

"Even now..." she said, her voice cracking. "Even now, you're holding me differently."

"Of course I am."

"I don't understand. Why don't you want me?"

"My darling... Trust me, I want you." He reached down and tilted her face up, so she couldn't help but look into his eyes.

"Well, then..."

"But you need to get your strength back. You're still weak and unwell."

"I'm not that unwell."

"Elise... you getting better is the most important thing. Making love... all of that, well, it can wait until you're ready."

"But I am ready."

"No, you're not."

"Isn't that for me to decide?"

"No."

"Harry!"

"Sorry, that came out wrong. What I meant was, you're not always the wisest person at knowing what's best for you. That's how you became so ill in the first place – because you overdid it. I'm not going to let that happen again."

She sat up and looked down at him. "Do you have any idea what you sound like?"

"A loving husband?" he said hopefully.

"No." She clambered out of bed and headed towards the bathroom. "An overbearing tyrant would be nearer the mark." She slammed the door against his still open mouth and he heard the lock turn.

She'd never locked the bathroom door before and he jumped out of bed, limping quickly across the room.

"Elise, unlock the door," he called.

"No."

"Elise..." he threatened, "open the bloody door, or I'll break it down."

"Don't be so ridiculous."

"I'm not being ridiculous. You've just come out of hospital. What if you faint again? What if you become unwell in there? I won't know, so I won't be able to help you. Just unlock the bloody door... right now... I mean it." There was silence for a few moments and then he heard the lock click. "Thank you," he said, more calmly, before turning and sitting on the chair by the bathroom door.

'A tyrant', he thought. *'An overbearing tyrant' at that.* He just wanted to protect her; to keep her safe. Was that so unreasonable? He listened as water ran into the bath. Was it safe for her to bathe alone? He wasn't sure. How could she even think he didn't want her? He ached for her. He couldn't remember the last time they'd made love. Seeing her even semi-naked was arousing to the point of breathlessness, but he wanted to be certain she was well first. And he knew he was still fretting over the sight of her and Griffin, locked together. He shook his head. Christ, if Elise was feeling rejected by his actions, she should try being inside his head, living with those constant images, reminding him of his inadequacies. That was something she'd never have to do. He would never look at another woman, but he'd never be able to forget that sight. Or the sight of her lying on the floor, the fear that had gripped him, that she might be dead, that he might have lost her forever. How could she even doubt his love, his desire? He just didn't want to be responsible for a relapse, or for hurting her.

He gave a half-laugh and shook his head. *But you're hurting her now, you bloody idiot.* And really, what did it matter about Griffin? What did it matter that those thoughts, those images, burned into his brain and would until the day he died? Nothing mattered except Elise. He got to his feet and turned to stand in front of the bathroom door, then opened it slowly. Inside, steam rose from the bath, even though the government-restricted amount of water looked less than luxurious. Elise was lying back, her hair tied up in a loose bun and her head resting on the edge of the bath, revealing her long, pale neck. Her eyes were closed, but the tear stains down her cheeks told him all he needed to know, and the breath caught in his throat as his gaze wandered down her body.

He closed the door quietly and stepped across to the bath, leaning over and kissing her gently. Elise's eyes shot open and she sat up.

"I'm sorry," Harry said. "I'm being an idiot."

She didn't reply, but moved forward in the bath. He took his cue without hesitation and carefully, awkwardly, clambered in behind her, settling down with some difficulty and pulling her back into his chest. "Forgive me?" he asked. She nodded her head once, nestling back.

"Only if you'll do something for me," she replied, twisting slightly as his arm tightened around her.

"Anything."

"Anything?" The playfulness had returned to her voice.

"Yes."

"Really?"

"Yes. Whatever you want."

"No more cotton wool?"

"No more cotton wool. Whatever you want, we can do."

"Well then… Could you wash my hair?"

Harry tilted his head back and laughed. "Are you serious?" he said, looking down at her. "You want me to wash your hair?"

"It feels so awful, I just can't bear it."

"But wouldn't you prefer Rose to help you?"

"No. I want you to do it."

"Okay. On your head be it… quite literally, I expect."

Half an hour later, Harry sat on the bed, with Elise nestled between his legs as he tried to towel-dry her hair.

"It takes so long to dry," he said. "I don't feel like I'm getting anywhere back here."

"That's because it's so thick. Hang on…" She picked up the

hairbrush that was lying next to her on the bed and started to pull it through the matted strands of hair. "I hate this bit," she complained. It took a while, but eventually, she put down the hairbrush and then started to braid her hair.

"That's complicated," Harry said, watching closely. "I've never really paid attention to what you do with it before."

"It just keeps it out of the way while it dries. I can't stand having wet hair dripping all over the place." She finally finished and tied the end with a band, and a ribbon.

Harry pulled her back into his naked chest. "God, you're beautiful," he said, looking down at her upturned face. She pulled herself closer and he leant down and kissed her, running his fingers, featherlike, across her skin and down her body as she sighed into his mouth.

"That was…" she murmured.

"Hmm… Wasn't it?" They were both trying to breathe normally, but were struggling. Harry lay beside her, his fingers stroking her, keeping her arousal intense, on the edge. Her eyes were closed and the pulse in her neck beat rapidly. "Do you want more?" he asked, gently, his breath caressing her shoulder.

"Yes, I do. I always want more, but… Would you hate me if I said I'm tired?"

He stopped the movement of his fingers in an instant. "I could never hate you, no matter what you said, or did." He knew the truth of that statement better than ever. "I'm sorry if I've tired you out. Are you all right?"

"Oh, don't be sorry. What you just did was incredible and I'm absolutely fine. But I'm going to be sensible and say that I should probably have a rest."

"Good." He kissed her gently. "I'm glad you're being sensible."

He pulled away from her slowly, but she took his hand and pulled him back. "Thank you," she muttered.

"Oh, don't thank me," he said. "It was entirely my pleasure."

"I meant, thank you for letting me be myself."

"I wouldn't want you any other way. You're perfect."

"No I'm not."

"You are to me." He twisted on the bed and turned her to face him. "I'm sorry for being such an idiot, and for hurting you. I hate the idea that you thought I didn't want you. I was so scared…"

"You had nothing to be scared of." She gently ran a fingertip down his cheek. "I'm all right."

"Elise, seeing you lying on the rug downstairs… I've seen so much death in my life. I know what it looks like, and you were pale, such a deathly pale." She heard the hitch in his voice. "I thought…"

"I know what you thought. You thought the same thing as I did when William came and told me about the plane crash; the same thing as I thought when you didn't come back from the war; the same thing I thought every time you left me to go back to the trenches. I know that feeling, Harry. I lived it."

"I suppose I never have, not until that moment and it scared me… so damned much. The idea of you being dead there on the floor… it's going to haunt me."

"But I wasn't dead." She took his hand in hers and pressed it to her lips, kissing his fingers. "I'm here."

"Never leave me," he whispered, seeking reassurance. She leant across and kissed him, her tongue seeking his, but she didn't reply; she didn't say a word, and even as he delved into her, Harry began to wonder again…

Chapter Twenty-two

Summer 1944

It was still only eleven o'clock in the morning and the heat in the kitchen of the house on the outskirts of the village of Chavenay, was becoming unbearable. As the morning wore on and the sun beat down, the temperature continued to rise and Amy licked her dry lips, unsure whether the cause was thirst or nerves. She sat at the table watching the dust motes as they floated across the chinks of sunlight breaking through the closed shutters, wondering what it must be like for everyone upstairs...

It had taken David just over a week to get together three men from other cells, who he knew he could trust, and for them to travel into Paris. It was a week during which Amy had been moved from one apartment to another, never staying anywhere for more than a day or two. She'd spent most of the time by herself, sometimes only seeing David fleetingly, or not at all, and only knowing of his presence during the nights by an indent in the cushions on the sofa, or a damp towel left in the bathroom. He'd brought her some clothes to change into the day after they'd fled the Gestapo. They were new and they fitted her perfectly, which didn't surprise her in the least – after all, he knew everything about her, including her dress size, evidently. He'd also kept her supplied with food, which she quite often found simply left for her, sometimes with a note, sometimes not. She'd offered to help, feeling useless and in the way, but each offer had been met by a blank refusal.

Then one morning he'd announced he was happy with the set-up and he'd be gone for a few days. A few days became nearly a week and then he returned and collected her in the early hours of the morning, telling her that Luc and Claudette had been captured. After a terrifying drive out of Paris, they'd settled in this house, and David and the three men had begun to question their captives. David had been adamant that Amy shouldn't witness any of the interrogations and she'd remained downstairs during each day, preparing food and drinks for when the men or David needed them. David had said from the beginning that he'd give it four days and, if he hadn't got the information he needed, he'd kill both of them and take Amy back to England. Tomorrow would be the fourth day.

From upstairs, she could hear footsteps, harsh words being spoken, and occasionally, a muffled cry which made her shiver, despite the heat. She knew Claudette was in the other bedroom and had heard her crying, while someone spoke to her for several hours the previous day. This morning, they seemed to be leaving her alone and focusing on Luc.

After a while, everything went quiet again, and she heard a heavy tread coming down the stairs. She got to her feet, expecting one of the men to appear, wanting a drink or something to eat. She was surprised when David appeared. He normally stayed upstairs all day, coming down only very briefly in the evenings. Over the past few days, she'd seen a different side to him, a very different side to the man who had professed his love for her. But now he looked beyond exhausted and flopped into a chair at the table.

"He's never going to talk," he said, rubbing his hands over his face.

"Would you? In the same circumstances, I mean..."

"No, probably not."

"What about her?"

"She's being a little more forthcoming." Amy waited for him to continue. "According to her, the whole thing has been planned by Luc. She fell under his spell, evidently."

"Do you believe her?"

"I don't believe she's under anyone's spell, but she's told us about an agent that Luc double-crossed and gave away to the Germans before she even got here. So, I suppose that sort of backs up her story. I'm still not falling for it completely, though."

"She cries a lot, you know. Even when there's no-one up there with her."

"Well, she would, wouldn't she? It doesn't alter the fact that she's betrayed her country."

"How could she do that?" Amy sat opposite him, and pushed a cup of coffee towards him.

"As I said before, you'd be amazed what people will do" He raised his head and leant on one elbow, his chin resting on his upturned hand. "I'm less worried about her. Right now, it's him giving me a problem."

"Oh?"

"Yes." She saw a shadow cross his face. "He wants to talk to you." Amy could tell by his reaction that she must have paled. He got up and came around the table, crouching down next to her. "Are you all right?" he asked, his voice filled with a concern she hadn't seen in him for days now. She almost felt relieved to see that he hadn't lost that side of himself in this part of his job. She nodded slowly.

"I'm fine. Why does he want to talk to me?" She was surprised by how quiet and small her voice sounded.

He took her hand in his, looking into her eyes. "I imagine he thinks you've got some influence over me. He believes we're lovers, remember? I haven't disillusioned him."

"I see."

"I know you didn't want to speak to him. You don't have to do this, Amy."

"But you think it might help?"

He shrugged. "I don't know. It might. I'm not getting anywhere."

"Then I'll do it," she said softly. He looked down at her hand and lowered his lips to kiss her fingers. "But if I'm going to do it, I want to do it now and get it over with."

"Okay." He looked up into her face. Her eyes were wide and intimidated and he wondered whether this might be another mistake to add to his already long list. "But only if you're sure."

She nodded. He got to his feet and went to the bottom of the stairs. "Give me ten minutes, then come upstairs, all right?" She didn't reply and he turned back to face her. "Okay, Amy?" he said. She got up and nodded her head again, just once. He paused, then retraced his steps, standing in front of her. "I can tell him no, if you want." His voice was so gentle, it took her breath away.

"No," she said. "I'll do it."

He placed his hand on her cheek, slowly caressing her. She leant into his touch, letting out a quiet sigh, and his eyes widened. It was the first time they'd really touched in ages, and her response surprised him. He allowed himself to hope, just a little. "I'll be there," he said. "I won't leave you alone with him." She smiled, but there were tears in her eyes. "Just remember what he is," David continued. She looked at him quizzically. "I told you it wouldn't be tea and cucumber sandwiches. Our methods aren't pretty. But you have to keep in mind what he's done, how many people are dead because of him."

"Is he… is he injured?"

"Not as badly as you would have been if they'd captured you. Just think about that when you get upstairs." She paled again and he took a deep breath, pulling her closer. "Don't think of him as your cousin," he whispered in her ear. "That man is gone." He leant back and looked into her eyes. "Okay?" She nodded and he let her go, turning and walking up the stairs, calling "Ten minutes," over his shoulder.

She sat back down at the table, her fingers twitching nervously, then she stood and walked up and down in front of the range, but found herself sweating, so she crossed to the window by the front door. The shutters had to be kept closed, but she put her face next to the gap and allowed the sunlight to fall on her skin, closing her eyes and thinking of home, and lying under the oak tree, with the light shining down through its branches. Someone was there with her, lying next to her, but they were a shadow. She couldn't tell if it was Ed… or David.

When she judged that ten minutes must have passed, she rubbed her damp palms down the sides of the skirt and walked slowly up the stairs, opening the first door on her right. The inside of the room was in semi-darkness and she looked around, taking in the scene before her. The furniture had all been pushed up against the wall to her left. On the bed, two of the men were sitting, watching her. In the large space in the middle of the room, there was a single wooden chair, on which sat Luc. His ankles were tied to the legs of the chair and his arms were secured behind his back. He looked up as she entered and she couldn't prevent a small gasp from escaping her mouth. He had a large, swollen black eye and his lip was badly cut, with blood running down his chin. There was dried blood from a cut on his cheek and his hair was matted into a wound on his forehead. She turned to her right and saw David, leaning against the wall, staring at her. The other man wasn't there and she assumed he must be with Claudette. At a nod from David, the two men on the bed got up and left the room, Amy moving to one side to allow them to pass out through the door, which one of them closed behind him. The atmosphere in the room was stifling, and it wasn't just from the heat.

"Hello, cousin," Luc said, his voice slurred.

"Hello," Amy replied, surprised by how clear her speech sounded, even to herself. Moving forward into the room, she kept her hands behind her back, so he wouldn't see them shaking.

"I certainly never expected to see you here," Luc continued. "I was very surprised when you turned up at the bar." So he had recognised her, after all.

"Likewise," she said, trying not to show any emotion. They stared at each other for a moment. "Why, Luc?" she asked, simply.

"Why what?" He had no intention of making this easy for her.

"Why betray your country, your parents, your family… all of us?"

He laughed, throwing his head back, then focused on her again. "Betray you? Ha!"

She took a step back. "What happened to you?" she asked.

"Nothing happened to me, you little idiot."

"Well, you certainly weren't always this much of a bastard."

She saw his eyes widen slightly. "Grown a little backbone, have we?" She ignored the sarcasm in his voice.

"No. It was always there. You were just to stupid to see it."

"Don't you dare call me stupid." He struggled with his shackles, anger filling his eyes.

"Well, I'm not the one tied to a chair, am I?" She turned away and took a deep breath, not daring to look at David. After a minute or so, she turned back. "So, why?" she asked.

"Because I've always hated you."

"Me?"

"Not you specifically… I'm not even sure I've ever really thought about you." He looked her up and down. "I can see no particular reason to do so. No. I hate all of you. My parents, your parents… All of them." Behind her, she felt David take a step closer into the room.

"But your mother… She dotes on you."

"That whore?" Again he laughed. "She'd slept her way around the village before I was ten. Do you know how humiliating it is, when every man in the village, every dad at school, has fucked your mother, and they talk about it quite openly, comparing notes?" Amy swallowed hard. "And what makes it worse is that your own father just lets her do it."

"Did it ever occur to you that maybe he loves her?"

"That's not love, that's servitude. He's just a weak man. I mean, look… at the first sign of trouble, off he ran, straight to dear old Harry." Amy felt herself bridle. "Harry… who's been bailing my dad out for the last twenty years, because he's too useless to make a go of the farm himself." Amy's mouth fell open, but she closed it again rapidly. "You didn't know, did you?" He looked at her. "Well, your big-hearted old dad has been sending money for as along as I can remember." The resentment in his voice was obvious. "But, do you know what? A few years ago, just before the war, I wrote to your dad, asking him to help me out with a business idea… Guess what dear old Harry said to that? A flat 'no'. Who the hell does he think he is? Sitting on all that money… I just needed the capital to get going, but no… he wouldn't help the likes of me."

"I'm sure he had his reasons."

"He had his reasons, all right. I'm not good enough, evidently." He looked at her and laughed again. "Well, who's laughing now?"

Amy stared down at him for a moment, then walked to the other side of the room and, pulling out a chair, she dragged it to the centre of the room and sat opposite him, leaning forward and looking into his face. "Just tell them what they want to know, Luc," she said.

"No."

"Then why did you ask to speak to me?"

He looked at her, then smiled. It didn't have a very pleasant effect on his battered face. "I don't know, really. Old time's sake, I suppose."

"We don't have any old times to reminisce over, not really."

"Perhaps I thought you'd put in a good word for me." He nodded in David's direction.

"I think you over-estimate my influence."

"You're his flavour of the week, aren't you? And I am your cousin, your own flesh and blood..."

"Tell them what they want to know, Luc, and I might be able to convince them."

"I don't even know all the names," he said. "I just deal with the lower ranks, and they pass the messages up."

"Well, tell them what you do know."

"And how do I know I can trust you? I could tell him everything I know and he'll still kill me."

"If you tell him nothing, he'll definitely kill you. This way, you stand a chance."

"If I agree," Luc said, staring at the floor. "I won't do it here. I want to be taken to England first."

"But..."

"Those are my terms."

"Who are you to dictate terms?" David's voice was cold and harsh. He stepped forward, placing himself between Amy and Luc, then he bent down, his face inches from Luc's. "I wasn't born yesterday. And we're finished here." He turned and held out his hand to Amy, who looked up at him for a second, before taking it and letting him pull her to her feet.

Outside, in the corridor, she leant against the wall while he locked the door. She opened her mouth to speak, but he put his fingers to his lips, silencing her, and led her down the stairs, where he motioned that she should sit in a chair at the table.

"I'm sending you home today," he said. "I'll get you on a train back to Agen and Thierry will arrange for your passage back to England."

"But…"

"Enough, Amy." The tone of his voice made her look up sharply. "I'm not arguing this time."

"What are you going to do?" she asked.

"What do you think?"

"Why can't you take him back to England and get the answers that you want?"

"Because he'd probably try and kill me or escape, or both, en-route. And giving me the information in England isn't of much use. I need to know who else is involved, and I need his contacts and I can't check them out from there. If he won't tell me here, he's of no value to me, so I'm better off without him and killing him shows any others who are involved that I mean business."

"He's my cousin, David."

"I told you to forget about that." He stood in front of her.

"How can I?"

"Because he betrayed you to the Germans, perhaps? He knew who you were – we know that much now. He gave you away to a man who was going to arrest you, torture you and probably kill you… Does that help? Do you honestly expect me to let him live after that, whether or not he gives me the names?"

"So you're doing this for me?" He couldn't miss the anger in her voice. "Because if that's your excuse, it's a pretty poor one."

He placed his hands on the back of the chair behind her, leaning down so she could feel his breath on her cheek. "I don't need an excuse, Amy. He deserves it anyway. But for what he did to you, he deserves for it to be a lot more painful than it's going to be. With what I have planned, I'm being generous to him, believe me. Do you know what they do to female agents that they capture?" She blanched and shook her head. "Good. You don't want to." He stood up. "Now. We've got a few things to finish up here. Go and pack and be ready to leave by four."

Amy stood by her small suitcase at the station. It was quiet, with very few people on the platform.

David stood facing her, looking down into her worried eyes. He pulled her into a hug, savouring the feeling of her body next to his one last time, until she pulled away from him. "Thierry knows what to do," he said. "He'll get you home."

"Will I be all right… on the train, I mean?" He smiled inwardly. It was the first time she'd shown any fear for herself and in a way, he welcomed it. She finally cared about what happened to her. He'd been hoping she might… one day.

"Yes. You're not carrying anything. There's nothing to give you away. No-one will even suspect you. Trust me. You'll be safe."

"When will you…?" she asked, forgetting about herself again.

"Later tonight," he answered, knowing what she meant without her having to ask.

"Can't I stay? At least until…"

"No."

"Can't you…?"

"No."

"You don't even know what I was going to ask."

"I don't need to. The answer's no. Everything has to take its course now."

"It was always going to, wasn't it?"

He sighed and smiled down at her. It was a smile she didn't return and he knew, all of a sudden, that she probably never would. "It does tend to in my line of work."

"I don't think I like your line of work."

"Then it's just as well that you don't have to do it any more. This was always going to be your one and only mission and you can go home safely now."

"And it's just as well I never have to see you again." She heard his breath hitch in his throat. "Because I never want to, David. Not as long as I live."

Chapter Twenty-three

Summer 1944

The evening sunlight pooled across the terrace and Harry closed his eyes, squeezing Elise's hand. She was so much better now; almost back to full health and they were enjoying the summer weather and each other, perhaps more than ever before. Harry had almost forgotten his fears. They'd seen nothing of Griffin, and Elise didn't seem to mind his absence from their lives. He'd also managed to put aside her lack of an actual spoken answer to his plea that she should never leave him. He hoped that her actions and words, both then and since, as they'd made love almost daily, with a renewed energy and passion, were her real reply.

"When do you think it will be over?" she asked, interrupting his thoughts.

"Who knows?" he replied. "But I suppose we should be happy that the end is in sight."

"It's been nearly four weeks since the invasion."

"That's not very long in war, darling." Harry opened his eyes and smiled at her.

"I suppose not."

"I know. It's easy to get impatient, isn't it? It seems like we've been waiting so long for our boys to get back into France, and now they have, we just want it all to be over and done with. But you have to give them a chance."

"Would either of you like a drink?" Rose walked into the garden from the sitting room, her pregnancy now much more obvious.

"Hmm." Harry sat up a bit, looking across at his daughter. "A whisky would be lovely, thank you."

"Do you mind if I have a gin and tonic?" The voice at side of the house startled them. Harry turned and leapt to his feet.

"Amy!" he cried, as Elise also jumped from her lounger and they both crossed the terrace as quickly as they could. Elise got to Amy first and pulled her into a tight hug.

"Why didn't you call, or write and let us know you were coming?" Elise said.

"It was all very last minute," Amy replied.

"Got a hug for your dad?" Harry asked and Amy moved towards him, letting him pull her in close. He felt her shoulders shake and a slight dampness passing through his shirt and onto his chest as she sobbed into him. "Hey…" he whispered, leaning back to look at her. "What's wrong?"

She shook her head, unable to speak. Harry nodded and pulled her in close again, wrapping his arm around her. Elise looked on, concerned. "Just happy to be home, aren't you?" Harry said and they waited for a momentary pause before Amy nodded her head.

"I'll get those drinks," Rose said, going into the sitting room.

"Come and sit down." Harry released Amy and led her across to the chairs on the terrace. Lowering her into the nearest one, he stood above her. "Is everything all right?" he asked, quickly, handing her a handkerchief from his trouser pocket.

She nodded, wiping her eyes. "I'll be fine," she said and looked up at him.

"Promise?" She didn't reply or move. "We'll talk tomorrow," Harry whispered as Rose came back, bearing drinks.

"How come you're home so suddenly?" Elise asked, settling back on the lounger.

"I've been unwell…" Amy had worked out her excuse on the long journey home through Spain.

"What's been wrong?" Elise sat forward. "Why didn't you tell us?"

"Oh, it wasn't anything serious." Amy took a sip of her drink. "I was just a bit anaemic, and run down."

"Well, I hope they don't expect you to go back any time soon." Elise reached over and took Amy's hand, squeezing it.

"No. I've left the FANY. They agreed that my health came first and said it was best if I came home."

"Good." Elise noticed the tears welling Amy's eyes again. "Oh, my poor girl," she said. "We'll soon get you better again."

Amy gulped. "I don't suppose… I don't… suppose there's been any… any news about… Ed?" she asked.

"No. Nothing," Harry replied. The sadness weighed down on him.

"Look, there's no need to think about any of that right now," Elise interrupted. "Why don't we go upstairs and run you a bath. Once you've had a good night's rest, you'll feel much better in the morning." Amy nodded her head and allowed her mother to lead her into the house.

The following day, Harry managed to snatch some time alone with Amy, while Rose took Elise to see Charlotte, just to discuss a few of the details for the dance, which was only a month away, under strict instructions from Harry that she wasn't to get too involved.

"Do you want to talk about it?" he asked her outright, as they sat in the sitting room after lunch.

"There's not much to tell, really." She picked at the stitching on her skirt, not looking up at him.

"Where have you been?"

"France."

Harry's sharp intake of breath didn't go unnoticed. "Are you supposed to tell me that?"

She shrugged. "I think you can be trusted… and I'm not sure it matters much now. You still can't tell mum, though." She attempted a smile, but it didn't work.

"How was it?" he pushed. She didn't reply and he nodded. "I'm here when… if you want to talk about it," he said.

"I kept thinking that I'd come home and you'd have heard something definite about Ed," she said after a long pause. "One way or the other."

"No."

"We'd have heard, wouldn't we, if he was a prisoner?"

Harry couldn't deny her question, but he didn't want to admit it to himself, so he said nothing.

"How much longer do you think we'll have to wait?"

"Maybe until the end of the war. I don't know."

"Mum seems... different."

Harry shook his head. "Of course," he said. "You wouldn't have got our letters."

"What letters?" Amy sat forward. "What's happened."

"Your mother's been ill. We wrote... well, Rose wrote to start with, and then when she didn't get a reply, I had to write, although of course I didn't expect you to answer... or even get the letter."

"Dad, what's happened?"

Harry explained the events surrounding Elise's illness.

"Is that why Rose has been a bit 'off' with me? She barely said a word to me last night, or this morning."

"Probably."

"She must think I didn't care two hoots. But I didn't know, Daddy. Not that I could have done anything, or come back to help. Oh God. This is awful. How is mum...? She's okay now, isn't she?"

"Calm down, Amy. Your mother's fine now. There was nothing you could have done anyway, even if we could have contacted you."

"But how can we explain why I didn't get in touch?"

"We can't for the moment. We'll just say that the letters must have got lost."

"Two letters? That doesn't seem very realistic." Amy thought for a moment. "I know, we could say I was transferred to another hospital a few months ago."

"But then you'd have told us."

"Yes, and *that* could be the letter that got lost, rather than both yours and Rose's. Then yours wouldn't have got to me at all, which probably seems more rational."

"Hmm..." Harry thought for a moment. "It might work."

"It's best to just drop it into the conversation, and not elaborate too much."

"What's this? The British Intelligence School of Lying, Lesson One?"

"Don't..." Amy turned away.

"I was joking."

"Except that's what it's like, sometimes. Thinking on your feet, working out the best way of deceiving someone, making them believe you're something you're not." He hoped she'd elaborate, tell him more, but she stared down the garden and they sat in silence for a little longer.

That evening, just before dinner, Matthew called and spoke to Rose for some time. She took the call in Harry's study and afterwards, she came into the sitting room, looking paler than usual.

"What's wrong?" Harry asked, getting up from his chair.

"Oh..." She looked up and noticed the fear in his eyes. "Nothing. Don't worry."

"Something's happened," Harry said. Behind him, Elise and Amy looked on, both concerned.

"It's nothing."

"Rose..." There was a warning tone in Harry's voice, which she knew better than to ignore.

"It's just that Matthew wants me to stay here."

"And what's wrong with that? We've enjoyed having you. Haven't you enjoyed being here?"

"Yes, of course I have."

"And he comes down most weekends..."

"Yes, I know."

"So, what's the problem?"

"It's the reason he wants me to stay here."

"Is this something to do with those rockets?" Amy asked. Harry turned and looked at her, raising an eyebrow. "I read about them in the newspaper earlier," Amy explained.

"Yes," Rose confirmed. "They're very random, evidently. It's not like during the Blitz, when there was a bit of notice, an air-raid siren and you got the chance to go into the shelters. These things just seem to arrive out of nowhere. They drop down and… and… He said the damage is unbelievable. He was on duty the other night when one fell and he said the injuries were like nothing he'd ever seen before… and so many…" Her voice cracked as she rubbed her swollen stomach and Harry moved quickly across the room, putting his arm around her.

"This is all wrong," he said, an she looked up at him quizzically. "No-one should suffer like that… no-one. But wars happen and when they do, it's men who should fight, not women and children. It's not just us; we're bombing them too, and it's all wrong… all of it. Matthew shouldn't have to be tending to innocents, and you shouldn't have to be hiding down here to protect your unborn child, although I'm damned glad you are. Matthew's right. You're staying, so don't you even think about going back to London to be with him. He'd never forgive you and neither would I."

"Oh Daddy…" Rose threw her arms around his neck. "I do love you."

"What did I do to deserve that?" he asked, kissing her forehead.

"Oh, I don't know. You just have a way of making everything seem all right again."

Harry glanced over Rose's shoulder and saw Elise wiping a tear from her eye with a small white handkerchief. Amy, on the other hand, was staring into the empty fireplace and he wondered, yet again, what she'd witnessed. He knew that lost look. What had she seen or done to give her that faraway stare?

Both Elise and Rose seemed to believe Harry when he explained over dinner that Amy had been transferred and that's why she hadn't responded to their letters. Elise was really more concerned with Amy's health than anything else, so her absence from her own sickbed was of much less importance.

Over the coming days they fed her up on as much good food as they could muster and fresh vegetables certainly weren't in short supply, but she didn't seem to improve at all. She'd lost weight and her skin was pale and missing its former glow. In their quiet moments, Harry, Rose and Elise discussed this and Harry put it down to Amy's continued mourning for Ed, although he doubted this himself, recalling the lost look in her eyes when he'd talked to her about France, which was there whenever she thought no-one was looking. He wished she'd speak to him, but he knew how hard it could be and he wondered if there was anyone else he could talk to about what she'd been through; anyone who could fill in some of the gaps and help him to help her recover. He couldn't bear to see her go through what he'd experienced, but he knew the signs and she was headed in that direction.

Chapter Twenty-four

Summer 1944

The early August evening was warm, the sun lowering in the sky as the guests arrived at the village hall. Charlotte and the rest of the committee had done a marvellous job with the decorations and, following the D-Day landings, everyone felt a little more optimistic, more like celebrating than they might otherwise have done. The village hall was resplendent with home-made bunting, and there were tables of cakes, sandwiches and drinks to keep everyone going through the warm evening.

It had taken a great deal of persuasion to get Amy to attend the dance, but she'd eventually agreed, probably to appease Elise, and definitely because Harry had asked if she'd do it for him, being as Elise wanted her to. She'd found her red dress at the back of her wardrobe. She hadn't worn it for years and, while it reminded her of Ed, she thought it went well with her dark hair and didn't make her look as pale as some of her darker dresses would have done.

Matthew had managed to get the whole weekend off, with an extra day, so he wasn't going home until the Tuesday evening, and had arrived just after lunch. Rose was overjoyed to see him and they'd spent the afternoon walking in the fields, only returning just in time to change quickly and join everyone else in the walk to the village hall.

The band they'd hired started the evening playing a few classics, but, as the night wore on, they picked up the pace, which pleased the youngsters, and gave the older villagers something to talk about. Anne was home for the school holidays and her young man, a Naval Officer named Patrick, was on leave and visiting for the weekend. Amy, watching from the sidelines, thought they made a handsome couple. He was much taller than Anne and, with dark, slicked back hair and a neatly trimmed moustache, his film-star looks didn't go unnoticed by several other young ladies. The shortage of men was evident, as women danced together, giggling over who should lead, but Amy chose to sit alone, even when Harry, William, Matthew and Patrick – at Anne's suggestion – offered to dance with her.

Everyone was very surprised when Griffin arrived at the dance, being as he'd had nothing to do with the committee since Elise's illness, and hadn't been seen much around the village, other than coming and going to his offices. Everyone that is, except Sophie, whose eyes lit up as he approached her immediately upon entering the room. They talked in whispers for a while, before going onto the dance floor. From the way in which Griffin held Sophie close, while she wriggled her hips into his, it soon became clear to Harry that Henri had been right about his wife, and that Griffin was Sophie's lover and, judging by their increasing intimacy as the dance progressed, had been all along. The expression on Henri's face told Harry that he'd drawn the same conclusion. Harry went to Elise, who was sitting behind the refreshment table, although she'd been forbidden from helping. He pulled her to her feet and took her hand in his.

"What's wrong?" she asked, noticing the expression on his face.

"That." He looked out onto the dance floor, where Griffin and Sophie were entwined, his lips on hers.

"Oh." She was very clearly disappointed, and he felt the familiar clenching ache in his chest.

"I'm sorry," he said, instinctively.

"Why on earth are you saying sorry to me?"

"Because I love you and I don't want you to be hurt, even by him."

"What are you talking about, Harry?" She turned to face him properly.

Harry swallowed hard, trying to keep control of himself. "I know," he said simply.

"What do you know?"

"About you and him."

"Me and him? Me and who? Harry… I don't understand."

"I saw him kiss you. Months ago, when you got the letter from Jack. I saw…" Harry blinked and took a deep breath. "I saw him holding you, touching you and then kissing you. Surely you remember? You were there… you were in his arms."

"Oh, God." She paled, and put her hand to her mouth. "Come with me," she said and led him from the room, through a side door and out into an alleyway which ran along the side of the village hall, dividing it from the playing fields beyond. Once outside, she looked either way to check no-one was there. "I didn't know you'd seen," she said.

"Well, I did."

"And you've waited until now to say something?"

"I've tried quite a few times, but the moment hasn't been right, what with one thing and another. But why didn't you say something to me?"

"Because it wasn't worth mentioning, not if you hadn't seen it. It didn't mean anything. The fact that you did see it… Oh, Harry… what must you have been thinking all this time?" She looked up into his eyes.

"I knew he'd been pursuing you for months. I didn't know how you felt about him, though. I hoped, when he stopped coming around, and you didn't seem too bothered, that you might not have been too interested, or that maybe you'd got over him."

"Harry, I was never interested in him, so there was nothing to 'get over'."

"But, you doted on his every word. I heard you in your meetings."

"No. You heard me appeasing a man who was incredibly difficult if he didn't get his own way. It was easier to do that than to argue with him." She placed her hand on his chest. "Why on earth would I be interested in him?"

Harry hesitated for a long moment. "Isn't it obvious? He, like most men, can give you things… can do things, that I can't…"

"Stop right there, Harry. I've never wanted anyone but you, not since the first day I met you."

"But, he kissed you… he was holding you in his arms."

"To be honest, until I felt his lips on mine, I wasn't even really aware of what was happening. I was so upset by Jack's letter, I couldn't even think straight. All I could think about was Sylvia and that poor, poor child and Jack, and how he must be feeling. Then Robert kissed me, and I just didn't know what to do. I didn't understand why he would do something like that when I was crying, and upset… it felt so wrong… and then, I looked up and you were there, and I realised he was still holding me and I was repulsed by him and couldn't get away quickly enough. Running to you was like running home. I was safe, because you were there."

"What if I hadn't been there, though?" An awful thought crossed Harry's mind.

"But you were. Haven't you noticed that? Whenever I need you, you're always there."

"I hope I always will be." There was a slight question in his voice, as though he needed confirmation from her.

"So do I. I'm sorry, Harry. I'm so sorry. I wish you'd spoken to me before now… I could have explained. Is that why you were so distant for all those weeks?"

"Partly."

"And the other part?"

"You were ill, my darling… I could hardly put my needs before your health."

"I don't deserve you," she murmured. "If I saw you being kissed by someone else, I don't think I'd be as generous, or as calm as you've been."

He ran a finger gently down her cheek. "I've been anything but calm… I've been falling apart, Elise."

"Oh, Harry…" She leant up and kissed him and, before she knew what was happening, he was pushing her back against the wall, holding her there with his body while his tongue parried with hers. He poured so much of himself into that kiss, touching her cheek, then running his hand down the side of her body and behind, pulling her closer. He leant back slightly, ending the kiss, her swollen lips evidence of his arousal, where he'd bitten and nipped them between his teeth. Breathing heavily, he looked down at her.

"I'd take you here and now," he whispered, "but I've got no intention of being caught out by one of our own children, who might just come looking for us if we don't go back in there soon."

"That's a shame." Her eyes twinkled.

"We'll continue this later." He took her hand, and went to go back into the hall, but then stopped in his tracks. "I have one question, though," he said. "Why did you seem disappointed when you saw them dancing. I know it's not very flattering to be replaced in his affections by Sophie, but was that it? Was that the reason your shoulders dropped and you seemed so saddened when I pointed them out to you?"

"Good God no. I was sad because of what it'll do to Henri. Nothing else. I'm not interested in being flattered by the likes of Robert Griffin." Elise was indignant.

"Good." He kissed her hand and looked into her eyes. "So, if I told you that you were the most beautiful woman in that room…" Harry rested his forehead against hers.

"Then I'd wonder about your eyesight, but I'd love you for saying it," she replied, raising her eyes to his.

"My eyesight's just fine." He kissed her cheek. "Come back in and dance with a lame old man?"

Elise smiled up at him. "I can't see anyone matching that description… so you'll have to do instead."

Harry opened the door and they went back inside, where everyone still seemed to be focusing on the exhibition that Griffin and Sophie were giving. He led Elise out into the middle of the dance floor.

"Lean on me, if you need to," Elise offered.

"I always lean on you…" He held her in his arms and they swayed in time to the music, ignoring everything else around them.

It was a little after nine-thirty. Harry and Elise were in the kitchen, helping to organise more refreshments with Rose and Charlotte. It was a warm night and people were getting through more drinks than the committee had anticipated. Amy, sitting by the stage, at the front of the hall, was beginning to wonder whether she could sneak off home in their absence. She'd been right. She shouldn't have come to the dance. She was fed up watching everyone else and, not wanting to join in herself, was studying her fingernails, trying hard to forget about what might have been. She saw a pair of black shoes standing in front of her and sighed, looking up and wondering who had come to pester her this time. Then she felt the air being sucked from her lungs.

"Can I have this dance?" the familiar voice asked. She shook her head and opened her mouth, but nothing came out and, ignoring his offered hand and the gazes of those around her, she ran from the room, just as Harry and Elise entered from the kitchen, laughing.

"Amy!" Harry called, seeing her running out through the main entrance, and then he glanced around to where she'd been sitting. The tall figure standing there turned and ran his fingers through his tousled blond hair, a look of confusion on his face.

"Oh my God," Harry whispered. "Eddie... Can it be? Eddie?" He began to shake, sliding towards the floor, and Elise grasped his arm, looking around for help.

"Ed!" she cried, but he was already by Harry's side.

"Let me help," William offered, taking Elise's place opposite Ed, and the two men helped Harry to a chair.

"Eddie," Harry kept saying, over and over, his voice almost inaudible. Matthew had joined the group and William moved out of the way to let the young doctor help Harry.

"No, no, it's Ed," Elise said quietly in Harry's ear as someone handed her a glass of water to give to Harry. He took a sip, then seemed to recollect himself.

"Of course," he murmured. "Ed." He looked up into Ed's face. "My boy... Oh, my boy," he cried, tears running down his cheeks. "We thought... we..."

"I know," Ed said. "I know."

"We need to get Harry home," Elise whispered to William.

"I'll fetch the car," he offered, and left the crowded room via the front door.

"And Anne, can you go and tell Rose what's happened?" Elise added. Anne disappeared into the kitchen, returning a few moments later, with Rose and Charlotte behind her. Rose crossed the room and threw her arms around Ed, holding him close.

"My God," he said, looking down at her stomach. "I had no idea. Congratulations!"

"Thank you." Tears were flooding her eyes.

"Sit down," Ed said, guiding her to a seat.

"Where's Amy?" Rose asked looking around the room.

"She ran…"

"Ran?"

"Yes. I'll find her in a minute, once we've got Harry on his way home." He knelt down next to her and lowered his voice. "I think I might have overdone the melodrama, just turning up like that. I saw the poster for the dance when I came into the village and guessed everyone would be here. Harry thought I was my father; I think it's given him a bit of a knock."

"Poor Daddy." Rose looked across to her father, who was sitting with Elise alongside him, his hands shaking, his cheeks still wet with tears. "He'll hate this, with all these people."

William appeared at the door and signalled to Elise that the car was ready.

"Let's get going," Elise said quietly, trying to get Harry to stand. Ed went over and took Harry's arm.

"Can I help?" Patrick was on hand, with Anne standing close by. Between them, Patrick and Ed helped Harry outside and into William's waiting car.

"Thanks," Ed said to Patrick, looking at him uncertainly. He helped Elise climb in beside Harry.

"We'll manage fine here," Charlotte said to Elise, who was looking at the village hall with a worried expression on her face. "You stay with Harry."

"Rose," Matthew said, "I want you to go home too. I'll follow on foot." He opened the passenger door and helped Rose in, kissing her gently, then William pulled away.

Charlotte turned to Ed. "It's so good to see you," she said, giving him a hug. "I'm sorry. You haven't been introduced to Anne's young man." She indicated Patrick, who shook hands with Ed. "He's on leave for a few days."

"This is Ed," Charlotte continued the introductions. "He was posted as missing last Christmas." He noticed her eyes glistening. "We'd just about given up hope, you know."

"So I gather. Look, Charlotte, I hate to cut and run, but I'm going to try and find Amy. Are you coming, Matthew?"

Anne placed a hand on his arm, stalling him for a moment. "Give her some time, Ed," she said gently. "It's been a tremendous shock for her."

"Yes, and she hasn't been well," Charlotte added.

"She's been unwell?" Ed was now frantic. "I've got to go." He turned and, forgetting all about Matthew, started running back towards the house.

Up in her room, Amy lay on the bed sobbing into her pillow. How could this happen? How could he still be alive? It was like all her dreams had come true and yet, when faced with the reality of it, she didn't know how she was ever going to explain what she'd done. He'd never trust her again. He'd never want her again, that was for certain. She lay still, listening to the sounds of everyone returning. William's voice was clear from all the way downstairs, while Elise's, Rose's and Harry's were a whisper. She heard Rose's footsteps pass her door as she went to her bedroom, then her parents' bedroom door opened and closed a few times, and then she heard her mother's footsteps go back downstairs and a conversation between her and William. After a few minutes, she heard the front door open and slam, and she heard someone running up the stairs, and a knocking on her door.

"Amy." It was Ed, his voice full of concern. "Let me in." She remained silent. "Are you there? Amy?"

"Come away, Ed." It was her mother.

"But I need to see her."

"You will. In the morning. Just leave her be for a while. She's had a huge shock."

"How do we know she's even in there? She could be anywhere... Should I go and look for her? She might be up at the tree." Amy heard his footsteps move away from the door.

"She's here," Elise said, calmly. "I was worried too, but Harry noticed she'd kicked her shoes off at the bottom of the stairs, and her shawl is hanging over the bannisters."

There was a moment's pause and his footsteps came back towards her room. "Oh, yes." Then another hesitation. "But..."

"In the morning, Ed." Elise's voice was firm, and Amy was grateful for a few hours' peace in which to work out what to tell him.

Chapter Twenty-five

Summer 1944

"I'm so sorry about last night," Harry said. He and Ed were sitting alone over breakfast the following morning. Harry looked down at his hand, lying in his lap, which still shook slightly. "I made rather an exhibition of myself, I'm afraid."

"Don't be sorry, Harry. It's all my fault. I should have called or sent a telegram. I thought I'd surprise you all."

"You certainly did that."

"Just not in the way I'd expected."

Something in Ed's voice made Harry look up. "She'll get over it," he said.

"I thought she'd be happy to see me." The disappointment in his voice was obvious.

"She is, you idiot." Harry smiled. "She's been through a lot lately. Seeing you is probably one shock too many. She'll be down later and you can talk." He poured Ed some more coffee. "In the meantime, you can tell me where you've been for the last eight months."

"That's simple." Ed took a sip from his cup. "France."

"France?" Harry couldn't hide the shock in his voice. The irony of Ed and Amy being in the same country, and neither of them knowing it, wasn't lost on him.

"Yes. I was shot down on my way back from a night op, but my bloody chute didn't open properly. I was falling far too fast and, to be honest, I thought it was curtains. I hit the ground with a thump and broke my right leg, although I didn't know that at the time. All I knew was that I was, to put it bluntly, buggered. I couldn't move at all. I just lay there for the rest of the night and most of the next day, hoping someone would find me, even if it was a German. I decided being in a POW camp would be better than dying in the middle of French field."

"So who did find you?"

"A young boy, believe it or not. Later that afternoon. He was probably no more than about eight years old. I've never been so glad that you made me learn to speak French in my entire life. He told me to lie still and keep quiet. He packed up my chute like a professional and hid it away, and then ran off. A while later, when it was nearly dark, he came back with two men and they carried me back to a house, which it turned out belonged to one of them, who was the local doctor. They put me up in his attic. I can't tell you how painful it was getting me up there, but they managed it. I think I must have blacked out at one stage, because I don't remember all of it."

"Pain does that," Harry commented. "So what happened next?"

"Well, cutting a long story short, the doctor, Pierre, he fixed me up… He had nothing to work with. It wasn't like we were in a hospital or anything, so he just had to improvise. He got me blind drunk, so I wouldn't feel too much pain, and he couldn't afford for me to cry out, then he set my leg and put me in a splint. It seems to have mended all right. I stayed there for a couple of months until I was fit enough to leave."

"So, what happened then – that must have been around February or March?"

"Yes. Pierre arranged for me to be passed to the Resistance." Ed looked away and then turned back, a smile on his face, which didn't go anywhere near touching his eyes and made Harry shiver. "And that's when the fun really began." Ed's voice was a little too bright, too carefree and Harry knew something was wrong. "I got passed from one cell to another, dodging the Germans, sometimes by just a whisker, but I ended up in a farmhouse with this group, just outside of Amiens. They were going to hand me on to another group, but things kept going wrong and I ended up staying with them for a while. Then the invasion happened…" His voice trailed away to nothing. Again, Harry felt there was something wrong; something Ed was hiding beneath the bravado of his storytelling.

"And this is your idea of fun, is it?" Harry said.

"Well, Pierre had told me I had to keep my leg moving, so I did…" Ed smiled. "Anyway, eventually, I caught up with some Canadians, and they passed me back to a bunch of Brits, and I found myself on a troop ship back home. I reported back to base and, after I'd been debriefed, they gave me a weeks' leave… and here I am."

"I get the feeling you're not telling me everything." Harry's voice was serious.

Ed looked up at Harry. "Now you know how we all feel," he said. "There is more to it than that, Harry, but it can wait." Ed sat forward. "I've got more important things to talk about." Harry raised an eyebrow. "Charlotte told me Amy's been unwell. What's wrong with her?" Ed stared at Harry.

"She's fine… Well, she will be, now that you're home." Harry sat back in his chair. "It was a terrible time for her when you went missing… Well for all of us, but especially for her. She… she went away for a while."

"Went away? Went away where?"

"Ed, I can't tell you her story. She has to do that."

"Okay… And she was unwell while she was away?"

"I don't know that I'd call it unwell as such, I think she just found it difficult. Look," Harry paused, "I don't really know the full story myself. She's hardly spoken to us since she got back. If you want to know what's been going on, you'll have to ask her."

"If she'll tell me."

"I'll try." The voice at the door made them both stand and Ed turned, a genuine smile forming on his lips.

"Amy," he said, moving towards her, but she backed away and out of the door again, shaking her head.

"We need to talk," she said.

Ed glanced at Harry, warily. "Okay," he replied. "Do you want to walk?"

She nodded and they headed out of the door.

Chapter Twenty-six

Summer 1944

They walked in silence. Amy kept her hands in the pockets of her full pale blue skirt, avoiding the need to hold Ed's, and to prevent him from trying to hold hers. She had to keep from any kind of contact or intimacy with him until he knew what she'd done and could decide how he felt. Overnight, when not tossing and turning, she'd resolved to tell him everything. Just one look at him last night had told her that she still loved him more than anything, and she wanted to be with him as much as she ever had, but she couldn't live a lie. He had to know all of it and, if he didn't want her any longer, then she'd just have to live with the consequences of her actions.

When she looked up, she found they'd walked up to the oak tree.

"Perhaps we should go somewhere else…" she suggested.

"Why? I like it here. The memories of this place are… perfect…" He smiled. She looked at her feet. "Okay," he continued, sounding hesitant, "something's wrong, isn't it?" She nodded, but still couldn't look at him. "Then sit down and tell me about it." He plonked himself down on the dry grass at the base of the tree and waited. After a few minutes, she joined him, but neither of them spoke. "I'm sorry," he said eventually.

"Why are you sorry?"

"Because of what I've put you through."

"You didn't ask to be shot down."

"No, obviously. But I can only imagine how awful it must have been."

"I don't think you can."

"Well, I know how I'd feel if it was you." He reached over and took her hand and she let him. "Tell me what's wrong," he urged. "Who knows, it might help."

"I doubt it, but I have to tell you anyway." He wasn't sure he liked the sound of that and took a deep breath, which he only released when she started talking again.

"Hearing that you were missing," she began, "was like losing part of myself."

"I'm sorry."

"You can't interrupt," she said. "This is going to be hard enough without you interrupting me."

"Sorry."

"And don't keep saying sorry." She sighed and he tightened his grip on her hand. "I felt so lost," she continued eventually, "and I certainly didn't want to stay here. Everything… everything reminded me of you and made the pain so much worse." She heard his intake of breath but ploughed on anyway before he could speak. "I decided to apply for a transfer straight away, but it seemed to take ages and, while I was waiting, this man came to visit me at the hospital. David Harrison was his name and… well, he worked for the government, he said, and they were looking for people like me who could speak French. I thought it sounded ideal."

"So they wanted translators?"

"Not exactly, no." She didn't look at him. "I went for an interview in London and they approved me and I started training at a big house in Cranleigh."

"What kind of training?" She glared at him. "Sorry, I'm interrupting again." Her eyes narrowed.

"The training was quite tough, but I enjoyed it. It gave me something else, apart from losing you, to focus on. After a couple of months, they told me I'd been picked for a mission."

Ed sat up straight. "A mission?" he said sharply. "What are you telling me, Amy?"

"I was parachuted into Southern France—"

"What?"

"We…"

"Who's 'we'?"

"David Harrison and I. We had a specific task, which was in Paris. We travelled there by train a few days later, but while we were on the train, a German officer came into the compartment. David needed to avoid having his case searched, as it contained a lot of money and some papers, so… he… he kissed me." Ed dropped her hand and she looked up at him. The expression on his face was unreadable, but now she'd started she had to finish. "He needed the German to leave, so we put on a bit of a display… It was…"

"What?" Ed urged. "Good?"

"No! Difficult was what I was going to say. But the German left and we got on with the job in hand."

"You mean you carried on with the 'display' behind closed doors?" The sarcasm in his voice was cutting.

"No, Ed. That's not what I mean at all." They sat in silence for a few moments. "We talked about what had happened, and then discussed the mission. That's all."

Ed stared at her, then swallowed hard. "Okay, so this David kissed you, and presumably touched you, to throw the Nazi off your scent." Amy looked at her feet, not daring to raise her face to his. "Is that it?" he asked. She shook her head. "There's more? What are you not telling me, Amy?"

"He kissed me again."

"When? Why?"

"The second time was also part of the mission. There was a woman David suspected of leaking information to the Germans. We had to throw her off our scent, make her think we were lovers."

"Were you?"

"No! Ed, how could you?"

"I'm starting to wonder the same thing about you." He paused. "You said 'the second time'… Was there a third?" Her shoulders fell and she nodded her head, almost imperceptibly. "And that wasn't anything to do with the mission?"

"No," she whispered. "We'd been in danger. A lot of danger. We were being chased… We'd just reached safety and… and he kissed me."

"Did you kiss him back?"

"I don't really remember. I think I might have done."

"How can you not know?"

"Because I was terrified."

"Did you want him?"

"No, Ed."

"Did he want you?"

"He said he did."

"And did he have you? Did you let him? Is that the bit you're saving up to tell me?"

"How can you even ask?"

"Because I'm wondering if I know you at all…"

She paused, accepting his comment. "He knew about you and he knew how I feel about you. He said he wanted a future with me, but that he'd wait for me to get over you first."

"Then maybe you should do just that." He glared at her.

"Ed… Don't say that. I was frightened… He was…"

Ed got to his feet, pacing up and down. "I don't think I want to hear any more," he said, running his hands though his hair.

"Why are you being like this? I didn't expect you to like it, but why are you being so…? I thought you were dead."

"Thought or wished?"

"Ed," she sobbed, "how can you say that?"

"It's not as easy as you seem to think." He stood in front of her staring down, his eyes hard. "Do you think I don't understand fear, Amy? Do you think I don't know what it feels like to be so afraid you can't even breathe?" He moved away, just a step or two. "Falling out of a plane with your bloody chute refusing to work is pretty damned frightening, I can tell you… I've done things in these last few months… seen things. I'm not proud of some of what I've done. I've hurt people… I've…" He turned suddenly. "Fuck it, Amy, I'm not going to tell you what I've done… I thought I could. God knows, I need to. I can't, though… not now." He paused and she noticed the tears in his eyes. When he spoke again, his voice was so chilled, she hardly recognised it. "Through everything, all that I've done, I've been loyal to you."

"So have I."

"Really? It doesn't sound like it. When I was falling through the sky, watching the ground approaching far too fast, I thought I was never going to see you again and it was the most terrifying moment of my life, but I didn't feel the need to go around kissing every French woman I came into contact with, just to prove how scared I was."

"I did not kiss every man I met."

"No, just the one, evidently. Still, one is enough… unless there's something else you're not telling me?"

She didn't reply, but allowed the tears to track down her cheeks.

"No? Well, being as you're so clearly over me, I suggest you go back to him, because he's welcome to you," Ed whispered and turned away, walking slowly down the hill towards the gate.

Chapter Twenty-seven

Summer 1944

Ed walked around the side of the house to find Harry sitting alone on the terrace. Rose and Matthew had gone for a walk and Elise was with Polly in the kitchen.

"What's wrong?" Harry said, sitting forward as soon as he saw Ed. "Where's Amy?"

Ed went to walk past, but Harry stood just in time, blocking his way to the house.

"Ed, where is she? What's happened?"

"She's up under the oak tree, where I left her... Unless she's decided to go and do something else completely irresponsible and selfish, which wouldn't surprise me in the slightest." He went to walk away, but Harry grabbed his arm.

"What the hell are you talking about?"

Ed sighed. "Nothing, Harry. It really doesn't matter."

"It really bloody does. What on earth's happened?"

"I don't want to talk about it."

"I wasn't aware I was giving you an option..." Harry still had a firm grip on his arm, but Ed pulled away, releasing himself, his fists clenched.

"Leave it, Harry, alright? Not now." He turned and walked into the house. Harry watched him go, then picked up his stick which had been leaning against the table, and set off.

It took him nearly half an hour to reach the field and, at the gate, he looked up and saw Amy sitting beneath the oak tree. He climbed up to her, but her head was bowed and she didn't notice him until he cast a shadow across her. She looked up and her face crumpled.

"Daddy..." she cried.

"Oh, sweetheart." He used his stick for support and, with a great deal of difficulty, lowered himself to sit next to her, taking her in his arms and letting her rest her head on his chest. He allowed her to cry, each sob breaking his heart, until she'd calmed enough to sit up a little. "What's wrong?" he asked eventually, reaching into his trouser pocket for a handkerchief, and giving it to her.

"Nothing."

"It certainly doesn't look like nothing. And having got down here, I'm not getting up again until you tell me what's the matter."

She looked up at him. "It's all gone horribly wrong," she said.

"Could you be a bit more specific?"

She wiped her eyes and, in a rush of words, gulps and more tears, told him everything she'd told Ed.

"And I didn't even get to tell him about Luc..." she wailed at the end of her story.

"What about Luc?" Harry looked into her eyes. "Tell me, Amy. What about Luc?"

She recounted the story of her mission, Claudette's role, the chase through Paris and how that tied in with David's kiss, Luc's capture and interrogation and her final goodbye to David at the station.

"And now Ed's gone off," she finished. "He was... horrible. He's so angry with me."

"Angry with you?" Harry was feeling pretty angry himself. "Why the hell is he angry with you?"

"Because David kissed me, of course."

"Oh. So, having been chased around Paris by the Nazis, you found yourself finally out of danger, with the man who'd just saved your life, and, when he kissed you in the heat of the moment, you were supposed to do what? Slap him round the face? Throw him out onto the street to be captured? It might have been a little different, if you'd thought Ed was safely tucked up at home, but you believed him to be dead anyway." He looked down at her. "Oh, come here," he said, pulling her back for another cuddle. "It'll be all right."

"How can it be?" she wailed. "I mean… It's not just Ed, is it? When I got back to London, I went to see the man at the office, which is what I was instructed to do, and he told me I'm not allowed to let Uncle Henri or Aunt Sophie know about Luc. They have to wait to be told through official channels, evidently, probably not until the end of the war. But what's mum going to say when she finds out? I was partially responsible for the death of her nephew… for Uncle Henri's son…" She put her head in her hands. "Oh God. What have I done?" Now, her silence over the previous weeks began to make sense.

"You are not responsible for Luc's death. Luc is."

"But…"

"Not another word, Amy."

"And Ed…"

"Ed's being an idiot. He'll work it out."

"You didn't see his face, Dad. He looked at me like he hated me."

"If he hated you, Amy, he wouldn't care what you did."

"And what about mum, and Uncle Henri and… oh God, Aunt Sophie…?" Tears tracked down her cheeks again.

"Leave all of that to me."

He helped Amy back to the house just before lunch. She went upstairs to have a wash. Elise was alone in the sitting room and Harry went and sat beside her.

"What's going on?" Elise asked.

Harry took a deep breath. "There's something I've got to tell you," he said. "And you're not going to like it."

"Okay." Her voice was wary.

He took her hand in his. "Please, please just remember that I love you. And don't hate me."

"Harry, you're frightening me."

"I don't mean to."

"Then tell me what's wrong."

He paused, then began: "Amy didn't take up nursing with the FANY. She joined them so that she could work with the SOE."

"What are the SOE?"

"It's a government department."

"I don't like the sound of this."

"Just hear me out, please."

"Okay."

"She was approached by them and they trained her, and eventually, back in May, they parachuted her into France."

"What?" Elise shot to her feet.

"Come and sit back down." Harry tried to keep his voice calm. "I need to finish the story."

She did as he asked and he took her hand again. "I'll let her explain the ins and outs of her mission later, but she went to France with a more senior officer and they ended up in Paris, where their job was to infiltrate a Resistance cell and find out who was leaking information to the enemy." He took a deep breath. "There's no easy way for me to tell you this, my love." He brushed her knuckles with his thumb. "The person they were looking for… the traitor, turned out to be Luc."

"Oh my God." He saw her eyes flicker and wondered if she was going to faint.

"Are you all right?" She nodded her head just once. "The man Amy was working with sent her home again and… Luc was…"

"Killed?" Elise asked.

"Yes," came the whispered voice from the door. Amy stood there, tears still falling down her face. "Oh, Mummy. I'm so sorry."

Elise leapt to her feet and ran across the room, clasping Amy to her. "Don't," she said. "Don't be sorry. Luc was always a fool. This is not your fault. I just want to know why you did it? Why did you go? And why didn't you tell us?"

Amy glanced at her father and Elise didn't miss the look exchanged between them.

"Wait a minute," she said. "You knew?" She glared at Harry. "You knew?" she repeated, raising her voice.

Harry nodded his head. "I guessed. Amy couldn't tell me, but I guessed."

"And you didn't tell me?"

"I couldn't tell you."

"I begged him not to, Mum. It wasn't his fault, you can't blame him. They made me promise that you weren't to know. I think they might have realised dad would guess, but they said it was imperative that you shouldn't know… because of Sophie and Henri. I might have been in danger if they'd found out. I made dad promise, Mum. Please don't blame him… I couldn't bear it if you argued because of me…" she sobbed. "I'm responsible for so much else going wrong. I couldn't bear that too."

Harry crossed the room and looked down at them both. Elise stared up at him. "We're not going to argue," he said, not taking his eyes from Elise's. "And none of this is your fault. None of it, Amy. Do you understand?"

"Mum?" Amy asked, looking at Elise. "Tell me you're okay with this. Tell me you don't blame dad."

Elise took a deep breath. "I can't lie to you Amy. I'm not happy that your father lied to me, but I don't blame him. He had to protect you, so I understand why he did it and we won't argue about it." She felt Amy's shoulders drop and the relief pouring from her daughter. "But what about Henri and Sophie?" Elise asked, looking up at Harry. "What are we going to tell them?"

"We can't tell them anything," Amy replied. "I was given orders that they'll have to wait to find out through official channels. It's killing me to know that he's dead and they have no idea, but I can't do anything."

"But we must be able to tell them something, surely?"

"No," said Harry. "Amy's been told what to do. We can't go against that. This isn't about us, or Henri and Sophie… It's about Amy."

Elise walked away from the two of them, towards the window, looking down the length of the garden.

"This is hard," she said, suddenly turning back into the room. "How do we face them?"

"The same way dad's faced you every day for the last few months, I suppose."

Elise looked at Harry. "So, how do we do it?" she asked.

"Just by knowing we're doing the right thing," Harry replied. "For Amy."

Later that evening, just before dinner, they all sat on the terrace. Ed still hadn't come downstairs and Harry decided his sulk had gone on long enough. He asked Matthew to go and fetch Ed, but was surprised when Matthew returned just a few minutes later.

"He's gone," he said.

"Gone?" Harry glanced briefly at Amy. "What do you mean, 'gone'?"

"His bag, uniform, clothes... it's all gone. It's like he was never even here."

"What? All of it?"

"Yes. The wardrobe, shelves, cupboards... everything is completely empty." He moved forward, holding out an envelope to Amy. "This was on the mantlepiece."

She took the envelope from him, glanced at everyone and went into the sitting room. A few minutes later, they heard a cry and Harry, surprisingly, was the first through the door. He found her on the floor.

"Matthew!" he cried.

"She's fainted," Matthew said, as he knelt down. He picked her up and placed her gently on the sofa. "Amy," he called, patting her hand. "Amy?" Her eyes flickered opened. "There's a good girl." Amy glanced around the room, her eyes locking on Harry's.

"He's really gone," she cried.

On the floor beside where she'd fallen was a folded piece of paper. Harry bent awkwardly and picked it up.

"May I?" he asked and she nodded.

Amy, he read to himself,

By the time you read this, I'll have gone back to base.

You can have your freedom, to do with as you please, with whomever you please, which obviously isn't me any longer.

Our time together was magical, and I'll never forget you.

Ed.

"The bloody idiot," Harry said, loudly.

"What's going on?" Rose asked.

"Is Amy all right?" Harry asked of Matthew, who nodded his head. "Good. Excuse me," he continued. "I'm going to make a phone call." He folded the piece of paper and left it on the table before walking quickly out of the room.

Elise took Rose's hand and sat next to her on the sofa. "Let me try and explain…" she said.

"Do you have to go tomorrow?" Elise asked as she got into bed, settling back on the pillows.

"Yes, I'm catching the early train. I don't want to let this lie. I'm not sure how much more Amy can take and I'm going to get to the bottom of this. I don't understand what's going on and I need to if I'm going to help her, and Ed, for that matter."

"Who are you going to see?"

"The man who's really responsible for all this." Elise sighed. "What's wrong?" Harry turned onto his side, facing her.

"Oh, nothing."

"It's clearly something… tell me."

"I feel guilty, talking about it now, with everything else that's happening… Amy… Ed… Luc…"

"What is it, Elise?" Harry said.

"It's us, Harry."

"Us?"

"Yes. We haven't spoken properly since the dance… since we talked about Robert kissing me. You were unwell when we got home, and we didn't get to speak about it… And since then we've both been so wrapped up with Amy and Ed… I'm not…"

"You're not what?" Harry sounded worried.

"I'm not sure how you feel about things… about us…"

Harry took a deep breath. "I love you, Elise. I love you completely. That's how I feel about us. I've always loved you, no matter what happened between you and him, even in my darkest moments, when I was imagining the worst. That's why it hurt so much… to see you in his arms." He reached over and pulled her closer, feeling her body next to his. "I always knew that, even if you wanted him, even if you left me for him, I'd still love you. I'm yours, Elise. I always have been… and it doesn't matter what you do, say, or think, I always will be… Does that help to answer your question?"

Elise nodded her head. "I didn't want him, Harry… and I'd never have left you; you know that, don't you?"

"Yes. I do now."

"Ed could do with taking some lessons from you," she whispered. Harry raised an enquiring eyebrow. "His reaction to hearing about Amy being kissed by this other man… it's so different to your reaction to seeing me being kissed by Robert…"

"He's young," Harry said. "He's got a lot to learn about being in love. I just hope he isn't doing anything stupid; something Amy can't forgive him for." He sighed and shook his head. "I think there's more to Ed's story than we know. I think something happened to him while he was in France… something he's not telling."

"Do you think you can help?"

"I need to see this man in London first, for Amy's sake… Then I'll deal with Ed."

Elise snuggled down into his embrace and he held her tight. "I love you," she whispered.

"I love you more."

London was busier than Harry had expected and, as he stood outside the official-looking building, with sandbags piled up at the windows, he was bustled and jostled by passing pedestrians. Deciding he'd be safer inside, he passed through the large double doors and into the quiet seclusion of the bland interior. A man standing behind a desk raised his head and looked at Harry, who moved forward.

"I'm here to see David Harrison," he said.

"Do you have an appointment?" the man asked, looking down at a piece of paper in front of him.

"No." Harry's reply was simple, but the expression on his face was compelling.

"Then I'm afraid..."

"Tell him Harry Belmont is here to see him," Harry interrupted, staring at the man.

"I'm afraid he won't see you, sir."

"Would you just try... please?"

"Very well, sir." The man sighed and picked up a telephone, dialling two numbers. He waited a moment then said, "There's a Harry Belmont here to see you, Major." There was a pause. The man looked at Harry, raised his eyebrows and replaced the receiver. "He'll be down in a moment," he said, unable to contain the surprise in his voice.

"Thank you," Harry said.

The footsteps on the stone staircase alerted him and he turned to see a tall man descending, probably in his late twenties or early thirties. He wore a pristine uniform, his hair was greying at the temples and his eyes looked tired. He was very handsome, without a doubt, but he wore it without arrogance. Harry found himself liking the man, even before David had approached and not tried to shake the hand he no longer had.

"Hello, Mr Belmont. My name is David Harrison. There's a room here we can use," David said, opening a door to their left. "It will save you the trouble of the stairs."

"Thank you." Harry entered the room, which was small, furnished with two wing-backed chairs placed either side of a fireplace, and a coffee table in between, the walls filled with bookshelves.

"Can I offer you a cup of tea?" David asked.

"No, thank you," Harry replied.

The two men sat down and David looked closely at Harry. "If you don't mind me asking," he began, "how did you…?"

"Find you?"

"Yes."

"I called an old army pal of mine. Name of Newby. I knew he worked with your lot, although we don't stay in regular contact… Just Christmas cards really, these days. But I knew if I asked, if it was important enough, he'd tell me what I needed to know, and I just needed an address, that's all."

David nodded. "And why did you need my address?"

"Because of Amy."

David sat forward. "What's wrong with Amy?"

"Everything."

"That's not very helpful. It's worrying, but not helpful."

"I know. If I understood it myself I might be able to explain it better. I think she's struggling to come to terms with what she's done."

"What she's done? I'm sorry, I don't understand."

"In France."

"I can't discuss that." David shut him down.

Now Harry sat forward. "You can, young man. And what's more, you bloody well will." David raised his eyebrows. "You took my daughter to France and put her in danger. Now, she's struggling to cope with what she did. I need to understand it if I'm going to help her."

David didn't take his eyes from Harry's. "All right," he said eventually. "I'll talk to you. But only for Amy's sake. And anything we say within these four walls remains between us."

Harry nodded.

"What do you want to know?" David asked.

"What happened? She's told me quite a lot, but I have a feeling there's more to it. Something she's not telling me."

"Well, being as I don't know what she's told you, that's hard for me to say, but if there are things she doesn't want you to know, it's not really my place to tell you."

"I just want to help her."

"I understand. Tell me what you know and I'll see what I can do."

Harry outlined the story he'd been given by Amy and David sat impassively, listening.

"I imagine it was a huge shock to find out that Luc was Amy's cousin," Harry finished. David looked out of the window behind Harry, then into the empty fireplace. "Wait a minute," Harry said slowly. "Are you telling me you knew?"

"I knew she was Luc's cousin, yes. I didn't know he was the mole. I firmly believed that was the female agent. Taking Amy was necessary, in case my plan to trap the female agent didn't work. I'd hoped that having his cousin there might bring Luc onto our side and help us to bring her in. Of course, discovering that Luc was the mole changed all that."

David looked at Harry's face again and shifted uncomfortably in his seat. "So… Let me get this straight. You, knowingly took my daughter into enemy occupied France, up against this man, who would give her… give his own cousin away, to the Nazis? You knew of their relationship and you took her anyway?" Harry raised his voice.

"Yes. I knew of their relationship, but – I repeat – I didn't know Luc was the danger. I thought that was the female agent. I saw Luc as being someone who'd help us, not someone who'd endanger Amy. I was using Amy's family tie to Luc as insurance."

"Well, that backfired, didn't it?"

"Yes." David didn't take his eyes from Harry's. "Spectacularly. And I'm not proud of it."

"Well good. Because if anything had happened to Amy, as a result of you getting it wrong… I'd have found you and killed you myself."

"You wouldn't have needed to." David averted his eyes, just for a moment. "I don't think I'd have come back."

Harry stared at the younger man, his anger diffusing as quickly as it had arisen. "Did you kill them both?" he asked.

"Yes. But none of that was Amy's responsibility."

"She thinks it was. And she's convinced her uncle and aunt will never forgive her."

"They'll never know she was there. But she didn't do anything to contribute to his death. She spent most of her time trying to persuade me *not* to kill him."

"She did? Even though he'd given her away to the Nazis?"

David nodded. "Yes. Don't get me wrong. Nothing… absolutely nothing Amy could have said or done would have persuaded me not to carry out my orders when it came to Luc Martin, but that didn't stop her trying… well, begging, actually. She was kinder to him than he deserved. He was responsible for the deaths of three of my agents, plus countless French resistance fighters and at least five British airmen… men like Ed… none of whom made it back home. Not to mention the fact that he laughed when he gave Amy away to the Gestapo. He actually laughed… I pulled the trigger myself, just for that." Harry noticed the knuckles on David's fingers whiten as he clutched the arms of his chair a little tighter. It took a few minutes for David's hands to relax slightly. "How's she been since she got home?"

"She's confused… upset. She's close to breaking point. I think the whole episode turned out to be very different to how she expected it."

"Well, that makes two of us."

"I realise you didn't expect to take her into that much danger. I understand that now."

"That's not exactly what I meant." Again David stared out of the window for a brief time, then looked back to Harry, clearing his throat. "I gather Ed's back…"

"Yes. How did you…?"

"I've kept track of things."

"Oh. Yes, he's back. Or at least he was. He's gone again"

"Now I'm the one getting the feeling there's something you're not telling me."

"He didn't react well."

"What to? Surely he's glad to be home."

"Amy told him… about you and her."

"Me and her? There is no 'me and her'."

"But there was, according to Amy." He noticed a sparkle cross David's eyes.

"Well, I hoped there might have been at some point in the future, when she'd laid Ed's memory to rest, but the last time I saw Amy, she made it very clear she never wanted to see me again." He noted the look of surprise on Harry's face. "I may have saved her life, but I was about to kill her cousin, and that, in her view, was inexcusable." He leant forward. "What did she tell Ed then?"

"That you'd kissed her."

"And that's all? He's left because of a kiss? That was part of our cover…"

"Not all the time it wasn't." Harry looked embarrassed. "She said there was one occasion when it wasn't strictly necessary."

"Well, it was necessary to me."

"But not to your cover."

"No." David got up and walked across to the window, staring outside and picking at some loose paintwork with his fingernails. "This probably isn't what you want to hear, but I fell in love with your daughter before we even went on the mission. So, taking her with me was the second most unprofessional thing I've ever done – the first being to get the whole bloody mission wrong in the first place. I tried very hard to stick to the cover, to be honourable in my behaviour towards her. I think I succeeded for the best part, but on that night… dear God, we came so close… as close as I've ever come to death, and I've been in some scrapes before. It was one of those spur of the moment things, when you realise that death has been standing, tapping on your shoulder and you just want the person you love the most in the whole world to know how you feel before it's too late, even though you realise they'll never love you back." He cleared his throat. "She made it clear to me that she still loved Ed, and I respected that. It wasn't easy, but I couldn't compete with a ghost, so I decided to bide my time and hope that, one day, she'd leave her memories behind and, maybe learn to love again. My only wish then had to be that, when the time came, I'd be the man she'd choose. Then, that hope was shattered on the platform at Paris Montparnasse when she told me she never wanted to see me again. Even then…" He lowered his head, staring down at the pavement outside. "Even then, I suppose I kept hoping she might… one day…"

"I'm sorry," Harry said.

David turned around and walked back across the room, re-taking his seat. "You say she told Ed?"

"Yes."

"And he didn't react well…?"

"No. To be honest, it wasn't his finest moment. But I think something happened to him while he was in France that he's not talking about either. They both seem damaged and I can't help them."

"Sometimes there's nothing we can do. We just have to wait for time to take its course."

"I'm not sure they have time. I know…" He paused. "I know the signs. They're both in a bad place and I'm worried. I've seen it before. I know where it ends..." David raised an eyebrow and sat quietly waiting. "I have my own traumas," Harry said, quietly.

"I've read your file," David said.

"Not everything is in the file." David waited patiently. "I've only ever told Elise this," Harry continued, "and I don't really know why I'm telling you, except that I think you'll understand better than anyone else who wasn't there, who didn't live through hell with us." He waited until he felt a little more composed, then took a deep breath. "I killed Ed's father," he said suddenly. David didn't react, just waited, sitting quite still. "He was my best friend, and I shot him."

"Why?"

"Because he was wounded and he begged me to."

"I'm assuming there was nothing else you could have done?"

"No. I'd been shot myself, in the knee and the hand, trying to get to him. Oh, trust me, if I could have carried him back, I would have done, even though he wouldn't have thanked me… not with his injuries."

"And only your wife knows about this?" Harry nodded. "Not Ed, or Amy?"

"No."

"Do you think he'd blame you?"

"Yes. And I don't want him to think badly of me. We're very close. Or we were, until this…"

"He might surprise you… If you told him."

"After the way he's behaved over you kissing Amy, I doubt that. But that's not really important right now. I need to find out what's wrong with both of them, before it's too late. This isn't about me, or Ed's father, it's about them. I don't even really know why I told you, other than maybe to explain that I know how hard it can be to live with the memory of what you've done. That's why I have to to whatever it takes to help them."

"I hope they appreciate you, Harry."

"Ha… that's easy for you to say, you don't know me."

"Like I said, I've read your file." David laughed, half heartedly.

"What?" Harry asked.

"Oh, it's just something that happened in France, with Amy. I gathered then that you're not very forthcoming with information about your war, so I tried to bribe her with stories about you to get her to come home early, once I'd realised how dangerous Luc was."

"I assume she didn't take the bait?" Harry asked, looking slightly concerned.

David smiled. "No. If I remember rightly, she called me a bastard, and told me she'd waited twenty years to find out your secrets and she could wait a bit longer."

"Sounds like Amy." Harry looked at his watch. "I feel as though I've already taken up so much of your time." Harry stood. "Thank you," he added eventually.

David looked up sharply. "What are you thanking me for?"

"For saving Amy's life, of course."

David stood as well, but looked away. "Well, as you said, it was me who endangered her life in the first place. Saving it was the least I could do."

"We both know that wasn't how it was." Leaving his stick balanced against the chair, Harry moved forward, offering his left hand. David took it and they held on to each other for a moment.

"I'd like to help." David said, finally letting go. "Both of them."

"Thanks for offering, but I'm really not sure there's anything you can do." Harry turned picked up his stick and slowly left the room.

"I'll think of something," David whispered to himself as the door closed softly.

Chapter Twenty-eight

Summer 1944

"Was that all he told you?" Elise asked, resting her head on Harry's chest. The bedroom was dark and the house was silent.

"Yes."

"I don't really feel like we're any further forward. It still feels as though there are holes in her story… and his."

"And David's," Harry said.

"Why won't they all just tell us what's gone on?"

"In David and Amy's case, I'm not entirely sure they're allowed to. As for Ed, I don't know if he can yet."

"Are you worried about him?"

"Of course. It feels like he's washed his hands of all of us. He didn't even say goodbye." She heard the hurt in his voice.

"I suppose he felt as though he couldn't really come back here now. Not after…"

"But he could have said something to me before he left."

"You could write to him."

"I'm going to… but I'm going to wait a day or so. I don't want to write something I'll regret, in the same way that I hope he's regretting that stupid damned note he left for Amy. That was so heartless."

"She's been quiet all day. Rose and Matthew took her out for lunch, but they said she barely ate a thing."

"What does Matthew think?"

"He's putting a brave face on it, but Rose says he's worried about her."

Harry pulled Elise closer. "We've talked about Robert and the kiss, and how we feel, but you haven't said whether you've forgiven me yet," he said. She looked up. "For not telling you about Amy…"

She nodded slowly. "Of course I've forgiven you." She kissed his chest delicately. "I was angry, I'm not going to lie, but I know you were only doing as Amy asked."

"I hated lying to you, darling."

"You must have been frantic with worry."

"Just a little bit… only every waking moment."

"I wish I could have shared it with you."

"I don't. That was my one solace – that you didn't have to share the worry, especially when you were ill."

"And now, all this." She sighed deeply. "It just feels so… hopeless."

"Do you know? Even when Ed was missing, I didn't feel this desperate. Even when Amy was in France, I didn't worry about either of them as much as I am now. And I've never felt this helpless in my whole life. I just wish I knew what to do. I thought talking it through with Harrison would help, but I really don't think it has."

The next afternoon, after a lunch at which Amy still barely touched her food, they all sat in the sitting room, making the most of the last few hours before Matthew had to catch the early evening train back to London. He barely took his eyes from Amy and, although everyone could see he was worried, no-one really knew what to do, or what they were going to do without a live-in doctor in the house once he'd gone. Harry took a sip of his lukewarm coffee and replaced his cup and saucer on the tray. He was wondering whether a walk around the village green might help, when the doorbell rang. After a minute or so, the sitting room door opened and Polly entered.

"A Major Harrison to see you," she said to Harry.

Harry got to his feet quickly, feeling confused as David Harrison entered the room. He glanced around, his eyes settling quickly on Amy, and Harry noticed the immediate look of pity, deep sorrow and, without doubt, love, that filled his gaze.

"Major," said Harry, crossing the room.

"Mr Belmont." As on the previous day, David didn't try to shake Harry's hand.

"This is my wife, Elise." Harry motioned to Elise, who had got to her feet. David moved forward and shook her hand. "And my daughter, Rose, and her husband Matthew." They also shook hands with the handsome officer.

"Hello Amy," David said, glancing at her.

Amy didn't even look up and Harry wanted to scold her for her rudeness, but decided against it.

"How can we help you?" Harry asked, offering David a chair by the window, which he took, keeping his eyes fixed on Amy.

"I've come to see Amy. There are some things I need to tell her."

"There's nothing you can say to me that you can't say in front of my family," Amy said, finding her voice at last, but still not looking at him.

David hesitated for a moment. "Very well," he replied, then turned to Harry, who resumed his seat beside Elise on one of the sofas. "Is everyone here familiar with…?" he asked, looking around the room.

"Yes," Harry replied. "At least, the bare facts."

"In that case…" He looked back at Amy. "Amy," he said, his voice suddenly carrying more authority. She glanced up at him, taking note of the stern expression on his face, although his green eyes were still soft, still caring. "I'm going to talk about what happened in France. You may wish to join in the conversation at some point. If you do, please remember, no names, no places. I know this is your family, but remember what you were told when you got home."

"I remember."

"Good." His voice had softened, and she looked away again. "Is your family aware you came to see me yesterday?" David addressed his question to Harry.

"No. Only Elise knows about that… until now." He looked around the room to find everyone except Elise staring at him.

"Why Daddy?" Amy's voice was small and lost.

"Because I have to help you."

David took over the explanation. "Your father came to see me in the hope that I'd be able to shed some light on your situation, or have some information that might help him. But I'm not sure I helped at all and, when he left, I decided I needed to try and do more…" He paused, waiting until Amy looked at him. "I made you a promise to always help you if I could. You may not have come to me, or even sent for me yourself, but the promise still stands. I want to help… So, I went to see my boss."

"Mr W—"

"Amy!" David barked. "No names, remember?"

"Sorry."

"Don't worry about it. He's not my boss in any case."

"But, I thought…"

"That was all for show." The other occupants of the room watched the conversation, with no idea what they were talking about. "We pretend he's in charge during interviews. It allows me to observe people more easily, because they're paying attention to him and ignoring me."

"Clever," said Matthew, from the window seat he was sharing with Rose.

David smiled and turned back towards the rest of the room. "However, while I pretty much run my own show, I do have a boss of sorts, and I went to see him straight after Harry left me. I sought and was given permission to come down here today. I'm going to see Henri and Sophie Martin as soon as I leave here. I've been given permission to inform them of their son's death."

"Oh, thank God," Elise sighed. "We won't have to pretend."

"No, you won't." David glanced at Amy. "I thought it might help."

"What will you tell them?" Harry asked.

"Certainly not the truth. That's one of the reasons I'm here. You all know the truth – or as much of it as Amy has given you. I'm going to give you the official version and I'm afraid that's the one you'll have to stick to publicly, but it's the best I can do."

Harry leant forward. "What's the official version, then?"

David paused for a moment, running his thumb down the seam of his trousers. "Luc was a collaborator… and that's putting it politely. Normally, when a collaborator is killed, the resistance make a point of letting everyone know what they've done and why they've been executed. A placard will be placed around their necks and the bodies will be put in plain sight… that kind of thing. It's a warning to others. My men wanted to do that with Luc, but I talked them out of it. Knowing what he'd done, it took some persuading." He kept eye contact with Harry and cleared his throat. He didn't want to look at anyone else in the room at that point. "I don't know if you're aware, but the Nazis have a reputation for killing people in a certain way." Harry shook his head. "They use a single bullet to the back of the neck. Well… a couple of hours after Amy left, we took Luc and the female agent out to a barn near to where we'd been questioning them, and used a German gun I'd… um… purloined." He paused. "To anyone who found the bodies, it would've seemed as though the Nazis had executed them, not the resistance. The story I'll be giving his parents is that he was working for the resistance and was captured and killed by the Germans."

"It's a better epitaph than he deserves."

"It is."

"You're making him sound like a hero," Rose put in. "When he wasn't."

"I know, but this is the best I can do."

"But it's still…" Amy looked across the room.

"Don't, Amy." David's voice was little more than a whisper. He got up, crossed the room and crouched before her. "Stop trying to protect him, even in death. He was a ruthless killer. I've already explained this to your father, but I don't think I told you that he laughed when he gave you away to the Gestapo. He shook that Nazi's hand and they laughed together." He lowered his voice even further. "He didn't deserve the relatively painless death I gave him; as your sister says, he didn't deserve to be thought of as a hero… and he certainly didn't deserve your pity. So stop it. Now."

"He laughed?" Elise muttered, the shock in her voice obvious. Harry took her hand and squeezed it. "You knew this?" She turned to him.

"I only found out yesterday."

"I'm not sure I want to protect his memory any more," Elise said.

"It's the only way I can tell his parents anything," David replied getting to his feet again. "Otherwise it will all have to stay a secret until the end of the war."

Elise took a deep breath. "I suppose this is for the best. I'm not sure it's fair... especially not to Amy."

"They can never know she was there," David warned.

"Obviously," Harry replied, looking around the room. "No-one but us can ever know that."

"And Ed," David added.

"He knows nothing about Luc," Harry said.

David looked at Amy. "You didn't tell him?"

"She didn't get the chance," Harry replied when Amy couldn't.

"I see." Harry wasn't sure that David did see at all.

"I'm so sorry," Elise said, filling the sudden silence. "We haven't offered you anything to drink. I can get Polly to make some fresh coffee."

"Please don't worry about me, Mrs Belmont."

"Call me Elise."

"Personally, I could do with something stronger than coffee." Matthew got up and strode to the sideboard, where he poured himself a whisky. "Anyone else?" he asked, turning to face the room, just as a shadow appeared across the open french window. "Ed!" he exclaimed and everyone turned, as one, looking at the figure standing in the doorway.

Ed looked around the room, his dark eyes settling for a moment on Amy and softening, before travelling on to David. "Who's this?" he asked, although Harry sensed he already knew the answer to his question.

"This is Major David Harrison," Amy replied. Harry saw Ed's lips tighten and his fists clench. Getting up quickly, he stepped towards Ed.

"Come in," he said calmly.

"What's the point?" Ed said, going to turn away.

"Ed?" David said, his voice commanding and unemotional.

"What?" Ed turned his eyes on David again.

"I'm only here to tell Harry and Elise – and Amy – of my orders to inform the Martins about Luc's death."

"Luc's dead?"

"It's a long story," Harry added, putting his hand on Ed's arm. "Please, come in. Have a drink." He nodded to Matthew, who poured Ed a whisky and brought it over. Ed stepped across the threshold and took the glass.

"Thanks," he said. "How did he die?" he asked, having taken a large gulp of the amber liquid.

"I killed him," David replied.

Ed stood with his mouth open. "What the f… Sorry." He glanced at Elise and she shook her head.

"Don't worry," she said.

"You're entertaining the man who killed your nephew?" Ed asked.

"He saved Amy's life," Elise said. "Sit down, Ed." She got up and came over to him, encouraging him into the room, and lowering him onto one end of the sofa, then sitting next to him. Amy, on the other sofa opposite, looked at her fingers, shaking in her lap. "You need to hear what happened," Elise said and looked up at Harry. "Can you tell him?" she asked.

"Amy?" Harry said, offering her the chance. She shook her head. "All right," Harry continued, and he sat on sofa next to Amy and slowly told Ed everything that she had told him. Every so often, David – who had resumed his seat by the window – interrupted, adding details, or correcting specifics. At the end of the story, Ed was staring hard at Amy.

"Why the hell didn't you tell me this?" he said.

"You didn't give me the chance. You ran out on me, remember?"

She had a point – one which he couldn't deny. He turned to David. "And what the hell were you doing taking her there? You knew the danger."

"Here we go again," said David, rolling his eyes. "I've explained this to Harry already. I knew that Luc and Amy were related. I did *not* know that Luc was the mole. If I had known that, I would never have taken her. She knows this. Harry knows this. Everybody knows this."

"You still endangered her. I've been in occupied France, for Christ's sake… I know what it's like. How could you put her in that position?"

"If I'd had a different option, I'd gladly have taken it."

"How on earth did you persuade her?"

"I didn't have to. She wanted to go."

"She *wanted* to? I don't believe you. That doesn't sound like Amy…"

"You really don't get it, do you?" All eyes were now fixed on David. He had nothing to lose as far as his future with Amy was concerned – that was gone now – and Ed needed to know the truth. "Amy accepted the mission, the danger… the chance of death, because she believed you weren't coming back. As far as she was concerned, she had nothing left to live for."

"Is this true?" Harry asked, looking down at Amy and taking her hand. She didn't respond, but glared at David. "Is it, Amy?" he badgered.

"It's true," David replied. "She's the only person I've ever taken or sent into occupied territory without a cyanide pill. I knew how she felt and I didn't dare let her have one, in case she just decided to just take it. That's why I couldn't let her be captured. Unlike every other agent, she had no way out, and none of you want to know what the Gestapo do to female agents they capture." He took a deep breath. "I couldn't let that happen to her," he whispered.

"Knowing that… knowing how she felt, surely you endangered her even more by taking her," Ed said.

"No. She was never alone outside of our safe houses, not even for a minute."

"That's not true, and you know it," Amy's voice rang out and she sat forward. "Don't lie to my family. You've revealed something I wanted kept a secret, so don't you dare lie to them." Her eyes were alight with anger.

"I'm not lying." His voice was calm and quiet.

"But you did leave me alone. You put me on the train in Paris… and sent me down to—"

"Names, Amy," David said patiently. "Be careful."

"Alright!" she yelled. "You put me on the train, and I travelled back to the south, to our… mutual friend. On. My. Own. You weren't there. Then he arranged for my passage home through Spain. And I did that… On. My. Own. The Gestapo had been alerted to me by then, so there was much more danger, and I think we both knew that, but you left me… On. My. Own. So don't you dare say I wasn't alone, because I was!"

"But you weren't." He held up his hand as she went to speak again. "Let me finish." He stood and crossed the room, crouching down in front of her once more. "Yes, I put you on the train. That's absolutely true. And yes, I wasn't with you – that's true also. I remember you asking if you'd be safe on the journey, and I was so relieved because it meant you'd started to care about yourself again. But I knew you'd be all right." She looked at him and went to speak, but he held up a finger. "Do you remember a man in the same compartment as you, a rather rough-looking man, wearing dark trousers and a navy blue coat, with short greying hair and stubble around his chin? He probably read a newspaper for most of the journey?" Amy nodded her head, slowly. "I can't say his name here, but he was the first contact I ever made in France. He's my greatest friend, and the one man I trust more than any other. I couldn't let you meet him, because I knew I might need him to look after you quietly at some point. It was him that I went to meet on that first day in Paris, while you stayed at the apartment. I wouldn't have let anyone else take care of you but him. I had to explain the situation, and the risks, and make sure he was willing to help. Looking after you could have cost him his life… He agreed… He didn't even hesitate. He knew what to do if the Gestapo came looking for you, and he carried the instructions for our mutual friend in the south."

"What instructions? You told me to tell him what to do… just to get me home."

"But my other friend had different instructions. When you got to the farmhouse, our mutual friend got you to wait for eight hours, didn't he?"

"Yes, he did. He made me sleep there overnight. He said it would be better to leave at dawn."

"Exactly." He ran his fingers through his hair. "Which gave me time to do what needed to be done in Paris and get the next train down south. I was about five hours behind you. I stayed in the fields behind the farmhouse until you left early the next day, then I followed you, all the way back to London. Once you left Paris, you were watched, the whole time, either by my dearest friend, or by me. I made you a promise that you'd never be alone, and you weren't… not once."

"I'm sorry," she whispered.

"Don't be. I'm sorry I gave away your secret, but Ed needs – no, he deserves – to know why you did this."

"I didn't even realise *you* knew."

"What did I always tell you?"

"You know everything." She rolled her eyes.

"Exactly." He stood and turned. All eyes, except Harry's were on him.

"So it's true then?" Harry was still looking down at Amy. "You really did do this as a sort of suicide mission?" He paused and, although she didn't reply, he knew it was the truth. "I knew your reasoning didn't make sense, but I was convinced it was about revenge… how blind could I be?"

"Wait a second, Harry," Ed said, getting up from his seat next to Elise. "Do you mean you knew Amy was going and you did nothing to stop her?"

"Oh, for crying out loud, Ed," Amy said, also standing, and moving across to Ed. "Will you stop blaming everyone. Dad guessed where I was going a few days before I left. Short of tying me to my bed, there was nothing he could have done to stop me."

"Then he should have bloody well tied you to your bed."

"Like I did with you?" Harry said, getting up and raising his voice.

"What? What does that mean?"

"I told Amy that I wouldn't treat her any differently to you, or George, or Peter or anyone else. She needed to do this and I wasn't going to stop her. Of course, if I'd known the real reason she was going, I would have tied her to her bed."

"And I'd have found another way, Daddy." Amy's eyes didn't leave Ed's, even though she spoke to Harry.

"You wanted to die that much?" Ed whispered.

She didn't reply. Harry crossed the room and stood in front of her. "You really did, didn't you?" he said, taking her hand in his. "I know what that feels like." She gasped, but he carried on, "I've been there, Amy, when I came back from the last war. I tried… and I never wanted that for you… not for any of you, and if what David says is really true… then I've failed you completely." He looked at their joined hands, blurred by his tears.

"Oh, Daddy, please don't blame yourself," she cried, throwing her arms around his neck. "I couldn't bear that. I just couldn't stand it any longer without him."

"Then why didn't you talk to me?"

"Because you were so determined to believe he was still alive."

"And you were determined to believe I was dead?" Ed asked. Amy loosened her grip on Harry and he stepped back slightly.

"No. I just couldn't bear to lose you twice." She looked up at Ed. "It was easier to accept it once, rather than keep hoping, and then to lose you a second time when it was confirmed."

"But you… you and him…" Ed looked at David. "When you were together in France… it was easier to think I was dead then, wasn't it?"

"You really think that?"

"Right now, I don't know what to think."

"The worst of me, clearly," Amy sobbed, sitting back down again.

"Ed." David stepped in again. "I think I owe you an explanation… and maybe an apology." He took a deep breath, looking around the room, his eyes settling finally on Amy – the place where they felt most at home. "I took Amy on this mission because I had to," he said at last. "I needed that family connection to make it work – or I thought I did at the time. But I had an ulterior motive…" He glanced at Harry and hoped he was doing the right thing. "I fell in love with Amy the moment I first met her." Ed looked from David to Amy and then at the floor. "She's the most incredible, beautiful, generous and compassionate woman I've ever met and I'll admit that falling in love with her was about the easiest thing I've ever done. Taking her on this mission was stupid and I shouldn't have done it, but knowing how she felt, I wanted to show her that she could live again, without you; that she could love again one day. I wanted to be the man she'd love. I wanted her to love me as much she loved you; as much as I loved her. As Harry explained, we were chased through the streets of Paris by the Gestapo. It was close… it was too damned close, and, as I've explained, I wasn't about to let her be captured by them." He paused for a moment, not once taking his eyes from Amy. "I carried a gun at all times…" He cleared his throat awkwardly. "If we couldn't have got away… if I hadn't been able to get us to the safe house, I'd already planned to find somewhere as quiet as possible and shoot her myself, rather than let them take her." David heard the strangled cry from Elise, but turned to face Harry, a look of understanding passing between them. "They're monstrous people… barbaric. You wouldn't want that for Amy; I know you wouldn't. My way was better. You do understand, don't you?" Harry nodded, just once. "Fortunately, we made it, so it doesn't matter, and I know how lucky I am that I don't have to live with that memory or the guilt of having killed someone I love… and for that, I thank God." The two men stared at each other for a long moment. "When we got to the apartment, the relief… it was like nothing I've ever felt before. So, I kissed her. I just wanted her to know, I suppose, that nothing else mattered. Nothing but being alive with her."

"And Amy?" Ed asked, eventually, his voice a mere whisper in the hushed silence.

"She apologised for not being able to respond to me in the way I wanted, but she didn't feel a damned thing for me, except maybe gratitude… and relief. All she could ever think about was you." He crossed the room and stood directly in front of Ed. "I'm sorry if this isn't what you want to hear, but you're being a bloody idiot over all of this. If I'd known you were alive, I would never have kissed her, I would never even have considered it… But then I think we've established that, if you'd been alive, she'd never have accepted the mission in the first place. I wanted her more than I've ever wanted anything, but she pushed me away… every damned time. Can you imagine how hard it is for me today, standing here in front of you all, with Amy, knowing how I feel about her, and talking about this? Can you?" He raised his voice just slightly. "She was never mine, Ed, always yours. We were never together, not in any sense of the word, and she never wanted me… but if you hadn't made it, I'd have tried to find a way back to her someday. I'd have found a way to take that chance, because she's worth it. I think I'd probably have been wasting my time, but that wouldn't have stopped me trying. You might not be able to see it in her eyes, but I can… She's still yours and she always will be; she's still in love with you, despite all your doubts, all your harsh words, all your insults. Despite you running out on her when she needed you most. Despite all of that, she's still yours and she's still waiting for you, and if you can't see it, it's only because either you don't want to, or you're not bloody well looking hard enough."

David broke off, breathing heavily and a stillness hung over the room until suddenly, without warning, Ed broke. His face crumpled, and he fell to his knees. David looked to Harry, then Elise, who immediately moved forward and knelt in front of Ed, pulling him close to her and hugging him as he sobbed. Harry stood beside them, his hand on Ed's shoulder. Amy was dumbstruck, but David didn't approach her. As much as he wanted to take her in his arms, he knew that would be a mistake, for all concerned.

"Sorry," David said quietly, "I went too far. I had no right…"

Ed was shaking his head, mumbling.

"I don't think that's the problem," Matthew said, coming and standing next to him. Rose went to Amy and put her arm around her sister's shoulder. "I think there's more to this than we know about."

David nodded. "Perhaps I should go," he said, but Ed suddenly became even more agitated.

"No," said Matthew. "I think he wants you to stay for some reason."

The two men sat down and watched while Elise comforted Ed, until he calmed and she could move him to the sofa. He was shaking and mumbling. Matthew mouthed 'drink?' to Harry, but he shook his head. Ed needed time. After a little while, Ed looked up, his eyes meeting with David's.

"Sorry," he mumbled.

"Don't be," David said. "That was my fault. I shouldn't have said all that."

"No," Ed replied. "You didn't say anything I didn't deserve. I am an idiot… as Amy knows only too well." He sniffed and Harry handed him a handkerchief. "I misjudged you," Ed continued, "and I judged Amy when I had no right to. God, the things I've said to you…"

"Why?" she asked quietly. "That's what I don't understand. Why did you think so badly of me so easily? That's not like you. You're normally such a fair person."

"But I'm not like me… not at the moment. Does that even make sense?"

"Maybe," Harry replied. "Do you want to talk about it?"

"I don't know. Do I? I think I have to, don't I? I'm just not sure how." He looked around the room.

"Would you like everyone else to leave?" Harry offered.

"No. I just don't know how… It's too much…"

Ed stood and walked across the room, standing in front of the fireplace. David felt awkward, wondering if he should leave, but Harry looked across and shook his head, holding David in his seat.

"I've told you already," Ed began quietly, "that I landed in France, that my chute didn't work and I broke my leg. I'll skip the rest of that bit. Eventually, I ended up with a group of resistance fighters near Amiens. They were a good bunch," his voice cracked a little and he cleared his throat. "Seven men and one woman… Helene." He turned and looked at Amy. "Before you ask, her lover was the leader of the group, so she didn't even give me a second glance – not that I wanted her to. They were so in love it was embarrassing at times. They couldn't keep their hands off each other…but it made me homesick, for here… for you." He looked down at the floor. "I was supposed to be passed off to another group, but the invasion happened and they were given orders to sabotage the railway lines. Dealing with a random pilot was bottom of their list of priorities. So, I decided to join in… It was better than sitting around doing nothing. We blew up several tracks and a couple of bridges. A few ammunition drops were arranged..." he turned to David. "Presumably by your lot." David shrugged. "Anyway, at the beginning of July, I suppose, we had to blow a line. It was nothing special... We'd done similar before, but this time, it went wrong." He paused. "The railway line went alongside a wooded area, so it seemed easy. The leader of the group, a man named Xavier, and his second in command, Alain, set the explosives. I was keeping watch. We were all done and everything was set, when suddenly a group of Germans appeared out of nowhere. They opened fire. We made a run for it, but I fell over – probably because of my dodgy leg. Xavier came back for me and he got shot in the neck." He turned to Harry. "I've never seen so much blood. It soaked my clothes, right through to my skin."

"I know," Harry said simply and Ed knew he understood.

"I knew he was dead. He was just lifeless." He choked. "Alain called to me to leave him and run. The Germans were approaching, so I did as he said. I left him behind. We got back to the hideout and Alain broke the news to Helene that Xavier was dead." He looked at his feet. "I've never seen grief like that." He raised his head and his eyes met Amy's. "She was wild. She attacked me. I couldn't stop her. I didn't want to really. I think she'd have killed me if the others hadn't dragged her off."

"It wasn't your fault," Amy whispered.

"It felt like it was." He waited for a few moments. "They passed me on to another cell that night. Within a week or so, I was with the Canadians and then the Brits, and then I was on my way home." He looked helplessly at Harry. "Now, listening to Amy's story... and David's..."

"It's not a competition, Ed. Your war has been very different from most people's. We've had this talk before. You're used to things being remote and fighting by yourself. To be suddenly responsible for someone else, placed in the company of others... that must have been very strange for you."

"It was." Ed relaxed a little. "But it was her reaction, you see. I couldn't believe how wild she was, how fierce. I mean, I was feeling rotten enough as it was, and she lashed out at me as if she wanted to kill me for taking her lover from her. And I felt like letting her do it, just so

I didn't have to live with the guilt of it… it's too much." Harry and David exchanged a glance.

"Grief affects people differently," Elise said.

"I've wondered every day since then, though, whether she's all right, whether she's recovering, or whether she still feels like that. I feel somehow responsible for her. This might affect her forever… and it's my fault."

"No, it isn't," Amy reiterated.

"Sorry… I've forgotten, did you say this was at Amiens?" David said.

"Yes."

"I thought so. I knew Xavier."

"Oh, God." Ed looked fearful. "Don't tell me he was a friend of yours."

"No, no. Nothing like that. I worked with him once, very briefly. He was a good man."

"And look what happened to him as soon as he met me."

"It was nothing to do with you, Ed. He was unlucky, that's all. He knew the risks. They all do. *We* all do." David looked at the clock on the mantlepiece, then got up, straightening his jacket. "It's getting late," he said. "I've still got to visit the Martins this evening. I'd best be on my way." He paused, then turned back to Ed. "I can put your mind at rest about one thing, though…" Ed raised an eyebrow. "Helene…" David continued, "she recovered, or so it would seem, anyway." Ed looked quizzical. "She's still working for the resistance, but she's not in Amiens any longer. I can't tell you where she is, but she's with another group now."

"Oh, thank God for that." Ed's relief was obvious. "I've had visions… nightmares of her grieving like that for years to come…" Ed crossed the room and shook David's hand. "Thank you," he said. "For everything."

"You don't need to thank me."

"You saved Amy… so I think I do."

"No. You don't." David glanced around the room. "Good evening, everyone," he said. His eyes fell on Amy and he let them rest there, taking her in one last time. She looked up at him and smiled. He smiled back, then turned and left the room. Harry followed him.

"I'm sorry about this afternoon," Harry said, as they stood at the open front door, David now clutching his cap, which had been left on the hall table. "It's been far more of an emotional ride than you bargained for."

"Don't apologise. I just hope I didn't do any harm in coming here. I only wanted to help."

"Oh, you've helped," Harry said. "Especially with that last piece of news. I'm sure you..." Harry stopped dead as he noticed the expression on David's face. "Wait... You lied back there, didn't you?"

"No."

"Don't lie to me now, David. I know that expression. I've been looking at it in the mirror for the last twenty-seven years."

David turned and looked down the garden towards the lane. "She's dead," he whispered.

"Who? Helene?"

"Yes. Please don't tell him. I hadn't realised until today that Ed was with the group in Amiens, but I was sent a report a couple of weeks ago, and it mentioned an RAF pilot. I didn't make the connection at the time, but then I had no reason to. She wasn't French at all, you see. Helene was her codename, and she was actually one of mine. A bloody good British agent – so good, even Ed didn't guess. Who'd have thought it?" He hesitated and turned back to Harry. "She killed herself," he added quietly.

"Oh God." Harry closed his eyes, leaning back on the doorframe. "Because of Xavier?" He opened his eyes again in time to see David nodding his head.

"As far as I know. She wasn't in any danger of being captured at the time, so it's the only reason I can think of. It won't help Ed to know the truth. It's better this way. Promise you'll keep the secret?"

Harry nodded. "I promise. I agree with you, it won't help anyone, really." He shook David's hand. "At the risk of sounding patronising, you're a remarkable young man."

"Coming from you, that's a compliment I'll gladly accept."

“And I’m sorry.”

“What for?”

“That things didn’t work out for you and Amy. I’m obviously not sorry that Ed’s back and I hope they manage to work things out, but I know how difficult it must have been for you to come here today… feeling the way you do. I hope, one day, you find someone…”

David shook his head. “Don’t, Harry.” He swallowed. “I think we both know that, sometimes you’re lucky enough to fall in love, and you fall so bloody deep and so bloody hard, that nothing will ever be as good, or as perfect again, no matter how long you look for it, so… to be honest, I don’t think I’m going to bother looking again…” He pulled his cap onto his head, looked up into the late afternoon sky, and walked slowly down the garden path.

Harry went back into the sitting room to find Amy and Ed sitting together. They weren’t exactly hand-in-hand, but at least they weren’t arguing, or at opposite ends of the room.

“I liked him,” Rose said suddenly.

“David?” Elise asked, looking across the room to where Rose was sitting cradled in Matthew’s arms. “Yes, me too.” Amy shifted awkwardly in her seat.

“It’s okay,” Ed whispered. “You can say you liked him too, if you want to. I’m not going to be an idiot about him anymore.”

She turned to look at him. “Why are you here? You made it very clear that I wasn’t good enough for you, you told me I was free. I assumed that was mutual. I assumed you’d—”

“If you’re thinking I’ve been with anyone else, you’re wrong,” Ed interrupted. “I swear on Harry’s life, I haven’t.”

Amy glared at him. “You don’t owe me any explanations,” she replied. “Like I said, I don’t even know why you’re here.”

“Because I was wrong. Leaving you was wrong. Saying all those things to you was wrong. Writing that letter… that was cruel, and wrong. Thinking I could live without you was wrong… I can’t, Amy… I can’t live without you.”

She shook her head, but didn't say anything. Instead, she got up and ran from the room. Ed looked across at Harry.

"Give her time," he said.

The next morning, Amy slept in late, and Matthew had returned to London but everyone else sat around the breakfast table.

"I meant to ask, how long are you here for?" Harry asked Ed.

"I've been told to complete my leave," Ed said. "My C.O. was concerned that I wasn't firing on all cylinders, so to speak. He was right, clearly. The squadron's been re-equipped with Spitfires while I've been away, and I need to be up to speed... quite literally."

"What are you talking about?"

"We're helping with intercepting these V1 rockets."

Harry nearly spat his coffee across the table. "That sounds damn dangerous," he said.

"It's not exactly the easiest thing. The Spits have been tuned to fly as fast as the rockets. We just have to get underneath and tip the wing."

"Tip the wing? What with?" Rose asked.

"The wing of the aircraft," Ed replied. "We just have to knock the rocket off its course – preferably into the sea."

They all stared at him. "Just...? You make it sound so easy," Harry said at last.

"Compared to fighting off half a dozen ME109s at the same time, it is. The rockets don't have an escort, so we're not being fired on at the time. It's really just about flying... fast and accurate. And in a Spit, that's a piece of cake... I've only been flying them for a couple of days, and they're amazing aircraft."

Silence descended while they all looked at him, seeing a different side to the man they thought they knew so well. He loved to fly; they all knew that. But this passion, this excitement, it was new to them all.

"So, you're here all week?" Elise asked eventually.

"I'm due to go back on Friday evening," Ed confirmed.

"Well, make sure you put things right with Amy before you go, won't you?" Harry said.

"I'll do my best."

"Wait, Ed!" Amy cried. "I can't keep up." The path to the field was dry and she slipped, but he pulled her along.

"Then try a bit harder."

"What's the rush?"

"There's something I need to tell you." She stopped dead and pulled him back.

"Then tell me. You don't have to drag me around the countryside, for crying out loud. You've been back here since Tuesday afternoon, pretty much ignoring me. You've had plenty of opportunities to talk to me, and haven't taken them, and you wait until the day you're due to go back to suddenly decide it's time to talk? I was enjoying a lie in, for heaven's sake, and you barge into my bedroom, throw some clothes at me and insist I get dressed, and then you haul me out here? What's the problem? Just tell me now."

He pulled her on again. "No, I'll tell you when we get there." He unlatched the gate and pulled her through, closing it behind them and dragging her along the hedge and then up the incline towards the tree.

Once they'd reached the top, he turned and they both looked out over the fields, panting from the walk.

"Okay, what was so important that you had to drag me all the way out here to say it?"

He stared down at her, placing his hands on either side of her face. "It's nothing much," he said and, as she went to open her mouth in complaint, he placed his lips over hers to silence her. "God, woman," he said, as he broke the kiss, "you never did know when to just shut up, did you?"

She narrowed her eyes and went to speak again, but he placed a finger on her lips and silenced her with a look. "Let me finish what I have to say," he whispered. "You know I'm rubbish at making speeches like this, but let me finish, then you can talk… all right?" She hesitated and then nodded her head. Ed took a step back and sighed deeply, running a hand through his hair. "I've been a fool, Amy," he said.

"I thought we'd already established that… several times over."

"You were going to let me finish?"

"Sorry."

Ed cleared his throat. "As I was saying, I've been a fool. When I came back, I thought I was the only one who was hurting, who'd seen death close up, and suffered its consequences, but listening to your story the other day..." He glanced up at her. "What you've been through, not just in France, but when you heard I was missing... Harry told me what you were like. Don't blame him, I badgered him until he gave in. It reminded me of Helene, and I don't even want to think about that... But then I got to thinking, and I realised that I stupidly came back believing everything would be exactly as it was when I left; assuming you'd be the same person, when really you'd been in hell the whole time. I came back, and instead of listening to you and loving you and making you happy, the way you should be, I behaved like an utter shit. He was right... David was so right. I let you down. I put myself first. I ran out when you needed me and I don't deserve you." He looked into her eyes, his own now darkening pools of blue. "He risked his life to save you, Amy. He told you and showed you, over and over again, how much he loved you, and you still remained loyal to *me*... or to the memory of me. And, idiot that I am, all I could think about when I got back here was that another man had kissed you and held you in his arms, and comforted you... all the things I wanted to do. Really, I should have been honoured that, although you had this man who loved you so much he was prepared to kill for you, to die for you, you still chose the memory of me... just the *memory* of me, for Christ's sake, over a life filled with his love for you. That's just incredible, Amy." He reached out and ran his fingertips down her cheek. "*You're* incredible. I'm not sure I'll ever be worthy of you, or your love, or your loyalty, but I want to spend the rest of my life trying to prove that I am... to both of us. That is, if you'll have me...?" He looked at her, doubt clouding his eyes.

"Are you...?"

"I'm asking you to marry me, Amy. I nearly died in France, and you were the only thing on my mind... as I fell out of that plane, all I saw was you. I don't want to lose you again. I don't want you to be free; I want you to be mine." He waited but she remained silent, looking up at him. "I said you could talk once I'd finished... Well, I'm finished..."

Still, she looked at him. "And you're choosing *now,* for once, to say nothing?"

"You really want to marry me?" she whispered eventually.

"Oh, God, yes." He grinned, pulling her close. "Please… please, just say yes."

"Just 'yes'?"

"Elaborate if you must, as long as the gist of it is yes…"

"I honestly can't believe you want to marry me after everything that's happened between us. It's been… There's so much… I mean, we're… We haven't… And you're… Things are still so…"

"Amy, just say yes, will you?" He kissed her.

She giggled into the deepening kiss. "Yes," she murmured, and the rest of her words were lost.

Epilogue

Autumn 1945

"That dress is absolutely stunning," breathed Charlotte, watching Amy and Ed standing outside the church, smiling beneath the early autumn sunshine. "Where on earth did you get it?"

"Harry and I took a trip up to London with Amy last month," Elise explained. "We left baby Laura with Matthew and Harry, and Rose, Amy and I went shopping. We had a marvellous time. We were starting to think we'd never find anything and Amy was threatening to get married in her pyjamas, but it was Rose who found the dress, and it didn't need any adjusting at all."

"Well, she does have a splendid figure. She looks incredible." The two women stared at the young couple. "It's so long since I've seen Ed out of uniform. He looks so handsome in a suit – I'd forgotten."

"He was officially discharged two weeks ago."

"So now what?"

"I'm not sure. He and Amy have said they want to talk about it when they get back from their honeymoon in the Lakes. We'll be down in Cornwall by then, so they're coming to visit."

"Will they live up here?"

"I've got no idea what their plans are yet," Elise admitted.

"What about John and Lillian?"

"They've bought a cottage down in the harbour. It needs a little work, but John's already made a start, so we'll be neighbours."

"That'll be lovely. We'll miss you, though."

"Oh, we'll still come and visit, just as often as we did before."

"Well, if you don't decide to keep the house on. You know, if Amy and Ed decide to live somewhere else, you'll have to come and stay with us whenever you visit."

"We will. Oh, Harry, don't they look lovely?" Harry and William walked over, and he took her hand in his.

"Perfect," he said, turning and looking back towards the church. Elise leant her head towards his.

"He'd have been so proud," she whispered.

Harry kissed the top of her head. "Thank you for saying that," he murmured into her hair.

Amy stared out across the Borrowdale Fells. "Can't we just pitch a tent and live here? It's the most beautiful place I've ever seen."

"It's very tempting, my love." Ed pulled her closer. "I'd live anywhere with you, you know that, don't you?"

"Hmm." Amy raised her face to his, opening her mouth to his kiss.

"Plymouth isn't our only option. We can do everything we've talked about up here, if that's what you want." Ed held her in his arms, looking down into her eyes.

"No. We'll go back and talk to dad, and see what he thinks. But I'm certain we've made the right decision."

"As long as you're sure. You seem so relaxed and happy up here."

"Just bring me back here often, please? It feels like coming home, even though I've never been here before."

"Anywhere with you feels like home to me. But, yes, I'll bring you back as often as you like." He bent his head and kissed her again. "Only right now, we're going to walk back to our hotel, then I'm going to run you a lovely hot bath, and once I've done that, I'm going to take you in every way imaginable, until you're begging me to stop."

Amy smiled up at him. "You're rather assuming I won't fall asleep before you even get me into bed... I find hot baths after a long walk very relaxing, you know." She placed her hand on his chest.

"Who said anything about going to bed? I was talking about taking you in the bath – at least the first time..." He grinned.

"Considering how long you've known me," she teased, biting her lower lip and tracing her fingers delicately up to his neck and round behind his ear, making him shudder, "I can't believe you think I'd ever beg you to stop."

"No, I don't believe you would."

"How are you settling in?" Ed asked.

"We've been back a week, and it feels as though we were never away, and certainly not for six years," Harry replied.

"I think we have John and Lillian to thank for that," Elise said, clearing the plates from lunch.

"Speaking of John, did you manage to arrange for them to come over this afternoon?" Ed asked.

"Yes." Harry got up from the table. "I think they're glad to escape the dust of the renovations."

"Oh," Elise said, coming back into the room. "And we haven't told you yet, Rose and Matthew are due to arrive on the three o'clock train. I've arranged for John to collect them from the station and then he and Lillian will bring them on here. They should get here by about three-fifteen." She glanced up at the clock above the fireplace. "So, just over twenty minutes."

"Oh." Amy looked up at Ed, who'd just got to his feet. "I didn't know they were here this weekend as well."

"It's not a problem, is it?" Harry had noticed the look that had passed between them.

"No, of course not," Ed replied.

"Why do you want to see John and Lillian?" Harry asked, opening the door into the sitting room.

"It's this idea we've got. We need John's advice... and your's," Ed said.

"Now I'm really intrigued."

"I didn't realise you'd have such a houseful. It can wait until another day, if you think it would be best," Amy offered.

"No, I'm not waiting any longer," Harry said. "I want to know what you're planning."

"Well, you won't have to wait much longer," Amy replied as she sat on the comfy sofa. Ed joined her.

"How were the Lakes?" Elise asked. "It's been so long since we've been there."

"Oh, you should go back, Mum." Amy's face came to life as she described the hills they'd climbed and lakes they'd rowed… well, Ed had rowed. "I think I could live there. It's just the most perfect place on earth."

"I'm quite jealous."

"I'll take you back," Harry said. "If you want."

The front door opened and they heard Rose call out, "Hello, we're here!"

Elise went out into the hallway, followed by Harry, where they met Rose, who was carrying Laura in her arms. Matthew followed closely behind, with John and Lillian bringing up the rear.

"We've left the cases in John's car for now," Matthew said. "I'll fetch them in later."

"Oh, it's so lovely to see you," Elise said, taking baby Laura from Rose while she removed her coat. "She seems to have grown so much in just a couple of weeks, doesn't she?" Elise turned to Harry.

He smiled at the two of them. "Come on in, everyone." He showed them into the sitting room, where Amy and Ed were now standing by the fireplace.

"Hello," Rose said, going to her sister and giving her a hug. "How's married life treating you?"

"Perfectly." Amy looked up at Ed.

"Hmm." Matthew came and shook Ed by the hand. "You two look deliriously happy. Stop it, both of you, or you'll give marriage a bad name."

"Don't listen to him," Lillian said, kissing Amy on both cheeks.

They'd all settled into chairs, with Laura resting on Harry's lap, staring up into his face and, when Elise brought in the tea, Rose moved to sit next to her father on the sofa.

"I hope you didn't mind us intruding this weekend," she said.

"Of course not," he replied, leaning into her a little. "You're always welcome and it's lovely to have you all here." He glanced across at John. "The people who mean most to us, all under one roof. It doesn't happen very often."

"Matthew and I have a particular reason for wanting to see you, and we decided that Amy and Ed being here gave us the perfect opportunity to discuss things with you."

"Gosh, this weekend gets more and more intriguing," Harry said, looking from Ed to Matthew.

Ed shrugged and turned to his brother-in-law. Matthew gazed down at his hands for a moment, then looked up again to find everyone staring at him. "I've been doing a lot of thinking," he began. "As you know, I've got a good job at St Thomas's and, I think, if I play my cards right, I could make Chief Surgeon in another five years or so." He paused, but no-one spoke. "But, I'm not entirely sure that's what I want anymore." He looked at Rose.

"We don't know if we want Laura growing up in London," she continued. "We've got a lovely house, but almost no garden and, both Matthew and I grew up in small villages, so we don't really want her to start life in the city."

Matthew took over again: "So," he said, looking directly at Harry, and then turning to Ed, "we have a favour to ask. It's quite a big one."

"Just ask," said Harry, glancing at Ed, who shrugged his shoulders again, looking perplexed.

"We want to buy your mother's old house," Matthew said, turning to Harry. "I know you haven't completely decided what to do with it yet, but Rose would really like to bring up Laura in the same place that she called home for so long. I've already had an interview at the local hospital and they've offered me a position. The pay isn't as good, but selling the house in London will give us more than enough to buy the house..."

"But we're also thinking about Ed..." Rose interrupted. "What if Ed and Amy... I mean, I know you kept the house to provide somewhere for Ed to live. We don't want to tread on anyone else's toes."

"Ed and Amy have their own plans, which they haven't told us about yet..." Harry said, looking at his younger daughter.

"I suppose if we tell you what we've got in mind, that might help," Amy said, nudging Ed. "You tell them... It's more your idea than mine."

Ed shifted in his seat and looked around the room. "Well..." He cleared his throat. "I hadn't anticipated doing this in front of an audience, but here goes... I got the germ of this idea when I got back to my squadron last year, but Amy and I have spent a lot of our time since then trying to work out the details. Even now, we're not really sure how to go about it, and that's why we wanted to ask your advice, Harry... and yours, John." He turned to find John watching him closely. "I'd better start from the beginning, so it makes more sense." He felt Amy's hand find his and squeezed her fingers tightly. "There was a chap in my squadron. We called him 'Sunshine'. His real name was Raymond Jeffers."

"Why was he called 'Sunshine' then?" Elise asked, looking confused.

"Raymond was shortened to Ray... Ray of Sunshine... Sunshine. The RAF isn't very original with its nicknames, I'm afraid. It was the best we could do. The name suited him though. He was very much a glass half full chap. He wasn't like the rest of us; didn't go out drinking and fooling around." He gave Amy's hand another squeeze. "He'd married very young and they'd had twin girls within a year of the wedding. He doted on all three of them. I used to go and stay with him sometimes, if I only got a 24-hour pass and couldn't get home. After I started seeing Amy, I didn't want to go out drinking with the lads anymore, and Ray had a lovely family." Ed looked at Harry. "I suppose in some ways, he reminded me of my father." Harry raised an eyebrow. "He'd gone to university, but not because his parents were rich or because he was lucky like me and had a wealthy benefactor; he'd won a scholarship to Cambridge and worked his way through." Ed turned to John. "He read English, like you." He looked down at the floor. "He wanted to teach after the war. I think he'd have been good at it." He fell silent for a moment.

"What happened?" Harry prompted.

Ed looked up. "Oh, sorry," he said. "When I got back to base, I learnt that he'd been shot down a few days beforehand. He wasn't so lucky, though, his plane was blown to pieces. He didn't have time to bail out." Silence descended and all eyes fell on Ed. Amy leant across and rested her head on his shoulder. "The squadron leader was having a whip-round for his wife and children. I put a couple of thousand or so into the kitty, which I think shocked them all a little, but that wasn't really the point… The whole episode got me thinking." He looked up at Harry.

"And you decided you want to do something more?" Harry asked.

Ed smiled. "Yes. Amy and I have been thrashing it backwards and forwards for months. We've come up with the idea of starting a school for the children of dead servicemen… the ones who didn't make it back… the ones who weren't as lucky as us." He looked from one man to the other. "We're not saying it'll be a huge concern, but we both appreciate the value of a good education and we want to do something to help. We toyed with the idea of starting a trust and just paying for their educations, but Amy thought we could do more… and I agree." He turned towards John. "We'd need you to help us with that, though."

"Where are you thinking of basing this school?" John asked.

"Plymouth. We don't want to be too far away from you, but we think the school needs to be near a big city. But don't worry, John, I'm not asking you to come there every day and teach. We just want you to both help us set it up. We'll employ the staff, with your help, of course. And Harry, we'll need you to help us manage the finances. We found a property for sale just to the north of Plymouth a couple of weeks before the wedding. I've checked with the agents and it's still available. It's not cheap, but I think it'll be big enough, and I'm hoping they'll be open to offers. I was wondering if the two of you could come and have a look at it with us… see what you think and give us your advice. And we'd like you both to be governors, if you'll agree."

Harry and John looked at each other, then Harry glanced at Elise. "I obviously can't speak for John," he said, "but I'd be privileged to help you both. I think it's a marvellous idea."

"I couldn't have said it better myself," John echoed. "I'll help in whatever way I can."

"We can discuss the details later in the week, and maybe arrange to go and see the house," Ed said, and turned to Rose. "But you don't need to worry about treading on our toes. Harry can feel free to do whatever he wants with Margaret's house. Thank you for thinking of us, though."

"I think your idea is wonderful," Rose said. "You'll both do so well. I know you will."

"So, Harry," Matthew said. "We'll need to discuss a price for the house. We can get it valued..."

Harry looked across at his son-in-law. "Really? After all these years? Matthew, you don't know me at all, do you?" He smiled. "The house is yours. I don't want any money for it."

"Daddy, I have my trust fund and the money from selling the house in London. We can afford to buy the house. You don't need to do that," Rose said, turning towards him.

"Yes, I do. I'll get the papers drawn up whenever you're ready, and don't waste your time arguing with me. Save your money for this little one, who seems to have decided I make a very comfy bed." He kissed the top of Laura's sleeping head. Then he turned back to Ed. "I'd like to talk to you a little later as well... both of you."

"What about?" Ed sounded worried.

"I think I'd like to invest in your school."

"Harry, we're not asking for your money. You've already given us more than enough. We just want your time... your advice."

"You have that. But I think this sounds like a good investment. You wanted my financial advice and as part of that, if the figures stack up, I'd like to invest. When I found you with your mother, I invested a quarter of my inheritance in you, the same as I had in Rose, and then Amy, when she was born. Those were the most sound investments I've ever made... but the quarter which I kept for Elise and myself has been very wisely invested too. I'm still a very, very rich man, Ed."

"We'll talk about it when you've seen the property," Ed said, rolling his eyes. "You might decide it's not such a good idea and change your mind."

"I doubt it."

Amy nudged Ed again. "Oh, yes... there's one other thing," he said. "We need a name for the school. It hasn't been a difficult decision in the end, but we toyed, for about thirty seconds, with naming it after my father..."

"That sounds like an excellent idea to me," Harry said.

"Yes, except I share his name, and that felt very wrong to me. I didn't really feel I could name it after myself."

"Why not? That seems fine."

"Well, we felt the school should be named after someone more appropriate. Someone who makes a difference to everyone they meet. Someone the children we help can look up to as an example of how to live their lives. We'd like – with your permission – to name it the Harry Belmont School."

Harry looked around the room at the smiling faces watching him. "And if I refuse my permission?" he asked.

Ed stared at him. "We'll probably do it anyway. You've given me so much, Harry but, other than Amy's hand, I've never actually *asked* you for anything... Please don't refuse me this. We won't do anything to besmirch your good name, I promise."

"That's not what's worrying me. I'm not sure I..."

"Harry, if you're about to say you're not worthy, then just stop talking, right now," Elise cut in. "I think this is just splendid."

"Whose side are you on?" She crossed the room, sat on the arm of the sofa and kissed his cheek.

"Yours... always."

Printed in Great Britain
by Amazon